PRAISE F~~OR~~
QUINN CON~~NOR~~

T0029563

"*The Pecan Children* is a revelation in ingenuity: lyrical, compelling, and unexpected. A haunting tale that pays homage to a disappearing past. A wishful story where the sanctity and sanctuary of home gets trapped in a loop and becomes fractured. There are splintered visions of what was and what is, and the story ends up giving us heroes but no fairy-tale ending. Readers will be drawn to the heartbreak of this work about a bygone era that is lost except in remembering. What a thoroughly mesmerizing read!"

—**Leah Weiss**, author of *If the Creek Don't Rise*,
for *The Pecan Children*

"Cleverly ensnaring their reader like vines of Southern kudzu, the emotional and temporal fractals in *The Pecan Children* make for an eerie, delicious book about loyalty, loss, and the haunting nature of unsated want. It is unlike anything I have ever read before, singular and seductive."

—**Katie Lattari**, author of *Dark Things I Adore*,
for *The Pecan Children*

"This suspenseful, eerie ode to doomed Southern towns lulled me into a spell with its atmospheric beauty, then had me gasping when I realized what was happening. Quinn Connor has created an iconic addition to the canon of stories about hometowns and the fearful, hopeful hold they have over us. Like fast-growing kudzu, *The Pecan Children* wraps itself tightly around your

heart… At some point, you'll try to glance up from these pages and find yourself transfixed instead."
—**Sara Flannery Murphy**, author of *The Wonder State*, for *The Pecan Children*

"A Southern Gothic, pecan-scented fever dream of a novel. Beautiful, haunting, and very unique."
—**Ann Dávila Cardinal**, author of *We Need No Wings*, for *The Pecan Children*

"Quietly suspenseful, mysterious, and magical, *The Pecan Children* is about forgotten places and the people who stay behind. We are transported to a rural Arkansas town in decline, being sold off parcel by parcel, run by its annual pecan harvest, and about to be swallowed up by a lurking darkness—a place that could be and reminds us of so many places across America. An intricately woven narrative that expertly juggles all its moving pieces, Quinn Connor shows us an American South haunted by a history buried long ago and teaches us that the past is never really forgotten."
—**E. M. Tran**, author of *Daughters of the New Year*, for *The Pecan Children*

"*Cicadas Sing of Summer Graves* is pure alchemy—it breathes in a mystery and exhales magic. In Prosper, Arkansas, up is down, history is alive, fantasy is reality, grief becomes horror becomes salvation. I loved getting sucked into the slow, sticky Southern summer with these rich characters, watching helplessly as they struggle with love and loss and legacy while the past haunts them at every turn."

—**Eden Robins**, author of *When Franny Stands Up*, for *Cicadas Sing of Summer Graves*

"Readers should prepare themselves to get lost in a dreamy, lush narrative, riddled with stirring subterfuge, captivating characters, and a visceral sense of place. *Cicadas Sing of Summer Graves* is a lyrical swarm of history, friendship, tragedy, and the limitlessness of reality. June, Lark, and Cassie are like sirens calling from a distant shore, luring the reader further and further into the depths of understanding. You won't be able to put it down."

—**Lo Patrick**, author of *The Floating Girls*, for *Cicadas Sing of Summer Graves*

"Eerie and deeply atmospheric, *Cicadas Sing of Summer Graves* immediately transported me to a hot, sticky lakeside summer, where the story wrapped around me, pulled me under, and wouldn't let go."

—**Nichelle Giraldes**, author of *No Child of Mine*, for *Cicadas Sing of Summer Graves*

"A liquid Southern Gothic that laps against the land of the living until old secrets that can't be washed away are revealed. Seductive, haunting, and beautiful."

—**Willa Reece**, author of *Wildwood Magic*, for *Cicadas Sing of Summer Graves*

ALSO BY QUINN CONNOR

Cicadas Sing of Summer Graves

THE
PECAN
CHILDREN

QUINN CONNOR

sourcebooks
landmark

The Pecan Children is a complex story of magical realism that includes brief scenes of child endangerment and neglect, a major house fire, death of a parent, acts of violence, and dubious consent between adults. We have tried to address these serious issues with utmost sensitivity and our deepest respect for those impacted by similar real-world trauma. Please take care when reading.

Copyright © 2024 by Quinn Connor
Cover and internal design © 2024 by Sourcebooks
Cover design by Erin Fitzsimmons/Sourcebooks
Cover photos © Magdalena Wasiczek/Trevillion Images,
Anan Kaewkhammul/Shutterstock

Sourcebooks and the colophon are registered trademarks of Sourcebooks.

All rights reserved. No part of this book may be reproduced in any form or by any electronic or mechanical means including information storage and retrieval systems—except in the case of brief quotations embodied in critical articles or reviews—without permission in writing from its publisher, Sourcebooks.

The characters and events portrayed in this book are fictitious or are used fictitiously. Any similarity to real persons, living or dead, is purely coincidental and not intended by the author.

All brand names and product names used in this book are trademarks, registered trademarks, or trade names of their respective holders. Sourcebooks is not associated with any product or vendor in this book.

Published by Sourcebooks Landmark, an imprint of Sourcebooks
P.O. Box 4410, Naperville, Illinois 60567-4410
(630) 961-3900
sourcebooks.com

Cataloging-in-Publication Data is on file with the Library of Congress.

Printed and bound in the United States of America.
VP 10 9 8 7 6 5 4 3 2 1

For my mother, Helene,
who passed her gift of words to me.
—A

For Angela Barrow—
Mama, there are no words.
You make my dreams possible.
—R

ACT I

CHAPTER ONE

A SCREECH SHREDS THE DELICATE MEMBRANE OF THE night.

A great blue heron hoists itself free of the river, and Sasha winces. That sudden thrill of sound yanks every nerve—the urgent, mechanical blare blasting in her ear.

When will this ever *end*?

It's the train, howling like a heartbreak as it passes into, or really through, the town. No trains stop in the old pecan town now, and no roads lead there, either, not since the storm that took out the only highway. Sasha's small riverboat, that eternal go-between, chugs doggedly back and forth, the only way in or out.

Her grip on the wheel is a vise. She wants to duck, to cover her head; that noise feels like some miserable thing beating itself brainless against her skull. "Any minute, folks," she assures the nearest shadows. She eyes the shore just to make sure it's getting closer. The passengers are as hushed as the midnight that enwraps them. No one replies, skeptical of the promise—or stunned by the train's devouring shriek?

Sasha pushes damp hair away from her face and drags in a rallying breath. This is her river. She is the principal actor here on this floating stage, and nothing will touch her. She recrafts, with effort, her breezy nonchalance. It is the role she most loves: the woman well walled.

The river swills around the riverboat's paddle. It's a sticky night, gnats stalking the deck lights, the air still and slick. The banks of this river have a muddy relationship; sometimes they draw close, seeking their other half, other times shoving apart like haughty sisters. This evening is too dense for even Sasha to read the inscrutable smiles and frowns of the silty land ahead.

The rich, sludgy soil of this country around the river is slightly reddish, as if all the blood spilled has soaked in, this ground struck blow after mighty blow. The first people who loved this place, the Osage and Quapaw, were mostly forced away, and the news hasn't been great just about ever since. Since the first pecan trees stuck their roots down in this rocky ground and held on, it's a place where people have made it work. But nothing works out here now. Sasha knows that. It's only her sister, Lil, one of the last holdouts among the struggling orchard keepers out here, who just won't let go.

The train fades to an echo on the horizon. Sasha usually likes to gab to the people on the boat, but she can tell it's not a jawing kind of night. She watches the swatch of brown slurry illuminated by the boat light on the river, then glances back at the town and its rocky ridge. A flare of light catches her eye. Something is burning back there, a bright tower of fire cutting the dark. The scent of it will reach them soon, even this far out on the water. Its brilliance sears into Sasha's vision, and she stares far longer than she should.

No doubt it's just somebody's controlled brush fire. But it's a big one. Sasha struggles to drag her eyes away.

Later, Lil would certainly ask her, *How close is the fire to home?* That's the question that always haunts an orchard keeper. They've seen the destruction drought and cigarette butts can make of fine, healthy trees. But it must be several miles away from their land, with the town between them, so Sasha drags herself back to the river.

The bank gives up its retreat, and the boat finally starts gaining. Sasha docks. The light on the boat is loose, and it shivers over the land, flashing here and there in a lazy teeter. She leans on the rail as passengers file away toward the parking lot.

For one wild, intoxicating instant, Sasha's feet itch with possibility. She could tie this baby up, jump over the side, and chase after these lucky sons of bitches with someplace else in the world to go. She could flee. She could hitchhike straight out of here to that sweltering, flatter-than-flat city where the fresh starts are. Leave the dying trees and the bloated river and the broken-down road the state seems in no hurry to fix and that *train* and just—

Something draws her back, her gaze magnetized to that home shore, and she sees…nothing. She scopes the shadowy trees, body ringing like a bell. Silence, and nothing. The hillside blaze from only a moment ago is nowhere to be seen. It feels as if the breathlessness of the evening has choked it out, midnight's fingers snuffing it in the second she turned away. Now not even a sigh of smoke.

Only the bank. Only the river. Only the night.

She drifts a moment longer in this strangeness, squinting into eerie darkness. That desire to escape seems to leak from the soles of her shoes, restlessness displaced by a deep disquietude and a longing to be home quick.

Sasha doesn't wait any longer. Late-night stragglers hoping to cross over are out of luck. She tosses the rope at the dock and starts back alone.

∛

Every morning as the sun rises, Lil walks deep into the Clearwater orchard. In their canopies, the precious pecans hang undisturbed, pretty and healthy in their heavy green cradles. Sometimes, when the light hits it just so, the orchard seems to extend forever, beyond its prized fifty acres, bleeding into the sunset.

Lil picks her way into the oldest part of the orchard, far past the barn where the strongest of the trees grow. It's the deepest place, with the coolest shade, past where anyone should go. It's not easy to get to this place. It's difficult to push through the thickets that grow so mottled, and through the trees that aren't set in clean, mandated rows. Here, they grow at their own whim, thick clutches of gnarled roots covering the ground, until walking feels treacherous. But she knows the way through, and she twists and ducks through foliage until she pushes into the clearing.

And stops.

Where the shade is thickest there's the pond, like a black moon set in the ground. Every morning, Lil comes to sit at the mossy edge. The water is always cool, the sun blocked off by the canopy of the single pecan tree that grows on its bank. At the pond's edge, the air feels different. The noise of the world is dampened; even the wind blows more gently here, in her most sacred place.

She dips her fingers in the water and drips coolness along the back of her neck as she scans the ground. Overnight, two pecans have fallen from the tree and nestle at its base. They aren't the usual tawny brown; each is the color of prehistoric amber, brighter and more vibrant than any other fruit from any other tree in the orchard. Their strangeness still arrests her. Lil gathers them up, smelling the perfume of earth, the sharp richness of the treasure inside. All of her days are spent on the work of the pecan orchard, and she's eaten more pecans in her lifetime than most people would eat in twenty. And yet she can only imagine how they would taste, these pecans from *this* tree.

"Not today," she murmurs. "Maybe one day." Instead, she tosses them, one by one into the water; each winks like a gold coin, falling with soft splashes.

Task done, she brushes dirt off her knees and returns to the sunlight, where her truck is waiting, the back loaded with a new delivery of fresh pecans from elsewhere in the orchard.

Her ride into town only seems to get longer these days, and she makes it with a canvas bag of her best pecans shaking in the truck bed. The fences of every property that she passes could use some upkeep. So could the one road that leads to and from town. It's been closed for …

How long has the road been closed?

It's not that it was ever such a great road, just WPA-poured concrete over an even older dirt track, leading to the bridge that stretches over flat fields toward that western horizon. Nestled in the shadow of an improbable ridge, on ground too rocky for most crops, the town has never been wealthy or as big as ones now closer to the interstate, but it is old and quaint, with a main street people like to walk down on sunny days.

But not many people have come to visit since that unseasonable, unprecedented hurricane took out their road, leaving behind a whole new map of topographical features—gravel mountains, fissures as big as the Grand Canyon, pocks and sinkholes and gashes.

When had that storm hit?

The road and the bridge had definitely already been wrecked by their thirtieth birthday. Lil and Sasha always had a party out in the pecan orchard. Lil made the punch boozy enough to accommodate a little rainwater. They'd hung lights in the more patient of the trees. There was enough Pop's Barbecue for a hundred. But by then, people were getting out of town any way they could. The Clearwater birthday crowd was decidedly sparse. Autumn hadn't even been there with her famous four-tiered pecan praline cake, always made from last harvest's tender papershells, and Sasha had been so quiet.

So that had been...

Whenever it was, it's a huge pain in the ass. Getting shipments out is harder than ever.

Lil twists the dial on her radio, but it can't quite grasp a station through clouds of static. She gets nothing but far-off voices that slip away like silk. The patchwork of farms with distant houses is more disheveled than it used to be when she, Sasha, and Autumn were young and would go running over fresh-painted fences and through pruned rows of pecan trees owned by neighbors. So many of those families have sold, so many trees left heavy with nuts that only the squirrels dine on. It hurts to see it; all neighbors she used to know by name, whose kids she grew up alongside. They held on as long as they could. The money doesn't come steady, and the work keeps her sore and sunburned. But whenever Lil considers doing the same, giving up and moving to some city—*No.* The rest of the world can crumble as far as she is concerned. Lil is here to stay.

The town is quiet today, from the library to the firehouse. With a population of more than twenty-five hundred at its height, plus those scattered across the fields and orchards beyond the town streets, this place has had some heft in the past, but there's no knowing how many live here these days. A few people wander the streets, and a promenade of some of the older ladies are making their morning stroll through the square. A rich autumn mess of damp leaves gathers into gutters and curbs.

When Lil parks in front of the Corner Market and Feed Store, the lights are on—if flickering. Su isn't rumbling around inside with her broom and scowl. She probably just stepped out for a smoke. Lil heaves the canvas bag of pecans off the truck. She hip-checks the swinging glass door open. No one mans the counter, but it hardly matters if no one is browsing the canned goods and basic toiletries.

Lil drops the canvas bag on the end of the counter that still bears a very old taped flier proclaiming, FOURTH OF JULY FIREWORKS AT THE RIDGE. Her back is grateful for the reprieve. Nabbing a scrap of receipt and a pen from a coffee mug full of them, she braces her elbows on the smooth wood to write down the weight of the week's batch, and the total cost. Su's the best for handling her shipping. But at the best of times, Su is absent-minded about getting Lil's final payments, and lately, she's worse than ever. Still, Su's the reason Lil has at least half of the regular shipment orders she gets. So she perseveres. The fan turns aim-lessly, stirring up the dead air.

Pay up sometime or I'll start charging interest, she jots. A glint of bright orange catches the corner of her eye. The candy hasn't been restocked, but there are a few Reese's. She snags a packet.

Also I took some candy, she adds at the end of her note. Maybe that will get Su's attention.

Plastic crinkles from beside her head. A Snickers is plopped on the counter next to her truffles by someone with square nails and scabbed knuckles. Lil freezes, skin at the nape of her neck prickling.

"Not such good service here, is there?" Theon teases.

He always manages to sneak up on her, appearing the second she stops looking. Lil straightens, signing the note with more pressure than it needs, ink blotting like blood from a scratch, and tucks it under the corner of the pecan bag.

He watches her. Leans on the counter next to her. His tie is striped horizontally, train tracks that narrow to a point at his throat, a target Lil longs to strike. "Spot me the price of a candy bar?" He pulls one of his pockets inside out to show its emptiness.

"Starve," Lil suggests. She can't remember how long it's been since he rolled into town. In a way, she feels as if he's always been there, roaming about and snapping up family orchards from desperate, aging farmers who can't pay the bills anymore. He is a rangy coyote, draped in costly wrinkled suits.

As always, no matter what she says, shouts, or spits, Theon is just amused. "You're cruel, Lilith. But consistent." Happy to turn her back on that smirk, she stomps down to the entrance again. His hazy reflection trails her. "If this pokey old place isn't paying you anymore," he calls, "my offer still stands."

"So does my answer." Lil pushes open the door into the sun-brushed air and onto the pavement, worn from years of feet. She jangles her key in the car door. "If you don't stop coming around, I'll start punching." A girl can dream.

"That's okay." Theon observes with animal-bright eyes as she wrestles the sleepy door open. He rips open the candy bar and bites it in half.

Despite herself—she is reliable as a bull at ignoring a challenge in red—Lil pauses halfway to her seat. "I'm getting sick of seeing you around, Theon."

"But I'm patient," he replies with that same amused grin. Like he knows the punch line of the joke and it's on her.

"I'm stubborn," Lil says.

"You can change your mind anytime, Lilith." Theon tosses the rest of the candy in the grass. "I'll be here."

She slams the door, flips him off through the window, and starts her truck.

CHAPTER TWO

IT IS A GROGGY MORNING AFTER A LATE NIGHT. THAT squeal of the train still rings in Sasha's ears, and she sits up in bed, almost knocking her forehead against her bedroom's low gable. That steam engine's approach is like a strike; it might as well run on tracks straight through her ear canal.

There's no ferry today, as Sasha only drives it three days a week. Grumbling, she rolls over to check the messages on the answering machine she keeps up in her room.

The recording crackles. *"Hey Sasha, Su here. Can you cover a shift at the shop this morning? Thanks, honey, buh-bye."*

It's a new message, but Sasha has to replay the time stamp to be sure. It's only the most recent in a line of identical requests from Su. There's a whole tape full of the same: Pop over at the barbecue place, Cara at the school, Freddie at the library, Tammy at the hardware store, etc. None of them are very creative in their requests, just asking for her to cover the same shifts in endless cycles. Ever since she moped back into town after the breakup, the local businesses have been scraping together hours for her to work. Along with running the ferry almost on her own, she's got about a dozen odd jobs. Not that Sasha minds. The variety is good for her. As in, it distracts her from being the lesbian-outsider twin sister of the town's foremost orchard keeper. And it keeps her out of Lil's hair, out of the orchard that was somehow always Lil's and Mom's only, and not Sasha's at all.

Clearing her throat, Sasha drags herself free of the bed, tapping the low slant of the roof a couple of times for good luck. The house is old, and maybe a little creepy to somebody who doesn't know it well, but the place definitely has a soft spot for her. It was so excited when she came home that it took one look at her with its wide French windows and immediately dropped half the shingles off the front of the roof. "You look like a bald-headed old lady," Sasha had muttered to it the next day, when she'd clambered up there to do some patching.

Crumpled jean shorts off the chair. Tank top from the drawer. Chunky sweater off the floor. The weather doesn't know what it wants to do these days, the shadows cool and the sun blazing hot. She claws through the ends of her toffee-colored hair a few times, then gives up on it, knotting it back in a bun. "*You are so beautiful, as soon as I stop looking at you, I forget what you look like,*" her great-aunt told her once. Her and Lil's faces are similar, but Sasha's features are more catalog-girl generic, which means people usually feel a little more comfortable looking at her. Then they mistake her for the friendly sister, next to Lil, who stomped her way through high school with rips in her jeans and a silver barbell piercing her tongue. But, to be honest, neither of them is too friendly.

She grabs her camera bag on the way out of her room, slinging the strap over her shoulder. Is it likely she'll see anything worth shooting in a shift stocking shelves at the grocery? No. But she never regrets hauling her equipment around, just in case. It'll only be a few more rolls of film, and she'll have finally gotten somewhere with this project. She'd definitely be getting close to something. Just porting her camera around feels like grasping hold of her other self, her *truer* self: a cool, gay, slightly emotionally messy photographer in the big city. And how pathetic it feels to be in the *x*th month since her *temporary* move home, Sasha prefers to ignore.

Lil is coming in the front door just as Sasha clatters down the creaky old steps. A warm fall breeze is roving through the house, and Sasha can smell the fireplace, even though they haven't lit it yet this year.

Lil is wearing clunky boots and a beat-up leather jacket over shorts and a ratty tank top. Her shaggy morning hair is half-caught in her collar. One of the biggest shocks coming home, honestly, had been Lil's hair, which used to grow down her back, thick and glinting like a night river. She's chopped it short, and it makes her dark eyes wider, giving her a soft effect—if you don't know any better. No matter what she alters, there are parts of Lil that will never change. The way she walks into a room and men surreptitiously wipe their faces and straighten their ties. The way she can hold a grudge as stubborn and long as the trees. The way she will take any tool—beauty, a hacksaw, an old tin can, a sister—and find a way to wring usefulness out of it. She is a bottle of strong spirits; time will only distill her.

Lil offers her a couple of pecans, the crinkle of broken shells still caught between her fingers. A snack of fresh sunshine and sweet earth expertly cracked between her knuckles and her palm. "Heading out?"

"Yeah." Sasha scoops the warm pecans from Lil's palm and pops them in her mouth. "Did you see Su at the store? She left me a message to cover."

"No. I left a note though. If you're stocking, she's low on candy." Lil rests her shoulder against the doorframe. Sasha chews, the pecan flavors falling one over another: the bitter tang of flesh, the warm savory nut, a honeyed sweetness. Lil goes on, "I saw Theon."

Sasha frowns, then—"Ouch." A fragment of pecan shell stabs her in the gum and she spits it into her palm. The tender flavor of the nuts mixes strangely with a coppery dash of her own blood. "That ass is *still* hanging around town? Is he on the clock with somebody for this harassment?"

"He didn't even make me a new offer. I wouldn't have taken it, but the last number he gave us was insulting." Lil scatters husk bits on the porch through the open front door. "So keep an eye out today. He might sniff around you too."

Sasha grimaces. "He's such a creep." He hasn't approached Sasha yet; he seems keenly aware of whose orchard it is, who belongs here and who doesn't. Something in that realization stings, and Sasha moves on. "I might go out to the Keller Orchard later."

Lil nods, a line furrowed between her eyebrows, a familiar twist of sympathy and probably a little judgment. It's hard to tell with Lil, the line where her hurt turns to anger. "Nice old people. I think they moved out to Nashville. They told everyone it was to be near their youngest, Caleb, but Mrs. Keller confided in me that it's because they couldn't afford the place anymore. She cried so hard the day they left."

It's the kind of everyday tragedy that offers no easy response. Sasha finds herself just wincing, humming vaguely. These miserable, dime-a-dozen pains built into this land—Sasha has a hard rind against them. Can Lil's heart really afford to dwell and break and rage over every departure? Sasha's heart, burdened with other sorrows, cannot. "Well...it's the next spot on Dale's list." One of her million or so half-done projects since coming home has been going out with Dale, the local land surveyor, to all the moldering properties that frame the town for appraisals. Lately, he's been sending her out on her own to get photos for him. Sasha takes a leap: "Want me to pick you up on the way over there?"

Lil looks tempted and a little amused at first—she's never been all that good with a camera, though she was once one of Sasha's very first, most amateur subjects. But her smile fades as quickly as it's born. "Better not. There's a broken bit of fence near the gate, and I think the shaker is breaking down. There's so much to do..." she trails off.

"Right. No, I know." Sasha feels a pang of guilt at even posing the invitation and thus reminding Lil how overwhelmed she is. At the same time, Sasha hasn't worked in the orchard in years. It's so fully Lil's space; she suffuses it like a perfume until you can't walk among the trees without feeling her presence. Sasha is never invited out there, and she never quite volunteers either. If Lil wants the help, she'll ask, won't she?

It hasn't always felt this way. When they were children, Lil would sneak into Sasha's room at night, and they'd become nothing but voices, twin whispers and muffled laughter in the dark.

But Lil has been a little more stubborn and solitary since Sasha left for New York. Sometimes Sasha hears her murmur in her sleep from her bedroom a floor up and wonders what she won't say while awake.

"Let me know if you see him," Lil says after a pause, eyes finding Sasha's, a key to a lock. *Or anything else out there*, she adds silently.

Sasha nods. "You got it."

Lil wanders into the kitchen. There's a distant sound: a stream of water washing into the coffeepot's echo chamber.

Sasha lingers there, listening for another word from her sister, just long enough to catch the machine's classic burble as it starts brewing. Then she shoulders her camera bag and sets off down the road in the only direction that it now runs: toward town. The other way goes past another property or two before it hits the CLOSED sign and the silent bulldozers beyond. She scuffs up dust walking on the shoulder even though a car hasn't passed the house since she woke up. She passes the familiar neighbors: the Preston Orchard, the kudzu-covered columns of the old Devereau house that has been turned into at least three apartments now. Across the road, there's—

Odd. Sasha pauses there, her bare ankles tickling in the dust. There's a light on in Honeysuckle House. The Finch house. It's crumbly redbrick, one of the finer houses in the town, and maybe the oldest. The Finches were town founders, which means they were a poor hick family somewhere else who got here when the getting was good. Mayor Finch retired the year after Sasha moved away, but people were always hoping his son, Jason, would step up. That was before, though. Nobody's been living there since Uncle Russ had to go to hospice.

She can see into the old parlor with its stuffy upholstery and heavy curtains. She used to tag along here with Lil when Jason's parents weren't around, gawking at its museum interior, at the jeweled candies glittering in crystal dishes. Perhaps those sweets are still waiting in there, tropical fruit colors long desiccated, collecting dust.

The light left on inside flickers.

Frowning, Sasha pulls out her camera and snaps a picture.

Ͼͻ

"Come on. I don't expect you to like it, but I do expect you to cooperate," Lil murmurs, stroking the rough, healthy bark of a tree clamped in her beat-up shaker. The machine is missing a few teeth, but she hopes she can get one more season out of it. Just one more. Nothing but a handful of hulls, and a shower of leaves wants to fall from the tree. Lil switches off the shaker and retrieves her favorite pole, shaking it in the canopies instead.

It's a tentative noon, the heat beginning to fade like an old letter this time of year, and the ache in her back is probably going to get worse. But the harvest isn't stopping, and she needs every good harvest she can get.

Lil was taught the history at the heart of her work by older keepers. Before a technique for their propagation was invented by a man named Antoine, a gardener enslaved in Louisiana, pecan trees naturally flourished all along the rivers. Every fall, they sustained the first communities that called the land home—and were companions to them, offering shade and nourishment when they were forced to walk through strange, unknown country.

Trees are as unpredictable as any other living thing. Kudzu, aphids or rosette, drought or scab: these could kill a harvest. But there wasn't always a reason. Some years they produce multitudes, and suddenly, they stop. For years at a time even good living trees might go dormant for unknown reasons.

Lil has her own ideas: healthy orchards dry up when good keepers must leave, replaced by indifferent ones.

A faithful keeper can spend decades acquainting herself with each individual tree. The health of its branches. How many decades it has stood; how many more it might last, long after its caretaker is gone. Used to care, suddenly deprived, maybe it takes time for land to remember it is meant to be wild. She's seen it often enough. Beyond the old Cooper place, beyond the abandoned Winston trees, lies anonymity. The silence, the unmoored storylessness of real poverty. The houses out there are abandoned. Broken-down trucks and old farm equipment bake like dinosaur bones in parched grass. The pecan trees out there don't produce so much as a blossom, and they stoop low, their bare branches poised in protective barricades. The Coopers are gone; the Winstons haven't produced in years. The Kellers now too, their land left to fester.

But row by row, species by species, Lil's trees are flush this year with healthy pecans. Each morning when she checks the nets that lie below the trees, they are teeming with ripe nuts. It's certainly a mast fruiting, plentiful and rich. The husks are smooth all over, no cracks, and the healthy ones fall onto the grass with the lightest prod of her pole. The wonder of it still fills her.

Lil pauses halfway through topping off another bag and braces her hands on the small of her back, feeling her stiff muscles ache as she breathes in the sweetness of pecans all around. It's fine. She'll rest when the harvest is over.

Lil has lost count of how many times she's promised herself that she'll rest later. A day of rest would be a blessing, nothing to do but walk around with Sasha, snapping pictures. When Sasha first returned, Lil believed it would be a new start, the two of them bearing the burdens of the family land together. Sasha's first night back in the house, Lil enjoyed the best sleep of her life, her soul shored up with the presence of her sister sleeping in their old room. Only Sasha doesn't ever want to stay. In a way it's like she never came back at all. She spends her days doing odd jobs for everyone in town. Everyone except Lil. Sasha shows no interest in the orchard's upkeep, in Lil's struggle to stay afloat.

It's a stone in her shoe, a constant, quiet ache. But Lil is too sharp even at the best of times, too prone to passion, and Sasha too untethered. In an argument, Sasha won't fight. She'll flee. *At least*, she reminds herself, *Sasha is here*. That's all she needs.

It has to be.

The wind shifts, the leaves rustling in an idle gossip. There's a different stir in the air now, and Lil glances back at the house—

"Hey!" He's standing on Lil's back patio, waving broadly.

Jason is in the orchard.

Even though he shouldn't be there, hasn't been there in years, he's impossible to mistake; no one in the town, or maybe the world, is as blond as he is. In summer, his hair brightens to the color of a crisp lemon. It's like he absorbs energy straight from the sun, and there on her porch, he glows with it. Now he's here, cool and breezy in his linen pants and boat shoes.

All at once, everything inside of her flares at his sheer audacity.

Lil throws down her pole and stomps across her ground. How had she not felt him here until the moment he called? It's unsettling. She should have known the instant he crossed her borders. "'Hey'? That's what you have to say to me? 'Hey'?"

At least Jason has the decency to cringe. "Surprise," he tries. The waving hand now pushes into his hair. "I'm kinda glad you, uh, dropped your weapon back there."

"Ballsy of you to come here without an invitation." *Though he had one once, hadn't he,* the most honest part of her whispers. "What do you want, Finch?"

Jason snorts, bends his head. Shaking it, a stubborn smile still hanging on, he seems about to make some classic retort (never very clever, that last word he always wants to claim), but he doesn't speak. Only keeps shaking and shaking his head like that, looking down at the graying and thirsty wood of the back porch. There's something awful and endless about that motion, like he might never stop, like a door swinging free on a loose hinge. Finally he looks at her again, and his dark, coffee-bean eyes are glassy. "Uncle Russ died," he says, in a cracked teenage-boy voice she hasn't heard in a long time.

Lil gasps through the ache that blooms in her chest. Uncle Russ was Mayor Finch's quirky bachelor brother. By far the jolliest family member, Russ was known to sleep outside with his vegetable plants if they were ever struck with blight. He raised the best tomatoes in the county and made his tobacco money off the miracle potions he whipped up for other people's gardens. He'd moved into Honeysuckle House to take over the family land after Mayor Finch died and Jason's mom relocated to Mobile. "When?" Lil asks.

Jason swallows, gaze escaping quickly out toward the orchard. "Early yesterday morning." Uncle Russ had been in hospice for more than a month—long enough that everybody had gotten a little comfortable; nobody believed he might really die. The look on Jason's face makes it clear he still can't imagine it. "Took me all day to get down here from Durham."

"I'm sorry." Russ used to invite her to sit with him whenever she picked up some elixir or other for the trees. They'd kick their feet up on the porch, watching for fireflies and sipping sweet tea that tasted like golden sunshine, and she hadn't even known—

Lil tries to breathe normally. "Come inside if you want."

On closer inspection, Jason's New-England casual is rumpled, face worn from travel—and older too, different in indecipherable ways. He stands in her kitchen, fiddling with the novelty salt and pepper shakers: two swans, their necks intertwined. "I knew you wouldn't want to see me," he admits. "But I—uh. I didn't want you to hear about Russ from somebody else. And I—" His voice stutters out. His hands are shaking. "That house, Lil. God. It's so quiet in there."

That's what happens when people leave. Lil doesn't say it. For once, she can hold her tongue. She lets her thoughts, her anger, turn cool and distant. Like the pond. "Sit down." Lil washes dirt and sweat off her hands.

"I just talked to him a few days ago." Jason eases into the chair as if he's afraid it will shatter under him. "He was doing well."

She fills the kettle, sets it to boil on the gas stovetop where Mom used to make countless meals; where Sasha perfected the few Puerto Rican recipes learned from their father in the brief time they spent with him; where Lil has cried, late at night—the only time she will let herself feel the weight of solitude and work. The low hiss fills the kitchen as she stuffs dried lavender into a teapot and braces her hands on the counter, which is still slightly crumby from her morning toast. She doesn't know what to say.

Jason traces a faded paisley in the pattern of the tablecloth. He doesn't know how to be still. "He was really tough," he says finally. "Guess everybody around here is."

"We have to be," she replies and pours boiling water over the lavender, the smell wafting up around her.

A pause. She fiddles. Russ's face floats behind her eyes and she swallows back tears. She was never good at grieving in front of other people. Even when Mom died, Lil couldn't shed tears at the funeral. Only after, when she was alone, did she let herself…

When she turns back with the mugs, Jason is hunched over the table in what used to be his chair, resting his forehead in his palm. She sets one mug down and retreats to the counter.

"I know—" She expected it to be difficult to say, like coughing up a knife. But in the face of his pain, her old resentments begin to feel small. "I know he was really proud of you. Loved bragging about you. Any time you called him, everyone else in town heard all about it."

Jason squeezes his lips together like she's struck him. The mug, a hand-painted ceramic made by Sasha's first real girlfriend, is probably burning his hands. "Russ was the only Finch I could ever really talk to," he manages. "He always said he'd come up to see me in Durham but—his health just wasn't…" He loses his place again and swiftly washes the thought down with boiling tea. "Um—ow." The bracing punch of a burned tongue summons a sort of choked laugh. Apparently recovering, he takes a hard pivot. "I heard Sasha's back?"

Lil keeps lingering at the counter. "Who'd you hear that from?"

She can feel his eyes on her back now. "Lou." Lou, who runs the junk shop and brews his own eyebrow-sizzling variety of moonshine, was Uncle Russ's best friend. "He's always had a soft spot for her."

Lil twists around to face him. He still has a tiny bump in the cartilage of his nose; she remembers the football that put the kink there. She sips her tea for strength. "I'll tell her you say hi. Or you can find her somewhere around town. She's usually out." A polite person would invite him for dinner, but Lil has never been accused of politeness.

"Okay." Jason is watching her again, maybe discovering those hard-to-define differences in her face too. He scoffs quietly. "You still hate me, don't you?" He stands up to peer at her, and even though he hasn't really made a move toward her, he's still too close. "Hey. I don't want bad blood with you. You know how I—"

I don't hate you, she longs to say, almost does, has to swallow it back.

"I'm not having that fight with you again," Lil replies. She puts down her mug and comes toward him. "Not today. For Russ. Also not ever, and that's because of *you*."

They glare at one another for a long moment. Then Jason takes a step back. "Understood," he says tightly. "Then I'll see you around, Lil." He turns to go, head ducked, and he doesn't look back.

"Sure," she relents. She doesn't breathe right until he's gone and the screen door has bumped closed. She slumps against the counter, and at the faintest jostle, a couple of fresh, healthy pecans spill from the bowl she keeps there.

CHAPTER THREE

W HEN SASHA REACHES THE OLD KELLER FARM-house later, it grins toothlessly at her from between the withered gnarls of the pecan trees. A *Grey Gardens* gloom surrounds the place, the windows of the top floor broken out, the front door boarded over. It looks like it's been abandoned for about a hundred years. Kudzu—that blanket of invasive plant they say is slowly swallowing the whole of the South—already sprawls in a heavy tangle across half the roof and one side. That choking vine will put that place down before too long.

It has depth, that greenery, a swampy density. No air reaches the inner chambers of those vines. When Sasha and Lil were teenagers, Chuck Vickers dove into a kudzu hill and never came back out. His friends waited and waited, laughing, rowdy and amused, then assumed he'd snuck off somewhere without them seeing. The town only realized later. Suffocated, everybody said. But Sasha lay awake in her bed after, imagining him eaten up, vines forcing their way under his eyelids, under his nails, sucking him dry, just like the land—

Sasha forces her mind back and moves to the end of the cracked cement driveway, long brown grasses tickling her legs. There are no cars parked out here, the place a bleached husk. "*If you ever get a funny feeling about a place, just give me a call and I'll meet ya out there,*" Dale had told her. She tries not to call him in too often, especially after his double knee replacement. With her own array of life experiences—from being out with girlfriends in bars full of aggressive men, for instance—Sasha doesn't spook easy, anyway. The potential of encountering squatters or meth cookers hadn't stopped her from taking the job. But this place? A Stephen King shiver creeps up her back just looking at it. It has a gobbling look, like the kudzu that devoured that boy all those years ago. Maybe she takes another step, and this dead grass heaves her down by the ankles.

With a deep breath, Sasha steps off the driveway, picking her way through the tall grass to scout toward the property line. She'd be covered in ticks and red bugs if not for that bug spray she'd soaked her legs with as she left the grocery store.

The trees are silent spectators, their gaunt forms twisting away on every side. This orchard doesn't speak with humans anymore; they gossip about her deep underground, their root systems whispering, *Intruder.* Dead leaves melt to mulch under her sneakers. She touches one of the orchard's trunks, and bark crumbles away under her hand. Bad blight. One look at this hollow carcass and Lil would keel right over. Pocketing her lens cover, Sasha leans back. Her viewfinder holds the bony fingers of the orchard's upper branches. The Clearwater orchard will *never* look like this, not in a million years. Sometimes Sasha imagines that under the earth, there is a single place where all the roots of the town's trees meet, a sweet, husked heart at the center of everything. If there is, the Clearwater orchard lies the closest to it. Sometimes, more and more in recent decades, something—a death or a sale or a sin—lops trees free from that heart, and they wither, just like this.

A chill breeze is kicking up between the trees, their shadows stretching away toward the backwoods. Sasha photographs what's left of the weaving drunkard of a fence on the west side of the land. After early trips out to places like this with Dale, Sasha tried to tell Lil about it, things she was learning about the land around here. Something in her is drawn to this decay, this weirdness. But for Lil, thoughts always turn to what had once been and was now gone. A family that had moved on, or a property that had once produced. Sasha's photos aren't a road back for Lil but a closed window.

Just for something to do with her hands, Sasha snaps a photo of the house. Immediately she senses a shiver of movement there, the vines jangling together. The sound of the shutter startled something. The kudzu rustles like dead hair as the thing crawls around, stuffing itself under the house. A possum? Sasha backs away, and—

Snap.

Her heel has cracked a fallen branch on the—wait. No, Sasha realizes, eyeing the gray shards pinned under her foot. It's a bone, the thin femur of some little animal, left here from a picked-over kill. She leans down to peer at it. And there's another, just a foot away. Nearby, a narrow rib cage.

Sasha backs up a step, her legs suddenly unsteady under her. Now that she's looking, there are bones *everywhere* here under the trees. Little skulls, scattered teeth, tufts of fur. Leftovers from the meager hunting of some small animal—maybe whatever is now hiding under the house.

So that's the smell that hangs over this place, the soft twist of decay. Not the trees, but the brown blood curdling at their roots.

The long honeyed afternoons of summer are long gone out here, and twilight is a fast fade. Sasha finishes the job, but it's hurried. After that, the only pictures she takes are for Dale's survey. She rushes through them, skin jumping. Her body urges her to bolt, and there's none of the usual calm to be found in the routine of the work. Everything in her longs to be gone. Even as they crowd the ground, she never steps on the bones.

By the time she starts the walk home, the final crickets of the season have started up their lonely serenades from the woods. Holding tight to her camera, she doesn't look back at that slack-jawed old ruin again.

☙

Sometimes when Sasha is out—which is frequent—and even Lil is tired of shaking trees and shelling pecans, she sits in the kitchen window and makes her calls. It's one of her least favorite chores. Worse than laundry, but just as necessary. Lil uses the same beige phone Mom had installed herself over the kitchen table, its coiled cord bouncing. The paint still bears drill holes from her first attempts. She rests her cheek on the table, next to her mug, and checks names off her list, reduced to dial tones and answering machines.

"Hi, Mrs. Franklin, it's Lil. Just wanted to confirm that you're coming to the quarterly town hall. As you probably remember,

I want to have a good show of support for the town council, because they're supposed to be discussing additional funding programs for small farms..."

"Hi, Cork, it's Lil. Just wanted to see if you'd heard anything about those funding programs. I know it got taken off the docket for the last meeting, but it's already autumn..."

Bureaucracy bores her. But there are still plenty of people left—fewer each year, it seems—who care about the town's future, who want to see orchards like Lil's succeed. She can already picture it: showing up at the next town hall with an army of grandmothers behind her, packing the seats with baked goods and fancy hats until the council has to listen to her. Lil's speech is almost done. If she can just get enough people there listening, then maybe—

Maybe. She holds that possibility like a prayer deep under her ribs as she makes every call except the one that she should. The most important one.

Jason only just got back to town and already she owes him an apology. She is thrown right back in time like it hasn't passed at all. Jason is just as she remembers. He hasn't gone to seed; he's kept his lean track star muscle and his politician's mouth. But that doesn't mean Lil knows him anymore. People change when they leave home. They blossom; Sasha came back from New York more confident and artistic than ever. Lil might be the only one who is caught in time. She can look at Jason and be sixteen again, feel his varsity jacket on her shoulders. Lil straightens and takes the phone, dialing the number she still remembers—only these days, it won't be Russ's rusty voice on the other end, but Jason's. Still. She can do this.

She has punched three numbers in and is nowhere near ready when the wind, the branches in the orchard, and even the house stills. The world around her slows to a wary halt.

She sets the handset back into the cradle, her chair screeching when she stands. Outside the window, there is nothing to see but the line of trees and a crooked bit of fencing she's still fixing. No movement. But there's an alarm going off inside her.

Then, like a hidden picture, an optical illusion, Theon appears behind the tree line.

Lil rushes out of the kitchen and onto the porch, charging down the steps. But there she stops, because he isn't on her land. Not yet. He stands on the edge of the property, where the fence is broken, his hands braced like he's thinking of leaping over it. When he sees her, Theon smiles and backs off a little, pacing the edge of the boundary.

Once, when Lil and Sasha were ten, a developer had come to their land. Lil only remembers the vague impression of height and stretched buttons over his stomach. Mom shuffled the girls upstairs, but Lil and Sasha creeped on sock feet to the top of the stairs. They knelt against the rail where they could see Mom's slender legs and ankles under the dirty cuffs of her jeans.

"A good offer for the land. Best you'll get. Take the money. Move to Memphis, raise those cute girls there." Lil doesn't remember the whole conversation, just phrases that flashed at her amid babble, and Sasha's tawny, curious eyes and quiet breathing. *"There's no man of the house. Tough industry—that's just the truth. Product's good, but no profit."*

Mom didn't say anything while the man talked. Not a single word. But Lil felt that Mom's silence wasn't a lack of things to say but an abundance of emotion and energy, of horror. She couldn't move or she would explode.

When she finally spoke, her voice was unrecognizable in its chill. *"Leave and don't come back."*

Lil forces herself to take another stride forward. And Theon reaches over the fence and rests a hand on the nearest tree.

She *feels* it. Warm, square fingers on her cheek and she can't hold back a shudder. Theon drags his fingers down the bark, a lover's caress she feels against her ribs. Lil breaks into a dead run straight at him. When the orchard doesn't let him in, doesn't accept his touch or his smile, Theon raises his hands and backs off. He's out of sight before she reaches the fence.

CHAPTER FOUR

THE NEXT AFTERNOON SASHA WORKS THE FERRY, LOU is aboard, and he sits beside her at the helm, the river breeze rustling in his hair. Luckily, he hasn't brought any of his moonshine along this time; even the smell of that stuff might be enough to tump them right over. "Well, I'm going to get my suit taken in for old Russ's memorial," Lou tells her sadly. "I've been on that Atkins diet, and all my clothes are just falling off me."

Sasha's hand is loose on the wheel. The river is drowsy and compliant for once. "Don't lose too much, Lou." She checks him over. "There's not enough of you to go around as it is." That summons a quick whip of laughter. He has a handsome, dark brown face, the ponderous forehead of a scholar incongruously combined with a Peter Pan smile. Lou's probably an older man, maybe pushing even sixty-five, but he looks younger.

Lou's curiosity and repair shop, a town institution for forty years, is all strangeness and clutter, teetering piles of rusting treasures displayed according to his own private design. Everything inside is theoretically for sale, but Lou makes better money with his canny repair work. Mostly, folks go in with things that need fixing, and though Lou always charges fair for his work, the things he repairs aren't likely to break again.

"I just don't know what I'm going to do without Russ to talk to all the time." Lou wipes absently at his face. "Me and this town just keep getting smaller. Next thing you know the Finch trees will be going fallow just like all the rest."

"I'll miss him too." Sasha lays a hand on his shoulder. "But we aren't all gone, are we?"

"No." Lou's voice is warm and melancholy. "No indeed."

"And there's still Jason Finch to take over for Russ at Honeysuckle House," Sasha points out.

Lou waves his hand in dismissal. "That boy's changed. He's got some kind of fire in his belly that means he can't stay. Even if he wants to." Sasha has no answer to that, and Lou continues. "Anyway, it's those orphaned trees that are the problem." His hand passes over and under his eye, weaving the story between them. "Something's rotten down there in the roots, and it moves fast. The nuts stop falling, and instead there are hungry children. Children of the trees with heartwood eyes. Voices like the wind." He sounds hoarse for a moment, air through a screen door.

Sasha scoffs, trying to laugh off the chill in her gut. "What are you talking about, Lou?"

"I've told you before, honey. The trees bear them," he murmurs, staring out over the water now. "More and more every year." He glances at her shocked expression, then away, weary. "I've been doing all I can, but y'all never seem to notice what's broken around here."

She puts her hand over his for a moment. She can't quite grasp what he's saying, but a thread of guilt pulls taut in her gut. "We Clearwaters can get a little absorbed in our own problems. I'm sorry, Lou."

When he looks at her again, frustration sparks in his eyes. "Sorry enough to say so but not enough to do more, I guess."

Sasha isn't sure how to respond, and she's still fumbling when they dock on the other side of the river. She offers Lou her hand as he hoists himself up onto the ramp, but he merely gives it a dusty pat on his way by.

She sighs, putting her hand over his for a moment. "I know."

They make dock on the other side of the river, and Sasha offers Lou her hand as he hoists himself up onto the ramp. Never one to need much, he merely gives it a dusty pat on his way by. The other passengers follow him off—first the young woman, her toddler on one arm and a bucket of cleaning supplies on the other, then a snooty First Presbyterian lady who used to work in the school office. It was a light trip, and Sasha is about to clip the rope back in place—But oh, she must have forgotten this last passenger, a wizened old casino-lover shuffling off toward Tunica. And following them, a pock-faced teenager with a guitar case. They don't take her hand or even meet her eye as they move up onto the ramp and diffuse away like mist. It irks her a bit. She pulls the rope taut again—

The last man aboard is slow, his body bent with fatigue as he creeps down from somewhere at the back. He is deathly pale under his wool cap, his cheeks desperately hollowed. Not someone Sasha recognizes from town. She checks the empty parking lot, but Lou is long gone. Their eyes lock as her last passenger stops in front of her, much too close, lipless mouth parting—Sasha had automatically closed the gate *again*. Frozen deep inside, she pulls the rope back yet again and, out of habit only, offers him her hand.

The hand that makes a hard and fast grab for hers is blued and veiny, cold as if it has just been submerged in an ice bucket, or in the deepest currents of the river itself. There is a dark brownish stain at the cuff of the hand that snatches at hers, at the flesh right above her digital watch, which has been on the fritz, just four flickering zeros. He leans into her weight as her gaze flashes down from those eyes, *those two burned holes in a blanket*, as Russ used to say sometimes. She'd never known what he meant by that.

The pale stare does not leave her. The eyes are fixed on her even as he shambles up the step. The weight on her arm increases, increases, becomes untenable, like her arm will snap from bearing this man up. She grits her teeth, shoves the cry back down her throat and bears it and bears it and—

He is gone, finally, and now she's alone again. Antsy, heart pounding, Sasha paces the length of the riverboat. She checks every seat, every corner. She climbs to the second level and bends low to glance into storage compartments at moldy life preservers. Empty. All empty.

There is no one to return with her across the river. She shoves off and gets the paddleboard moving again, anxious energy clotting in her arms and legs. The river is still mirror-smooth, a golden-brown sheet in the afternoon light. Sasha spins the wheel to depart with nervous, jerking turns, and spares only one glance back.

A familiar figure stands on the far bank behind her, watching, auburn hair snapping in a wind Sasha cannot feel. She, in her scribbled sneakers and oversized Zeppelin shirt, is somehow more solid, more real to Sasha than any of those who just left the boat. Sasha ditches the wheel to hurry back and stare out over the growing distance between them. She hasn't seen her in ages and ages. Where has she been?

"Autumn!" Sasha shouts, waving in huge arcs over her head. She feels better, the horror of the moments before fading into a dream at the sight of her. "Hey, Autumn! I'll loop around and get you, okay? Just wait there."

Autumn doesn't seem to hear. And she doesn't wait, either. By the time Sasha eases that heavy old boat around and chugs back, she's already gone.

☙

As a teenager, Lil liked falling asleep outside, under the shade of tall trees. When she hit her teenage years—and her teenage years hit back—when the inside of the house felt too tame and soft for her sharp edges, Lil would spread out a blanket under the trees, where she was finally able to breathe. She'd feel silk nighttime breezes, hear the coo of the far-off train. She'd entertain fleeting dreams of catching one. But she never would. Because curled against the roots of those trees, it was as if she grew roots of her own. She felt right within herself among the trees. It wasn't *nice*. The hard limbs bruised her. Bugs bit at the lines of her socks; sometimes nighttime things skittered just beyond the fences. And yet, she was safe. She never overslept there; the trees dropped pecans on her head if she was going to be late for school.

She falls asleep under the trees again today. She doesn't mean to, but she must have. Because she wakes up to a change in the sunlight, near the fence. Lil's neck aches from the angle and she eases up. Her caning pole is nearby, laid neatly against the tree she slept under.

It's only when she stands up that she feels a tether at her ankle. Lil trips, catches herself on her knee and twists around. The fence at the border of her property is still broken in one place, a stone's throw from the front gate. That's right; she'd come over expecting to fix it and gotten sidetracked, then sleepy. And under the break, a thin line of kudzu has encroached while Lil was dozing. Creeping past the broken post, it has slithered into the grass and threaded around her ankle.

Lil kicks once, twice—she pulls at its tendons and the vine shreds under her hands. As soon as she's free, she attacks it, fighting its weak hold on the ground. She rips up young, tender roots, and grassy dirt clods come with it. Even the hammer she'd brought has been partially covered. She untangles the handle. It's just a lone scout testing a border, easy to stamp out. She tosses the leash of leaves back over the fence and all the little scattered bits with it.

Lil scans the ground. How had it come so quickly? How had she not seen it until it was over the border?

Her breathing isn't quite steady. Her hands feel useless and shaky, and they shouldn't. She won. It's fine now.

She's only a little tired.

"*I'm so tired,*" Mom murmured many times over endless nights, stretched on the couch with one daughter under each arm, her body smelling of sweat and earth. "*I don't think I can even make it up the stairs today...*"

But Lil's the one who can't quite get herself up and moving

now. This harvest feels like it may never end. She's still staring
when the Clearwater truck trundles up the road. For a stupid
second, Lil mistakes the shadowy figure driving it for Mom,
recognizing the cut of her jaw, the familiar curl of feathery hair.
The next moment, she remembers. Lil waves, and Sasha pulls to
a dusty stop, reaches over the dash, and pops the passenger door
open. She tucks her camera back behind the seat to make room.

It's too late in the day to fix the fence now anyway. She'll do it
first thing in the morning. Lil jogs toward her, swings herself into
the cab, and flops down in the passenger seat.

"You okay?" Sasha laughs, brushing dirt from Lil's arm. "Did
round two with Jason involve mud wrestling, or what?" She and
Sasha have been running counter to each other for days, catching
each other up in brief sentences exchanged halfway up or down
the stairs.

"I haven't seen him again." Lil fiddles the dial on the radio.
Still nothing. "Just took a nap." Sasha has brought the smell of
the river with her, and wind in her hair. "How was the ferry?"

Sasha stares out the windshield, her fingertips running over
the skin of her other arm. "Autumn hasn't been home in forever,
has she?"

It's been a while since Lil thought about her. "No. Not since
before the road closed. Main Street isn't the same with the bakery
shut." Sasha always had a soft way she talked about Autumn, a lilt
when she says her name, like it means hope. "I figured you were
in touch with her. Why?"

"Right." Sasha frowns, kneading at her forehead. "We may
have been in touch a bit." Had she called? There were no saved
messages from Autumn on the answering machine. "Not since

the road…right; she didn't even make it for our birthday. Was that—before the road?"

"It must have been." Lil remembers past birthdays so clearly, Autumn in her apron from the bakery near town square, embroidered honeysuckle vines on the faded blue denim. The cake, always a towering masterpiece under the trees.

"What about her little place above the bakery?" Sasha wonders. "Just empty? Can't imagine anyone would rent it from her these days." It's getting hot in the truck, like the sun is suddenly roasting them through the roof.

"Why do you ask?" Lil watches thoughts flicker across Sasha's face. Sasha hasn't mentioned Autumn in a long time. But it's easy enough to conjure an image of those two class cutters in their high school days, swinging their legs off the bleachers, Sasha's head in Autumn's lap as they cackle their way through some half-remembered in-joke.

They pull up beside the house and Sasha gives an airy, deflecting shrug. "I thought I saw her on the river today."

"I wish she'd stayed around," Lil replies. "Her baking would bring some stragglers back to town for sure."

Sasha cuts the engine and hands Lil the keys. "I wonder if she knows about Russ." Something in her seems to brighten. "Maybe she'll come for the service."

If anything draws friends, enemies, and lost loves home, it's a funeral.

CHAPTER FIVE

THE DIRT SASHA TOSSES ONTO THE CASKET IS BRITTLE, just a handful of dust. Last prayers float around the little huddle of mourners. This cemetery is nothing special, no sprawling New Orleans necropolis of poured cement mansions. Here, the little stones poke up from dying grass; this is just a yard like any number of cemeteries along that old sun-parched highway that doesn't reach here anymore. They'd be last in line at the Last Judgment, that's for sure. Sasha swears she can feel her second-grade teacher's postmortem stare on her from a few rows back. She feels sad, but also tired. Maybe mostly tired. They've had to do this too many times.

The soil plunks against the coffin lid. Lil stands beside her, wearing her tear tracks like a badge of honor. They already did their rounds among the grievers together, quiet exchanges with the farmers and shop owners who came to honor Russ. It's a smaller crowd than expected.

The speaking is over with, all the eulogies said. Sasha spots Jason; this is the closest she's been to him in a long time, since her visits home after college, when he was still considering a life in town. Once he was essential here, the last Finch of Honeysuckle House, captain of the volunteer firefighters—but that was a long time ago. Now he just feels like Russ's nephew from out of town, his shoes a little too shiny for the dust out here. With a soldier's poise, he stands in huddles of Russ's friends, his golden head bowed as he leans down to listen to something one of the tiny old women is saying to him.

She and Lil stand quietly together. Lil doesn't stride off on her own to hug grandmothers and exchange condolences now. She is rooted to Sasha's side, to the hole in the ground. "This is wrong," Lil breathes.

Sasha had somehow missed Lou at first, but there he is, crouching down beside the grave with two glasses of bourbon, one untouched. She puts a hand on her twin's back. "I know."

They stay that way for a moment, Lil collecting pieces of herself. She presses her fingers to the bridge of her nose. "Even Jason. The look on his face. I've never seen him like this." She casts around, eyes flitting between the scattered townspeople. Her back stiffens. "What's *he* doing here?"

Jason is standing under an oak tree with someone else now, someone Sasha hadn't noticed during the service. Theon, Lil's personal tormentor these days. Sasha hears all about him when he comes by, proposing Lil sell the Clearwater land. Those visits seem to come more and more frequently. She grinds her teeth. The two men cut starkly different figures: Jason's broad shoulders and straight back, Theon's slouch and sneakers.

"He didn't know Russ. He doesn't know Jason. He shouldn't be here." Lil's eyes blaze on Sasha. "He *shouldn't.*"

Sasha folds her arms. Theon's creeping around is starting to set even her teeth on edge, and Sasha is famously the mellow sister. "Should we go beat him up?"

Theon leans in to catch Jason's gaze again, which has slid from him back to the grave. His face is impassive, and he keeps a healthy space between them as those around them melt away. Sasha can't make out the words, but she catches the tonal ramp of a question. Jason hesitates, but his eyes don't leave Theon's this time. They stand there, strung between question and answer. "That ass is after Honeysuckle House," Sasha realizes. "He *gate-crashed* the burial to get at the Finch Orchard."

"He senses weakness." Lil watches Theon reach out for a businesslike handshake, and slink off into the crowd. Jason is left standing on his own, wiping the hand absently on his pants leg. He scrubs his face again, at tears or sweat or both.

Sasha squints across the plot at him, past Lou pouring a last drink out for his friend, past the dwindling mourners. "So what are you going to do about it?"

Lil straightens her back, her face grim, but determined, tears dry. "Whatever I can."

❧

Long ago, after home games when Jason would be surrounded by friends, Lil used to wait in the emerald glow of fireflies under the bleachers, and watch. She could have joined them, slotted into place under his shoulder if she wanted to be that kind of a girl, the kind that wore varsity jackets and got engaged at graduation. (Back then Lil despised that kind of girl. It felt daring to hate other girls when she was younger, rather than callous.) Lil waited, in those days, until that moment when the crowd that washed Jason out to sea ebbed. She spotted his dark eyes, flashing up, and knew he was finally taking a breath, finally not answering a question, not laughing at someone's joke. And she'd move, snatch his hand, and they'd vanish, quicksilver, into a world of their own. And he'd be hers. Finally.

Jason is older now. Lil is older, too, and uncomfortable in the dress she'd bought for Mom's funeral, scratchy and ill fitting as grief itself. But just like she always has, she lingers in the shade, watching the throng around him, waiting for that moment when he surfaces.

He may just be a familiar stranger, a face that she knows wearing all sorts of new expressions she can't totally track anymore, but she still remembers *this* weary look, this particular smile. Jason is trying so hard. He will never pull himself away.

Mrs. Grady and Cork are embracing in front of Jason, blocking the other well-wishers, and Lil takes her chance. Just as Jason shuts his eyes and inhales, the first private pause he's had all day, she presses her hand into the crook of his elbow and tugs him out of the place where he's been rooted, from under the dissolving canopy of the old oak.

Jason looks a bit dazed, sun dazed or grief dazed, reeling, like someone who's just been yanked off a carnival ride. "Oh. Hey," he says. There's a tension in the way his hands remain in his pockets, as if he's resisting lifting them to fend off a blow. They hadn't parted on the best terms last time. "Thanks for—um—being here."

"Come on," Lil murmurs. "They'll be okay. You've done him proud." Maybe it's because of the long, drawn-out torture of a day like today but he doesn't question her, following with the easy trust of a child. Sensing her gentleness, one hand strays from its pocket to take hers.

All at once his cologne, peppery and sweet, hits her—and it is Russ's. Russ only ever wore that one scent, the one Jason picked sometime in college. He'd given Russ the first bottle, wrapped in bright-red paper one Christmas Eve, and Russ had chuckled that he'd better wear it since there was a lady present. Then Jason turned to Lil, the lady present, and handed her a bright-red parcel too. She felt like a happy fool bundled up in flannel with a mug of mulled wine, Jason and Russ—

Lil breathes through the hot flush of tears behind her eyelids. "Come with me," she says, and leads him away from the funeral. Jason looks parched and pale, like he hasn't thought about food and water all day, and it's only half over.

The atmosphere is heavy with Russ's absence—she'll never hear his ragged laugh again—but the air tastes just the same as it did before they laid him down. The world hasn't noticed one of its best people is gone.

"I have to get over to the reception," Jason manages, when he spots her truck waiting for them. "I don't really have time to—"

"We're going to the reception. You don't look like you should be driving."

He weighs this, scowling slightly now, then jumps in on the passenger side. "Thanks," he says when she joins him and turns the key over. "I'm dead on my feet."

"It's a long day. He'd want you to take care of yourself too." She leans over him to pop open the glove box. Sure enough, there's still a couple of granola bars in there, stashed for emergencies. She tosses him one. "You can eat on the way."

For once in his life, Jason apparently doesn't have it in him to argue. He promptly shoves half the bar in his mouth. "Losing him is like being on those endless shifts down at the firehouse." Groaning, he rubs the back of his neck. "Can't go home, can't sleep—but there's no *actual* fire, because he's gone…so there's nothing I can *fix*. Just go through junk in the house and wait around."

Lil digs under her seat for her aluminum water bottle and hands it to him. Shade dapples the windshield. "It was like that when Mom died. Boxes and boxes, bills, and old papers…" Mom is still everywhere in the house—the pressed flowers in frames on the wall over the stairs, a hall closet stocked with her best coats. One photograph of her and Luis, their father, the man she'd loved…almost as much as the orchard.

"Exactly." Jason drains her bottle in a gulp and a half like a quarterback at halftime. "Honeysuckle House has been in the family so long, all the junk is probably what keeps it standing up," he says gloomily. "Easier to just burn the old place down than empty it out." He leans his head back against the seat, eyes shut for a moment. "What a mess."

"Speaking of messes, what did Theon want?" Lil can drive these roads blind, but she keeps her eyes forward.

Jason rubs at his eyes, distracted. "Who?"

"I saw him talking to you. Guy in the really wrinkled suit." The roads feel especially empty usually, but there's a small crowd of cars behind them, headed for the reception as well. "Probably the only one that you didn't know."

"Oh, right." Jason fumbles her water bottle into one of the truck's cup holders, sighing. "Asked me to call him. Sounds like you know more about it than I do."

"He's always after me to sell my land." Lil grips the steering wheel a little tighter. "He's a snake. Buying up all the old properties for low prices."

He's watching her now; she can feel his eyes on the side of her face. There's a pause, like he's tasting a few different words before he spits any of them out. "Did you think about it?"

It's hard to read his tone. Maybe he wishes she would flee this old trap like he did. And maybe it fills him with fury, to think she would, when she wouldn't do it for him when he asked her to leave with him years ago.

"No," Lil replies. "I wouldn't think about selling to him."

"Then who?" He sighs. "What small-time operation would buy this eaten-up land?"

"I don't know. I don't even know what he does with it. As far as I can tell, the properties he's bought are just rotting." Lil swallows down the anger that always feels close these days. "Someone needs to do something. This town, Jason…it's changed since you left. It's like no one cares anymore. Everyone's just ready to give up on it."

Jason gazes out the window, watching the worn-out parade of Main Street buildings pass them by. "What are you asking me, Lilith?"

"Nothing." It isn't true. There's a question beating away in her throat, desperate for freedom. But they're pulling up to the country club now, a stately old dowager with cracks in her facade. "Not today at least. But—" She shuts her eyes. "Come to me. If you need anything."

In a gentle move, she feels his hand around hers again. They're close in the car, the musky glow of Russ's old cologne all around them. "Thanks for the ride."

Switching the car off, she faces him again. "Are you ready?"

He is ready. He squeezes her hand, then releases it, and they go inside together.

CHAPTER SIX

SASHA WAKES TO THE SMELL OF PRETZELS. IT'S SO near, the buttery tough skin baking, that she could be inside the oven herself, tacky dough knotting around her, expanding in hot bands against her skin amidst the roar of the convection fan. She sits up fast, writhes in her sheets.

It's just her room, the same as ever, a fly beating itself brainless against her window. She sniffs again, and the fly throws itself at the pane. Does it smell that too? Cheesy jalapeño pretzels, plain ones covered in thick crystals of sea salt, sweet ones with cinnamon sugar wreathed through the dough. Pretzels. Pretzels. Pretzels. It couldn't be Lil baking downstairs; she doesn't have the patience. And pretzels only remind Sasha of one person. There's only one person she used to split them with behind the bleachers at high school football games, fighting over the nacho cheese.

Sasha checks the time—late, obviously—and hops up. Her nose aches like she's inhaled cayenne pepper. She's trying to get out to the bathroom when she sneezes *hard* and knocks her head against the door frame. "*Argh!*" she screams at the house. "I am having a confusing morning!"

Lil arches an eyebrow at her when she comes downstairs, coffee in hand as she pores over some papers. "You look rough."

Sasha stumbles past her to the door. She's too hot, desperate for some fresh air. The pretzel smell has only intensified, taking on an interesting golden saffron edge. "I have a brain tumor and will almost definitely die," she announces piteously as she goes out. "At least you'll inherit everything just like you always wanted."

"You'll be remembered as a martyr," Lil calls after her. The door slams. Sasha jogs down the road, toward town. She trips over several cracks in the pavement, ones that seem wider and deeper than ever. Her mouth waters.

Town lists around her as she walks. The old timber place that still has smoke pouring out of the stack, even if she never sees anyone go in or out. The faded POP'S BARBECUE, EST. 1946, with a single car outside. The little blue building with an angel out front that sells home furnishings that haven't changed in thirty years. Lou's junk shop, with a light on. Su's grocery.

And then the bakery, a sandy building in a row of two-story shops, built more than a hundred years before, with the same bright-red door. It's been shuttered for a long time, no one there to write specials on the chalkboard, no one to unfold the patio furniture that leans under the awning, gathering scarves of orange leaves. The sign says it's closed, but light glows from inside. Someone is moving around in there.

Sasha tries the door; it's open and the smell of pretzels blooms afresh in her nose, in her mouth, her throat. She steps inside. The place is almost all kitchen—three tables feel like a crowd in the tiny sitting area. The display is empty, no careful cardstock labels for the old favorites like pecan pie, or slapdash Post-It notes for spontaneous specials like bourbon fig cheesecake. But the kitchen isn't empty.

"If you're a robber, just know I'm broke," a familiar voice calls from the back.

The double doors that lead to the kitchen swing open and she steps through. Her auburn hair is swept into the world's messiest, most lopsided ponytail, and a hunk of pretzel is tucked in the thin curve of her lips like a cigarette—she was always trying to quit, back then—and flour or sugar dusts the knobby heels of her hands and wrists. When she looks up and sees Sasha, she breaks out beaming.

"There you are," she says, her voice warm. Like Sasha is welcome. "Come on. I need your thumbs."

Autumn. Autumn is back.

"It's you," Sasha says dumbly. She sways back, thudding against the wall, then transforms the fall into a lean, very nonchalant, there against the bare brick. Her head pounds. "But I thought—you're here?"

That *had* been her on the bank that night, watching. No mistake—Autumn had been there.

Then how did she cross the river?

"I'm here," she confirms, biting her bit of pretzel in two and offering her the other half. "Since someone isn't answering my calls anymore."

Sasha charges her, grabbing her in a hug that is too tight, too much, enough to lift her right off the ground. The bite of pretzel hits the floor and bounces away. "I missed you," she grumbles out against Autumn's shoulder, hoarser than ever. She feels almost angry about it.

Autumn chuckles and pats the top of her head, sprinkling her with flour. It showers in a faint cloud around them. "Come make cookies with me. I'm doing the thumbprint kind."

Sasha lets her go. She's still feeling unsettled, a little off balance, like Autumn's arrival might signal an earthquake. But Sasha gives her a double thumbs-up, and they go into the kitchen, where baking sheets are laid out and waiting. Strawberry jam glows in a jar by the window, ready to fill the centers.

Autumn has sometimes said she's never more peaceful than when she's baking. When she ran the bakery, she'd wake in the pitch black of 3:00 a.m. to spend very quiet, lonely mornings with the ancient receiver radio's buggy antennas tuned to jazz as she cut chilled butter into flour or whipped eggs to a stiff meringue or wrapped long logs of oatmeal cookie dough. Autumn never planned what she made each day. There used to be one kind of focaccia (unless she was very stressed, in which case there might be five), and whatever assortment of cakes, pies, tarts, and donuts struck her. Then she went to culinary school, others took over the space, but…there was no possible replacement for her, so for a while now, the bakery has just been floating in stasis, unused, waiting for her to come back. "Wash hands," she commands with the sternness of a teddy bear. "And present your thumbs."

Sasha washes with the bergamot soap by the sink, then holds her hands out to Autumn. "Thumbs ready." She wants to ask her things, but the questions feel odd somehow, and so she doesn't ask, *Where were you?* or *How did you get back?*; she asks, "How

have you been, Pip?" It was an old nickname, short for Pippi
Longstocking, for the braids she wore as a child.

"Not bad," she says. "My parents are on their retirement RV
trip around the country. They're sending me polaroids from the
Grand Canyon." Sasha has always liked Autumn's parents. They
used to grow pretty decent hemp. "Maybe a little homesick. You
though, I thought you'd never move back home."

"Well, I'm just back for a little while," Sasha reminds them
both. "You missed this place?"

"Yeah. This is still my favorite oven. And my favorite sous
chef." There's a tray of pretzels cooling on the rack. But she leads
Sasha over to a pan full of cream-colored dough balls, rolled into
perfect spheres. "Come on." She snags Sasha's arm, positioning
her thumb over the cookies. "Mine are too small. My Achilles'
heel." She presses their thumbs down gently, together. "You never
returned my calls. As I mentioned."

"You know how it is. I'm working a lot. And service is bad out
here." Sasha hadn't gotten any of those calls. Had she? It's true
that she doesn't have the best track record with follow-through...
All her previous relationships are proof enough of that. Sasha
squishes a dough ball, then another. She rests her other hand on
the counter, and a tendril of russet hair tickles her cheek. "Giant
thumbs are terrible at dialing numbers into telephones."

"Fee fie fo fum. What have you been up to? Fighting with
Lil?" Autumn teases.

"Constantly." Sasha shrugs. "Also doing a bunch of odd jobs
around town. I basically run the ferry service now too." She hesitates. "Actually—I thought I saw you the other day by the river."

Autumn's work pauses. "You saw me?"

Sasha nods, reading the stillness. But then Autumn keeps on. "If you're running the ferry, I should get you a jaunty captain's hat."

Sasha laughs. "I think that would suit me." It feels so comfortable to be there, like they can just fall back into step again. "I'm also doing this photography project and helping Dale survey some of those old orchards west of town. It's pretty creepy out there."

"I used to play in those orchards." Autumn's smile turns a little dreamy. "Mom didn't like it though."

"I get it. It feels a bit..." But there are no words, only a sort of twist in the gut, which some might interpret as the wriggle of fear and Sasha chooses to call a thrill. She leans around to catch Autumn's eye, smirking. "Want to go play out there again?"

⌒

Danger feels far away to Sasha as they wander along the train tracks toward one of the nearer properties on Dale's list. They finished the cookies first, of course, and ate them too hot, with jam spilling onto their fingers. Autumn is a twinkle of light through lush leaves; something about her keeps Sasha's dark thoughts at bay. It even seems like the kudzu has retreated, thin fingers only gently caressing the trees on the far side of the railroad. The sun crashes down on the rails, drawing out a scent of crushed wildflowers, rust, and, below that, an old ambition, faded from a century past. The few houses here are shotguns, small shuttered husks. The ground is a mix of hard dirt and trash, beer cans, and tires. It's tired. The stray cats that live out here stay away from people.

"Why did we never hang around out here when we skipped school?" Sasha wonders as they pass the rotting timbers of an abandoned barn. She hoists her camera strap on her shoulder, raises the lens. "I guess we always had the tree house as an out-of-bounds hangout." Their secret place, the tree house by the creek, cypress knees nudging out of the mud and reeds below. That had been their major repository for dark secrets.

"Yeah. I don't know." Autumn is kicking around what looks like an old horseshoe; Sasha snaps her picture. A little delinquent with her scuffed shoes and weathered denim jacket, she catches Sasha in the act and sticks her tongue out. "It's…" She tilts her head into the sun. "It's dirtier, smaller than I remember."

They wander the railroad, an easy amble, weeds growing up through rusting bars. A faded stop sign lies dangerously close to the track. The properties they pass grow more and more dilapidated, one with a rocking chair that creaks along on its own. Any paint that ever touched these old skeletons is long gone, flaked off in the sunlight.

"Do you remember—" Autumn begins and abruptly cuts off. She frowns. Something in the tall grass startles and darts for the trees.

"You know I never remember anything. What?" Sasha nudges, watching her through the viewfinder.

"That weird little legend people used to talk about. You know." Autumn turns with a spooky wiggle of her fingers. "About what falls out of the abandoned trees. It's funny, I haven't thought about this stuff in ages, but now that I'm here, it's all flooding back to me. All these old stories I'd forgotten."

Sasha frowns. "Lou was trying to tell me something about that on the boat. Something important. About—kids." It's been on her mind since then, along with a wriggling discomfort that she's missing something, failing him.

"Yeah." Autumn pokes along down the tracks a little further. "Some of the grannies used to talk about it. They said in the old days, some trees stopped dropping pecans, and then later, people found babies sleeping under them instead.

"Granted"—Autumn turns back—"I remember some different versions. There's also one where the rich matriarch of an orchard wanted a child so badly, she prayed to the trees until they gave her one, but as payment, the harvests stopped and she died penniless. Sort of a cautionary be-careful-what-you-wish-for tale. But the more common story is about babies, born of otherwise barren trees. I like that version better," she admits.

Feral, angry children lost in abandoned orchards that never bear fruit, children of the ground with no one to love them, who shiver on cold nights and grow up nursing their own bruises. To Sasha, it follows the same vein as fairy changelings and lost boys, just with added local flavor.

"Did you ever find a baby out here, Pip?" Sasha asks lightly, only it doesn't feel light.

"I used to play with these kids that I never saw in school." That wasn't so strange; it wasn't as if every kid in the surrounding area went to their school. Just…most did. Wisps of hair float around Autumn's sharp face, river-colored eyes. She's all points and angles in a way that really shouldn't appear as friendly and open as she does. "I haven't thought about that old story in years."

They reach the property line of the old orchard on Dale's list, and Sasha walks the boundaries, checking the old markers, taking a measurement or two the way he'd taught her. A few unharvested

Pawnee pecans litter the ground, crunching under her feet in a way that makes her jump. It smells like leaf mold and damp earth, and they're quiet.

There's almost too much to say for small talk. She's been home longer than she meant to be. The photo project has taken too long; Sasha hasn't even bothered sorting through her film yet. Her last breakup is no longer raw. She's running a little thin on funny anecdotes, her main social currency. Maybe Autumn has met new friends, better company that's a little easier to love.

Once upon a time, Autumn never did anything Sasha didn't hear about—and very little Sasha wasn't there for, right at her side. Now, both of their lives are full of fresh, new pages the other hasn't written on at all.

Sasha glances back. "How long are you staying?"

Autumn fixes her with curious eyes. "How long are *you* staying?"

"Oh. Well, I mean—" Sasha shifts between her feet. "I meant to leave after our birthday but then there was everything with the road and Theon and..." *Which* birthday?

How long has the road been closed?

They stare at one another, the great boughs creaking overhead.

"What's that?" Autumn darts down the tracks and crouches down. When trains were more frequent, they'd blow through town like hurricanes. When the horns wailed, kids rushed up close to put copper pennies on the rails, which rattled as the locomotive blurred past. They'd traded the pennies around, warm and pressed completely flat. If a train comes now, they'll hear it in time to move, right?

"Autumn," Sasha calls, walking more quickly toward her. She doesn't respond, but beckons.

Sasha follows like she's bound on a string.

When she reaches her, Autumn's face is pale with apprehension as she stares at the center of the tracks, where something is tied with rough, homemade twine. At first, it's easily mistaken for an art project; three slender sticks are tied together at a point a foot high, and full colored leaves wreathe around the base. It's almost pretty.

Except the skinned body of a squirrel hangs from it by the neck. It isn't a sculpture, but a strange, clumsy gallows. Or an offering on a crude altar.

Numbly, Sasha snaps a photo. Its black beady eyes are still slitted enough to reflect light, and its mouth is cracked open.

"Poor thing. Who would do this?" Autumn flutters like she wants to take it down.

"Don't touch it." Sasha pulls her back, picturing maggots and foaming mouths. "There's nothing you can do for it anyway."

"Right. Yeah. Diseases." Autumn stands and leans against Sasha's shoulder. "I didn't know anyone else ever came out here, except you."

"They don't," Sasha admits, somewhat soothed by the weight of her there. She almost wants to slip her arm around her, to sneak her hand into the pocket of that tattered old blue jean jacket—but she doesn't. The idea turns to vapor and dissipates with a breeze. But they still don't move yet, or get back to the surveyor work. They just stare up at the trees together, the sour stink of decay tickling Sasha's nose.

She's not even quite sure what she's staring at. High up in a wizened oak, a twitch of movement catches her eye. For a split second, a small face with blank dark eyes glares out at her from between the limbs of the tree. She blinks—and it's gone. It's got to be a trick of pale roundish bark and knots in the wood. Too much folklore in too quiet a place.

"Tell me next time you come out here," Autumn says. "I want to join you."

CHAPTER SEVEN

L IL REMEMBERS THE FIRST TIME SHE FOUND THE pond. She and Sasha had been playing hide-and-seek, and it was Lil's turn to hide. She rushed past the barn and dove deeper into the orchard. As Sasha's counting faded, Lil's path took her between narrow crevices and hulking roots. She tumbled through the brambles without meaning to and landed beside the pond.

The pond was perfectly round. To her, it looked like a vinyl record sunken in the ground. When she touched the deep midnight water with her finger, it was cold as snowmelt. But what transfixed her was the tree, growing the prettiest pecans she'd ever seen, the bright gold of Grandma's necklace that Mom kept in her jewelry box. Game forgotten, Lil gathered up a handful and ran to bring them to Sasha and Mom, to show them the miracle.

Mom was in the kitchen fixing breakfast. But when Lil held up her treasure, Mom dropped a plate of eggs and smacked the pecans out of her hand. *"Don't you touch those."* Lil ran to her room and cried into her pillow.

Only later, Mom took her hand while Sasha was sleeping. She led her back through the trees, and sat down with her on the banks of the pond.

"I'm telling you because I don't want you to be scared," Mom said, plucking up a nugget of golden manna between her fingers. She stared down at it. "We're stewards of this place." Lil hadn't known what that word meant, but she trusted that Mom knew everything. That's what a child thinks at five. So she listened.

"This is not a normal pecan tree. We didn't plant it. Neither did your grandparents or great grandparents. This tree takes care of itself. It has this whole pond to itself, all the water it needs. There's only one thing we can do for it"—Mom's eyes went flat—"and that's to never let anyone in."

"Why can't I eat it?" Lil asked. She'd wanted to, had been about to before Mom shouted and the shock of terror on her face had stopped her. "What are they?"

"They're an offering," Mom said. "The tree is like an arm that the pond reaches out to us. They're meant to be a gift. But the gift is too great for anyone to bear. So you must not try." When Mom told her to throw the golden pecan into the water, Lil did without hesitation.

Today, sitting on that familiar bank, there's only one golden pecan to find. Lil strokes over the smooth hull of the little treasure. The invitation. The ambrosia-laced trap. Once more people knew about the tree. They tried to sneak over fences to steal a handful of gold, convinced a single pecan could grant their wishes. But now, the center of Lil's life is forgotten by the world. The old ways are dying, the myths and legends aren't being honored, and Lil's guarding a treasure no one even remembers to want. The rules have been passed down so long, and even the full consequences of eating a golden pecan are lost to time. But she knows all too well that they don't grant wishes.

Lil stands, task done, and hikes her way back out into the main orchard, into the sunlight.

Sasha's out, as usual, stumbling through her life like some wayward ghost. But before she reaches the house, down the road, she hears the soft tread of a runner. The jogger turns off the highway and lopes up to the fence. Interesting to see him here. Lil walks down to meet him at the gate. He waits for her as she crosses the long yard.

He's still a little winded when she makes it to the fence line, and he gives her a fierce look. She can smell his sweat, salt and citrus. "Fine," Jason pants. He's dressed for a run, hair bronzed against his forehead. His hand wraps around one of the pickets. "Let's talk about how to save the damn town. I'm suffocating in that house."

Lil rests her elbows on the fence too. He does look tired, like he's run the whole way here. "Come inside. You look like you need some water."

☙

Jason stands by the table, amid the ghosts of his past self, high school Jason daring her to drink hot sauce, postcollege Jason making coffee the way she liked it, keeping quiet so they didn't get caught—twenty-three was still young enough to be scolded if Mom caught them making out in her kitchen.

"Glass of water," she reminds them both. "You—you remember

where the cups are." Obviously. The silverware is in the same drawer it's always been in, the glasses in the cupboard, the cracks in the wall plaster. It's all the same.

Jason hesitates, then goes to pull down a cup from the cabinet. It has a faded old Girl Scouts of America logo on it, from way back in Sasha's scouting days. He fills it, drains it, and then fills it again. "Everything's the same at my house too," he says, almost bitterly, as he leans back against her counter. "Like I never left."

It isn't constant heartbreak anymore to think about Jason and the way he left, bound for law school, for a bigger world. Enough time has passed that the ache doesn't follow her the way it did at first, when they were twenty-five and wine-drunk in the middle of the last, greatest fight. The warm light of the kitchen, still smelling of burnt caramel and vanilla creme. Jason flushed with anger and rejection, pleading that *he's not leaving her; he wants her to come to North Carolina with him.* Lil snapping at him that *if he wants to go, then go*, because if he ever knew her, he'd know her roots were set deep, and to leave would be to rip herself in two.

For a long time, she wasn't able to think of crème brûlée without a current of furious hurt coursing through her. But time went on. At this point, resenting him for it feels more like a reflex than a reality.

"Are you swamped with casseroles?" Lil asks. "Almost every grandmother in this town has a crush on you."

"So many. Remember Dorothea's cornflake casserole?" Jason swoons back, nearly knocking his head on the cabinets.

"Isn't that the one that she always insisted was better served cold?"

Jason makes a face. "Like revenge?"

Lil chuckles. "So you said you want to save the town."

"I said we could talk about it," Jason corrects, straightening up. The space feels cramped once he does. "You weren't exactly subtle on the way to the memorial."

"I didn't mean—" She's almost as bad as Theon, isn't she? "It wasn't what I meant to do, bringing it up there. But I'm not sorry." She leans against the fridge, facing him. "I don't want to leave. I can't just sit back and watch my home die, but I can't do anything about it alone. And this is what happens to small towns, isn't it? People move away, farming gets too hard, and they die." She has to be careful; she feels every potential minefield in this conversation. "That isn't a comment on you, so don't take it that way." Is that too harsh? God, this is hard, when talking to him used to feel more like mind reading.

"No, I get it." Jason refills his water glass, his arm brushing hers. "I always thought I'd come back here after practicing law for a few years and try to get on the town council or something. Hell, run for mayor. But the town can't even get that road repaired."

"Do you think it's possible to change the course of things?" Lil asks.

He considers her, expression wry. "You can't stop time."

"I'm not trying to *stop time*," she interjects.

His mouth twists. "Or maybe time can't stop you. Either or. I know I'm not dumb enough to tell you what you can't do, Lil."

It makes her glow despite herself, so Lil smirks and teases, "You're definitely dumb enough. We wouldn't have fought so much if not."

Jason snorts. "Yes, that was completely because of my stupidity and had nothing to do with how damn bullheaded you can be."

A foolish, involuntary smile pricks at her lips. She bites it back. She's missed this.

"Hey." Jason catches her hand. "I sort of miss your bullhead."

His thumb warms the rough calluses of her palm. It's hard to explain what exactly drew them together that first time, when Jason was concealed like he's always concealed, beneath his glamour of respectability. But then, and now, and probably always, when Lil allows herself to look, deeply look at him, she sees the burning. Even in high school it was there, the house fire blazing inside Jason Finch. He hides it well, and no one else ever seems to notice. But it always made perfect sense that he worked so many shifts at the firehouse, maybe just trying to quench himself. They are gasoline to each other. The kitchen feels tight, like a closet, and he's close enough that she could have dragged him against her. His hand would be rough at the nape of her neck, his mouth would be urgent, his body—

"You will not *believe* who I found in town today and who's coming to dinner!" Sasha sings, spinning into the kitchen to douse them. She stops hard at the door, nearly tripping over her own feet in a moment of uncharacteristic awkwardness. "Oh." She glances back, clearly evaluating if escape is still an option. Everyone knows it's not. "Hey, Jason."

"Hi, Sasha," Jason sighs, and his mask falls back on, and the moment is over.

☙

The evening creeps on, the air dusty, the sunset faded. Inside, candlelight burns close and, for Sasha, with a brightness like raw joy. Autumn is back! Here at home! Even the house itself feels pleased to see her, the old spaces sighing with a dwindling evening breeze.

Jason is welcomed tonight too. Sasha notes Lil's eyes on him as they all sit down to eat. Sasha pours dark wine into crystal cordial glasses, and Lil presses happy kisses to Autumn's cheeks. They talk about the harvest and Jason's law practice and Sasha's survey work for Dale. They reminisce (gingerly) about simpler adolescent escapades, Lil's smile a slice of warm danger.

Autumn beams, jokes, but sticks close to Sasha's side. It's probably the most she and Jason have ever talked; they were in different universes in high school, Jason in student council and every sport, Autumn happy to skate by on average grades. Of everyone at the table, the prom king and the slackers, only Sasha could bridge the two worlds: somehow she was always popular *and* a total screwup.

"The money-laundering scheme to buy all those kegs for the bonfire was me," Sasha brags. "No one guessed because I was repeating Algebra 2 for the third time."

Jason looks tempted to bang his head on the table. "You were the *student council treasurer*."

"Exactly!" She pours him the last splash of wine, winking. "The kegger was my major campaign promise."

Autumn raises her empty, wine-stained glass, cheeks flushed. "Sasha for president! Kegs for all!"

Time turns runny, and midnight closes in on them without Sasha noticing. Jason finally stands and admits he has to go. Autumn, always on baker's hours, can't seem to keep her eyes open as she follows Jason out the door. There's a determined set to Jason's shoulders as he's swallowed by the darkness down the steps. He and Lil aren't even looking at each other, but Sasha feels the tension.

"Lunch tomorrow?" he murmurs to Lil, like he thinks Sasha won't hear. She does. And she sees Lil's nod too.

"You sure you don't want to stay?" Lil says to Autumn as they all walk to the door.

"My place above the bakery misses me," she replies, and Lil sweeps her into a hug. "And I want to make cinnamon rolls in the morning."

Sasha grins eagerly. "That's a good reason."

"Come back," Lil demands against her flurry of hair. "Don't let Sasha hog you."

Sasha gives the truck keys a chivalrous spin as they all step out onto the porch. "I'll drive y'all home. C'mon   "

But she pauses. Something has stopped her. They listen. There's a shushing sound in the air, like the song of river reeds in the wind. Or maybe that's what the ocean sounds like; it feels like a lifetime since she's heard that insistent crash of waves.

"Is that the train?" she asks, voice dropping. She searches the night for the source, for a car speeding or just a thatch of rustling grasses. It's not clear—

"Look." Autumn points. Sasha squints past her into the blackness, and it takes a moment to even understand the spot of light pricking at the night.

Jason is hoarse. "Fire."

The house is far enough down the road that it only winks at them through the trees, more road and projectiles of black smoke than visible blaze. But it's got to the whole house, one of the empty properties, swallowed in an inferno.

Lil palpably shakes off the afterglow of the evening, striding
out to the truck. To go single-handedly fight the fire, apparently.

"Wait," Sasha calls, darting back into the house. "I'll call it in."

It takes two calls to connect at the firehouse. "Hey, Cesar."
Sasha hurries out. "There's a giant house fire out here. Can't tell
which house, but you can't miss it if you drive out toward the
roadwork." She listens to the scurry at the tiny station. "We're
going out there now to try to slow it down."

They pile into the truck, Sasha and Autumn crouching in the
tailgate with a pile of fire blankets that Lil always keeps there.
Autumn presses her hand to her mouth. "I'm too tipsy for this."

Lil drives, her truck coughing with every pothole that sends
them jostling against each other. It's such a dark haze out on that
country road that the headlights barely cut through to the next
tree. The horrible rushing sound grows, and soon they turn down
a gravel drive. The house, all alight, beckons them down the
road with a gaping grin. Kudzu clinging to the sides writhes in
glowing tangles. As they pull up as close as they dare, a half-hung
porch swing blazing on the rotten deck collapses, hitting the ashy
timbers below with a *thunk*.

"Cesar is on the way," Sasha reminds them as Lil cuts the
engine. "We don't have to save the day or anything."

Jason rolls his eyes once again at this repeated news. He and
Cesar have apparently never gotten past their various rivalries.
The noise here and the light are so intense that they're cut off
from the dark road, from any approaching siren.

Even the orchard itself, barren as it is, even seems to lean
away, leaves choked in smoke. Jason takes charge, and for once,
Lil allows it without a fight, letting him direct their movements.

He dives in closest, dragging away the debris that's most likely to catch, while the others brace themselves at the far edges, ready to smother any stray sparks. Lil glares down the fire, between it and the trees as if her will is enough to stop it, fear only showing in the way her mouth trembles.

It's like staring down a demon. Sasha loses sight of Autumn around the side of the house. Sparks flare dangerously close in the grass and she pounces with her blanket, stamping them out. But it's startlingly stubborn, hot even through the blanket. Jason drags a dead tree branch out of the way, silhouetted against the flames.

And then—the sound of an engine cuts through the roaring fire.

Sasha turns, waving at the fire truck as it cruises up the road. It's moving slow—potholes, maybe—and finally, it turns onto the dirt driveway of the property. Lil dashes to Sasha's side, face bright with relief.

For a moment, the truck idles. Then it shuts off and Cesar is the first to step out in full gear. The driver, Shiloh, hangs out the window, frowning.

"Lil?" Cesar calls over the distance, bracing his hands on his hips. "What are you doing out here?"

"Your job," she yells back, turning back to the house. "Which you should be—" She cuts off. Silence rings in her ears. "Sasha," Lil breathes, yanks at her shoulder. "Sasha, look."

Behind them, the house crouches, decrepit in the darkness. Only it isn't burning. Autumn is sprawled on the ground in front of her blanket, staring up with huge eyes at the intact wood frame. Jason's hands are still grasped around an old tire. Bewildered, he tosses it aside. The porch swing, still haphazardly aloft, creaks.

Cesar joins Sasha and Lil. "Yeah, we, uh, followed the sound of shouting." He pulls his gloves off, folding them into his belt. "Pretty...big fire."

"This is wrong," Lil murmurs. "It was—it was on fire a second ago. We all saw it."

"We saw it from the orchard," Sasha snaps, dropping her blanket. "We drove out here; we've been fighting it."

"Well it looks like you got it." Cesar's face is pinched. He pulls Lil aside. "Look, I don't know what this is," he whispers, close to her cheek. "Is this some kind of joke?"

"It's not a joke," Lil insists. She rakes her hands through her hair, smudging soot against her forehead. "Cesar, do you think I would joke about something like this?"

"Technically Sasha called," Cesar points out. "Hi, Sasha."

Blandly, she raises a singed hand to him.

"If you're going to blame her, at least do it far enough away that she can't hear." Lil yanks away. She's the one on fire now, flaring toward the house.

Of all of them, Jason looks most lost, his arms slack. "What the hell," he breathes.

"Jason." Cesar sniffs, stands a little taller, his size putting Jason to shame, if Jason felt things like shame. "Are you in on this too? Wouldn't have thought you'd find something like this funny." His eyes dart between Lil and Jason.

Somehow, even in deepest distress, Jason manages a haughty glance past Cesar at the fire truck. "Took y'all forever to get out here," he says, more to Shiloh in the truck than to Cesar. Jason trained Shiloh years ago. "Someone could have been hurt."

The decrepit old door to the house is slightly ajar, and Lil shoves it open. But she doesn't go in. Sasha follows her, leaving Jason and Cesar to glare at each other.

Lil's breathing has turned unsteady. Even the old welcome mat, which should be ashes, is back under her feet. One of those custom ones that reads, Welcome to Grandma and Grandpa's! in big curling letters. It's not even scorched. "You saw it," Lil whispered. Behind them, the boys have raised their voices. "It was real. Just a second ago. Right?"

"Of course it was real. We saw it from the orchard. All the way up the road." Sasha's hands sting. "We fought it."

Lil turns to look at her, lips pressed together, eyes full and fearful. *I know*, Sasha thinks. *And I don't know what's happening either.*

The porch creaks as Autumn joins them. "We need to go," she says. "Before Cesar and Jason start dueling or something."

"Okay. Okay." Lil wrenches herself away.

The inside of the house still smells faintly of smoke.

CHAPTER EIGHT

IT'S ONLY AS HER TRUCK CRUNCHES TO A STOP IN THE gravel parking lot that Lil realizes she can't remember the last time she went to Pop's. It's the best smokehouse in town, probably in the state, with tarp walls and a tiny worn-out interior. The wide timber posts are littered with recognition, magazine features, local and national awards. Outside there's a window for orders and picnic tables with tablecloths of red-checkered vinyl. The air smells like woodsmoke and honey. There's always a line out the door at lunch, and though he serves customers until the cupboards are bare, Pop usually closes well before three. Sasha worked here as a teenager, somehow never rushed as she counted out change at the register or stacked mile-high sandwiches with smoked pork watched by fifty pairs of impatient eyes. In his heyday, Pop had kept the smokehouse going seven days a week— and isn't it sad when towns start using the word "heyday," which can only be defined once it's over.

Pop himself is older now, with bad knees and no staff, so he can't get up the gumption to smoke every day anymore. When she drives by, she usually looks whether the single bulb over the door is turned on, meaning he's there, but lately it seems like Pop's is closed more often than not. Only today, it's open, the tables out back humming. A few townies raise their hands to her from their places in line as she passes. The sky is the kind of bright clean blue that only comes in early fall, and Jason waits for her. He's wearing a faded firehouse shirt, fingers busy organizing the complimentary sugar and Sweet'N Low packets people use to sweeten their own iced tea.

Lil stuffs her hands in her pockets, swings a leg over the bench, and plops down. She's still exhausted. She had been too wired to sleep. All night, she felt the creep of kudzu scratching at her window, the lonely howl of the train. When she finally passed out, she only fell into fevered, gasoline fantasies that felt too real, and woke up to Jason's phone call, reminding her to meet him for lunch. From the window, Pop bellows an order number.

"I already ordered for us," Jason says, not looking up from the mixed-up white and pink packets he's organizing. "If you're not in line by eleven fifty-five, you're doomed."

That little aside sends a prickle of irritation up the back of her neck. As if she doesn't know that. As if she hasn't eaten here more at this point than he has. "It's cute that you remember that," Lil replies, swiping a pink sweetener out of the tin and deliberately slipping it back into the sugars. "Got any other hot tips for me? Where should I go for a good book, the library?"

Jason finally deigns to glance up at her, but it's only to roll his eyes. "I didn't sleep a wink last night after all that."

Lil resists the urge to droop against the table. "I didn't either. Did you order me something with caffeine?"

Jason opens his mouth to answer, but Pop thunders across the yard, "Finch! Order up!" He jumps up and soon returns with two enormous platefuls of smoked ribs, a miniature tureen of sauce, a side of baked beans, a pile of pickles, and two huge Styrofoam cups of long-steeped iced tea. He pushes her little paper tray over and gets to work on his own. "Too hungry to talk," he says around a bite.

It's as good as always, so tender it falls apart like paper in the rain. Lil pops a pickle in her mouth. "We weren't drunk. We didn't imagine it. I know that much."

Jason scoffs, tossing a sand-blasted rib bone onto his plate. "That fire," he murmurs. "I've only ever seen a fire like that in my dreams. I thought it'd eat us all alive."

"Have you ever seen one vanish into thin air?" She tosses one on his plate too.

He doesn't answer right away, long enough for her to look up at him. Even in bright noon light, his eyes are very dark, no sun catching there. "Why do you hold on so tight to this place?" he asks, voice a smoke-broken rasp.

Lil balls a napkin in between her hands. "Jason. You know." The midday light, golden syrup gilding the trees. Mom humming as she cracked pecans on the porch, Sasha complaining that her fingers are cramping. Thunderstorms that shiver down Lil's spine. The night in the pond, Jason's fingers digging into the soil behind her, learning to move together that first time. "Don't you?" Lil shrugs helplessly. "You know how special it is here. You know I can't just leave this place."

Jason is the only person outside the family who has seen the pond in Lil's lifetime, if not the golden pecans. Still, he's seen more of her than even Sasha, maybe. She chose the Clearwater orchard over *him*. He is quiet, reading her face. Then he nods swiftly. "Then I think I need to show you something."

"What?" Lil asks, but he's already standing, leaving the bones of their lunch, and offering her his hand. "Fine." She pushes herself up. "Let's go."

☙

They jump into Lil's pickup, and she turns to him with a raised eyebrow. "We're going up to the old cemetery," Jason instructs, hair blowing back from his face as they turn out. "Park in the ferry lot."

Situated at the top of the ridge, on a long bluff overlooking both the town and the river, the town's tiny necropolis could never have been a good idea. It's a logistic nightmare, only a narrow one-lane road, the ground too rocky for easy below-ground burials. No, the early Methodists must've known it wasn't the best place for a cemetery, but they'd done it for the glory, so that the dead here would be up high, expectant, among the first to rise on Judgment Day. Jason and Lil park and take the long winding stairs up the ridge. Soon their hike turns—in fits and starts—into a race.

"There's a reason the Finches have always been buried in the western churchyard," Jason pants, hooking a switchback in the stairs to pass her. "This is so damn…inconvenient up here."

"I think it's a nice run." She jogs forward, looping around him and bounding up the next few steps. "Relaxing," she taunts over her shoulder. They careen up the path neck and neck, Jason a glint of gold in her periphery, until the gates are visible at the top of the ridge.

Unlike the sparsely shaded stones of the newer cemetery, this place is cramped with graves, mausolea, and stacked burials huddled together beneath old withering trees. Kudzu twists over the gates and slinks across the ground. Jason steps carefully across a dense green tangle straying into the path, leading the way between the silent stone structures. They are watched on all sides by stone monuments.

"I went on a jog this morning and found myself up here," Jason explains. "I guess I just wanted to see the whole town."

"It's a beautiful view." Clearwaters historically have made their final homes here, in some dark corner. Mom used to take them to visit occasionally; Lil has a stark memory of a little boy's grave, some distant relative who died by drowning. The oldest of the graves are long since cracked and devoured. "But what do you want me to see?"

The twisted shadows of bare branches fall across Jason's back, pass like ghostly antlers over his head, and she pauses on the path, the scent of dead leaves caught in her lungs. For a blink between shade and light, he doesn't look quite right, too thin, too quick, too—something. "Jason?" she calls.

"Come here. Look."

They sit on the low stone wall. Below them is the town. The river gleams away over her shoulder, Sasha somewhere down there humming some tuneless river song. Right under them, there's the central square, the courthouse, and the stately columns of Town Hall, where everybody's favorite ineffectual, semicrooked mayor, Marshall Braxton, is no doubt indulging in his after-lunch nap at his desk. Nearby is Su's grocery, First Methodist, and the park. Down Main Street, Autumn's bakery sits at the corner across from the closed-down five-and-dime and Wade's ancient shoe store, whose display hasn't changed in about twenty-five years. Wade wasn't at Russ's funeral, was he?

The town has a single stoplight. Off that intersection are their elementary school and the old neighborhoods, where most houses have at least one pecan tree in their front yards, and those with larger backyards have a few more tucked away. That's also the way to the new high school—new, because it replaced an older one around 1928—its football field ever verdant, bounded by bleachers. Players scrimmage on the field, sunlight glinting off their helmets. And beyond the school are fields and the long curving boundary of the ridge.

But the other way, through the stoplight, is west, where the six blocks of real town give way to pecan trees on every side. The railroad to the south snakes closer to the highway, as if it's squeezing the old orchards. And the kudzu, lurid and clutching, is creeping in, running up trees and down hills, over houses and into wells, turning the world into walls and carpet of unbroken acid green. Up here, Lil can see its boundary point, and it catches her breath how much closer it's gotten: the Finch orchard is the last line of defense, now that the Winstons and, in their wake, the Coopers, packed it in. It's too far to really make out, but she knows those trees out there, now lumpy with scab. Left untended, their roots don't have enough zinc to send upward. They get rosette. The leaves darken, turn spotty. The husks crack.

She squints past all that, at the anonymous empty places where the kudzu has taken hold. Any people who might still be out there, miles out, don't come to town. It's always fire season there, where the ground is so parched it begs for a lit match.

Then there's the old WPA bridge, cracked in two and half sunk when the highway was destroyed in that storm. The repairs are ongoing, subject to endless delays, either funding issues from Town Hall, or weather, or men quitting at the site. But they're working today; Lil can hear the distant call of voices, the occasional industrial clang. Any day now, they'll finish laying the new road and the town will take its first deep breath in who knows how long.

Any day now.

Her entire life is below her, everything and everyone. It looks like one of Lou's model train set up here on the ridge, watched over by the quiet dead.

"What did you want to show me?" Lil asks again, catching Jason's eye. He's been watching her. "What?"

"Look at the library," he murmurs.

The town's library is just off the central square. It is a repurposed old house, a squat off-white building with the pillared porch that faces the courthouse. At first, it's hard to make out what Jason is talking about. But in that bright noon light, there is some gentle shimmer around it. A shimmer, and above, a darkening billow of smoke.

The library is on fire. Before her eyes, a char runs up the back, flames busting through windows. Lil lunges instinctively forward, but Jason puts a hand out to anchor her. There's a palpable rumble as the roof shifts, like at any moment the whole thing might cave in. She can't see them, but the books inside must be peeling apart, the air noxious with melting glue, running ink, curling and blackened pages.

"Why isn't anyone doing anything?" she growls at him. A breeze carries over the chemical smell of smoldering insulation, and with it she can feel the heat of that fire creep over the back of her neck.

But Jason just shakes his head. "Look again."

Her fury rises, but Lil looks.

The fire is gone.

Desperately, she glares at Jason again. He's still holding her hand, tight as a vise against his knee. "This morning, it was the same house fire we fought last night, blinking in and out like a light."

"What—how could—I don't…" Fires that vanish one minute, consume the next. She scans the town again. Empty football fields. Quiet streets. The light is off at Autumn's bakery. The library looks perfectly safe again. This is hardly the first time this land has shown her sights that defy her senses. But the pond and the tree are known to her. This? She's never seen this in her town before. She doesn't know what it means.

"What do you think?" Jason asks, still watching her. He's so… calm. Why isn't he bothered by what he's shown her up here? Denial?

"I don't know." Behind them, the trees sigh and release a shudder of leaves, the wind pushing them against their ankles. "But I'm going to find out."

ACT II

CHAPTER NINE

AUTUMN WAS STONED AT AN OUTDOOR MUSIC FESTIval when she had her epiphany. Some muzzy melody strung along in the background, an indie band she didn't know who mixed accordions with electronics. Autumn floated, half-shut eyes falling on a girl in the crowd with a pierced navel and toffee hair, raising a clunky camera to capture the band.

Matt hissed, poking at the micro-wrinkles under his eye. "I swear they're getting worse. Tell me honestly, can you see them?"

"Not really." She stretched her arms in the cool and pleasantly waxy strands of grass. Clouds plodded across a blue New Mexico sky. Onstage, an accordion wheezed.

"Your skin is amazing," he said, his gentle hand, slender fingers, one turquoise nail, carding through her swampy bangs, looking for frown lines. It was so hot that day, humid from the bodies of a hundred sweaty music fans. "You promise you'd tell me if these wrinkles were noticeable?"

"Promise."

For all the ways being high softened the edges of the world, like Vaseline smeared around a camera lens, it also brought her such clarity. Because lying on that grass, while Matt complained about aging and their friends moving to the suburbs, Autumn remembered her hometown for the first time in ages.

She's been busy. Culinary school. Work. Life. Mom and Dad moved away. She hadn't had anyone to call, any friends left to visit.

But in that instant, the feeling of home returned, fresh and new. The flowers Mom grew on the borders of their small brick house. The family library of albums, something perpetually spinning on the record player. Dad fussing over a babka. Sasha's eyes, very close, which whispered a sleepover confession that often played through her mind, the last words she'd hear before closing her eyes: *You're the only one who really knows me, Pip.*

The only one.

When Autumn heard that old echo, her comeback was always a swift and bitter bite: *If that's true, where the hell did you go?*

Autumn hovered, her body strung as tight as a guitar string. The beginning of a suspicion stirred in the back of her mind.

A question she did not want to ask, much less answer.

How long had it been…?

☙

The day after the house-fire-that-wasn't, Autumn rises, groggy with lack of sleep, and stumbles her way downstairs to her old bakery. She never gave up the prime Main Street location. Now, as she turns on the oven, she's grateful.

Autumn spent years honing her skills in the bakery before striking out to try her luck outside of the support of parents and loyal grandmothers coming every Saturday morning for her challah bread. So she knows the world from behind her counter. What Cork liked to order with his coffee, and what nuts Cynthia liked in brownies and abhorred in cookies. Who couldn't resist a cinnamon roll and who could only be swayed by old-fashioned apple turnovers.

She knows where everything goes. The two red patio tables she kept folded up in the alley with matching chairs. That old cash register that had to be smacked in just the right place to fully pop open. Even her emergency handle of bourbon kept in the drawer under that cash register. It's all miraculously as she left it. Only a little dust.

Most people might have sold the bakery. Autumn rented it out rather than sell, but she hasn't had a renter in a while. And by the look of their little town, she isn't sure she'll get another anytime soon.

As the oven heats, she forms a dough. It'll be focaccia today. Focaccia is her thinking bread. Any stress, problems, questions, crushes—they are all baked into sweetly spongy bread with olives and mozzarella, finished with garlic and herbs and indecent amounts of olive oil. It was Dad's thinking bread too. He taught her the recipe at six, using her fingers to press divots into the dough. Mom, without fail, hung on his shoulders whenever he pulled a batch out of the oven, teasing until he let her and Autumn pull off crusts that breathed steam.

By the time she's sliding the first loaf into the oven, she is more alert. But the night before doesn't make any more sense.

She's feeling it again. The same seed of suspicion that drove her here, the heaviness of a question that she does not want to ask. Only—

Only what was that question? It's as if she can't hold it in her head. She's all jumbled. She's been thrown off since she got back.

Now, maybe it's been replaced altogether with: How can a fire snap at her fingers one moment, and the next, be gone?

Autumn stops. She presses the heels of her hands against the cool steel counter. Sasha hasn't called.

Despite having so much time pass without Sasha in her life, Autumn is reattuned already, and it's weird that they haven't talked about what happened. Not that she knows what to say.

While her loaf bakes, Autumn steps out the back door into the alley where her dumpster sits empty and her trusty metal patio furniture has been waiting all this time.

The alley gives way almost immediately to a wide greenbelt where the weeds stretch tall, leading to trees. The openness of the space used to let her breathe. Sometimes she'd hear teenagers, or find broken bottles if she wandered there. Not today though. It's an early hour, and the world is beginning to awaken. The best part of being a baker is that she rarely misses the glory of a sunrise in full bloom. It's happening now, lifting the gauze of the early morning. There's nothing like sunrise to banish the night-time thoughts that creep in under windowsills to whisper all her despairs in her ear.

In the grass, near the seam of the tree line, something flashes by.

Autumn pushes off the building. She ventures nearer—but the ghost of smoke, of batting at illusory flames hooks in the back of her mind. Once, she would run around these woods like a stray, finding her own playmates, without fear. Now, she doesn't remember how it feels to be so fearless.

She takes a step—a branch cracks under her foot and a figure in the grass rockets up.

It's a child. He's small, can't be older than five at his size, his slenderness. Like a little forest creature with a mop of shaggy hair. Could he be a child who lives out beyond the tracks, some family still scrounging out there? Aren't his parents looking for him?

"Hi," she murmurs.

He sniffs the air. The aroma of baking bread has followed her outside.

"I'm Autumn," she calls as gently as she can across the distance. Someone needs to care for his clothes; she can spot a tear in his faded shirt collar. Red-brown eyes watch Autumn. "I've got bread," she tries. "Would you like some? There's plenty—"

And just like that, he takes off, sprinting into the woods, nothing but the soles of his shoes flashing at her.

"Wait!" Autumn calls, but he's already gone.

For a long time, she stays, watching, as sunlight illuminates the trees. But he doesn't return. Nothing moves out there. She can't understand the feeling that stirs in her, that this child is in need. Her heart pulls toward the fallow fields, and she thinks of the skinned squirrel. It may not be as safe out there as she remembers.

Autumn returns to the bakery, pulling her bread out of the oven not a moment too soon.

If she leaves it wrapped in cheesecloth on one of the red tables in the back alley, no one else has to know.

☙

The uneasiness of the night before lingers all through the day, clinging to Sasha's clothes like the smell of smoke. The ferry runs four times: there and back, there and back. Her shoulders itch, neck tickling every time she's facing the other bank. She'd considered going to see Autumn at the bakery this morning, maybe even inviting her out on the boat for the day—but something stopped her. Yesterday, she'd been joy-drunk to see her friend. But it's like the antennae on her emotional TV is constantly shifting out into static these days.

That disconnected feeling within, a kind of numbing that she usually masks with a joke, with a hasty one-off, feels like something that began here in the town where she grew up. Here, she is grounded enough if she keeps busy, if the things that matter are held up an inch before her eyes. There's the elementary school where Sasha pushed Lil on the swings; there's the Baptist church where they rescued the records of "devil's music" waiting for a bonfire; here is home. Mom was here.

And out *there*? Out there, maybe because she's *out* there, there's no mask locked onto her face. She managed to have things: her place in the group show in Queens, showing her photos. A few kind oddball people who, bizarrely, wanted her around. Linda, a sculptor with a studio apartment and a great teaching gig, with books on art theory up to the ceiling and a wide-open, miraculously undamaged heart. Sasha would dive in, seize on to those bright-hot flares of the missing thing, wrap her fingers around an opportunity or a person or a place that seemed, for a moment or two, *real—*

But just as she secured her grasp, really sank her teeth in, whatever it was that had drawn her in was just gone. Those big-city folks, her rich art types, couldn't understand her origin story. Of course they'd struggled, just like everyone does. But Sasha had different hurts, the pain of a small-town queer coming of age, of a mom who seemed to gravitate toward her sister instead of her, of the silent broken heart. Someone in New York would laugh at something a little too hard or say something glib about where she was from, and a vast canyon would open up in her. Sasha would be left in a room full of strangers—maybe one room, a bright, colorful apartment full of ideas, and just one stranger—full of expectations Sasha found she couldn't rise to.

Autumn comes from here. She should understand. Except there was that one time in the tree house, all those years ago, when Sasha reached, and Pip ran. Today the happiness of her return feels dwarfed by the horror of that bizarre fire, and Sasha can't risk seeing her, in case she turns out to be just another stranger.

So, as usual, she keeps busy. If there's anything Sasha's learned in this time at home, it's that there's always another task to be done around here, always something else to do so she doesn't have to brood. She docks on this side of the river, waving off her passengers. Then comes the waiting. It's the second to last run of the day, lights beginning to twinkle around her. On their side, there's the ridge, but over here it's only a low sandy bluff, and beyond, flat, flat, flat forever. Somewhere nearby, a crow complains in the trees. These idle moments waiting for the next run are almost enough to tempt her to develop a new smoking habit. She stares at the trees, that same wrongness from last night wrinkling over her.

"So where do I get a ticket for this thing?" someone drawls, and Sasha turns sharply. Theon is on the boat.

She has ridden enough deserted Q trains late at night to feign composure when a man skeeves her out. "It's a public service until the road opens back up," she says, looking past him at the bank. *Please someone else come*, she begs the empty lot. Ferrying Theon across the river should have been merely an irritation, but now that she is actually faced with the task of taking this man across on her own, it fills her with dread. "Never seen you on here before," she realizes.

He flashes a smile, a knowing one, like her casualness might fool everyone else, but would never quite fool him. "I usually take the train."

We don't have a passenger train through town, she is about to say, but her hopes have been answered with the arrival of a few others, who file aboard with barely even a glance. And it isn't worth getting into particulars with him.

Theon tips his head to a blank-eyed man passing. "Not a lively bunch, huh?"

For a long moment, Sasha thinks hard about just ignoring this too, but something in her can't quite turn her back on him. Every time Theon has made an appearance at the orchard or in town, he's approached Lil. Only Lil. As if Sasha isn't an equal inheritor of the Clearwater family land. Now he's come to see her, and Sasha is incapable of just staying mulishly silent. "It's the after-work crowd," she tells him, tossing the rope onto the dock and getting the little steamboat's paddlewheel chirring again.

He snorts, glancing back at the shrinking occupants of those few places on the benches. "More like the afterlife crowd." Theon slips his hands in his pockets, the picture of ease. "They might as well be headed straight over the Styx." When she says nothing, irked by him, he just laughs more fully. "Hell, maybe they are."

"What do you know about these people?" Sasha snaps suddenly. "What do you know about *any* of us?"

Theon pauses at her tone, cocking his head like a dog catching a scent. Water sloshes far below. When he replies, his voice is soft as twilight haze. "I know you don't belong here."

It's like he's seized her around the neck. Her hands are frozen on the wheel.

"They did a write-up in the paper the day you two were born. Did you know that?" He's leaning forward, elbows on his knees, a private conference. He puts his hands up to pantomime a headline: "Clearwater TWINS?!" His mocking hands fall, and he shrugs. "Your mom didn't know there were two of you. She only had one name planned. Didn't she get 'Sasha' out of a magazine?"

Trying to force a swallow, Sasha fixes her eyes on the flickering lights along the ridge. It's an old anecdote. He can't hurt her with it.

"In old times, they would've left you out in the woods to appease the spirits," he murmurs. His accent is flat, void. Like the voice in a recording or over an intercom. Like he's from nowhere. "I remember. One to keep, one to give away."

She can't let him say any of this. In a hard jerk, she forces herself out of that throttling stillness. "Do I need to toss you in this river?" she growls. "You're here by my say-so. The boat and the river are *my* places. So watch it, asshole."

Theon raises his hands appeasingly, but he doesn't shut up. "You're the part of this that makes no sense. *Her*, I get." It's just a strange flicker, but in the instant he speaks of Lil, he looks transported. "So my question is, what are *you* still doing here?"

Sasha sees the pecan trees of the orchard, their canopies blotting out the light in her old bedroom window. Growing up, they always rustled out there, invading her dreams. In the deep night, those trees are dark as onyx. They made the stars look so faint and numerous they barely twinkled, a dusting of flour on a dark pan. And in the center of them, Mom and Lil, their whispered, late-night conversations. The two of them, vanishing in the trees together, loyally tending their secrets.

Maybe Theon says something else, but Sasha doesn't hear.

A breeze slips along her cheek, carrying the tang of a bonfire.

CHAPTER TEN

Early in Lil's senior year of high school, Mom finds the brochure under her bed. Lil doesn't even know what she was looking for. Maybe she was simply fishing around for a lost sock on laundry day. But Mom waits until Sasha has left the house carrying Autumn by piggyback before sitting down with Lil under one of the trees, where she has chosen to read. She places the brochure on her lap and looks at her.

Lil freezes. On the cover, a shady building surrounded by trees is photographed in black and white tones. The University of the South, it reads. Est. 1857. Mom's expression is a little tight with discomfort, but well-meaning. Full of regret. Maybe it's how other moms looked at their daughters when they find love letters from a beau, or a packet of condoms in a hiding spot.

"Mrs. Stein gave it to me," Lil says defensively. "I forgot about it."

Mom isn't fooled. Her hair is loose under her wide-brimmed hat, a red ribbon stitched around the rim. The sun-worn wrinkles around her eyes and mouth are getting deeper every year. "Honey."

"I know," Lil adds, but Mom is going to want to *talk* about it now, even if Lil would rather yank out her fingernails. She's trapped in the conversation. It makes her feel wild and violent inside. "I'm not planning to apply."

Mom doesn't even try to pretend with her. She just nods, relieved at Lil's decision. Perhaps relieved she doesn't have to make a stand. It's easier to pretend this is a choice if Lil doesn't force it.

The wind dies around them. This time of year, the fall, it carries the scent of pecans everywhere, and leaf rot. Lil smells it on her clothes at the end of the day. Smells it on her body all the time. The smell wakes her up at night.

"I could get in," Lil says suddenly, impulsively. "Mrs. Stein says I'm at the top of the class."

"I don't doubt it." Mom hesitates. The silence between them is long.

Mom was young then. But she looked older every year. Carrying the weight of daughters and the interminable burden of the orchard. It's getting harder every year. Owning land is the ultimate privilege, the promise of security, the stolen inheritance of this country. For Mom, the land is her purpose, her legacy— her yoke.

"One of you has to take over." Mom is steady, but she fiddles with the grass between them.

"I know." *One of you*, Mom says. As if she didn't pick Lil out for it at five years old. As if she didn't trap her with the knowledge of the golden pecans and the pond before she knew what it meant.

"I wanted other things at your age too," Mom says.

Lil feels that rush in her ears. Jason is looking at colleges. Urging her to apply. *We could both go*, he'd suggested once. She swallowed down the horrible hint of longing and scoffed. *Never*, she proclaimed. *I want the orchard. It's mine.* Her options feel so limited. If she doesn't yell at him, she might have to cry, and Lil can't bear that.

"You're bright, ambitious. And I'm—sorry. But it has to be this way. A Clearwater must be the guardian of this place."

Sasha's probably off with Autumn in their tree house, whiling away a whole afternoon. Sasha got to apply to art schools; she sent her applications off last week.

"And Sasha…" Mom sighs. The brochure flutters in the wind like a waving hand. "Sasha needs to leave here more than you do. This place, these people…won't be good for her. She needs a different life."

Her words drift and settle heavily over her and it takes Lil a few seconds to grasp her meaning. Lil jerks her gaze up to Mom, shocked. "You…*know*?" They've never talked about it. Sasha and Lil have never even talked about it, even though once upon a time, they talked about everything. Mom, she assumed, was totally unaware. But maybe she's only feigned ignorance, the way she doesn't comment when Lil sneaks in past curfew and creeps out again to sleep under the trees. How much can three women in the same house know without speaking about it? How many secrets are cluttering up their spaces, both known and unknown?

But Mom just meets her eyes. She doesn't explain herself further, though she wears the same deep sadness that's spreading through Lil like molten lava. "I love you both. It should be her that goes," is all she says.

It's the only time they speak about it. And Lil throws out the brochure.

こ

Lil is sprawled on the couch, sweaty after an afternoon working in the orchard when Sasha comes in after dark and pauses just inside the door, an odd stillness in her. It seems like she isn't sure where she wants to go next: to the kitchen, to scrounge for leftovers? To slump onto the couch? Straight upstairs to bed?

"Good, you're here," Lil says from the soft cushions. "We should talk."

Her sister jumps, eyes catching on her in a momentary spark of shock. "Didn't see you there," she manages.

"Jason and I went to the cemetery on the hill and we saw more of those—those fires," Lil says. "We didn't imagine it last night."

Sasha paces past her into the kitchen, opening and closing cabinets. "Well, no shit," she calls through the doorway. "We weren't on, like, some group trip last night or anything." There's a grouchy pause; then Sasha peers around the frame at her. "You said you saw more of those fires just burning up town? In the middle of the day?"

"Yes, and it was just the same. Burning one second, gone the next."

"That's—some end-times bullshit right there." Sasha's shoulders are tense. She's worn emotions lightly all her life, but something is weighing on her now. "I can't even process that."

Lil follows her. "What's wrong?" Which means, *What else is wrong besides the erratic there-then-gone fires?* It seems they're shelving that bizarre revelation for the moment.

Sasha glares at the ceiling. "Jason's back for less than a week, and suddenly you're thick as thieves again," she says. "I've been here I don't even know how long now, and you barely say a handful of words to me a day."

Lil's cheeks heat. "I—excuse me?"

Sasha's nostrils flare. "While you were off playing Hardy Boys with him, Theon was being a total creep to me out on the river."

Even when she doesn't see him, Theon ruins everything. Rage lances through her at the thought of him accosting Sasha in one of her safe places. "What did he say to you?" Lil demands.

"He was just trying to get to me." Sasha's arms are tucked around her gut. "I took care of it."

"Well. Good. But it isn't my fault." Lil mirrors her.

When Sasha doesn't speak but doesn't leave, just glares, Lil gingerly picks up the argument. Tries to put the pin back in the hand grenade. "I would love to play Hardy Boys with you, Sasha. But you're out of here most days before lunch hits."

"How would you know?" Sasha retorts. "You're always out of the house at the crack of dawn!" She's standing by the coffeepot, which Lil always makes sure to leave on in the mornings for her, a mug waiting beside it so that even if they never really sit down to have a cup together, she knows Sasha will come down to it.

"Yes, because there's work to do, and no one's helping me do it," Lil spits out like her tongue is on fire, words she'd never meant to say. "In case you haven't noticed, there's a whole orchard to run, and you can't be bothered to lift a finger."

"You don't want me there." Sasha's voice is ragged, rising—and her voice never rises. She's always the picture of cool, always lounging, always smirking like she has some secret expertise no one can share. "You've *never* wanted me there!"

"That's all I want. But you keep leaving. You leave every day, Sasha." Lil swallows, her throat dry and painful. It isn't like fighting with others. This—with Sasha—is like clawing skin off her own back.

Sasha shakes her head, stubborn. "Mom didn't want me there either. That was your place together, without me." She holds out her hands, laughing harshly. "I wouldn't even know how to help you. Because I know nothing about the orchard. And—no. Don't say anything. You know it's true." She grabs a box of cereal from the cabinet, along with a bowl and spoon. The refrigerator door slams.

Lil finds her voice as Sasha is stomping upstairs, milk jug dangling from her hand. "All I know is that I try to reach out to you," she says to her retreating back. "If you can't see that, maybe you're the one with the problem."

She holds herself together as best she can and storms back out of the house. She rages through the trees to the wild heart of the property, into the brush and roots where the pond glimmers under the shade of its single tree. Her breath is coming out hot and hard as she flings herself down at the banks, shoves off her shoes, and plunges her feet in arctic water.

All at once, the anger soothes out of her. Leaves shift and sigh above her. Silent ripples move across the dark surface. It's cold, but too silky to bite, as if her and the pond are the same thing. One creature, existing at the center of a heartbeat. Far off, through Sasha's back window on the second floor, she can just barely catch a snatch of a Bangles song on her stereo.

It's not easy to admit. But here, her thoughts are clearer. Maybe Sasha isn't wrong. Everyone has their altars. Autumn worships at the feet of her ovens with baked offerings. Sasha gives reverence to the river. The churchgoers have Sunday prayers and after-service country club meetings. But this is Lil's place of prayer, where she is stripped to nothing but her barest self. She can always feel it with her no matter where she is, cold pleasure, a dip in icy water that keeps with her even on the hottest days of the year. The pond is Lil's. She is its, and it always reaches back if she reaches for it.

It is hard to be twins, a life halved and shared. Everything is split, and Lil tries not to be selfish. She never begrudges Sasha full shares over any sense of longing and connection to their father; Lil quiets that part of her heart, turns inward, and seeks the imprint of their mother. Sasha wanted the freedom to strike out into the world; and in exchange, Lil became the Clearwater meant by the Clearwater orchard. At least that's how Lil sees it. There's no telling how it seems to Sasha, what secret sacrifices Sasha has made for love. But they walk on set paths, and Lil can't go back now. Not even for Sasha. She doesn't want to.

The water shivers and *pulls*. Lil slips in up to her knees and abruptly catches herself on the cool mossy shore, clings to the grass and roots. Its love is greedy.

"No one eats as many pecans as that pond," Mom whispers in the air, in Lil's mind. "And it's still hungry."

"No," Lil says firmly. After a long moment, the pressure releases. She pulls herself free of its clasp, tucks her legs under her on the bank. Water laps harmlessly at the shore. A pecan falls close to her, skitters to a stop in the dirt like an apology, or a plea—who knows?

As always, she completes her end of the ritual, picking the husk up and feeding it to the water.

eɔ

When Autumn calls Sasha's phone, she gets that fuzzy voicemail message again, her voice just the right side of brisk—*Leave a message, and I'll call you back later if I like you.*

"Hey, Sasha." She packs chocolate chip cookies first, golden brown to perfection, soft in the middle, just the way she likes them. "Just checking in. I guess you're still out on the boat." Then biscuits with bacon and cheese, still warm in aluminum wrappers. "Call me if you get a chance. I'm going back out to some of those old properties, and wanted to see if you'd come." Her cell phone didn't have service out here, so she's stuck using that old corded phone.

Autumn pauses, all wrapped up in the phone cord. "Bye," she tacks on and hangs up. Oh, she's an idiot. It's just Sasha. There's no reason that talking to her should be hard; they drank their first beers together; they used to talk about crushes, giggling the whole time, even if Sasha never seemed to have many crushes. There's no reason Autumn should be babbling worse than she did when a woman with a shaved head slipped her number into her back pocket at Starbucks.

No time to dwell on it. The basket is as full as she can make it. Autumn hooks it over her elbow and slips out the back door. The air is chilly this afternoon, the sky a pinched gray above her as she crosses the greenbelt.

It's been a few days since she saw the little boy. But she knows what hunger looks like. When she returned to the bakery a day after she left him a loaf of bread, it was gone. And based on the direction he ran, she suspects where he could have been going. He was headed away, toward the railroad. She walked those lands with Sasha just the other day, with rusty car parts and abandoned houses.

It was in those fallow fields where she used to find playmates, children whose parents she never knew.

By the time she reaches the railroad, the basket, packed with so much optimism, feels heavier on her arm. She walks along the tracks, looking for what remains of those worn footpaths, or for some sign of life.

She's walked for a while before she comes upon a huddled old estate, unkempt with neglect, vines climbing up the toothless porch. It's the old Winston house, once the town's most glamorous, well-to-do family. They had a Tiffany chandelier in the front hall.

She steps off the railroad, pushing through the overgrowth for a better look at a once stately dowager reduced to a sorry state. How long had it been abandoned? Autumn vaguely remembered there being life inside it in her childhood.

She walks forward.

It happens so quickly, Autumn registers it all at once. Her next step falls on something hard, without the give of soil—the rustle of force bursting through leaves—a red flare of pain, a beast clawing open her leg—metal scything through air.

Snap.

Autumn's vision returns in a haze of black dots. She's on her side. A distant moan hums in her marrow.

Bottle-blue sky beams above her, leaf rot clogging her nose. And pain, her body locked tight and screaming.

The sound, the moan—it's coming from her, and she cuts off, gasping for breath that won't stay, can't make it into her chest. She can't seem to hold it, inhaling dust and moss.

She can't figure—

What's wrong?

She tries to move, forces herself to sit up—her leg yanks, red and hot—and she twists enough to see—

She is caught in the jaws of a vicious metal beast. It's chained to the ground, ancient and strong. Red slicks the sides of its iron teeth and stains her jeans.

Oh god. *Oh god.*

She's caught in a trap.

Autumn screams. Her body flinches, a stupid, agonizing tug, waste of blood, of life, of time. She forces herself to still, forces her teeth to clamp shut.

That's all you get, she tells herself viciously. Her eyes threaten to film over, her stomach heaves. *No one knows you're here. It is up to you. It's just pain. It's just pain.*

She swallows against her panic, every shake tearing into her skin. Unyielding metal digs into her like she's meat, without give, without mercy. When she's ready, when the worst has passed, she inches closer to it. It's nimble, not a bear trap, which could have killed her. It was made for something smaller. That's good.

Her leg isn't crooked. It may not be broken. That's good too. Blearily, Autumn tries to sit up, her head pounding, stretching until she can reach the trap and see the mechanism. Was it left to catch some big cat? Did anyone still hunt in these ruined trees?

"It's fine. I'm fine," she breathes. "It's fine."

It is gruesome. One look—vile—Autumn scrabbles at the

teeth and heaves, trying to leverage the jaws apart. But they won't budge. She isn't strong enough. She pulls, but her fingers slip and slip and *slip*.

"Fuck"—she curses and just like that she can't hold back the wave of panic—"Help"—and it's overtaking her and she's screaming again—"Help! Help, somebody!"

But no one answers. Instead, there's a flutter, a burst of birds fleeing somewhere in the trees, a skitter of animals dashing. And then it's quiet. Even the wind stills.

In the complete silence, her breathing is very loud.

Forests are full of sound, rustling leaves and the chatter of birds, squirrel songs and the velvet footsteps of deer. Trees are like cities, full of life, always stirring. Wind and creaking branches. There's never a still, quiet moment.

Only now, nothing moves. It's as if every living thing has scurried away or frozen in place, hiding in hopes of remaining invisible. She knows what it means. It's the vanished tide before the tidal wave.

It's the doomed quiet before a predator stalks through.

Trapped on the ground, pinned in place, Autumn watches the tree line. She always wondered, before, why a mouse caught in glue would chew off its own limb just to get free.

She can't see it, can't hear it. But she knows she isn't alone.

CHAPTER ELEVEN

THE RUSTED CHAINS CLINK WITH HER, SOFT AND TELL-ing as a bell.

Autumn jerks her gaze around, trying to keep her eyes up, wary of the shadows between thick tree trunks, of the pockets of darkness hidden in the veils of kudzu.

She can't run. She'll have to fight, if the invisible hunter makes its lunge.

She grasps around for something, anything, fingers grazing the wicker basket, crumbled napkins, oozing smashed pie—cold metal. The heavy sense of some enormous presence bears down on her. Watching, waiting to see her tear herself apart.

A butter knife from the bakery. When she yanks it free, it's smeared purple with blueberry filling and slippery, but it's real. It's something. Autumn tucks it into her bloodstained palm, blade out. She bends over the trap again, ripping at the vine-covered chain. It's stubbornly held, she can see bone-white roots almost fused into the links. It's as if the whole of the earth is pulling back against her.

She feels the phantom of hot breath, like a wolf sniffing the air, catching her scent. The pressure seems to close in.

"Please," she hisses. "Please, come on—"

The kudzu is stronger. It swallows whole trees, acres, orchards, miles, smothering them where the sunlight cannot reach, and it is going to swallow her too. Vines will climb the chain in perfect silence, embrace her body, and eventually, they will find her, years and years from now once it holds only her bones.

Autumn pushes against the jaws until her leg seizes in fire and the knife threatens to bend. She should have waited for Sasha. No one knows where she is, and who will there be to call when she can't be found? Will Sasha just assume Autumn's left again, drifted off on a wandering current? Will she wonder? Will she search? Autumn only just found her again, here, against all odds, after loving her in foolish, lonely bursts for ages, and now—

"What is it doing?"

Autumn freezes. Feels another pulse of hot blood down her ankle. It seems to have come from the canopies. A treetop whisper. And just like a startle of wind, it's suddenly picked up all around her, from all sides.

"What is it doing?"

"What is it doing?"

Autumn drops her knife and it's worse now, growing from a hiss into a chorus, and the trees themselves seem to stretch and groan.

"What is it?"

"Where has it been?"

Louder and louder—

"What does it do?"

"It bleeds."

"Does it grow?"

It's too much—Autumn clamps her hands over her ears, scans the trees, and *prays*—

From behind a trunk, something is watching her, eyes like buttons, small paws, and a face made of twisted, mottled bark.

A scream rips out of her throat. The thing is too still, staring at her there.

The face of bark leers. A hand-carved jumble of features, with knots for eyes above a fixed grin full of real teeth threaded into the opening. Dog teeth. The grain warps and whirls in her vision, the mask eerie and alive even as it stays perfectly still behind the tree.

Then it's rushing at her. She feels a cold prickle at her neck. She can't look down and see, at least not well—but she knows it's a serrated blade. "Not s'posed to be here," it growls in her ear.

She opens her mouth, and the knife draws tighter, crushed against her windpipe. "No one. Go way," it hisses.

"I can't," she whispers as carefully as she can, meeting those strange knotty eyes. It's small. It isn't oppressive, like the stalking force bearing down at her before.

"I can't get free."

The bark is rough. She hears a sucking sound. It's smelling her in long dragging snuffs. "Let you *die*," it suggests, quiet, weighing the idea. "Leave you for the hungry man."

Bile rises in her throat. That's the name of the predator with invisible eyes. She's sure of it.

But…even talking under its breath, this voice is…young. It wears old, worn clothes, pants secured with a length of knotty rope. Dirty shoes with no laces. Autumn looks, really looks, and underneath the shaggy hair, there's twine, looped into the bark mask and around the head, just over a tender ear. "Please don't," Autumn says as calmly as she can. "I'm hurt. And I can give you food."

It hesitates a moment longer, the woods grown deadly quiet around them again. The knife trembles against her neck. It's so close to biting into her. Then the masked thing takes a quick step, a hop, and the feet stamp down like it's going to crush her trapped ankle—

Autumn screams again as the metal teeth drag free of her flesh. She pulls herself back out of its reach, her elbows almost collapsing out of fear shaken together with relief. The knife is gone from her neck, or else she might've slit her own throat flinching at the pain.

"*Hush up,*" the thing says, still full of menace. It skitters away from her, ducking back to the place behind the tree.

"Wait," Autumn calls. "Wait, please. I have—I brought you some food." She can't be sure, not with the mask on. But her heart tells her this is the child who'd come to the bakery, enticed by the smell of baking bread. Even if she's wrong, it doesn't matter. She owes them.

The mask is impassive. She can see the knife glinting along the tree trunk. But maybe the voice has gentled very slightly when they say, "Leave real quiet."

"Thank you," she gasps. Standing is… Red burns over her vision, and her leg wobbles, but the bone isn't broken. It's just pain. She can limp, so Autumn flees. She only looks back once, before the trees close over the clearing leading to the Winston house and the trap. The grimy figure is still there, crouched curiously over the basket of food.

She turns away and moves, quick as she can, toward the safest place in town.

&

After her fight with Sasha, Lil watches the night for phantom fires, but sees nothing. The next time she meets Jason, it's at Honeysuckle House. It is a place made of history and venerable furnishings, fragrant wisteria curling up the ivory columns. She hasn't been there in years, not since Jason left for law school, but even the air around the orchard has an unchanged quality, almost stifled. It's the old, stale air of an empty jar with the lid shut tight. She's about to knock, but he opens the door a second before her knuckles make contact, and they rap on his chest instead.

"Hey." He grins at her; Jason is always cheery in the mornings. He's damp from the shower, like he got his run in and the sun supercharged him for the day. It's just how he's always been, even in high school; his car was always the first one in the lot. "Come on in."

If Jason has been working on packing this place up, he hasn't made it to the first floor yet. The place is entirely unchanged from the days (and nights) she spent there in the past. The fussy, expensive upholstery, the antlers and wood paneling in the den. Somehow it's too big for even the two of them to make any dent in its emptiness. Honeysuckle House is among the most elegant homes in town, even if it still can't claim the highest pecan yield. It's been featured in a number of magazines.

Jason seems to read her mind. "I can see why Mother got out of here," he says, with a little laugh. "After she married Dad, she still couldn't change a thing. Nana Finch wanted it all kept just the same." Marigold, Jason's mom, was always smiling, always out in her garden, debating with Russ about the best treatments for the vegetable patch. She was never here in the house, which meant that, as teenagers, Lil and Jason could usually find some corner of this old mausoleum to curl up in. "I need to sort all this out but…" He tosses his hands up as they walk into the kitchen. "I feel Nana's eyes on me, I guess. Coffee?"

"Well, since it's on." She slides onto one of the kitchen stools. There is a large window that opens onto an octagonal "breakfast room." The house was built with the assumption of dining fine, of cooks and maids and, hell, maybe even a butler. It was a sumptuous setting fit for Lil and Jason, who were all mythology and drama back then, before they cooled into a true long-term relationship with all the taxing trimmings. In the end, their lives drifted apart without anyone writing epic poetry about it, which would have been hard for teenage Lil to imagine.

"I can see why it's been hard for you to be here alone," she realizes as he pours coffee into a neat little cup for her. "It's not the same…and too much the same."

He leans across the counter, coffee mug between his hands. "And how is it over at the Clearwater orchard, huh?"

She stirs in milk and sugar with a glinting silver spoon. Fancy, yet terribly impractical, absorbing heat like a lightning rod. "Hard," she murmurs, as if the trees will hear. "I'm stripped bare, keeping it going. But it's beautiful," she adds in a rush. "This might be the best harvest I've ever seen. The flavor this year,

Jason, it's—" She almost forgot. Lil reaches into her pocket, pulls out the small handful of shelled pecans she brought, pushes them across the table at him. "See for yourself."

His eyes catch on hers, a flicker of light in their dark depths, some burning—almost too much. And it's almost sex, or maybe it's something else, but it shivers down into her as he rolls those pecans under his fingertips and then pops one in his mouth. He tastes it thoughtfully, and her cheeks warm. "Elliots?" he guesses, humming with a deep approval at the taste. "Where in the orchard are these from?"

"Good guess. You haven't lost your taste." Lil takes one too, crushing it between her teeth, and ignores the flush rising in her cheeks. "Figured you traded it all in for traffic laws, or whatever it is you studied."

He waves the jab away with a roll of his eyes. "I wondered if they grew near the place you took me once. Out there in the orchard."

Heat prickles over her skin. She knows the place he means. It's the only place he could mean. Lil showed it to him just once. They were drunk on shitty beer. She stumbled when she pulled him out of the house, away from the seventeenth birthday party she and Sasha were sharing—almost all Sasha's friends. Lil stole Jason away and brought him to the pond. What a foolish, danger- ous gamble. In front of the still inky water, they pushed out of their clothes as quickly as possible, skin to skin because it almost physically hurt not to touch him. He wore a letterman jacket. Blue briefs. They went skinny-dipping in water as cool and fresh as a full moon.

The memories still live in the pond even now, deposited in the silty shore, clinging like dew to the mossy stones. Her silent dare. His teeth gently dragging across her shoulder.

Across the counter from her, Jason's flushing a little. He reaches forward like he's reading her mind, grazes warm fingers against her hand, the knob of her wrist.

She remembers it with visceral clarity. Urging him to move, despite the little bit of pain. Her name on his lips, his voice coiled tight with need. The soft give of the soil under her head, the shades of shadow across his skin, his hair in the moonlight. They stirred waves in still water, ankles tangled in reeds. The two of them.

Lil shakes herself out of the past and raises an eyebrow at him over her coffee. "What did you want to talk about?"

"Right." She watches him drag his brain back from where they'd gone together just now. He winks at her, a winning, recovering gesture over the top of his coffee cup, which he drains quickly. "Let's go up to the attic."

It's quite a climb, through forgotten, decaying glamour: antique mirrors, dark with tarnish; a split ivory-handled hairbrush; clouds of old perfume. Through one door, she catches sight of an heirloom cradle and powder blue walls. Jason taps two times on the closed door of Russ's old room as they pass, head down. "You probably remember my mom was really active in town? Committees and charities. For the hospital, for the firefighters, whatever," he says, tugging a dangling rope to open the hatch to the attic. They have to tug together to get the creaking old ladder down. "As much as Hattie Winston or more. Your mom did some things with her too."

"Much to Hattie's dismay." Lil follows him up the ladder into heavy, musty air that smells of time. Their mother wasn't short on

friends in town. But there were always a few disapproving naysay-
ers, despite her place at the helm of the Clearwater orchard. It
was her status as a staunchly single mother with twins from a love
affair with a Puerto Rican man—the height of scandal to close-
minded bigots. Hattie Winston, an old-money housewife to a
former senator who'd done her life right, couldn't comprehend
that the Clearwater orchard, the town's crown jewel, remained in
the hands of a woman who, to Hattie, had done her life wrong.
But the quality of the Clearwater pecans demanded a level of
grudging respect, if not love from everyone, and Mom never
cared what anyone thought.

In fact, she seemed to take a little pleasure in being untouch-
able to the disapproving Hatties of their world.

"Take a look," Jason says, gesturing to a pile of open boxes
with neat handwritten labels. Lil kneels beside them and her
heart fills as she realizes what Jason is showing her.

She remembers the two of them, Mom and Marigold on the
couch, a bottle of wine open between them as they made banners
and signs. Mom's bare feet tangled in yards of canvas, stitching
leaf patterns around Marigold's bold red lettering.

Here in a box in Jason's attic are those red and gold patterns,
unfaded, laid out on white canvas.

She brushes her fingers along stitches last touched by her
mother. "The Pecan Festival."

Mom loved the Pecan Festival. She saved their best pecans
for it, carted them around to the local bakery—run by a gruff
old man before Autumn's time—the country clubs, the grocers.
Stands lined Main Street; the local shops depended on the business it brought them every year from out-of-towners. There were

musicians playing in front of City Hall, a parade, and at the very end, a grand ball on the riverboat. The air tasted of mulled wine and cider. Mom would lead the twins by the hand, scarves tucked up to their chins.

"Hold hands," she'd say, giving them money they didn't really need—because no one in town would've charged the Clearwater girls at the Pecan Festival if they hadn't insisted, not when Mom supplied the best of the pecans. "Stay together no matter what, okay?"

Lil closes her eyes, full of the urge to curl up in the banner, wrap it around her.

She feels Jason's cool hand on her shoulder. "The road is closed," he allows, tilting his head back and forth. "But—we have the riverboat. The casino's right there across the river. We can publicize."

"I must be losing my touch if you thought of the Pecan Festival before I did." Lil wipes surreptitiously at her eyes. She stands, bringing the banner with her. "I love it, Jason. It's perfect."

"Amazing." He hoists one of the boxes with a muffled grunt. "Let's save the town."

❧

Sasha spends her morning in a shift at the library for Freddie, yawning across the information desk and idly flipping books from cover to blurb as she shelves them. She isn't much of a reader, honestly—neither sister is. Too busy? Too self-involved, maybe.

In childhood, Sasha would read aloud to Lil, performances that became increasingly staged, with their stuffed animals recruited into a story time cast with a multitude of voices. Once Mom arrived to shut off the stage lights, they'd retreat under the covers, and Sasha's whispered dramatics would keep them up well past a reasonable bedtime. This probably led to Sasha's stint in drama club in high school, where she landed a couple of major roles in unforgettable productions of *The Wizard of Oz* (the Tin Man) and even *As You Like It* (Celia). Autumn ran the lights, and they'd sneak smokes with the rest of the crew of misfits after those endless rehearsals.

Still, Sasha reflects as she checks out a couple of Anne Rice paperbacks to take on the boat with her, her best work was definitely those bedtime one-woman shows she put on for Lil. And, maybe, without her to read to, novels just didn't have quite the same draw.

She feels bruised and exposed after that argument. Lil was so shocked, like Sasha had just punched through the parchment paper window of their playhouse. *If you can't see that, then maybe you're the one with the problem.*

You're the problem.

And Theon said, *I know you don't belong here.*

The sky is long blue rows of clouds scorched to fire at their edges as she trudges home, the books under her arm. She's deep in her own mind, so she doesn't see her until she's right on top of her.

Pale and covered in dirt and smears, Autumn sits on the porch steps, head leaning against the railing. Her ponytail is half-out and there's—*blood.* Blood and mud smear her legs, a terrible wound at her ankle oozing.

She opens her eyes as Sasha approaches and offers a wan almost-smile. "Can I come in?" she asks hoarsely.

"What—here," Sasha hurries over to hoist Autumn against her shoulder, half carrying her into the house. She settles her at the kitchen table and starts rummaging in cabinets at random for the first aid kit. It's in the same old place above the sink, and Sasha carries it over. Before doing anything with it, she pours Autumn a double brandy from the bar and sets it on the table. "What the hell happened?"

"Long stupid story." Autumn downs her shot, winces and rests her head on her arms. Her eyes peek out from her curtain of hair. Sasha pulls her leg up into her lap and opens the kit.

It's weirdly difficult to breathe as she rolls up Autumn's jeans, bits of denim sticking in dried blood. For a moment, Autumn hides, shoulders trembling. "I, um—have you checked your answering machine?" her voice is wet and choked. "I left you a message."

Sasha listened to that voicemail, but it was this morning, in the midst of rushing off to the library and her post-fight-with-Lil misery spiral. She peeked through the window at the bakery, but the front was dark. She should've knocked. She should've cared a little more. Sasha grinds her teeth.

"I'm sorry, Pip." She works as tenderly as she can, cleaning dirt and dried blood until she can see the wound itself, punctures and a ring of mottled bruising so terrible it's hard to imagine it'll ever fade. Clearly it has bled badly. Autumn tells the story in woozy bursts. A loaf of bread. A child. Autumn's tender, foolish heart leading her into shady, vine-choked woods. Sasha's own heart pounds.

How many other traps crouch under the kudzu?

"There's something out there," Autumn murmurs as Sasha

winds the bandage over the ragged but clean injury. "I was being watched."

Sasha's voice sounds calmer than she feels. "You mean besides by the terrifying Ewok child?" All the emotions of the past two days are collecting at the pressure point in her sinuses. She's definitely about to lose it. "What if he hadn't come around?" Her hands shake as she clatters the first aid kit shut. "How would I have found you?"

Autumn's eyes fall on her like she must be seeing through the eggshell holding Sasha together. "I don't know," she admits. "It's bad out there. Worse than I remember. How long has it been like this?"

"I mean, it's been going down for years. West of town was rough even when our parents were young," Sasha says, tearing medical tape with her teeth.

Autumn catches her arm. "No, Sasha, how long—" she breaks off, lips pressed together in a thin line. Sasha waits, heart running. "Never mind," she relents after a moment, hand sliding away from Sasha's. But something guarded lingers in her eyes.

Sasha waits, just in case she changes her mind. But Autumn's had a hard day; she doesn't have to talk if she doesn't want to. Not tonight. "You'll have to check all over for ticks whenever you shower." Sasha hovers, unsure where to turn next. "Want some aspirin? Another drink?"

"I'll take another drink." A tremulous fraction of that Autumn cheeriness is returning. "You fixed me up great. Thanks, doc." She taps her empty glass on the table, gaze skating away. "Can I stay with you tonight?"

"Oh, *I'm sorry.*" Sasha grabs a second glass from the dish rack and collapses into the chair beside her, pulling a sardonic smile onto her face with effort. "Did you actually think I was going to let you *leave*?"

Autumn snickers a little. "My hero. My knight in shining flannel." She nudges her glass to Sasha. "Go on then. Pour me another."

Sasha pours. She'll empty this bottle, turn on every light in the house, play the stereo as loud as it'll go—anything to chase the dark away tonight.

CHAPTER TWELVE

Once, Sasha and Lil shared the room with the low slanting ceiling and the view over the back acres. There was a single vanity for both of them, with their plastic jewelry and a big mirror, a communal bookcase, two sides of one closet, and two twin beds with matching flowering quilts. A macrame tapestry. A watercolor of hot-air balloons.

Lil moved out when they were teenagers. She was a cheetah in those days, scratching at the walls, trying to get enough space to stretch out. Jason, who was at least half the cause, helped her haul her mattress up the stairs and into the attic.

Lil took nothing else from their old room. She still sleeps a floor up in that huge not-quite-a-bedroom. It is still her domain, window ledges full of her houseplants, clothes in a big wardrobe. The master remains Mom's, even now.

And Sasha?

The childhood bedroom is hers. It's had a couple of updates. The macrame tapestry was taken down. There are more photographs now from her darkroom, ones Sasha liked enough to look at every day. One of them is from her show in New York, and someone had offered her a lot of money for it, which she'd turned down. It's of Linda, taken on a day trip to Philadelphia. They'd wandered down South Street and spied this guy tiling an alley. What he'd done looked like a shattered rainbow: wineglass bottoms, bits of broken porcelain, hand-painted ceramics. Sasha had photographed Linda there, her face captured in a mirror reduced to shards and then mosaiced there in that alley, so she could see fragments of her face at half a dozen angles. Reflected there, she was a *Demoiselle D'Avignon*, a woman in pieces: a cheekbone, a quizzical chin, one mahogany eye, keen and bright and on Sasha through the lens.

Sasha had hung it here and then immediately wished she'd sold it back in New York.

She'd also pushed the two twin beds together, and they fit naturally into one bigger bed. Just put king-size sheets on. It's always a slumber party in here these days.

That's where Autumn sits now in one of Sasha's softest flannels, her leg resting on a pillow to keep it elevated, another double of brandy on the windowsill next to her. The lamplight infuses russet flyaways all over her head and glows on her knobbly knees. She's watching the moonrise over the canopies when she stiffens.

"Look," Autumn murmurs. "On the hill."

Sasha follows her gaze. Up there, on the halo of hills that bound their town, something glimmers. A ghost light. No. Another house fire. It startles her, but almost immediately the fire snuffs out.

"It's just like the one we fought," Autumn says. "On and off again. What do you make of that?"

Sasha squints out into the darkness. With the fire gone as soon as it appeared, there's no way they'd find it now, driving around out in the night. "Just jot it down in our notepad of mysteries, Pip. I don't know."

"That notepad must be getting really full." Autumn watches for another tense moment, but the flicker is gone, and slowly, tension releases its grip on her. "Can't remember the last time I had this kind of sleepover," she tells the moon, the stars, the lost beetle tapping on the outside of the window.

Sasha hops onto the bed beside her. "Want me to braid your hair?" It sounds ironic, but it's not: Sasha actually learned to braid so she had an excuse to touch *this* hair, this hair that looked like fall and smelled like Christmas.

"Like old times." Autumn's hair is a little damp from the shower she's taken, blood and dirt and leaves all washed down the drain. She shifts enough to turn Sasha's way. Downstairs, Lil has come in for the night, her steps creaking around the kitchen. "Braiding hair, telling secrets."

Sasha stretches for the brush sitting on top of her dresser, then gathers Autumn's hair in her hands, dividing it into fragrant sections. "So. Tell me a secret." It's the kind of thing you ask without totally wanting to know; if you don't pry, then things are just as they were. But it's in those stories, those life experiences missed when the paths diverge, where the alienation lies between friends. Sasha has plenty of her own stories that, safely tucked away, can't distance her from those she longs to pull closer. She listens to the kettle singing in the kitchen, and her heart tugs.

"Glad you asked. I've traveled the world, dabbled in espionage, the trading of illegal baked goods…some real femme fatale behavior." The top of Autumn's head brushes Sasha's chin. One of her fingernails is broken. But she's smiling now, brandy-loose and relaxed. "I'm sure you remember the power of my…secret-ingredient brownies."

Sasha gets her gist immediately, remembering that one night in the tree house. *The* night. "I thought we didn't talk about that," she says, giving that hair a playful tug. She steadies her breath.

Autumn waves a hand, putting on a deep, dramatic voice. "What happens in the tree house…"

Stays in the tree house. All of the hours they passed there. It's a precious relic from those teenage years, one of the few secret places Sasha never shared with Lil, but kept for her and Autumn alone. They'd discovered it together, built in an oak beside a creek. It wasn't much of a house, just a floor and an approximation of a wall. It should have been condemned because of the sloped angle it held over the water. They were always one misplaced elbow from death.

They'd had so many times out there, Sasha digging her fingers into Autumn's ribs to make her laugh, or else listening to the radio, Autumn's head resting on her chest like it belonged there. Then there was that night. The *last* night, right before Sasha left for SCAD.

"What do you even remember about that?" Sasha laughs, tangling the strands between the fingers of one hand as she stretches for a scrunchie on the bedside table. She is careful. The laugh is a cover, because truthfully, even the mention of that night hurts her. "Those brownies were…"

They'd huddled out there, night damp, tickling their fingertips over candle flames to keep warm as they waited for something to happen. The tree house had creaked ominously in the wind, filling the night with a feeling of presence, like little feet in the brush below, or something sinister between the trees. And then, in several hot-air balloon lifts, something kicked in, and they were suddenly weightless, the tree house shot into orbit. No one could stop laughing, and thoughtlessly, Sasha had reached to touch the fanned flame of Autumn's hair.

"What do I remember?" Autumn muses. "I remember…skipping school because baking was more important. And I remember you"—she pokes Sasha's side, right where it's a little squashy—"trying to recite your lines from *Midsummer Night's Dream* to me. You were really into it, lady bard. I think you made yourself cry."

"Ha." No. Sasha had not cried then, but she'd cried the next morning after she limped home, a late, hungover huddle under her covers. She'd been so filled with bravado that night, with joy and youth and their perfect knowing of each other. And at dawn, covered in shivering dew, head pounding, Autumn had ducked out. Even this time, when Pip is bringing it up herself, she acts like she doesn't remember the most important strokes of that night. Maybe she really doesn't remember. And that makes Sasha not only an idiot—the unloved, gay weirdo—it also means that maybe everything that happened up there was inappropriate. Manipulative.

Sasha sniffs theatrically and jerks herself out of that memory. Because Pip doesn't remember, and so when Sasha visits that place in her mind, she feels entirely alone. "The life of a fairy queen is a heavy burden." She finishes her shining plait. "There you go. I've outdone myself."

Autumn feels for the braid with her fingers, and makes a small approving sound. "Please, continue pampering me." She flops back against Sasha's chest like she's an armchair. "It's been such a day."

"You've been through hell. You're probably in shock," Sasha hears herself say. She's *right here*, so close after so long apart, collapsing time into touch—and it's like they're back in that last night before they parted ways and everything was never quite the same again. Sasha reaches awkwardly, just grasping the corner of her quilt with her fingertips, and pulls it up over them, tucking Autumn in. "I bet you're exhausted."

"What does shock feel like, do you think?" Autumn plays with the end of her new braid as Sasha cuts the light. They are left in the night-light glow.

"How should I know? Like this?" It feels dark and charged in here now, yet Sasha gives her a swift tickle anyway. Autumn shrieks, half laugh, half pain, wrenching hard enough that Sasha apologizes quickly. "Sorry, sorry! That wasn't nice." Sasha hugs her tighter. Her own heart is pounding too, with Autumn right against her like this. Maybe teenagers can wrap up in a tangle of limbs and pretend it's platonic, but at some point, Sasha graduated out of this ability. Still, that's not fair; it isn't good to snuggle your probably-straight friend under false pretenses. She tries to stifle the heat pooling inside her. "You're still freezing."

Autumn wraps a hand around Sasha's elbow, a quiet bid for comfort. "I'm still scared," she admits.

A cool breeze drifts in the window, carrying with it the sweet scent of the pecans, of damp bark and fallen leaves. They're far from danger here. "'Sleep thou, and I will wind thee in my arms,'" Sasha murmurs, dredging Titania up from her deep memory. She searches for the next piece. "'So doth the woodbine the sweet honeysuckle gently entwist; the female ivy so…enrings the barky fingers of the elm.'"

Autumn sighs against her, just in time with the rustle of leaves from the orchard. If there are any fires burning out there in the night, they are beyond their view.

એ

Lil knows better than anyone that if she's waiting for Sasha to resolve a conflict like an adult, she's going to be waiting in tree rings rather than days. They move through and around each other like specters, and for once, Lil doesn't have the energy to build the bridge.

Someone clearly spent the night, probably Autumn, but Lil is already out of the house by the time anyone from the child-hood bedroom stirs the next morning. It gnaws, having to be the mature one when sometimes all Lil wants to do is burn.

Jason waits for her on the porch of Honeysuckle House, and he's killing time by pulling vines off the bone-white columns. Perched on one of the wicker outdoor chairs is a checklist and clipboard. Ah, yes. Student Council President Finch is ready to run the agenda, as usual. He has the toe of one beat-up old sneaker wedged into the balustrade as he hoists himself precariously up to snatch one of the higher tendrils of ivy from the capitol—which is how Lil manages to sneak up on him.

She shades her eyes against the light, which falls like a golden veil over the scene, smiling despite herself. "Your fly's down."

Jason jumps, then wobbles on his perch, threatening to tumble over on top of her. Then he rights himself and joins her, the vine trailing behind him like a party streamer. "No it's not," he says, giving her a swift kiss on the cheek. It could be friendly, but it leaves a scorch of heat behind. The heat Jason gives off is never more than thinly concealed, and she sees it now, a simmer in the eyes. "Morning. Ready to win everybody over?"

"No wonder you're in politics," Lil replies, scooping up his notes, a thorough checklist of all the people they'll need on their side, all the roles they'll have to fill to put on the festival. "Let's go. I'll read on the way."

She flips through Jason's near-impeccable initial plans as they walk, poking a couple of good-natured holes in it—his handwriting, the color of the pen—just to stir him up. They squabble. It's friendlier than they've been since the law school debacle, their old patterns reanimated. Bickering to feel alive, because they both loved a battle of wits, feeding off each other's energy. She can't help it. As gentle as Lil feels in the presence of her trees and her family, she had *missed* the unbridled freedom that came from Jason's adoration of the whole of her, even her sharpest edge. He was the only one who seemed to want the sheer volume of her love, her passion, her loyalty. Having him here, with her and on her side, was arnica to the bruise of heartbreak.

They wander into the center of town, past the grocery and First Methodist, toward the central square. The air is livelier today than it's been in what feels like forever. Two cars idle at the intersection, waiting for the light to change. The marching band must be practicing on the field because horns bleat in the distant air. Is it a school day? Her sense of time is measured in harvests lately, not weeks, and this harvest has been endless.

Lil spares a moment of guilt for the pecans she hasn't picked yet this morning, for the half day of work she'd done the day before. She'll rise early and play catchup tomorrow.

"So, volunteers. We'll need the firemen to build stalls before the festival and on extra shifts during. Plus, the kids always loved seeing a truck at the square," Lil says, passing the clipboard back. "Better hope they still like you over there."

"Everybody likes me. Or at least they do when they don't think I'm calling them out to fake fires," Jason replies, cutting her an amused look. "Do they like *you* over there?"

Lil offers a poison-apple smirk. "You'd be impressed by how many friends I've made." Not that she's had a long-term lover since Jason. The orchard will always come first for her, and in the years since he left, the work has only grown, the margins only shrunk. Still. Let him imagine what he wants.

Jason shakes his head, some of the amusement cut short at the suggestion. The heat from him doesn't dissipate.

The firehouse is a converted Main Street mansion; the most notable outside change is a set of truck-sized doors gouged out of the back. It's especially fresh-faced today, pale blue with a saucy red door, sprawling porch, and gables bordered with white, like lace from a bride's hope chest. Jason softens at the sight of it. Back when it was his kingdom, his twenty-four-hour shifts left the two of them as parched as drought-stricken grass for each other. Their reunions were an inevitable blaze. Every time.

Warm, Lil palms the back of her neck.

The crew today is small, and they gather to shake Jason's hand. It's like he never left. It's like Lil has fallen back in time.

"Not another prank fire, right, Finch?" Cesar says to Jason, offering Lil a conspiratorial smile.

"Much better," Lil replies, sweet as sugar, before Jason can start beating his chest. "An opportunity."

It goes well. Headily so. They get five volunteers for construction right off the bat, and that's before Jason launches into a soliloquy about duty. By the time they leave, their volunteer setup team is secured.

The day is beautiful. It's a perfect Southern fall: the final remnants of summer heat that won't let go mixed with changing leaves. And above them shines the crystalline sky that only happens in autumn.

For once, there's a light on behind the blue shutters of their squat, ivy-drenched library. So they catch Freddie next, the library's wisp of a keeper. He's stacking books in a cart labeled DONATIONS at his desk. He instantly volunteers to organize the book fair.

"I want to do this kind of outreach. I keep seeing new kids in here, and so many of them look uncared-for," he says, cradling a copy of *The Shining* like a baby. "Do you know, I don't think their parents are bringing them. It's like they're coming alone." Freddie was such a worrier, but Lil and Sasha used to walk to the library alone as kids. Mom made them hold hands the entire time.

They've barely stepped outside when they're flagged down by a couple of rotary club members who haunt the courthouse steps. The elders of town love Jason—think he's a promising young man—and they shower him with questions, ideas, and dreams for the Pecan Festival. He tries to keep careful note of each and every suggestion while maintaining eye contact and his sunny smile, even when Millie Preston reaches over with a skeletal hand and actually pinches his cheek.

"Let me offer some starting funds," warbles Cork, a widower known for wandering too late at night, wrestling two dollars from his wrinkled wallet. Jason starts to take it, but he hands it to Lil. "For you, young lady. No offense, young man, but she's got the better head on her shoulders."

They steal into the alley behind the library. Someone needs to empty the dumpsters; the air is thick with rotting meat. And yet, leaning on the brick, Lil meets Jason's eye and they both burst out laughing.

"*She's got the better head on her shoulders*," Jason intones. "I can't—he isn't even wrong." Lil can't remember a day as golden as this one for months. A day when the ache in her back isn't all she feels. A day when what she's trying to fix—a fence, a pecan shaker, a familial bond—doesn't resist with all its might. Lil never backs down from a fight; she and Jason would never have survived as long as they did if she didn't like to fight a little. But she's been fighting so long.

Lil catches her breath and suddenly, her laughter begins to turn. Tears. Even though she's so happy—she catches herself, a hand over her mouth.

"What is it?" Jason asks. He leans close to her.

"Nothing," she murmurs against her palm. Her eyes are full and she's smiling all at once. What is wrong with her? What is happening in her body? Hope isn't gentle, but a wild, powerful invader. "I just—I needed this." She takes a breath. A roach skitters between their feet, into the shadows. "I needed…this."

Jason sways into her space, eyes consuming her. Intense…and a little curious.

"What?" Lil asks.

Jason is wild-animal taut, eyes starved. Clumsily, like he doesn't know how to be gentle, he touches just under her eye. But there's nothing to feel. She hasn't actually shed tears. She isn't that far gone.

"Never seen someone laugh-cry before?" she prompts when he doesn't respond.

"Huh," he says. "I guess not. Lilith." He rarely used her full name in the old days. Only when the lights were low, his hands were on her, and he wanted her to beg. Those eyes like oil. Dark. Ready to catch fire.

Lil thrums with all the violent power of flint and stone, of lighters, of a match. There's work to do. She steps back. But she'll leave a bookmark nestled at this exact page. "Thank you. For helping. I know you probably can't stay until the festival, but—"

"Don't worry about that." He catches her free hand, sunny as ever. "I'll be here."

CHAPTER THIRTEEN

AUTUMN WAKES IN BED AND WATCHES SASHA'S SLEEP-serene face, the gentle parting of her lips. As quietly as she can, she slips from beneath the covers and tugs her socks on. She's particularly gentle with her injured ankle. This morning there's a chilly bite to the air.

Sasha flops over, easily sprawling to cover the whole space. But when Autumn looks back, her eyes are open, one hand stretched for her. "I didn't say you could leave," she complains, the visible hazel eye almost golden, like the exposed sheen of an acorn.

"Sorry, lots of baking to do. I have A Plan," Autumn explains, scavenging through Sasha's drawers for a sweater. The one she finds is a little mothy and much too big. But it's *so soft*, and it smells like home. She dons it like armor to combat the shard of fear from her ordeal yesterday, which hasn't totally left her. Its urgency has followed her into the new day.

Sasha grumbles into her pillow. "Why?"

Autumn chuckles and relents, returning to pounce on the

mound of Sasha and linen covers. She props herself up, peering over her shoulder. "Come with me and see."

"Well…" Long fingers brush just once through her hair. "Hold your horses. Let me check those bandages first." Letting Sasha care for her has never been a hardship. So Autumn sits back down to let her do it.

Later on, both dressed and Autumn's ankle rebandaged, a tousled and yawning Sasha accompanies her to the bakery, shooting worried looks at the way she's limping. But it's just sore; no real structural damage.

Sasha mans the counter and the espresso machine while Autumn gets to work. It looks, bizarrely, like they might actually have some customers in, so Autumn whips out some easy crowd-pleasers to get them started—chocolate chunk cookies, her quickest cinnamon coffee cake, an herb-loaded focaccia with cheddar sprinkles. A few of the essentials are prepped and waiting for the oven, so it isn't long before they have the doors open for this surprise Saturday crowd. She loves it, she really does, but of course people are coming the one day she doesn't want them, the one day she doesn't truly want to be open.

Sure enough, every time she pokes her head out into the storefront, Sasha is chatting with someone, effortlessly managing the register and running the place like it's her own. She's a natural. Though, by the sounds of it, and the messages Sasha flipped through on that ancient Clearwater answering machine before they left, Sasha's actually been sort of running the town for a while now. While her customer-facing baking fills the building—and the block—with enticing layers of aroma (puff pastry, apple cinnamon, roasting garlic), Autumn gets busy with what she actually came here for today.

Oatmeal cookies. Sausage rolls. *Many* sausage rolls. Hearty seedy breads and fruit, dried and dehydrated in the sun. Honey cake, which could cure all ills. Autumn whips up a special survivalist storm, not just her best food but the things most packed with nutrition: oats, grains, protein, and vitamins anywhere she can.

Because she's not giving up.

Even with cool fall air drifting in the open door, Autumn dabs sweat from her brow as she kneads dough.

"So you wanted one of these amazing brookies, two perfect scones, and two coffees? Great…" Sasha's voice drifts back to her from the front. She probably gets fantastic tips at whatever shift she was covering. Even in all her years outside this town, Autumn has never seen a face quite like Sasha's. With the warm tan of her skin, her pouting mouth, those pale golden eyes, she looks like some kind of Greco-Roman river spirit, a nymph brushing her hair on a bank. She's the taller sister, both of them more powerful than thin in build. Of course, both of them have a stark, raw beauty. Forces of nature.

In her youth, Sasha got so sick of hearing about her looks from the geriatric population of the town that she's now almost allergic to compliments. People are used to Sasha here, and something about her relationship with this place, with Sasha being quietly but stubbornly gay and not running the land she half owns, means she is often ducking into the background, her head down, trying to assure the world that there's nothing to see—but there's no doubt she must have turned heads those years she was in New York. If she'd had any interest in modeling, she would've been snatched up in a second, but Sasha always preferred to be the eye, happiest behind the camera.

Maybe that's why she likes Autumn, because Autumn never cared about her last name, the novelty of her being a twin, or even her beauty quite as much as she cared about *her*. The things she said. The way she laughed. How she could feel the world so deeply but wear her cares so loosely. Autumn never wanted anything from her, only more time.

Autumn dodged Sasha's question about the special brownie night—hypocritically, since she'd technically been the one to bring it up. In a moment of brandy-soaked bravado, she bulldozed her way into that forbidden territory. The night. The fireflies, the stir of heat in Autumn's stomach, the young confused fumble with Sasha out of the safe realm of friendship. They'd never been more than a step away from the boundaries.

It's been uncountable years. Out there in the world beyond town, Autumn has talked it through with friends, with partners, unpacked it many times over in her own head. So Autumn believed she was ready to talk about it with Sasha—only to open her mouth and be tongue-tied. Maybe it's just what Matt calls the Homecoming Effect. Truths that are accepted, even celebrated out in the world, can choke you in the town of your birth.

It's like, I'm at my parents', and they know I'm gay, but suddenly, I get the urge to make up a fake girlfriend. Just in case. Like an insurance policy, he once said morosely after Christmas.

She sighs, driving her foolish knuckles into the dough. Maybe in a century, they can talk.

After Sasha sells the last slice of quiche and all the snickerdoodles—besides the one hanging from her mouth—she starts to close. She hasn't badgered Autumn, hasn't asked what she's doing back there. Sasha isn't one to emotionally crowd; she probably senses that Autumn is working through what happened in her own way. She's sweeping when Autumn appears with the two heavy baskets, their insides lined with water bottles and all the things she made, many of her creations still warm.

Sasha glances up from the floor and immediately shakes her head. "No. No way."

"Yes. Yes way," Autumn replies. "You don't have to come, but I'm going."

Sasha groans, leaning the broom against the wall. "I knew you were going to say that."

❧

This time, they stay out of the woods, walking along the highway, then cutting toward the railroad on one of the dirt roads between properties. They'd follow the tracks and…hope for the best.

Sasha chivalrously hefts both baskets, leaving Autumn the job of carrying herself. It's slow going with the ankle, but it's lucky there wasn't a sprain. It's late afternoon now, and the day feels changeable, a weather system making the air charged and heavy. Though it was sunny and open in town, now they trip along beneath a low sky. It's very quiet out here, and Autumn finds herself avoiding the clang of her feet on the tracks, in favor of the soft ground between them.

"I don't know his name," Autumn murmurs. "We could… call out?"

"Um—forest children," Sasha shouts, her voice cracking. She clears her throat and gives it another try. "Little masked monster, where are you?"

They both wince. Breaking the silence feels wrong.

Nothing to do but continue to trudge forward, counting the rivets in the railroad tracks. After a couple of hours, they're several miles from town and may as well be a hundred. Nothing stirs in the tired landscape, the ground a mix of hard dirt and trash, rusted beer cans and fifty-year-old tires.

The pain in her leg is getting harder and harder to ignore, and sweat runs freely down Autumn's back. Finally, she relents. "Let's just sit a minute?" she suggests, unable to mask the fatigue in her voice.

Sasha lays down the baskets, then offers Autumn her hand, easing her gently onto the pine needles. Then she sits, throwing her legs out over the ground. "Good thing we wore long pants," she says. "We'd be eaten alive out here by creepy crawlies." There's no judgment in her tone, no frustration. Sasha is relaxed. She's not an I-told-you-so type. They'll walk as far as Autumn wishes, and then Sasha would probably give her a ride home on her back.

She picks up a cluster of pine needles and peels them away from each other with her long fingers. "Lil and I are in a fight," she admits, eyes down.

"Uh-oh." Autumn digs around for one of the water bottles for them to share. It is never good news when the Clearwaters are on the outs. They often bicker, but it isn't so often they go days in conflict. At least, that's how Autumn remembers it. "What about?"

"Honestly?" Sasha's brow is furrowed as she tosses one of the pine needles over her shoulder. "I think it was about me being jealous of Jason. Again." She doesn't look over, her voice low and embarrassed.

Autumn waits. With Sasha, it's better to hold the silence for her as she gets the thoughts out. Sometimes it takes a little while.

Sure enough, Sasha goes on. "I know Lil loves me. I do. But I don't think she really…likes me very much?" It is a tremulous confession, and Autumn brushes a hand across the wings of her shoulder blades.

"She did when we were kids. But ever since she moved out of our room and started spending every second out in the orchard, I don't know how I fit here." She snorts. "Which made living in New York a huge relief, actually."

"I bet it was a relief for a lot of reasons," Autumn murmurs. They haven't directly addressed Sasha's sexuality since Autumn's return, but it's been openly understood between them since Sasha told Autumn about her first girlfriend on a spring break from college. The same isn't exactly true in the other direction; Autumn has never told Sasha everything about herself. Eventually, things unsaid build up. Autumn has quite a pile of things she hasn't told Sasha.

"It was." Sasha glances at her. "But when I came back and the situation was so bad here, with the orchard, with losing Mom, I stayed. I thought we'd be closer. But we aren't, and now Jason is back and immediately he's the one she confides in." She stabs the end of a pine needle into the knee of her baggy jeans until it breaks. "She just—likes him more than me. Even if she thinks she doesn't love him anymore."

The hair on the back of Autumn's neck begins to rise. She knows this feeling: curious eyes hidden in the trees. They aren't alone anymore. "You're her twin," Autumn points out gently. "You're two halves of one biscuit."

Sasha smiles faintly at that, then grimaces. "I wish I had a biscuit right now. I'm starving."

Autumn sighs, waves of mingled disappointment and relief hitting her at Sasha's redirect. The topic is closed, for now at least. Autumn darts a glance toward the dense greenery of the woods only a few yards away. "I think he's watching us."

"Really?" Sasha asks quietly.

Autumn nods. There's a patch of shadow in the corner of her eye.

"Hey, if you're there, come on out," Sasha calls, her voice very gentle. "It's okay. We brought you some more food."

Silence, not quite the same silence they've been disrupting this whole time. A held-breath silence. Rustling. They share a hopeful look. But then it quiets again.

"You were really brave yesterday," Autumn tries, even as Sasha's mouth presses into a hard line. "I'm doing a lot better now. You helped me. I just wanted to thank you." She speaks more softly, putting all the conviction she feels about this into it. "But we can leave the food here, if you want."

A shape shivers in the grass, no more a disturbance than a rabbit. And there it is, back from the tracks about twenty feet: the mask, peering at them. Autumn can't help beaming at the proof that he's here, thriving in his own way. The kudzu hasn't swallowed him. "Hi. I brought a friend."

Sasha starts to stand, but Autumn catches her wrist and pulls. They've got to stay relaxed. She's lost this boy twice already, and she won't again.

The boy wears the same faded shirt and no shoes at all.

"I don't think I told you my name last time." Autumn keeps

her tone light. She reaches into the basket and pulls out one of the sausage rolls. She unwraps the foil, lets the smell bloom in the air. The boy inches closer. "I'm Autumn." She nudges forward, two pairs of eyes tracking her, and lays the gift on the tracks, far enough away that he might feel safe taking it. "This is my friend, Sasha." The little masked figure lets out a snappish combination of word-sounds he must've learned from the trees.

This time, since she isn't actively bleeding, it makes Autumn laugh a little. "I know, I know, you told me not to come back," she says, like they're speaking the same language. "But I had to. This is one of my favorite foods, and I think you'll like it too."

The smell of good food, the sound of friendly laughter: they're her most powerful tools.

And they work. The boy inches forward, close enough to snatch the sausage roll then retreat swiftly. His mask falls to the ground so he can cram half in his mouth. He chomps away, his small face very serious. He has warm, sun-kissed skin and shaggy brown hair, matted and hanging nearly to his shoulders. His baby face is smudged with grime. His eyes are a luminous amber.

"Where's the purple?" he says, a baby-lion growl.

"The...purple?"

"The—thing—the—" he frowns, lacking the words, bares his teeth. "Purple sweet...blood."

"What the hell?" Sasha breathes.

"Oh, the blueberry pies!" Autumn realizes. "I didn't have any more blueberries. Sorry. But I brought you some cookies with chocolate. Do you know about chocolate?"

For a moment, he just looks at her. Then he nods his head slowly.

"You'll love these." She grabs three cookies from the basket, hands one to Sasha, and scoots closer to the boy. He arches a little, a cautious move. But she stops before she's in reach, and carefully tosses a foil-wrapped cookie his way. He snatches it out of the air.

She unwraps hers and takes a bite. Oatmeal and chocolate with just a hint of cinnamon: what could be warmer on a cool day?

"Do you live around here?" she asks. "We do."

The little boy chatters like a squirrel, glancing back toward the overgrown darkness of the trees. He plops down in the brush to devour the rest of his sausage roll.

"So I'm Sasha, this is Autumn…" Sasha repeats, then points to him. "Who are you? What's your name?"

He dithers. "Umm—Wyn."

"Wyn?" Sasha clarifies, around a bite of her own cookie.

He shows her his teeth, not quite a grin. Several of his baby teeth are already gone, maybe knocked out. He couldn't be more than five or six years old.

Sasha shrugs, then shows him her teeth back. "Nice to meet you," she says.

Wyn tucks his foil-wrapped cookie into his pants, then wanders over to investigate the now open baskets, his head nearly shoved inside. Winnie the Pooh in a honeypot. "You know the liberry?" he mumbles.

"I love the library," Autumn says. "I went all the time when I was a kid. Do your parents take you?"

Wyn pokes his head back out. He has found another goodie, which is now in his mouth. He takes it out to peer at her. "What's a…?" He seems shy to try to say a word he doesn't know. "Don't know," he says instead. "Neel and me—Neel and me, we go to the liberry. Sometimes."

Autumn nods, not wanting to startle him. But at least he isn't alone. He looks like someone must be feeding him, helping him make masks, keeping him alive out here. "Is it just you and Neel?"

"Used to be Fran and Googoo and umm—" Wyn searches for another name, but gives up with a shrug.

Sasha gives Autumn an ominous look. Other children were out here, apparently, at least at one time. *And what happened to them?*

"Used to be?" Autumn prompts.

"Train." Wyn is gnawing contemplatively. "Don't—you better not touch those vines," he says finally. Sasha hastily drags her sneaker away from the kudzu edging over the ground.

"Wyn," Autumn begins and scoots a little closer to him. He's glancing over his shoulder. "Do you like living out here? Are you safe—"

"Get back, Wyn," someone shouts, fiercely enough that Sasha seizes Autumn's wrist. Standing a few yards from them, nearer the trees, is another boy, this one maybe ten or so. His hair is a dark mop of unkempt curls. Wyn stares wide-eyed at him. This must be Neel, Wyn's protector. "Get away from him," the boy snarls. Worst of all, he is brandishing a shotgun.

Autumn raises her hands. "It's okay. We're friends." She offers her kindest smile. "Are you Neel?"

The boy fires his gun straight into the air. "Get," he yells. He is even scrawnier than Wyn, a body forced to grow on scraps.

Wyn starts to cry.

"Now hang on," Sasha tries, though she is also on her feet and yanking at Autumn. "We're friendly—"

Neel reloads. Even at his age, he has the desperate, dead-eyed edge of a person capable of taking a lethal shot.

Wyn glances between Autumn and Neel, then scurries back to him.

Autumn lets Sasha pull her up, distantly aware that she's crying too. "We don't want to hurt you. We want to help you." The kudzu vines nearly trip her, and it's only Sasha's grip that pulls her clear of them.

"C'mon," Sasha murmurs, holding tight to her hand. "We'll come back."

"But he—I can't leave them here," Autumn pleads.

Wyn hovers by Neel now, watching the gun nervously. Tears track down his face.

"We don't need your help," Neel shouts, something wild in his face. "You'll bring the hungry man." And he points the shotgun straight at them.

That's the last straw for Sasha. "We have to go," she says firmly. When Autumn hesitates a moment longer, she scoops her up and starts walking, back along the tracks. The baskets stay where they are, where hopefully the boys will still take them.

Autumn looks back, but the figures are already going, Neel dragging Wyn to the safety of the trees, or whatever he considers safe. Autumn buries her face in Sasha's shoulder.

"We'll come back," Autumn promises herself more than Sasha. "We'll think of something else."

It's so easy to get lost there, out by the abandoned orchards that never seem to bear fruit, where something stalks in the shadows.

CHAPTER FOURTEEN

E ARLY IN THE MORNING, WHILE THE LIGHT IS STILL blue, Lil realizes it's been three whole days since she tended to the pond and the golden pecans.

Deep in her subconscious, Mom reproaches her for neglecting her most important duty. So she wraps up in her leather jacket, shoves into her Wellingtons, and hurries out of the house, into the trees. Honeyed light spills between new gaps in the branches as more leaves, more pecans continue their gentle rain. It's not just the pond she hasn't cared for; too many ripe husks crack underfoot on her way there. They're close to ready with the festival—the stands are already going up in the town square—but she'll need to pause the rampant planning and beg off for a day. Maybe Jason will even join her in the orchard. Like old times.

Lil pushes aside bare branches and reaches the quiet of the pond and the tree at its banks. There, the sight stops her in her tracks.

It's…bad. The shower of gold is everywhere, abundant as leaf fall after an unseasonable snow, and the pond has snuck higher up the banks than usual, slithering against the roots of the tree, shallow tendrils stretching toward the far brambles, hungry for every last morsel it can't reach.

"Now, now," Lil murmurs. "I wasn't gone that long." She bends and starts scooping them up, tossing handfuls into the water with heavy plops.

The last time Lil missed her duty for more than a day came not too long after her trifecta of loss: Mom passing, then Sasha's move to New York, and Jason's departure for law school. She barely remembered that whole November; she had lost the meat and bones of it to a raging fever. Her remaining recollections are grim. Crawling up the stairs on hands and knees to collapse, shivering, in bed. Her throat aching so badly she couldn't sleep, the glass on her bedside table bone dry. Eating only the summer preserves until they made her sick because the cupboards were otherwise bare. Strange-blooded visions of a faceless figure with antlers crouching at the edge of her bed. Being too terrified to close her eyes—it crept closer whenever she did.

Russ was the one who came for her, finally, when calls to her home went unanswered and she missed two deliveries to Su's Grocery. Her fever broke to the sight of him humming at her stove, warming a pot of his homemade chicken soup.

When she dragged herself back to health, even the empty house seemed flu-ish, the far papershell trees had scab for the first time in her memory, and the pond was eating ground, lapping at the edges of its solitary glen. So many golden pecans fell, she worked for an hour to clear them.

The house was so empty that winter.

Today's mess isn't nearly so dire. Lil works in silence. She has spent almost every day with Jason, sunrise to golden hour. He's just as excited as she is. Just as unable as she is to sit for long; sometimes they're both up and pacing the living room of Honeysuckle House, racing in contradicting orbits around the coffee table.

Lil remembers the breadth of his hands and wants to bury herself in between his ribs.

It still doesn't feel entirely safe to shine her want in his direction. But she can't crush the flowering hope that maybe it's different this time. Jason was passionate about their town once, spent days in the orchard with her once. Is it so wrong to think that just maybe, he's returning to her?

Finally, the ground is clear, and Lil cradles one final pecan, warm between her palms. She turns it over in her hands. Lifts it to her nose and her mouth waters, but she doesn't eat. Her own little ritual.

Maybe one day. Not today.

She tosses it into the pond and with a final ripple, order is restored. "Don't think I didn't notice you creeping," she says. "Calm down."

But then she feels it. Lil doesn't even have to see him to know that there's an intruder at her boundary again. She snaps around so fast her neck flares, and makes for the far fence, where it had to be newly mended, where kudzu has tried and failed to encroach. Of course he comes now, when her day is bright and beautiful. Of course it's today he chooses to ruin.

Sure enough, when she breaches the trees, there he is. Recognizable even from afar: a mistake on the canvas, a twisted smile and hungry eyes.

"Hey," she shouts.

Theon is resting his hands on the fence again, caressing it

absently, and he looks up when she approaches. When he grins at her, it's full of mirth. And something—wrong. She can't place it. A flavor that shouldn't be there. A sun that casts no shadow.

"Hi," Theon says.

Lil stops a few feet away. "What are you doing here?"

But Theon doesn't speak for a moment, only gazes at her, and keeps touching the fence like he's allowed. Though, of course, to him, someone who's gobbled up as many family homes and ripe orchards as he has, he probably feels entitled to everything he sees.

"What are you doing here?" She enunciates slowly when he refuses to back off, refuses to leave or to engage.

He chuckles. "You're so prickly in the morning." Finally, those hands are gone, off her property and stowed in the pockets of those stupid, ratty pants. He wears suits so badly, without care for the fineness of them. What is the point of it? Of biting into a candy bar and throwing the rest away, of buying land and letting it molder? Is the flavor of wastefulness really so sweet?

"Go away," she tries next.

"Nice out here today," he offers, kicking at the grass, idle and lingering. There's the note of wrongness again.

"How many times do I need to chase you off?" Lil snaps at him.

And in the face of her bite, Theon just smiles. A tiny burgundy stain marks the corner of his mouth. Mud cakes the cuffs of his pants, a new button is missing in his cuff. It's all wrong. But none of it is the exact wrongness that prickles at her. "You've got some dirt. On your cheek," he says.

And he *reaches* for her.

Lil isn't even close enough to touch, but she flinches back, shocked, her heart a queasy tempo in her ears. She wants to scream, bite, vomit, run. Theon's brow furrows with uncertainty, and it hits her: the true nature of the wrongness she senses. He's treating her like he's—she casts for a word that won't drive her to murder—*fond*.

No. She cannot do this. She cannot understand this, and will not.

Lil strides forward, slaps his hand out of the air, and spits, "What are you *doing*."

Theon freezes, a feast of contradiction: confusion, tenderness, intensity, hurt, and then—he rips his gaze away with enough force that he wrenches back a step. When he looks up, he's blank, and his smile bares his teeth.

"So touchy," he scoffs. "No point then, in me asking if you're going to sell."

"Is that seriously—? Is that why you're—" Lil tries. "No. Of course I'm not going to sell." The morning was so beautiful. Lil searches for the kindness she'd only just bathed in, for the light through trees, the sense of Jason's care, the warmth of Mom's pride—but she can't feel it now. She's worlds away. Trapped in a standoff.

Theon's jaw is clenched hard. The tiny rusty stain at the corner of his mouth repels her. "The Pecan Festival won't save you."

She shivers once. But doesn't shake apart. "Leave."

"No one will come. No one cares."

"*Leave.*" She dares break eye contact, desperate for some answer, some help. For Sasha flying down the driveway. For anything. There, against the tree abandoned last time she worked. *There's* help. Lil backs up.

Theon leans forward, gripping the fence again. His voice

chases her. Coming at her harsh and fast. "It's going to fail and they're going to leave." Her fingers grasp blindly. She finds the slender shape of the pole that shakes loose what wants to cling in the canopies. "You'll wish you gave it all to me because you'll be alone, working here until you die here and you rot here—"

Lil swings the pole as hard as she can, and it cracks across his knuckles and breaks into two.

Shocked, Theon looks down. Even though it should have shattered a finger, he makes no sound, no shocked cry of pain. Slowly, he raises his eyes to Lil again, gaze roaming over her face.

"Leave," she breathes.

One by one, Theon peels his fingers away from the fence. He makes a small derisive sound. "Bitch," he whispers. It isn't loaded with righteous fury, but something worse: promise. But he goes. Slipping his hands back in his pockets, easy as you please, he begins to amble down the road.

Lil stays until he strolls the far curve of the dusty, pockmarked pavement into town. But just when he's out of sight, when she begins to relax, Theon starts to whistle. Lil doesn't move. Her hand burns, her legs tremble. The wind carries Theon's song back to her as he departs.

∽

Sasha swore to Autumn that they wouldn't leave those kids out there in the woods, and she meant it. But it takes a few days to figure out their next step. For once, no one is leaving her requests to cover shifts around town. Everyone is around, doing their own jobs. Sasha and Autumn spend most of that time together, either at the bakery or on the ferry, where Autumn is awarded the title of skipper. Sasha is cozy in a white cable-knit. She always lets Autumn wear her sailor's cap when they're both aboard. Autumn is quiet, gnawing a thumbnail as she watches the water illuminated by the riverboat's big light. Her ankle is healing, but she is quiet, her expression wistful. Sasha can see that there's a windstorm of thoughts behind those big-sky eyes, but she doesn't press.

It's on the last ferry of the night that she remembers something crucial. They've only got two or three passengers tucked away on the boat, little more than denser patches of darkness in the evening chill. "I thought of someone who might know something about Wyn and Neel," Sasha says, spinning the wheel to dock.

It's like lightning, how Autumn reacts, turning to look at her with eyes full of hope. As if with just a few words, Sasha has fixed everything.

It's after eight and dark by the time they make the walk back to the center of town, but people are still milling around down there, chatting on park benches, eating ice cream from the general store. A Bible study has just let out at First Methodist, and some of the women are still congregated outside in easy conversation. It seems the evening is in no rush to turn to night out here. It's a good sign; maybe he'll still be open.

As they walk, Autumn gently bullies her way under Sasha's arm. *You belong there*, Sasha thinks to her, and it feels so true that it billows up in her chest, a fullness and a pain.

The junk shop is squeezed into a narrow and decrepit building just off the square, one of the historic storefronts. The post office and the shoe store loom on either side, both much larger and more freshly painted than this place. Hand-painted lettering curls

jauntily across the front window: LOU'S GOODS: PURVEYOR OF
DREAMS, EST. 1950. Lou had opened this place and the scrap-
yard out back with his GI Bill funds, and the shop has scraped
along all this time. As a Black man, even getting his GI benefits
was a heaven-born miracle, he liked to say, so there was no way
that either hell or high water would wash this place away.

One of the stained-glass lamps is lit inside, so Sasha pushes open
the door. Nothing smells better than Lou's shop, rich with age, old
paper, and forgotten treasures. There's no surface wasted, no corner
or shelf, nook, or cranny, that doesn't hold something that's special.
Special to somebody, anyway. Cookie jars, wedding china, copper
wire, comic books, playing cards, cigar cases, and cradles and clocks.
A violin. A porcelain-faced doll. Safes from banks that went under
in the Depression, their thick sides and ancient cranks and combination locks so old-fashioned they'd probably survived a hundred
years before that. A narrow display beyond the glass showcases a
constellation of engagement rings. They twinkle coquettishly, like a
line of wandering eyes, forgetful brides far from home.

Over the years, Lou has repaired every kind of appliance
and sold them again, helping a lot of folks who couldn't afford
something new. He'd repaired Mom's old landline from the house
at least twice. He's tinkered with Sasha's digital watch before, and
she curses that she didn't remember to bring it for him to look at
this time, since it's been flashing zeros at her for ages. He has a
better archive than their library basement, organized so minutely,
and so personally, that he can help anybody find anything they
wanted to know, and probably a lot more that they didn't.

"Lou?" she calls through the dusty darkness.

"Hey," Lou answers from deep within the labyrinth, his rusty voice faint from the comfortable old armchair he keeps behind the cramped desk. He lifts a tumbler with an inch of amber liquid inside. "Just pouring one out for Russ, you know."

"Hey, Lou." Sasha feels a pang of guilt that she hasn't come in to check on Lou since the funeral. It has to be really tough on him, to lose his best friend. Had Jason been in? Lou might want some of Russ's things from all the decades of debris in Honeysuckle House...if Jason is even cleaning the place out anymore. Could he *actually* be considering staying? Ruefully, she commits to suggesting that Jason let Lou take a look the next time she sees him around. "Thought I'd bring Autumn by to see the trains. Did you know she was back?"

Lou's face lights up like she just told him his birthday came early this year. "My little Pippi Longstocking is home, and she hasn't even brought me any pecan clusters yet?" He rises and starts the complex journey through the shop for a hug.

Autumn beams, darting over to wrap herself around his ribs. He really is getting thinner. "Hi, Loulou." She's probably the only one in town who could get away with a nickname like that. But it isn't just Sasha who'd let Autumn get away with anything. "I missed you."

"Well, now. I missed you too. I thought you were gone for good." He lays a hand flat on top of her head, as if he's checking for any last-minute growth spurts. "Are you getting along all right out there in the world?"

Autumn smiles at Sasha, keeping her close in orbit. "Home-sickness aside, sure." She softens. "I was sorry to hear about Russ. I wish I'd been back in time for the funeral."

"Oh, it's okay," Lou soothes, reaching up to one of the shelves for two more slightly dusty tumblers like his own. "These things seem to happen more and more often these days." He pours whiskey for them. "Let's just have another little memorial now." One of the trains toots from its overhead track, winding around just below the crown molding.

Autumn picks up the tumblers and hands one to Sasha. They drink in reverent silence. Autumn and Sasha's tooling around town used to bring them here. Sometimes, just to poke around or look for birthday gifts for the people—Lil—that were criminally difficult to shop for. Autumn liked to sit on the counter and ask about anything new that caught her eye. A Wonder Woman lunch box, the painted tin only a little dented. A string of antique freshwater pearls from some tiny Arkansas lake town. Lou saved her the best kitchen appliances: a beautiful retro blue stand mixer Autumn swore by, stainless steel tongs, even a marble mortar and pestle, because Autumn usually turned her nose up at spices that came to her already powdered.

"Come see the trains." Lou offers. They walk back to the second display room, many of the objects here not for sale. This is where Lou keeps most of his trains. They chug on at all levels, cruising along the walls, like a miniaturized subway system. In the center is a romanticized model of town, hemmed in by the rails. They hover over it, Autumn noting the new details, such as the hand-painted earth mover and construction workers toiling on the wrecked highway west of town. There's even a little ferry on the river.

Autumn is usually the last one talking, the last one laughing, when evening turns to night. But not today. Sasha is the first to break their comfortable reunion. "So, Lou. We had something we wanted to talk to you about."

He takes a seat, nodding to a set of barstools clearly placed for ideal train viewing. They rumble around them in predictable circuits as they talk. "What do you want to know?"

Sasha lets the whiskey burn soothe her nerves. Even these small trains fill her with some strange dread. "Do you remember when we were on the ferry that day and you mentioned those— children? Out in the fallow orchards?"

Lou fixes her with a keen look. "I remember, honey."

Sasha pauses, thinking through her next words carefully. "You know I've been doing some surveying for Dale? So we were out there…"

Autumn takes over the story the moment Wyn enters it, brushing her fingers along Sasha's wrist as if they're passing a baton back and forth. Like she can't bear not to talk about Wyn, like it'll conjure his little spirit. "They're too young and they don't seem to have anyone. He didn't even seem to know what a parent was. Do you know anything more? Have you seen anything lately?"

"Lately?" At some point during their tale, Lou's eyes have strayed to the little town on the table. He looks very weary as his trains circle like sharks. "Less and less nowadays. Used to. The town watched out for them, found homes for them when they were real little. But a lot of those folks who knew how to help died or had to move away. Russ and I did all we could, but his health… I hardly ever see any kids around here now." He goes to a dusty, unpainted shelf. On it is what looks like a hodgepodge nest fashioned out of sticks, decorated with tufts of feather and dirty string. "Cajun bird trap," he says, passing it to Sasha. Something in her doesn't want to reach out and take it, but she does anyway.

"What's it for?" Sasha asks, turning it over. Lou only shrugs. "I don't know. But I used to find a lot of things like that out there in those woods." He hunches down to clasp another. This one seems to be elaborated with hunks of hair.

"We saw one of these," Autumn says. They could have been beautiful if they weren't so like insects, skeletal and crouching. Built with intentions and expectations beyond their understanding. "On the railroad tracks. But it was more—*gruesome* than this." There was an echo of Wyn's mask in the craftsmanship too: the thread that bound teeth to the bark, the strangeness of the creative vision it must have taken to bring it to life.

Lou lays the bird trap down again, draining his glass. He levels a gaze on Sasha. "Helping those kids has been one of my life's callings. For so long, no one's cared a twig about it, just looked the other way." He lays a weathered hand over Autumn's. "You do one thing for me next time, huh?

"What is it?" Sasha has finished her own drink too, faster than she meant to. Something about holding those *things*—they left her gut knotted. Her hands tingle. They feel dirty, caked with dust or something more. And the sense of having left something undone, of an alarm screaming at the back of her mind, makes her ears ring.

But Lou's looking only at Autumn when he answers. "Don't walk on those railroad tracks, honey." His own trains rocket along in their dollhouse world, swerving through miniature landscapes where no one lives. Autumn takes a sharp breath and nods.

Sasha shivers. "Why not?" She asks the question, but the answer isn't one she needs. She knows it in her bones.

Lou's eyes are on the trains, mouth a grim line. "There's dangerous folk out there."

CHAPTER FIFTEEN

I
T'S TIME TO THINK, WHICH WOULD NORMALLY CALL FOR focaccia. But there's a new bite to the air, like fall is really settling around them now. Leaves hang in bright reds and golds, the shades of ripening apples, and Autumn can almost feel the trees taking the last long gasp before frost, their veins tightening, sap dribbling down into the safe vaults of the roots. She feels in herself the same need: the need to shelter and brace for a long, heavy, oncoming snow. She needs to ponder with baking, but this time, it just has to be pumpkin bread.

Lou's words whisper in her mind as her electric mixer whirs. *I hardly ever see any kids around here now.* The image of those strange offerings he has collected over the years. Wyn and Neel's faces.

Autumn closes her eyes, bracing her palms on the familiar steel counter. She tries, briefly, to conjure Dad, a whiff of his Irish spring soap, the steadiness of his hands. Or Mom's easy-like-a-Sunday-morning voice, her noodling on the banjo she loved but couldn't really play. Even as an adult, she can't totally shake the childish notion that Dad and Mom would know what to do, any more than she can shake the burn of resentment for the fact that they aren't here now, when she needs them. Maybe they would be able to explain why this place where Autumn grew up feels so different. So changed.

Maybe she'll go see Lou again, without Sasha this time. There are things she must say, and saying them in front of Sasha still feels impossible. But maybe she can try with Lou. They can talk over a slice of this pumpkin bread. It'll taste great with his bourbon. There is so much more she needs to say, and more she needs to ask.

By now, the children's basket of food—assuming they even went back for it—will be wearing thin. They'll be all out of sausage rolls. Autumn considers sneaking back to the tracks to try to find them again, but there's the distinct possibility that if she goes, she'll find the wrong end of Neel's shotgun instead. *We have to make a plan,* Sasha had said. *We have to go prepared.* It sounded very adult, very mature for Sasha, who usually liked to play fast and loose with life. Or at least pretend she did.

So far, their ideas are pretty scant.

Autumn leaves the front door open, for the breeze. It's quiet today, unlike when Sasha manned the front and the town filled her doors. Down the street, empty stalls wait to be filled with pecans and goods. A banner swings from between two street-lights. But the air feels dead, no cars at the meters, not a single neighbor walking their dog.

Then comes a sudden gust of wind from the west, as if someone has switched on a box fan. The door flies in and knocks against one of her display shelves. There's a sound of scuttling, a *thunk* as one of her bags of premade brownie mix hits the floor. Noisy rummaging. Autumn is frozen, listening to this bizarre, invisible burglary. There is a moment of quiet, as if the intruder has gone.

And then:

"Otto?" calls a tremulous, familiar voice, the best approximation of her name he can manage. He's only heard it once.

Her heart on a kite string, Autumn doesn't bother dusting the flour off her hands, leaves her batter half-whipped and pushes through the double doors. "Wyn?"

"Here." He pokes his head around the counter, hair and face dusty from the road. Her basket is by the door, much the worse for wear. "Neel—Neel's actually nice," he explains, peeping at her. It looks like his knees are scraped, maybe from tripping somewhere along the long walk into town.

Autumn kneels down. If he were another child, one with a kinder life, she'd wrap him up in her arms, she'd wipe dirt off his face and clean his cuts. Only even a gentle touch could scare him. He hasn't had a gentle life.

"I believe you," she says. "I think he was scared. I'm glad to see you again."

The one amber eye she can see watches her for a moment. Then Wyn sniffs several times. Curiously, he wanders from his hiding place past her toward the kitchen. He still has no shoes on, which means he walked miles on bare feet to reach her. He even returned her basket.

Autumn picks up the basket and follows him. "Hungry?" she asks, and he's nodding furiously before the word is even out of her mouth. So she sets him up at the table and makes him enough oatmeal for a family of four. She puts in cardamom and cinnamon, maple syrup, chopped apples, and, of course, toasted pecans from Lil. Wyn looks curious when she sets the large bowl in front of him but doesn't wait to ask questions about what it is. He gobbles it down, probably burning his tongue on the first piping hot spoonful.

That's when she realizes how much he actually trusts her.

"I'm making pumpkin bread today. I bet you'll like it," she tells him, when he's chasing individual oats at the bottom of his bowl. This feels like holding a baby bird, trying not to startle it into flight. "You want to help?"

But he is already clambering up onto a chair to peer down into the various bowls. "I will…help," he decides, looking very serious.

"Good. It's been a while since I had a helper." She brings over a little whisk for him. Up on the chair, she can see the grit and blood caked on his knees more clearly. "You whisk what's in the bowl together, and I'll—can I fix up your knees for you?"

Wyn glances down at his legs, then shrugs. He's much more interested in his new project. He prods the eggs and sugars in the bowl a few times with the whisk. Autumn digs out the first aid kit she keeps near the cash register, then dabs Neosporin gently on the scrapes. Wyn flinches at little, but doesn't complain. "Like this?" he asks, gouging at the eggs.

Autumn sticks a colorful Band-Aid on each knee, then straightens up. "Good," she says. "Now just give it a big stir! Stir, stir, stir! You can go fast." She holds the bowl for him as Wyn whisks enthusiastically. "We add that to this bowl of spices and flour, and then it'll be batter."

Wyn is a quick learner. "I sneaked away," he tells her, as he scrapes determinedly for every last drop of mixture. "Neel was hunting."

"Now we mix all that together." She gives him a wooden spoon. "I'd love to meet Neel again when he's not feeling so scared. You said he's nice to you?" God, it was hard to know how to ask a child things in the right way. She's a baker, not Mister Rogers.

Wyn nods hard, his mane of overgrown hair tickling the shoulders of his dirty T-shirt. "He takes care of... We look after each other."

"My friend Sasha, who you met, is like that for me." If only Sasha were here, actually. It's easier to improv with a scene partner. She leans on the counter, chin propped in her hands. "You know what, Wyn?"

He is busy with combining the gloppy orange batter. "Huh?"

"Plain pumpkin bread isn't enough now that you're here." She grins at him. "I think this calls for chocolate chips."

"Chocolate?" He matches her grin with a gappy one of his own.

Autumn scavenges through the pantry for her chocolate supply and goes for the massive dark chocolate chunks. "You told me you and Neel had other friends?" she asks over her shoulder.

"Uhh—yeah." Wyn mashes gamely at his batter, which is really coming together. "Trees."

She sets the enormous bag of chocolate on the counter, and he cackles at the sight. "Other kids, though. Didn't you have other friends that...went away?" she asks, frowning. There's no point in asking about any adults; it's obvious there are no parents in the picture.

"There were," Wyn says, reaching for the bag of chocolate, so far he nearly topples from his perch. She hands him a chocolate chunk.

"Ready?" she asks, picking up the chocolate to dump into his batter. He lifts the spoon out to make space, watching eagerly as more than enough chunks of chocolate pile onto the batter. Then he sets to work mixing again. This kid is a natural.

He pokes the chocolate in until she quickly shows him how to fold it. "Now, though, um—now it's just me and Neel and trees and nobody else," he finishes.

She stares at her hands as she says, "What about the hungry man?"

Wyn's spoon clatters to the ground, and when her head whips up, his face is the gray-white of unfired clay.

"Wyn?" Autumn's stomach knots at the look on his face. She shouldn't have said it. She wants to reel the words back in, replace them with warm spices and melting chocolate. But it won't be long before Wyn wants to return to the woods, and she has to know. "Is he what happened to your other friends?"

But he's petrified, and when he does finally try to answer, it's only in the chittering language of the forest.

"It's okay, it's going to be okay." Slowly, she gets him a new spoon. "Let's put our batter in the baking tin. Ready?"

By the time their pumpkin bread is in the oven and Autumn has sat Wyn down with a cup of warm milk, he seems a little more himself. She sits down with him, the scent of cozy fall slowly filling the room. "Wyn," she says gently. "Do you think Neel might ever want to come here too? Maybe..." she hesitates. "Come to stay in town?"

"Umm..." Wyn's face scrunches up. He can only shrug, swinging his feet under the table.

"I really think you should stay here with me until we figure some things out," she tries again. The thought of sending him back there, with traps under the kudzu, missing children, and some man is intolerable.

Immediately something in Wyn's face hardens, his eyes sharp. "I gotta—I gotta go back," he insists. "Neel."

"Right," Autumn agrees hurriedly. What the hell can she do? She gets up, maybe a little too fast. "Let me go call my friend, and she can drive us out there in her truck, okay? Then you won't have to walk so far again." He's watching her closely as she goes into the front to make the call.

For once in her life, Sasha actually answers the phone. "Hello?"

"You're home?" Autumn gasps, relief filling her.

"Just got back." Sasha is smiling; she can hear it in her voice. "What's going on, Pip?"

Autumn drops her voice. "*Wyn* is here. He came to the bakery."

"Holy shit. Shit, shit, shit," Sasha whispers too, pointlessly. "What do we do? I'll come over. Should I—call somebody? Lou? Town hall? Social services?"

"Just get over here as soon as you can," Autumn hisses, craning her neck to see into the kitchen. "I can't let him go back out there. There's something *bad* in those woods. We have to—" She's cut off as the oven timer starts to sing. "Oh, hell. Just come." She hangs up on Sasha and scurries back to Wyn, back to the steaming pumpkin chocolate chip bread they've made together—

But the kitchen is empty, the back door letting in a chill wind. Her oven sounds the alarm, and the little boy is nowhere to be seen.

ల

Sasha makes it over to the bakery in time for a steaming slice of pumpkin bread, the chocolate chips oozing. Autumn is very quiet, inconsolable, but distant; the grief isn't even on the surface, but somewhere deep within, inaccessible and hidden from view. Ever since Neel pointed that shotgun, since they went to see Lou, a door has been creaking closed within her, and Wyn's return to the wild clicked the latch. Though Autumn asked her to come, by the time Sasha arrives, she is definitely an intruder.

"I should have known he would run," Autumn says. "I swear, ever since I came back..." But she cuts herself off, casts Sasha an uncertain look, and changes the subject. "May as well have some cake."

It's as she is driving home from the bakery, after making Autumn a cup of tea and giving her a long, not-quite-returned hug, that something connects in her brain.

Autumn is hiding something from her.

If she's being truly honest with herself—since no one else is being honest with Sasha—Autumn has been hiding something since she came back.

So maybe Sasha can't use Autumn as the emotional security blanket protecting her from the ongoing conflict with Lil anymore. Sasha is on her own, a small boat in the dark river only she can cross.

Which is how Sasha ends up awake and in the kitchen at five in the morning, brewing the damn coffee and heating her favorite eye on the stovetop. She'd considered slipping on her work boots and heading out into the orchard to do Lil's chores for her, but somehow she senses that that would be an invasion rather than a help. Autumn isn't the only one who keeps secrets from her. So she's doing what she can. She chops this and that from the refrigerator, as if in a dream, a low blue light beginning to glow on the horizon's edge out the window. Her skillet is just heating as she hears Lil's perplexed step on the stairs.

Lil appears in short order, denim jeans and an olive-green sweater hanging off her haphazardly like she's heard the commotion and dashed into clothes, like she thinks it's some unexpected company downstairs.

For a moment, her eyes consume the entire scene: the diced peppers and onions on the cutting board, the egg carton. Sasha and her heating pan. Lil's gaze can shred you down to bits. So Sasha one-handedly cracks eggs instead of looking at her.

"What's this?" Lil asks, cautiously hovering in the door.

"*Tortilla de huevos,*" Sasha says, nodding at the steaming coffee-pot. That should pull Lil into the kitchen. Her own hands are full as she combines things in the big mixing bowl, beating plenty of air in. She gets the onions and peppers sizzling in the skillet, measuring out flour for her mixture and whipping it frothy.

Lil's face softens, butter in sunlight. "Wow. That takes me back."

It's one of Sasha's go-to bachelor recipes. She hasn't made it since New York, but it always reminds her of their harebrained twinscape down to Central Florida. Twenty hours on the bus playing gin rummy, then a midnight wander through the unfamiliar city, squinting from streetlamp to streetlamp at the waterlogged address in the letter from the bureau, which Sasha had stumbled upon looking for stamps at the beginning of that summer. They were only seventeen, but they'd scribbled a note for Mom, *We'll be back in a week or two,* and just gone. One of the few times Lil had gone that far from the orchard. During those long hours on the bus, Lil, offhand, had said it barely counted as leaving home if she was with Sasha.

They headed down through swampy Florida and found the address in the letter. The man they met was their father, and he had been surprised to see them, when he opened the door to two girls who could only be sisters, who could only have come from their mother. But he wasn't their dad in the way Autumn had a dad, who could pick her up from school and teach her how to ride a bike, and who Autumn ran to with all her problems, her joys, her tears. That was a kind of paternal relationship Sasha and Lil never quite grasped.

What they had instead was Luis, the cheerful, laid-back man who Mom had loved once, in a faraway dream. He had never seen the town or walked in the orchard. He was Puerto Rican, and Mom had met him on the island, when she went out looking for herself far from home. From the way his eyes filled with tears as he gaped at them in his doorway, it was clear that he'd really loved her, probably fought to keep her, maybe wanted much more than the month or so she'd been able to offer. Because the orchard had pulled her back.

Luis now owned a successful pharmacy in Kissimmee, and they spent more than a week with him in his neat stucco house. That was where Sasha had learned about *tortilla de huevos*.

Lil dips her fingers into the skillet, snags a pepper, pops it in her mouth. "You got the hang of this better than I ever did."

Sasha soaked up that time with Luis like a parched plant. She saw so much of herself in him, in his easygoing, puckish energy, his determined lightheartedness, his creativity. Maybe because she felt differently about the orchard—and yeah, about Mom—than Lil did, she'd craved those lessons from Luis just a little bit more desperately. Now, she sautés with one hand and mixes her eggs with the other. "I thought it might be a nice start to your day," is all she says.

"It is," she says, eventually. "Thank you." And she moves around the counter, taking a seat at the table. "Did you ever reach out to him again? I don't think I have, since Mom."

The skillet sizzles pleasurably when Sasha adds the eggs. "Every once in a while." In her third year at SCAD, she'd sent him a card when he married the pretty, fun girlfriend they'd met on the trip down there. When her photographs were up at the gallery in Queens, she'd sent him an invitation to the opening on a whim, and he'd called her to thank her and let her know that his wife was going to have a baby soon, so he wouldn't be able to make the trip. That telephone call had meant more to her than she'd wanted to admit, especially with Mom gone. And, more than that, the soothing knowledge that she had blood out there in the world beyond this town.

Sasha watches her tortilla. "I was harsh the other day. I'm— sorry." She was sorry, it was true, but more for the simple fact that they couldn't see eye to eye on so many things. She wasn't strictly sorry about the true things she'd said. But the clash of their truths, each deeply held, was terrible.

After a moment, she hears Lil moving. Her feet padding across the floor. Then Sasha feels her nudge up against the counter. Lil watches the tortilla with her. "Me too. I never want to fight. Not with you."

"Well, we *are* twins," Sasha points out, grinning at her. "Weekly fights are probably appropriate. But—no more dead air." As the flourish on the end of this sentence, Sasha hefts the skillet and gives it a mighty toss. It does not really make sense to flip *tortilla de huevos*, more a substantial egg pie than your average diner-style omelet, but she's always been one for flair.

Lil applauds her successful pan flip. "Hey, I never forgot. End of the day, you're stuck with me. It's you. And me." She moves to help clear up what hasn't been used, filling the eggy bowl where the raw stuff had been with soap and water. "I saw Autumn's place is back open. Is she here to stay?"

Sasha serves up slabs of the steaming tortilla, carrying them to their kitchen table. She hesitates. "Autumn is...something is up with her." As briefly as she can, in their shorthand, she catches Lil up on the children from the abandoned orchards and their talk with Lou. The toothy trap out in the woods. The train tracks. She watches Lil's eyes fill alternatively with horror and indignation as her gears work. Lil, the fixer, grappling for a solution and failing to find one.

"I've never known there to be secrets between you and Autumn," Lil says finally. "I mean, it's Autumn. And you."

"She's holding something back." It's so early in the morning, Sasha's stomach isn't sure what to think of her breakfast now that she's made it. She spears a bite. "I think maybe she's always held things back from me." Something Lil and Autumn probably have in common, but for the sake of making up, Sasha keeps this thought to herself.

"I guess she never really said why she came back." When her plate is empty, Lil doesn't brush Sasha off, doesn't dash for the work. Instead, she sets her fork down and leans back, resting her head against the wall, nursing a second cup of coffee. The earth feels steadier under their feet when they are aligned. When her eyes meet Sasha's, they're open and readable. "She'll tell you eventually. Maybe she needs some time, but she always comes back to you."

Sasha shrugs, lip twisting. She grabs their plates and lays them in the sink. The sun is up now, shy and rosy over the tree line. In the mudroom off the kitchen, their work boots sit side by side, Lil's a good deal more worn.

Sasha steps into hers. "Let me help you out with the harvest this morning," she offers, trying to make light. "I feel like we have a lot to catch up on."

At the sight of Sasha in her work boots, Lil's whole face glows. She stands hurriedly, for once, the last to be ready to face the day. "Oh, do we ever."

CHAPTER SIXTEEN

It's just like old times. Lil and Sasha haul empty gallon baskets out to set at intervals along the trees and get to work picking through the husks on the ground. There's no need to bargain with the finicky old shaker today, or even break out the cane poles to rattle the treetops. Pecans fall plentiful enough to the ground. While the daily rigors are old hand to Lil, Sasha folds right back into the rhythm of it. They learned the land young, climbing trees, napping in their shaded branches, the chalky smell of pecan blossoms all around. The orchard's care isn't the kind of thing you forget, not after doing it for eighteen years straight. Together, they clear a section of the Elliots—good small pecans that are perfect for baking.

"Maybe a nice gift for Autumn," Lil suggests. "At this size, they're perfect for pies. Barely even need to be chopped."

"Good idea," Sasha says breezily, shading her eyes. "Hopefully all the baking for the festival will be a nice change of pace for her."

The worst of the work is simply bending, over and over again. It used to be easier as children, Lil thinks. Closer to the ground.

Bones like rubber. Easy to bend and bounce back, all day long. Mom used to send them out in matching coats and boots, and would tell them to stay on one tree at a time and not to leave her sight. Lil and Sasha rarely listened; the world was too big and exciting, so they were prone to wandering off, playing witches in the barn, or cats in the brambles, or lost girls among the trees, gathering pecans for their dinner. Once, they found a baby frog, which Mom grudgingly let them raise in a bowl—for one afternoon before he leaped to freedom from a low window.

Now, Sasha whistles little snatches of tunes, takes surreptitious breaks to rub her back, and fills her baskets without complaint. Lil moves fast, methodical, with one eye on the fence line as she works. Theon doesn't show his face, but she still feels his stain.

The sun is nearing afternoon when they pack it in for the day for hurried sandwiches, showers, and fresh clothes for the ride into town. Sasha's braid is still wet when they pile in the truck.

Lil lets Sasha twiddle the radio dial, looking for music, but there's still nothing but static. Sasha swears she hears Led Zeppelin in the noise, and Lil's in a good enough mood to let her.

The energy as they reach the center is palpable. Speakers are being tested, crackling in random jolts. It looks like the entire fire department and most of the church folks are down here today, making this somewhat slapdash festival happen.

Lil parks at the bakery, where there's a light on. Autumn is surely in the back. And Jason sits at one of the little red tables, head tipped back into the weakening fall light, until the truck pulls in and he snaps back up, eyes finding her through the windshield. She breathes in, a giddy rush of cool air, and turns off the car. In unpracticed unison, she and Sasha hop out, crunching down onto the gravel parking lot.

Jason has a mountain of supplies arrayed around him, plus the clipboard. It seems that the picnic table is his current HQ. "Can't wait for you to see," he says. His smile is a little long-suffering, maybe from coordinating volunteers all morning. "Things are really coming together out here."

"Hey, Jason," Sasha offers, though she's glancing back at the bakery. In her hand is a plastic grocery bag full of pecans they'd gathered that morning. "Lil said y'all were hoping to have a party out on the river. Great idea. I'll get the boat polished up." The riverboat isn't terribly big, and the party tends to feel a little cramped, but it's always served them faithfully before. A closing party on the river is a Pecan Festival tradition.

"Really? That's going to be fantastic." He grins at her, eyes crinkling. "As if you needed another job though." She rolls her eyes in agreement, and they both laugh.

The bell over the door chimes and Autumn leans out. She has a bit of a crowd inside, people milling over full display cases, and suddenly everything smells like vanilla and mulling spices. "Am I dreaming, or are there two Clearwaters on my doorstep?" she asks. "I should have made something special for the occasion."

If Lil hadn't known from Sasha that there were bandages under her jeans, hadn't known about the blood and the wild children, Autumn's meringue-light smile would have utterly snowed her. "Autumn, thank you so much for taking on a stand on short notice," she says.

"'Short notice' is kind of this festival's middle name." Jason laughs. "Whatever you're working on right now smells amazing. Makes me hungry."

Autumn startles, and for a moment it's as if she doesn't even recognize him, she's so strained and suddenly pale. It must be the toll the past days have taken on her. But Lil can't blame her. Too many nights alone in the Clearwater house, too many unanswered calls as folks move away have taught Lil the horror that ensues with certain change, when a familiar, beloved place twists itself into a stranger. But Autumn's spell doesn't last; her answering smile comes a second later.

"Thanks." She rummages in her pocket and pulls out a folded and floured sheet of paper, covered in her messy scrawl: *hummingbird Bundt cakes, caramel buns, nutty bunnies, praline brownies, spicy nut mix, cookies, hand pies, maple bars.* "This is my final lineup for the festival, but if there's something you'd suggest I don't already have listed, just let me know."

"You're my hero." Lil hands the paper to Jason, who will invariably file it away, alphabetically, numerically, and possibly color-coded. The man likes his organization. "It wouldn't be the same without you."

"That's me. Local hero." Autumn's tone is a little flat. She's already turning to Sasha, flower to the sun. "Are you going or staying?"

"I'm with you, kid." Sasha gives Lil and Jason a little salute, then bounds into the bakery.

Lil and Jason walk toward the square, where most of the action is. "Cesar has been on my last nerve all day," he admits. "But the guys built the stage after you left last night in record time. I couldn't believe it." Jason takes a deep breath, stopping them just before they reach the middle of the chaos. As soon as they enter the fray, there will be two dozen people simultaneously asking them questions. Facing her, he leans against one of the majestic old trees. "How are you? I feel like I haven't seen Sasha in forever."

"Good. Really good, actually. As of this morning." Lil tucks her arms around herself. "If you haven't seen Sasha, it's because she hasn't really wanted to be around me." The respite is nice. Lil doesn't always think to give herself a respite. "Fighting with her felt so wrong. And I can usually fight with anyone. I can fight with you."

He smiles, his thoughts probably going with hers to their most memorable, heated play-fights. Flirt-fights. Even the real, bitter, no-way-back fights. "You and I always kind of liked fighting," he remembers, winking at her. Those Jason Finch winks will be the death of her.

"But Sasha?" Lil shakes her head. "It's not like that. It's like fighting myself. Knocks me in my most vulnerable places."

"Well there's no one quite as stubborn as you are—except maybe her." He catches the elbow she aims at his gut, snickering. Then he looks more earnest. "It's a low-stakes game though. You could say anything to her, and Sasha would still lock herself in a burning house for you and throw the key down the sink."

She leans on the tree, shoulder to shoulder with Jason. "Yeah, well. You think I wouldn't do the same for her?"

He gives her a very serious glance. "Oh I know you would."

They survey their work together. "Hey." He turns his head to look at her, cheek against rough bark. This brings his eyes very close to her. They're warm as they run over her face. "Come over for dinner after we get everything set up tomorrow night." His mouth twists, rueful. "It'll probably be late, but you know we'll be starving."

She raises an eyebrow, but she's smiling too big to hide it. It's dangerous. Stupid. But it's nice to know the person who always saw the heart of her—even when he seemed to hate her—hasn't lost his knack for it. "Not if you're cooking. I remember what you did to those scrambled eggs."

He winces. "How did they get so...gray?"

"But I'll bring something over," she compromises. "That'd be nice."

He chuckles. "I'm actually reasonably okay at using the grill these days. I'll make rib eye."

"Deal." She pushes off the tree. "Shall we? Lots to do before you poison me tomorrow."

Looking immensely satisfied with himself, Jason follows her into the festive chaos.

☙

Much like the bustling town outside, the bakery is full of activity. Sasha takes in the aromas in a daze. Clearly, Autumn has thrown herself into festival preparations. From the looks of that list she gave Jason, it'll take every hour she has left to get it all done in time. As for Sasha—she checks her digital watch, but it only blinks blank zeros up at her. Again. She gives it a couple of slaps, sighing. If the crowds Lil is optimistically expecting really do show up, Sasha will be running the ferry six times a day at least, not to mention trying to get the riverboat ready for the grand-finale fancy dress thing they have in mind.

For now, she loiters in Autumn's kitchen, lulled by spices and the whir of the convection oven. Autumn has given her the very simple job of stirring some sweet-smelling goo with a wooden spoon, and she swirls it absent-mindedly. The back door is open several hopeful inches, just in case a small and mysterious guest happens to reappear.

"Doesn't it feel a little strange to be getting ready for this cutesy town froufrou when there's so much shit going on? The fires?" Sasha wonders aloud. The instant it's out of her mouth, she wishes she hadn't said it, hadn't even thought it. It was this kind of seasonal tradition that kept the sinews of the town from atrophying completely. *Don't prod it,* something in her urges. But she has to find out what Autumn is keeping to herself. Or at least invite her to share.

Autumn puts down her scoring knife. She has been working miracles as Sasha stirs her goo. Beyond Sasha, cities are being built in brown sugar and egg, and row after row of sweet-smelling confections are leaving the oven. Even now, she's devoted to carving leaves out of raw pie crust, to top each and every miniature pecan pie.

"You're right," she says and brushes her hand against her hair, tightly bound under a net. "It's strange to be celebrating…under the circumstances." Sasha could see how hard Autumn was trying when they'd lingered outside, talking to Lil and Jason. She's holding herself together with candy floss. Her smile is full of cracks. Sasha knows without her saying that she's thinking about Wyn and Neel.

Sasha scoops super sticky marshmallow fluff into her mixture as the plot thickens here on the stovetop. "You think the Pecan Festival might bring the kids to town?"

"It's more likely to scare them," Autumn says, and her knife presses too hard. An easy fix, but she curses, balls up the misshapen leaf, and tosses it into the trash. "But Wyn says he's been to the library, right? So he must not be too afraid. I don't know. I don't know." She stares down at her baking sheet.

"Pip…" Sasha turns her back to the stove to face Autumn. She keeps her voice very gentle. "I—you know you can always talk to me, right? If there's something bothering you, I mean."

Autumn picks at the baking sheet. She spreads flour here and there in the corners, where it tends to clump. The back of her head tells Sasha nothing. Until the tense set of her back falls and she lets out a shaky breath. Autumn slumps across the room and pushes her face into Sasha's shoulder. "I'm that obvious?" comes her voice, muffled against her shirt.

Sasha loops an arm around her automatically, rocking them a bit. With her other hand, she reaches back to take whatever she was stirring off the heat. "You've just been a little quiet since we got run out of the woods."

"Here I thought I was being coolly aloof." Autumn tugs the netting off her hair and her messy bun droops down over one ear. "I'm bothered," she says eventually and extricates herself just enough that she can talk, so that her eyes aren't just a blue squint under Sasha's chin. They are as full and expressive as always. "And I want to tell you. I want to tell you everything." Autumn chews her lip. "I will," she adds. "I just need a little time to finish processing. Soon—I'll tell you everything."

"Hey. That's okay." They are very close together, near enough that Sasha can breathe the faint fragrance of Autumn's skin. Sasha shows her the blank hours and minutes on her digital watch. "All we have is time." And because she is on an emotional roll that day, coming up double sixes with every brave conversation she starts, she says, "You know, I think there's going to be a party out on the river at the end of the festival."

Autumn peeks around her at the goo, left cooling midsimmer on the stove, and they disentangle so that Autumn can reach the thermometer that waits on the counter and stick it in the pot. She hums her approval, exchanges the thermometer for a spatula and gives the sludge a few encouraging stirs. "I heard about that. It's a lot of responsibility for you and your riverboat. Will you need a crew, Captain Clearwater?"

"Sure will." Though a crew was not what she'd been about to ask for. Once again, they'd dodged each other, the latest feint in a long dance. Sasha holds the pot for her as Autumn steers the contents into molds.

Autumn salutes with her sticky spatula. "Then count me in as skipper."

Nodding, Sasha shoves down her disappointment. All they have is time.

CHAPTER SEVENTEEN

THE MORNING SKY IS SO LOW AND DARK, THE AIR SO close, that the day feels over as soon as Sasha enters it. The night before, after she and Lil left the bakery for home, she tossed in strange, sweat-soaked dreams. Mom came to her, through the house, spectral feet treading the familiar creaking path up to her room. Her legs were grimy, trailing reeds and waterlogged muck. She knelt down beside the bed, and they stared at one another. Sasha tracked the golden flakes in her eyes, like twenty-four-karat debris. Mom opened her mouth, and dark water dribbled over her lips. In a death-roughened voice, she said something to Sasha that she never had in life. *Meet me in the orchard.*

On the nightstand, Sasha's digital watch still shows a jackpot of zeros. Maybe she slept in, or maybe she didn't, but Lil is not in the house when she goes downstairs. So whether it's to go find her, or to simply shake the dread of the dream, Sasha throws on her khaki chore coat and goes out the back door.

"Lil?" Her voice seems to snatch on the branches. There's no answer. Sasha strolls. The atmosphere feels sharp and too warm.

It almost sizzles in her nostrils, like the clouds are full of lightning. Absently, Sasha checks the nets, stuffing pecans in the giant pockets of the coat. Some magnetism tugs her deeper. There's a warning in her gut. She was never welcome here, she chides herself. This isn't her place. Not this far in, not without Mom or Lil.

But the dream.

Gradually, Sasha realizes she is walking toward something, through pecan trees that grow larger and more gnarled with each step. It's like she's struck an artery and is now being sent into the heart of it, toward Mom, or the mother of the trees. She hasn't come here before. She knows, intuitively, that the barn is away to her left, and the wood and the railroad tracks somewhere far beyond that. There is no grass in this part of the orchard, the shade too great. Here, there is only dust and dry brush under her sneakers. It feels almost as if someone were calling her, but the sound is just barely beyond perception. *Lil?*

"Coming," she murmurs to the orchard and turns—

There, tucked into a grove is a perfectly round pool of water. Above it droops the largest and oldest pecan tree she has ever seen. Framed by tree roots, the pond is like jet. Not a single leaf floats on its surface. Cold emanates from the water. And everywhere, scattered around and in it are nuggets of gleaming gold. Sasha leaps back, her first thought that some heirloom from their grandmother's jewelry box has ended up broken and scattered out here. But as soon as she bends to collect the pieces, she's frozen. It's not rings, or links from a necklace. It's—what? Stunned, Sasha sits down on one of the mossy roots to stare into the pond, transfixed. How has she never seen this place before? She hasn't, has she? Her boot has crushed one of the golden things, and at the sensation, she moves it hastily. Beneath her foot is a glittering constellation of broken—pecan. A pecan, made of gold. They shimmer overhead, ripening from tender green to metallic gold in the tree.

Sasha grapples hopelessly with the unreality of the scene. There is something incredibly lovely, velvety, about the water. This pond is a twisted thrill in her chest, a shipwreck right here in the orchard. Heart pounding, she reaches to brush the pool with her fingers, just to make a ripple...

"Sasha." The tremor in Lil's voice breaks through the haze. Her sister's tones are known instinctively to her, learned over a lifetime of a tandem heartbeat. And right now Lil is terrified, calling for Sasha to leap up and run.

It's meant to shock her, the first screech of a siren. But she isn't shocked. It hits her like an alarm clock that's been ringing for a long time, right at the back of her skull. As if Sasha has been listening to her sister say her name in that way, in this place, for forever.

Her script is just as set. Her hand remains poised above the water. "Lil."

"Don't. You shouldn't." Lil's stumbling. So rare, to see Lil, in her independence and fire, stumble. "You shouldn't. Get back. Please?"

"Why?" Sasha stays where she is, frowning at her. "What is this?" The air has turned dreadfully cold, sending a shiver through her.

"Nothing," Lil says too quickly. "Nothing for you to worry about. Mom—"

She cuts herself off, but Sasha understands her. *Mom.* This is one of their secrets. Mom and Lil, always talking quietly together in corners of the orchard. Mom and Lil, pulling each other aside, changing the subject when Sasha's around. This is a secret. From her.

The rage is so bitter she tastes it in her mouth. "I should be *surprised*," Sasha snarls at her. "I should be completely thrown by the fact that you would have hidden whatever this place is from me *our entire lives*." She scoops up the shattered nut and tosses it at Lil like golden confetti. Dirt shoves itself under her nails. "And Mom too. But of course I'm not. Of course you did this." Hot tears trace her cheeks. "And then you still resented me for leaving! Who *wouldn't* leave?"

"So simple when you say it." Lil falls to her knees beside the pond at Sasha's elbow. Close enough to yank her away. She's restraining herself again. As if Sasha doesn't see perfectly well how Lil reins herself in around her. All the time, holding back. All the time, hiding. "What else was I supposed to do? You shouldn't *be* here."

"I should *be* in New York." Sasha wishes Lil hadn't sat down so near her. It's suffocating here, between tree and water. "Why not?" she asks at last. "In what logical universe is there a place that is okay for you and for Mom and not okay for me?"

Lil is staring at the water, not Sasha. "Of all the parts of the orchard, Sasha, I swear...this is the one part I'm supposed to protect you from." She wipes at her eyes. "There's only one, okay? Two of us, sure, but there's only one person who takes this task. I can't—I can't—" She shudders and a ripple moves in the water along with her. "I can't share it with you and be sure you're safe. No one is safe. Not even me."

"Safe from *what*?" Sasha snaps. "What is this place?" She picks up the nearest golden husk. "What are these?"

Lil looks at it. Her hand twitches toward it, a silent plea. "Put it down. Go back to the house. There's a million trees—just leave this one."

"Tell me now," Sasha grits out, each word a hard huff of breath, "Or I'm going back to the house, walking out the front door, and never coming back." It feels terrifyingly true.

"Maybe it's better." Lil's face is flushed and wild. "All I wanted for so long was for you to come home, but this isn't supposed to be part of it. The one thing, Sasha, this is the one thing I can't share when there's so much else I need you for."

Maybe it's better.

Maybe it's *better?*

Well, hell, maybe it is, then.

Numb, Sasha stands. She'll be the last passenger on the last ferry. Maybe Autumn will go with her. Otherwise, she leaves with nothing at all.

Lil watches her stand, and some dull horror visibly steals through her body. She looks away, but not before Sasha catches tears slipping down her face.

"Wait. Please." Kneeling beside the pond, Lil trembles. And Sasha feels the most stubborn part of Lil, the unshakable bedrock on which her sister is built, crack. "Of course I resented you leaving," Lil breathes out in a hush and the water shivers. "Do you really think I never wanted to go? Do you think I never wished I could? When you left. And Jason left me. I was *alone, I was so alone*—" She clamps a hand over her mouth. The whites of her eyes shine like a threatened deer.

"You made your own loneliness," Sasha bites out, the last spark of her fury in it. But at her sister's sob, she droops back down beside her, into the silty dirt at the pond's edge.

Lil turns to her, tears still shivering on her eyelashes. "Sasha, I want—" She cuts off. "Want is...not *simple*. I want you to be safe. I want you to stay. I want to tell you, but I want to honor Mom." She scrubs at her eyes. She looks young again, exhausted from a day of fighting her way through school, fighting with Mom—because they used to fight back then, didn't they? Even when Lil was determined to take over the orchard and follow in Mom's footsteps, it was never smooth between them. Sasha was the peacemaker, left out of their flaring rages. And their secrets.

She should have to search harder for her next words, but they're there, waiting for her. "Mom wasn't fair to you, Lil," she murmurs. "Maybe you don't have to do this job the way Mom did. You can... Maybe we can let her go."

Like she let us go.

They aren't words to say aloud, but they are something Sasha knows, a deep gut-truth. The pecan from the tree is still in her fist, and she opens it to look. When Lil called those years ago, to let her know that Mom was gone, that she died in the orchard, it'd been a solace to know she passed close to what she most loved. But now...

No one is safe.

"Mom ate one," Sasha says distantly. "This place killed her."

"Yes," Lil admits. "This is where she died." She takes a steadying breath, touches the ground to find herself. "And I don't know why. She always told me not to eat a pecan that grew from this tree. So finding her here was"—her face blanches—"awful."

Sasha can't speak. For Lil to have found her here, alone—it is beyond speaking.

"The pond is something eternal. Before language, before creatures," Lil says, fixing her eyes on the water, like she can only go so long without finding it. "The pond feeds the tree its waters, and the tree feeds the pond its pecans. They're one. A replenishing cycle."

It feels like a story Sasha heard long ago. Maybe she heard Mom tell Lil one night, when they thought she was asleep. Maybe it was whispered into her dreams.

"But what about the ones that don't make it into the pond?" Sasha asks, gesturing at the scattering on the bank. "What if people eat them? They're poison?"

"Mom said that they're an offering." Lil sounds skeptical, despite herself, despite devoting her life to this strange service. "The tree is an arm the pond reaches out to us. They're a—gift."

Sasha feels its weight in her hand. "Or a trick?"

"I don't know exactly. I think Mom…" Lil trails off. "I have ideas. About what Mom thought. Because of…well. What Mom did." She turns to Sasha, slow and exhausted. "I think I know what she would have wanted when she ate one. But it overwhelmed her. She always said the gift was too great for anyone to bear. Maybe"—she hitches a breath—"maybe she did it on purpose. Maybe at that point, she wanted to be overwhelmed."

They stare into the pond together for a few cold moments.

But Lil's eyes are soft on the side of Sasha's face. She's never seen her fearless sister quite so scared.

"Is it overwhelming you?" Sasha asks.

Lil doesn't say a word; she drops her gaze to the pecan, innocently glinting in the sun. *Yes*, Sasha hears anyway. *A little more every day.* Lil is built of stubborn pride and loyalty. She would try to bear the earth on her shoulders, a new Atlas, if the right person asked her to try.

Silently, Sasha lifts the pecan—at least this pesky thing, she can handle—and tosses it into the depths. Though it was heavy against her flesh, in the pond it is buoyant.

Swirling through the water like a feather, the golden burden slowly disappears into darkness.

CHAPTER EIGHTEEN

L IL AND SASHA LOAD THE BEST NUTS OF THEIR HAR-
vest into the truck, dropping them off with the various
vendors who need them—and Lil's mind lingers in the
chill waters of the pond.

She can't afford to be distracted now. The Pecan Festival can't
go on without pecans. So Lil fills her truck bed with pecans for
selling. Most of the vendors already have what they need. Nan's
for her trail mix, Big Bub's pecan-infused candles, soaps, scents,
and salts. There are raw ones to sell, nut butters to churn fresh.
Lil won't be free to think until it is over.

But Sasha is with her. They have no time to speak, but they
check each other every moment.

"Wow," Sasha says, like she can't help it, when they pull into
a spot near town square where they can see it all laid out before
them. The fruits of all her labor. Lil reaches out across the dash-
board and takes Sasha's hand.

Sasha returns the squeeze. "I have to go," she admits, hesitant.
"There's probably a line a mile long for the ferry." The town owns

two riverboats, and today they need the enormous antique paddle steamer. "I'll see you…" Considering Lil's plans with Jason that night, it is hard to say, so Sasha just shrugs, smiling with unusual gentleness. "When I see you."

"We'll talk," Lil promises and lets her go.

They go their separate ways: Sasha to the river, and Lil to the heart of town. The air smells like cinnamon sugar. It's the most crowded the town square has been for…ages. Booths line the street, bustling with activity, where tomorrow they will display baked goods and butters, liquors, and beaded jewelry.

The volunteers have the administration worked out amongst themselves, all stationed wearing their green ASK ME FOR HELP! shirts. Lil stops at their HQ first, taking note of their numbers. Agnes, the treasurer of the Rotary Club, is checking everyone in, confirming their time slots for tomorrow and the days ahead.

"This is great," Lil says to her, running her finger down a list of names she knows, the people who fill out her life here. "And Su doesn't need—"

"Su says she'll take two volunteers and no more at her pumpkin stand, because they'll mess with her system," Agnes warbles. "Don't you worry, child. We've got this. You go on."

So she does.

Overhead, one of Mom's banners, printed with a large icon of Saint Dorothy, the town's patron, *whomps* in the wind. There's a traffic jam of flags and banners going up in the square and the Ferris wheel and carousel are already being erected in the empty lot behind Elm Street, ready for tomorrow's crowds. There, Lil can finally make herself useful as one of the crew, helping assemble the tall mechanical beings of nuts and bolts. They are built like statues against the afternoon sky, icons of a strange god. But as she works, Lil feels the pond recede a little from her mind, because this sight is exactly what she dreamed of. The soul of the town has been brought out for display.

Things take longer than they should, those last stubborn wrinkles slow to iron out. She has seen Jason, here and there, but doesn't feel the need to approach him. Their time later, to talk, is coming with the nightfall. For now, they slide around each other, shoring up every chink in the project. The day blurs. Soon dusk is falling around them and it's a race against night to have it all ready. Occasionally she'll hear Jason directing people this way and that, many hasty instructions harmonizing with her own.

By the time everything is done, the sun has long ago set, and everyone goes home. Anticipation scrabbles in Lil like a dog eager to get off the leash.

"Everybody get some rest," Jason calls as he makes his way out. "You deserve it! Amazing job, y'all. This is going to be awesome." Just like at Russ's funeral, Jason takes time for people. He pauses to share a private word with anyone who stops him, usually makes them laugh, never hesitates to juggle his notepad out to scribble down what they're saying if they need something done. But his course is true, and Lil is happy to wait. Finally, he jogs up to her, windblown and grinning. "I spied on you all day," he confides. "You're a great organizer. Might need you on the campaign trail one day."

"Oh please. Like I could ever tell people to vote for you with a straight face," Lil lies. It's better than the truth: that a small part of her has always been startlingly ready to be his knight, to carry his banner and his cause. Even when she refused to go with him into the world, she had to wrestle down that loyal corner of her heart. "Didn't you promise me dinner?"

They take Lil's truck the short drive back out to Honeysuckle House. One person is not enough to revive the old place, and when she walks in, the entrance hall feels just a little dank. It hasn't even been long since she's been here. Hasn't it just been days? But the difference is palpable. Or maybe she just wasn't paying attention—not to the house, at least. The flowers in a glass vase from some well-wisher that seemed fresh last time are withered in their place on the entry table, black and curled on themselves. From the den, there is an oppressive musk, probably from those grand velvet curtains. Lil stops in the doorway, caught on the sight of cobwebs spun over the fireplace, pokers scattered all over the heavy rug like someone's been tossing them. At some point, he must've spilled coffee in a rush and not had time to wipe the dark stain up.

He rubs his neck self-consciously. Maybe it's the seasonal turn, but the house feels colder, grimmer than her last visit when they'd gone up to the attic. *Emptier*, a yawning mouth missing teeth.

"Letting the place go a bit," she says lightly. It isn't like him— but then again, her orchard got desperate for a moment there. It's pretty clear that he's been avoiding the work on the house in favor of the festival, and Russ's death seems to be catching up with the place.

"It's better in the kitchen," he says, reaching for her hand. "I got a candle."

With a chai-scented candle from Big Bub lit, they get to work on dinner. He ducks out to the back patio to light the charcoal. His steaks have been marinating all day. He lets Lil handle potatoes and broccoli and opens a bottle of wine. It's dusty, one of the faded labels from his parents, and in the crystal decanter, it's a brick brown.

They've worked together before in this kitchen, cutting vegetables elbow to elbow. Jason was a fastidious sous chef; she left the chopping, prepping, and dishes to him, traditionally. He didn't grill back then, and it's hard not to dwell on who taught him how out there, who accomplished more with his culinary skills than she ever did. Lil isn't jealous—a surprise even to herself—but she is hungry for this knowledge of him. How he's grown. If he's changed. What he's learned, what he thinks. She wants to catalog the new ranges and valleys of him, compare notes with the Jason she remembers.

So she asks, "How'd you learn how to grill, anyway?"

"When you become a lawyer, you mystically acquire all douchebag skills," he deadpans. "Ask about my golf game. I dare you."

Chuckling, she pushes at him with her wrist, knife blade turned away. "Bet you have opinions on wine now. And turn to the finance section first. I bet—oh no, I bet you belong to a country club, don't you?"

"I'm disinclined to make a comment at this time." He passes her with the meat, heading for the grill beyond the screen door.

Soon they're sitting down in the breakfast room (the dining room is all packed up, and the doors are closed). He tops up their wine. "To working our asses off to save the damn town," he laughs, offering his glass across the table. "And to…stealing a little more time with you."

In a haze, she tilts the belly of her glass against his, more of a brush than a clink. "To stealing time," she murmurs. The wine warms her throat even as it leaves her aching. She cuts into the steak and it's a perfect, tender red.

"It's good," she admits, letting the compliment seem dragged out of her, grudging but earned.

"Not as bad as those scrambled eggs?" he teases, spearing broccoli.

They're both absolutely famished after the hectic day, and there isn't enough first-date energy to stop them scarfing down most of their dinners in reverential silence. As they're picking the carrion, he swirls the dregs of his wine, thoughtful. "This is honestly not a night I expected to be in," he confesses. "I've been gone from here for a long time now."

Lil could have sworn she stopped pining for Jason sometime after the first year of heartbreak, but her heart is pumping like it never stopped. "I know," she says. "And I know you can't—you probably can't stay. I understand." She'll try to, anyway, when he eventually goes. The hopeful part of her whispers that this time is different, this time he'll stay, but she's not a child anymore, and she won't count on hope.

Still, she reaches for him across the table. "You've got to know what it means to me that you're here now." Words Lil thought she was too proud to share are rising inside her now. Her cup, running over. "Not just because I needed the help. I could get help. Hell, I could do it myself." *I'll do it all myself, if I have to*, she told herself like a prayer for so many days when she faced the gauntlet of the orchard alone. "But it's *you*. I'm so glad it's you."

He's watching her, rapt, consuming her words, dark eyes

taking her in like a black hole absorbing light. "I've been out in the world," he murmurs. "It feels like a myriad of experiences. But, Lilith, there's nothing for me like you. You've always been what I couldn't forgive myself for losing." He catches her hand, his grip rough.

"I haven't really forgiven you for that either," she admits and hides her smile behind the curve of the wineglass. "You know me. Better than almost anyone. So that's probably not a surprise." Blood is starting to race, in her throat, in her stomach, in her ears. "Maybe we both need to let that one go though. There's no one for me like you either."

There's a single shared breath between them. A tendon pulls taut in his jaw. At the same time, they move. She pushes into his space and he pulls, dragging her elbow along the table—a wineglass teeters, and they meet halfway, his mouth a firm wine-dark press. It's not a first kiss; there's no gentle exploration. This is his hands immediately grasping in her hair, pressing against the back of her skull like he wants to crack her open.

She shoves out of her chair, his hand clamps on her wrist—as if she'll leave—and she rushes around the table to crash into his lap, lock her knees around his hips, bringing herself near those dark eyes. Stroking his golden hair back, she can't help but laugh at the look on his face, full of desperate hunger, a perfect reflection of what she feels.

"Shut up," he breathes, hands shoving against her, begging for purchase under her clothes. "You're so—"

She doesn't want his words; they aren't what she needs. Lil bears down on him again and bites the swell of his lower lip. Her back hits the edge of the table—he swipes urgently to clear a path. Plates smash, food goes flying, and he lays her across the bared space, covers her, nosing against her neck. Greedy, he always has been the only one who ever matched her. Heat in her veins, Lil breathes out, shuts her eyes, draws her hands hard and slow along his back. She kisses him again, and he shudders.

This has always been their story. Her and him, explorers discovering the highs of life under her sheets; her and him, wrapped up together on nights when storms turn the air to a live current. Following his voice into the house from the orchard on the long days, kicking broken shells off her shoes on the way there. His smile when he sees her. The life she thought they'd have forever.

"Lilith. Lilith," he breathes like steam against her skin and she guides him out of his clothes. He tears at hers like they're a challenge.

The air carries a faint scent of flame, like the fire she's always felt burning away inside him. He runs the pads of his thumbs over her bare stomach. She holds his head against her neck, too close for their eyes to meet, taking great lungfuls of air but unable to breathe as deeply as she needs.

He crowds closer. "What do you want?"

Something in the corner of her eye flickers, foxtail quick and orange. "You know," she says against his mouth. "Come on."

The room is warm, though it's warmest in his arms, and she wraps herself around him. She wants to be a vine to cover him, hold her sway, to never let him go. He braces a hand under her, the other on the table. Some dish behind them shatters; distantly, water hisses, becomes steam. He picks her up and carries her into the living room. It's warm here too, when they lay each other out on the rug. Sweat pools on her back as she braces herself over him and they press together there on the floor of Honeysuckle House until their edges blur, his eyes boring into her. He's glowing in a flickering phantom light, orange catching highlights in his hair, on his skin. He bites at her breast, canines grazing, teasing her. Somewhere overhead there is a rumble, maybe from the house itself, but she can't bring herself to care, physically can't make herself look away from him. If this is a trap, she's willing to let it keep her. She wants to snap at his mouth until they both bleed and break, until they can curl together, their softest selves, sated and still. She wants to cry.

"Do you even know how I've missed you?" she tells him through the rush and roar in her ears. A blond cowlick is tickling her inner thigh.

He looks up at her from there, slowly. "Show me."

Something glinting flutters from above, burns when it brushes against her, and even the pain she cannot quite pay attention to—he's on his back again, pulling her down, hands on her face.

"Show me everything, Lilith." His mouth is hot against her temple, scorching her ear. Ash flutters around them like snowfall. "Give me everything."

CHAPTER NINETEEN

SMOKE RISES SOMEWHERE CLOSE, ANOTHER PHANTOM fire in the night. Sasha sits in Autumn's window seat, peering at the sky. She wraps her arms around her knees. How long has the road been closed?

The darkness feels loaded, some faint tinge of gunpowder on the breeze. A sharp hiss swiftly becomes a shriek—but it's only Autumn's kettle. Sasha tries to force herself to relax, but that's not the kind of thing that can be bullied.

It feels like she's just killing time tonight. And some hysteria in her sticks on that phrase. "Killing time." Like "stealing time." Why is time a victim of all these crimes?

How about "make time"?

Break time.

Autumn's apartment above the bakery hasn't changed at all since Sasha was last here. She fingers a flap of peeling wallpaper, navy blue, shimmering with weathered amber birds and rusty blooms. In the bathroom, there's a stained-glass window of a dahlia. Autumn filled this place with squashy secondhand furniture and lined the kitchen counter with old diner stools, where Sasha would perch as she baked. And here, nestled into the sloped gable, a window seat where the two of them used to sit in the evenings.

She finds Autumn when the sun is going down, her clothes smelling of that riverbed mud after running the ferry all day, and Autumn pulls her upstairs with a sad twist in her smile.

"There's always something special about your first apartment, isn't there?" she says. "After all these years, I almost forgot what it looked like. I was so young here…" She sits Sasha down at the breakfast counter and makes sandwiches on a loaf of fresh sourdough. Autumn always has odds and ends around from experimenting with baking mix-ins: tomato slices, fresh basil pesto, and mozzarella.

Sasha shifts uneasily. The day began with a revelation, and it seems like it's going to end with one too. Too bad she isn't ready for any more. It feels like she's about to be broken up with, and that reminds her of Linda, her similar sad, ironic smile that last day before they parted and all Sasha had left of three years was a photograph of a shattered mirror and a faded face.

Autumn has a purpose here. Whatever thoughts she has been distilling over the past days are done. She is ready to share. So Sasha waits.

Autumn sets Sasha's mug on the windowsill and settles across from her with the other one balanced on her knee. "I don't know how to say it," she says finally. The moonlight through windowpanes fragment her into segments. Her ear. A blue eye turned slate gray with the nighttime. It isn't just moonlight that gathers in her skin, the side of her face, the hollow of her collarbone. There's some inner fire there too, blood and blush, maybe. "I've been thinking about it for so long. Longer than you know." She taps one finger on the mug. Traces around the rim. "I came back for a reason. But at first, just being here shook me up. It disoriented me. My friend Matt calls it the Homecoming Effect…" She trails off. "But I've remembered now. What I want to say, even if I don't know how."

They gaze at one another. Sasha's tea is far too hot to drink, but she hovers her fingertips over it anyway, bathing them in the steam. "Just start anywhere," she bursts out at that. "First page. Last page. I don't care. Spit it out, Pip." She wants to nudge her feet against Autumn's, just to feel her, but the room is too still.

Autumn's expression is brimming with sadness, and no small amount of fear. "I've missed you. Even after how long it's been, I never stopped thinking of you. But I didn't think you'd be here. I really didn't—" She cuts herself off. "This isn't going to make sense," she says, more to herself than Sasha. "I don't know how to make it make sense—Wyn." She tries desperately. "I've been looking for him. And we talked to Lou, about the pecan children? I haven't been able to tell you, really tell you, why it mattered so much to me—" She pauses again. Swallows. "No. That's not right either, is it? That still won't make sense."

Sasha is reminded, suddenly, of her own stumbling attempts to tell Lil she loved women and not men, all the avenues into the topic that ended up being dead ends, all the convoluted stories she's told herself so long to excuse it. It was hard to find her way out. And, as Lil waited, patient for once, for Sasha to get to the point, it became obvious to them both that she'd known all along anyway. They'd been keeping that secret together. Sasha waits, putting the mask of Lil's patience over her own face, and lets Autumn untangle herself from her stories.

Autumn has turned inward, taking several deep breaths. "I'm spitting it out, I promise. Because really, the thing I have to tell you—the hardest thing—is this." And then, she reaches out, catches Sasha's fingers over the steam. She holds her gaze with rare intensity. "Sasha, there is something wrong. Here. With this place. This town. And it's been wrong for a very long time."

"Of course there is," Sasha says slowly, feeling dumb. "Same thing that's wrong with all of small-town America. Reaganomics, pressure on the small-time farmers to sell to corporations, no infrastructure, no opportunities..." She trails off, because something desperate is sparking in Autumn's eyes. It's a flicker of gold, and it shivers there like the gilded pecans in the tree, the tree that is an arm, reaching, offering something.

Something with a cost that is too high.

"Sasha, how long has it been since you last saw me?" Autumn asks.

"A year, maybe. The birthday before last." The day is a haze in Sasha's head, a memory so well-worn it's starting to have holes. "Why are you asking? You were there."

Autumn rests the tips of her fingers on Sasha's watch. "Really think. How long has it been?"

Sasha pulls her hand back, gut twisting. "Maybe we shouldn't talk about this," she says. "I don't—"

"We have to." Autumn is gentle even in her ruthlessness. And Sasha can't think. It wasn't so long ago, was it? "It isn't safe here. You've seen the phantom fires. We've heard from Wyn that the children like him are disappearing. So I'm sorry, but it's time to wake up." Autumn keeps her hand where it is, open between them, in case Sasha decides to reach out again. "Do you remember your thirtieth birthday party? The first one I ever skipped?"

"Of course I do," Sasha snaps. "That was my last birthday. That just happened."

It just happened. Hadn't it?

She scrabbles, searching back. She doesn't want to do this; she just wants to sit in comfortable silence with Autumn and not do this.

How long has the road been closed?

"No," says Autumn, who stood on the banks of the river like a mirage just days (weeks? months?) ago and found her way to town all on her own. Found her way back to Sasha. "I tried to call you after that. For a while. But you never called back. I used to wonder…but it wasn't that you were mad at me or done with me."

"Never." Sasha hears it from below her. Far below her, she sees the two of them, huddled in that window seat. "I could never be done with you."

"It was something worse." Each word rings like a slap. Sasha's floating, up in the crook of the gable.

A tendril of rosy hair, curling over her neck.

Don't say it, Sasha begs.

"Sasha. Your thirtieth birthday—that was twenty-nine years ago."

AUTUMNAL INTERLUDE

AUTUMN

May 1983

THE NIGHT AFTER GRADUATION, SASHA AND AUTUMN abscond to their tree house, accompanied by a flurry of fireflies and a tin of Autumn's first batch of homemade weed brownies.

"Tell no one," Autumn says with mock solemnity and pops the lid on the tin. Cocoa fills the air.

"I'll take it to my grave," Sasha promises.

Sitting cross-legged, facing each other in ritual, they toast the future with tiny squares.

It's a celebration of two things: Autumn's summer job at Ezra's Bakery and Sasha's imminent departure for art college. The idea of a Last Summer is difficult to swallow, but hopefully Autumn's *special* brownies will be the salve. At the very least they are one last "first" that Autumn and Sasha can share before Sasha ventures into the wide world and forgets all about her. They've never had edibles; may as well try them together.

Senior year was nothing like the others. The pressures of the real world consumed all. College acceptances, marriage proposals, whirlwind travel plans: it's the liveliest their graduating class has ever been. There are even a couple of hush-hush pregnancies in the mix, but the town is so small, everyone knows who got who pregnant. (Barb and Bobby; Johnny and Stacey.)

Even the Clearwaters, whose inheritance of the orchard has been assured since birth, aren't immune to the hype and fervor. At the eleventh hour, their English teacher begged Lil to apply to the University of the South. Lil scoffed, of course. She's attending the nearest college with an agricultural focus, for as few years as she can so she can return to the orchard. But Sasha's lackadaisical extracurriculars—student council, drama, the photography studio—suddenly paid dividends in the form of a robust and well-rounded college application. She has caught her bright future like a falling star. Ever since her acceptance letter to SCAD arrived, she has glowed.

No one offers Autumn many options. Except Dad, who hopefully mentions the neighbor's son, George, is single again. He says it like she doesn't know George, like she didn't attend all of her school years with him. George, who peed on the bus during second grade. George, who asked Lil to junior year homecoming (she went to spite everyone who laughed at him over it). She has no real college or marriage prospects, just a summer job at the bakery lined up. Everyone is changing around her. Except her.

"It's not free, even with the scholarship," Sasha admits. She's scribbling out her financial options for the years ahead. "Mom isn't really able to do much. But I think I can get a part-time job. Maybe a few part-time jobs. In a diner or something. I can wear an apron. Like you." Autumn laughs. But as she watches Sasha calculate the fixings of her future, she is swept away with a now-familiar dread: soon they will be in very different worlds.

Autumn eats another square and flops back on the ages-old wood. It complains like an elderly man with bad knees. "I'd go if I had something I wanted to study."

"Well, you're good at everything you like." Sasha reclines too so their heads brush.

"I don't know. Our teachers said I lack drive." She digs out her pack of cigarettes, flips it open, considers the neat cylinders within. "Maybe I'll try to quit smoking. Develop some drive that way."

"Great idea. Healthy." Sasha steals her pack and pockets it, grinning. "I'll help save you from yourself."

"My hero." Autumn rolls onto her side to look at Sasha. It's the easiest thing in the world, looking at Sasha. Sasha is the favorite book she keeps on her bedside table forever, partly in case she wants to read it, partly to use as a coaster. She's the smell of a favorite food Autumn wants to come home to after a long day. Food. Now she wishes she had fries, not just brownies.

On second thought, third thought, Autumn eats another square. Wind kicks up and Sasha's shirt flutters. The top button is a tug away from coming loose, and Autumn's fingers warm with the idea of pressing it safely back in.

Sasha moves her arm so Autumn can burrow against her shoulder.

She pats Sasha's stomach. "I have a confession. These brownies aren't making me feel anything."

Sasha opens a toffee eye at her and grins. "We must just not have eaten enough."

It takes under an hour for the tray to vanish, empty and discarded against the tree trunk.

A rookie mistake. Because when the brownies hit, it's with a vengeance. "Am I ever going to see you?" Autumn is distantly aware that she is asking Sasha a question she has sworn to herself was the secret of her own heart. It's not a burden she intended to place on Sasha. But it's too late, and she can't get her hands working well enough to scoop the inquiry back into her mouth. "What if you meet other people you like better?"

"Oh, poppycock." Warm and fond, Sasha drags both hands through Autumn's hair, wraps her fingers around the back of her head. "No one else would make me brownies this good. I think I feel them a little."

"I'm serious," Autumn protests, but she's smiling as she socks Sasha's shoulder. "Don't be cute."

"Can't help it." Sasha catches her fist, laughing. And then holds onto it.

"I mean, like—like—there will be people. To choose from. So many people who…study more. And you're so…Bobby Kaplan is obsessed with you. And Chuck Harlowe." She pauses suddenly, heated suddenly—and afraid. "You know that, right? They're desperately in love with you."

"That's just talk." Sasha laces their hands together. "Your fingers are so cold."

"I have poor circulation."

Sasha's thumb plays over the back of her hand.

"But am I?" Autumn asks again. Her words taste like syrup. The air is so sweet, and heavy. Maybe this is why Van Gogh painted swirls in the sky; Autumn feels swirls all around her.

"Are you...what?" Sasha asks, eyes glinting with mirth. Her pupils are as huge as ponds. "A wood nymph? A scamp? A Pippi Longstocking? Yes. Yes, you are."

"Am I ever going...?" Words are heavy too. "See you again. Am I ever going to see you again? Are you going to just...?" There are fireflies in the trees, and Autumn feels tender kinship with them because there is a light on somewhere in her too, and she cannot turn it off. It burns in her and is reflected in Sasha's eyes. She props herself up so that she and Sasha are nose to nose. "Will you forget me?"

Autumn thinks Sasha says no. She thinks maybe she starts crying a little, and Sasha coos and wipes at Autumn's eyes. And kisses her. Sasha kisses her mouth.

All Autumn *knows* is they are lying close, whispering, and then they are kissing.

They say things. They kiss more. Autumn has lain down in the red-hot embers of a banked fire and found them to be a warm bed. She has discovered that the thing that's meant to burn her only wants to hold her.

And then Autumn *floats*, outside of time, above it, and also possibly wrapped inside it like it's a warm blanket. Their conversation feels more like telepathy than talking, and Autumn can't quite grasp what they're talking about, but she knows it is as rich as fertile soil where good things grow.

Guess what I'm thinking, Sasha says and Autumn can't remember what she said, but Sasha exclaims that *you're right, that's exactly it, how did you know?*

But after that critical moment—Autumn's memory goes blank. The rest of the night is lost to her. *Too much weed*, Sasha would bemoan in the morning. *We should have paced ourselves.*

In the gray dawn light, they stumble out of the tree house, at once deadly ravenous and too nauseous to even think about food. The high flickers in and out like a faulty bulb for hours more. Autumn is shaky with fear and confusion. She half jokes that she doesn't remember, she sees the effect of her lie—the mistake—flinch over Sasha's beloved face, and they never talk about it again.

"I always wondered if I should tell you."

෴

December 1989

"I meant to ask," Boris says softly. "About your…life." They're lying in bed together, closer to morning than evening. Autumn still tastes the expensive wine the other graduates shelled out for—because if graduating culinary school that day taught their cohort anything, it was how to long for tastes beyond their means. Bottom-shelf wine and discounted cheese may never be good enough again.

"What's there to ask about?" she murmurs against his neck, too tired to move. "We're all together for like…80 percent of my days, so you already know everything. School, work, nap, school."

He graduated today too; they're two of a close-knit group of five, bonded by gas-powered fire, the blue of the crème brûlée torch. It's what she needed, after Mom and Dad retired and left town in an RV, after Autumn closed the doors of her bakery to see if she could cut it in the wider world. At twenty-five, she abandoned it all to finally do what everyone else she knew did at eighteen: better herself. Pursue higher education of some kind.

Culinary school can be a lonely and cutthroat place, but she met Angie. Boris. Bruno. Tabitha. Together, they survived, scrimping money, working night shifts at diners to get in all the real-life kitchen experience they could. Now, they are their own kind of family.

"Hey." Boris nudges her. "Are you falling asleep on me?"

"Mmmmm no. What was the question?" She tilts her head up at him.

"I never asked about your life, before school," he says. She sees, for the first time, a tiny freckle in his iris. His tone sounds like he's angling toward something, but she's too drowsy to figure out what.

"You know about the bakery." She misses those ovens, the blue KitchenAid mixer from Lou. She misses the smell of sourdough. She misses the gruff noncompliments of Ezra, the former owner of the bakery and her first true culinary teacher. The swears he expelled when a batch didn't rise, the shoulder pats he gave when her work pleased him. The kiss he dropped on her forehead when he left the bakery to her at twenty-one and moved to Florida.

"Oh my god, you're going to make me ask." He buries his face in the pillow. "I mean like…are you…? Was this…?"

"You want to know if this was my first time? You scoundrel!" Autumn pokes him, and he laughs, still a little tipsy, a little bashful.

"I know, I know." He colors, the blush she now knows goes all the way down his chest. "Sorry. I just want to make sure I was a gentleman."

"Oh stop. You know you were." Boris and Autumn aren't even the closest of the group, but tonight was a celebration. He has beautifully long eyelashes, and he loves her the way the rest of them love her: easily, without expectation. So there it is. With him, she hasn't so much lost her virginity as crossed it hurriedly off the list with a sense of relief. They'd listened to a record. He kissed her out of her clothes and folded his futon back into a bed.

"I'm fine. I liked it. A good first," Autumn says, a little surprised to discover it's true. She has wondered if Sasha was the exception or the rule. But maybe love and attraction aren't that simple.

"I know it was your first time with…a man." He trails off, staring at the ceiling, where cracks branch off from the corner, like the roots of some spindly tree. "But did you ever…?"

"Ah." Autumn rolls onto her back too. "No, this was my first time. I've never done that with a woman either."

He watches her. "You've wanted to."

Autumn nods. She isn't ashamed. She refuses to be; she'll paddle forever, keeping her head above that cruel cold water.

"Your friend. The one whose birthday you go home for." Once again, Boris's aim is startling and true.

"We only kissed once," Autumn admits. His sheets smell like them. He still has an arm around her, and even though she's lying on it, he hasn't asked her to move. Just strokes her side, reassuring her that she isn't alone. "We were high. I don't remember it all."

The trip went bad, Autumn hyperventilated and her paranoia took over the rest of the night—*Do you hear that, Sasha? Someone's out there, I swear I hear whispering in the trees—*

"So she was straight all along," Boris guesses.

Autumn laughs. It's dry, cold. Unlike her. "Oh no. She went off to college. Had her great awakening. She's out and proud. She has a real-life girlfriend and everything."

While Sasha embarked on her self-discovery, what had Autumn done? Nothing. Autumn stayed. Once or twice, she returned to the tree house alone and tried to summon her memories, if only to understand it. She even kissed George, the neighbor's son, and let him take her on five placid dates, not enjoying it, and wondering if it made her a—

For a long time, Autumn couldn't even say the word for a woman who likes kissing women. Her parents proudly voted for Jimmy Carter, Walter Mondale, and Michael Dukakis, and loudly proclaimed they had multiple gay friends they'd met on the road, and yet it took years for Autumn to say the word "lesbian."

Meanwhile, Sasha is kissing more women—beautiful, smart ones with sharp minds. Sasha comes home, and Autumn is still her funny little friend who can only stammer that she isn't really seeing anyone.

"Who needs it," Sasha said breezily, like it was easy. "No one deserves you anyway."

"So she's gay. But you aren't together," Boris cuts in, his forehead creased with confusion.

Autumn can't dispute it or explain it, so she pushes her face into his chest again.

Wait. Autumn wanted to burst the first time Sasha came home talking about the girls she was kissing—the first time one of them seemed to stick—the first time she had an official girlfriend. And the second time. And the third. *Wait, I'm still in the tree house. You only just kissed me. How can it be too late when you only just kissed me?* There's a hint of new distance between them. They can't lounge as carelessly on Sasha's bed when there are girlfriends. But Sasha still tortures her with arms slung around her neck, like it means nothing to Sasha to touch Autumn so casually. And Autumn touches her too, helplessly. Why are they doing this to each other?

"I get it." He brushes a tender kiss against the crown of her head. "I had a similar situation. My best friend growing up. Paul, he—he and I—we used to—" Boris breaks off, swallows, tries again. "He's married, actually. Nice girl. Got a cute kid." She reads in his face a multitude of heartbreaks, written in languages she doesn't even know. "I don't think he wants me in his life anymore."

Boris is a great friend to her. They talk a lot after that because he also likes kissing boys as much as he likes kissing her. Maybe, he says, it's not all that black and white for some people. Maybe, Autumn decides, she is an unfinished tapestry. Maybe she is free to keep unraveling and weaving as she discovers the new patterns of herself.

"I always wondered if I should tell you."

༄

April 1995

Autumn paces the tile floor, and perched on their kitchen counter, Victoria watches skeptically.

"I don't get why it's such a big deal. It's just a birthday," she tells Autumn. They're in the apartment they share, their one-bedroom home high in the Chicago sky like a bird's nest built in the tallest tree branches. It's been a year together, and Autumn still can't believe her luck.

Victoria wears earthy perfumes, magic, feminine musk that turns heads, and has sharp eyes, always slightly unreadable, her mind too fast to quite reach. She was top of her class in college, her future as landscaped as a French garden, the polar opposite of Autumn's lackadaisical mix of hopes, distant inclinations, and spontaneous choices. When they met, they were certainly unlikely. Victoria was twenty-five, working in finance and stopping for coffee at the nearest bakery—where Autumn happened to work the morning shift. She came more and more often for the free pastries Autumn couldn't help pressing into her hands. Autumn falls with her whole heart, captivated and honored just to be near her. It's tangling with a dragon, beautiful, dangerous, clawed—beyond her. Autumn never understands exactly why Victoria picked her and can only be grateful for it.

"I like your silly T-shirts," she'd tell Autumn, crowding her against the sink, wearing nothing but one of those T-shirts, She-Ra emblazoned on the front. "I like the way you bite your lip."

But the more time they spent together, the more Autumn lost her sense of helpless enthrallment in favor of something far more dangerous. Because Victoria, she has discovered over the past year, is secretly shy under her intelligence and red lipstick. She's like a cat, content to curl in Autumn's lap and demand her fingers in her hair. Sweet and brittle at turns, and awkwardly goofy, like she's still learning how to let go and *be*—Autumn is flush with first love.

And yet...she's torn. The moment Victoria invites her to come to an important conference in Seattle, followed by meeting

Autumn's parents in Northern California...Autumn is torn. "You're sure you need me at the conference?" she asks. "Maybe I could meet you after, when we get to Big Sur."

Victoria's lips are pursed. "It's been, what, thirty years? And you've never missed the twins' birthday? Surely they can spare you this year."

"But that's just it," Autumn says. Again. This isn't their first cycle of conversation over this decision. "It's their thirtieth birthday. That's such a big one."

"It isn't like they're coming out here for your birthday." Victoria catches her, hooking a finger in Autumn's belt loop to reel her in. "I know. I was there." She was. She'd gathered Autumn's friends—all her Chicago people, even the culinary school crew flew in—and hosted a surprise party at an exclusive nightclub that Autumn had no chance of getting in alone. They'd danced all night, snuck edibles past the bouncers, and Autumn had glued Victoria to her side, unable to stop looking at her. It was as special as she'd ever felt, because Victoria didn't like parties full of people only Autumn knew, and she must have hired a PI to track down as many of Autumn's friends as she had. But she'd done it, all of it, for Autumn, and sent everyone home with actual care packages to alleviate the inevitable hangovers.

Victoria kisses her, a welcome, beloved interruption. "Autumn," she says carefully. "When's the last time Sasha came to your birthday?"

"That's different," Autumn protests, nudging their foreheads together. "It isn't just about their birthday. It's mostly their birthday. I make the cake. But it's usually the only time of year I ever go back there now."

But Victoria is too smart and she doesn't buy it. "Your parents are in Big Sur. They sent you an entire disposable camera just to share their trip with you." She arches an eyebrow. "Who else do you have to visit at home? Except…?"

Sasha is home this time, maybe even for keeps. She left New York and her New York girl and moved back into the Clearwater house. Back to the town and the tree house.

Autumn bites her lip. Face-to-face with Victoria, it's so difficult to admit. But Autumn has always loved so easily. Too easily, sometimes, with no thought to guarding her heart. She's felt it most keenly with Sasha, who was so far ahead of her for so long, confident in her college coming-out and her girlfriends. By the time Autumn knew what she felt, Sasha was comically out of her reach. Oh, it haunted her. Autumn *dreamed* of chasing after her through the trees, watching her strong, straight back as she vanished into the horizon. And now she wakes up in Victoria's arms. She loves Victoria wildly, to distraction, and in secret, her love is twinned by tumorous guilt.

"What if she needs me?" Autumn asks finally.

"What if she doesn't?" Victoria's counter is cruel. But fair. "Also," she adds. "I want my girlfriend with me." Not unlike a dragon, Victoria has a little possessive streak. Sometimes Autumn hates it, and sometimes she wants to wrap herself up in it, in the proof of Victoria's love, her desire.

It has crossed Autumn's mind that Victoria might have known the birthday was coming. That Victoria's work trip—some conference—for that exact week might not have been entirely innocent. But not even Victoria could force the whole world to bend, just to keep Autumn occupied during the one week of the year she is normally spoken for.

"You really want me there? I won't be a distraction?" Autumn presses.

Victoria's answering smile is slow and sweet. "Oh, you'll be a distraction."

Sasha is a tether, tugging Autumn southward, past-ward. But Victoria is her present. Precious, worth keeping.

So she kisses her again, smiles against her lips. She'll do her best to keep what she has. In the morning, she'll call Sasha. She'll tell her then.

"I always wondered if I should tell you."

☙

August 2002

It's late in the evening, a single june bug dazedly spinning itself against the front door light, when Autumn finally carries the last box over the threshold and closes herself up in her new apartment.

Everyone warned her that moving in the midst of summer heat—in Texas, no less—was a terrible, terrible idea. But Autumn is from the South; she knows all about heat. And breakups are a heat-death that consumes all.

The one-bedroom is very dark. She's left the light on over the kitchen oven, and it floods over the breakfast bar, right into the tiny living space where the kind movers positioned her couch, the only piece of real furniture that felt like hers enough to take it from Victoria's. It's green fabric, a vintage fade that Victoria allowed because Autumn unapologetically loved it. Squashy in all the right places. Sturdy enough to hold the weight of two women and their love. Probably still had popcorn somewhere under the cushions, too deep to ever pull out.

Victoria is magnanimous, and much wealthier, so she offered Autumn her pick of their shared items. As ruthless as she can be at work, with subordinates and rude strangers, she still isn't ruthless with Autumn. But Autumn didn't want their things. Better to start over, with her clothes, her books—and overwhelmingly, her kitchenware. The last box is…

Autumn peeks. A weird mix of scarves, cheesecloth, and her favorite oven mitts. She dumps it on the couch, on top of the box containing her cookie press and her cake-scaping tools. The cushions wheeze.

Autumn feels empty. But the cleansing fire of the breakup hasn't burnt her down, at least. Her leaves are gone, branches bare, bark scorched, but she stands anyway in the wreckage, still alive under the ashes.

This is her choice. She'll stand by it.

With a nebulous plan after culinary school, Autumn jotted herself down into Victoria's day planner. She spent seven years as Victoria's most devoted high priestess, as Victoria's shelter from a sharp world, letting her make all the biggest decisions.

But this cruel, final one, is hers.

"I don't think you've changed at all," Victoria teases her, the first time the two of them find a new little gray hair growing at Victoria's part. Autumn says it makes Victoria look presidential. Calls her Madam President for days. It's the first of the silver sprinkle of winter flowers that come with spring's fervor during the last year they'll ever spend together.

Months later, holding a glass of red wine, Victoria looks down at Autumn, who wears the same threadbare shirt she bought at their first concert together, who has the same job she's had since she was twenty-nine and wooed this dragon with pastries. It's what they've been fighting about: Autumn's job, spurred by Victoria's newest promotion. "I don't think you've changed at all," Victoria accuses her. "You're not even over your first crush yet. Don't you want more for yourself?"

And another time, in the dark butter of nighttime, one of Victoria's hands slips around her hip. "Autumn?" Her voice is soft, like it hasn't been in the weeks they've spent fighting. "You're not... I don't think you've changed."

And Autumn, staring out the window, having swallowed a stone that sits in her stomach: dread in its purest form. "You say that a lot."

"You see it too," Victoria presses herself against her back and pleads. "It's not just the job stuff. I don't care—I mean, I *do* care about that, but it's not what I mean. It's *you*, your face, your body; it's been *seven years*—"

"Stop," Autumn cuts her off. It's out of character enough that even Victoria, who would argue with God if given the chance, doesn't respond.

Another night, one of the very final nights, watching Autumn cook: "You haven't been back to your hometown in a while," Victoria says. She still likes watching her work, even if she doesn't understand why Autumn refuses to open her own bakery—the very smallest and meekest of Victoria's ambitions for Autumn. "Maybe you should go there. See the bakery you used to run."

Autumn barely listens, because risotto takes her whole attention, because she's tired of Victoria's need to hammer Autumn's life into some more acceptable shape. (It's *Autumn's* life. Even if Victoria thinks she knows better.) "Where?" she asks absently.

"Your hometown," Victoria's voice rises above the mushroom-scented steam, baffled and suspicious. "Your childhood *home*, Autumn."

And then the memories flood back. Not that Autumn has forgotten. She simply hasn't thought of that old town in a while. Home, yes. Home, of course. The papery smell of pecans housed in the tall canopies, molten praline cooling in bunny rabbit molds so she can sell them at the Pecan Festival, Sasha's hair slipping out of her ponytail. "Oh, right."

She never went back. Ditching the thirtieth birthday turned into ditching them all. Or maybe Sasha stopped extending the invitation. Regardless, Autumn goes months without thinking about it, without even thinking of Sasha, other than occasional twinges of regret for how neither of them have reached out to the other.

"No," Autumn says. She needs to stir less. She's making the risotto too starchy, too gluey. But she has to have something to do with her hands, or she'll turn around and spit at Victoria: *If you don't think I'm good enough for you, if you're ashamed of your deadbeat partner, just say it. Put me out of my misery.* "Maybe I'll go next year."

The end of her and Victoria's relationship is marked with fights breaking out like lightning storms as Victoria's patience fades and Autumn feels, once again, outpaced by someone more beautiful and capable. Sasha all over again. It's too difficult to be outgrown, so Autumn, for the first time, made the decision for both of them.

"No more," Autumn says softly one night. She's bought Victoria an orchid. No idea why. What does one buy their girlfriend after seven years, to express their forgiveness, their desire to be amicable from afar, but to never be in the same room again? It sits on their coffee table, pink petals, a gentle, swan's-neck curve in the stem.

Victoria doesn't protest, because they both know Autumn is right. Victoria is fire and fury, growth and ascension. Time, years, love, fingerprints, bruises, tears, cities…and Autumn is unchanged.

As for leaving Chicago, it is the right choice. Even breaking all ties with her old life, her old friends, for a new apartment in some state she's never lived in is right.

Because Victoria is correct about one thing: there are natural, normal ways Autumn *should* have changed.

She pushes enough boxes to the floor that she can curl up on her couch. It's getting harder to ignore. When Autumn presented her driver's license, the agent gave her a long, strange look, eyes flicking between the birthdate, 1965, and Autumn's face.

"I have good genes," Autumn jokes. "And hair dye." Because she doesn't know what else to say. She's almost forty, starting over, but she doesn't look it. Not a single gray hair. Not a wrinkle. Not a word from her best friend.

It's dark in her new apartment, where in the cold light of the breakup, Autumn admits what she hasn't been able to, surrounded by friends and wrapped in Victoria's love: something isn't right.

For the first time, on that shitty couch, in her lonely new living quarters, she does what Victoria always wanted. Autumn begins to consider her future. In case the impossible is somehow possible. In case she wakes up tomorrow and still looks twenty-five.

Outside, the june bug must still be tapping on the light.

"I always wondered if I should tell you."

☙

January 2015

"To New Year's Eve!" Chloe screams over the noise of the club, about one shot and three minutes from climbing onto the table. "With the best people in the world."

It's cold out in Greenwich Village, where none of them can actually afford to live—but can afford to party, here and there—the first snow of the year already underway. Autumn is sandwiched in the middle of the booth, surrounded by her favorite people, and the year is turning around them. She doesn't know the club; to her it is indistinguishable from all the other long, black-boothed bars in Manhattan with low lights, high-priced whiskey specialties, too few wooden stools, and ample spillover into the street. But Chloe knew the bouncer (she's very like Victoria, sometimes), and so here they are, in a sea of the city's queerest and most glamorous, full of optimism.

They toast, Matt and Autumn lock elbows and pour back their shots together. He kisses her on the cheek, a wet, limey smack.

And...Chloe is on the table. She's gorgeous tonight, with most of her tattoos, including the Taurus under her collarbone, on display, in her element. Autumn always thought Chloe would have liked the Club Kid era. She's the lightning rod of their little group: Matt, Autumn, Ellis, and the Ryans. She was the one Autumn met first, at the bakery where she'd become head pastry chef. It's how she finds all her friends: luring them in with pastry.

And the countdown to a new year begins.

Autumn's proud of what she's found here. Chloe with her solstice parties and astrology charts. Matt and his constant search for antiaging skincare: fountains of youth found in plastic bottles. The two Ryans and their annual enthusiastic Super Bowl party (cats allowed). Ellis's ever-changing video game obsession—and their insistence that Autumn would definitely like *this* one. Occasionally it crosses her mind: what Sasha would think of the little queer crew Autumn has found, these brightly colored birds of a feather flocking together.

"Another year," Ryan P. demands of the world, of their friends. Tequila makes him loud, but it also makes him really cuddly, which is why he's sitting on Ryan G.'s lap. "Another drink too, where's my—" Ryan blinks at his empty hand and scours the club. "I think that guy stole my drink. Chloe, fight him."

Obligingly, Chloe hops off the table, but before she can actually fight anyone, Matt slides Ryan's dirty, dirty, *dirty* martini over the tabletop at him, eyes glinting mercury with mirth. Matt's still agonizing over his smile lines, even though they all swear they make him distinguished. Autumn doesn't bother picking through her hair for grays anymore. She knows there isn't a point. Instead, she resigns herself to the odd, inexplicable truth.

If she really isn't aging, there are worse fates. Technology, Pride parades, Friendsgiving, Pixar, Asian fusion donuts: there's a lot to be grateful for, so much sweetness to love in life.

"Are we making New Year's resolutions?" Ellis asks, scooting closer to Autumn so Chloe can join their booth again. "Or is that too much? Is that stupid?"

Matt looks up from his phone, where strangers seem to be messaging, and his eyes soften. "I'll make a resolution with you."

Ellis snorts. "I resolve to find you a boyfriend so you stop telling me about your hookups." Matt's cruising his dating apps, because he's at the sweet, raw time after coming out when living itself feels new and he's desperate to make up for lost time.

"Matt, you can always tell me about your hookups," Chloe soothes him and turns, viper-quick to Autumn. "It's Autumn who needs someone."

"Hear, hear," Ryan raises his glass, one arm still looped around Ryan, to keep him from sliding to the ground.

Autumn laughs, waves them off. "I'm fine. I like being single."

"But you're so cute," Matt protests. "And perfect cuddling size."

"I made her an account," Chloe says, stealing an olive from Ryan's martini. "Her profile gets lots of likes."

Matt stares. Ellis stares. The Ryans stare. Autumn stares. "Are you...catfishing people as me?"

Chloe's smile is slow around the olive. "It's not catfishing if you're the one who shows up on the date."

Autumn tries to be careful about dating as she suspects that she can't promise anyone forever. But there's still love to be had and life to live. Victoria still checks in, here and there, still beautiful, her sweep of hair cut short into a silver bob. She's married to a virtual goddess now, a celebrity in the baking industry. Autumn unironically owns all her cookbooks. They are fierce social advocates for gay marriage and tied the knot the very day it was legal. Victoria looks like she's never lived a day in fear, but Autumn knows it isn't true.

"Well…let me see my profile," she decides.

"Later." Chloe ruffles her hair and slips out of the booth. "Dancing first. Go into the year as you want to go out of it, yeah?" She's a devastating dancer. Once, she'd told Autumn, she wanted to go to school for it, but she broke her ankle, lost her scholarship, and…well. *"My mom didn't really have the money."* Autumn still recalls the banked pain in her eyes. *"But I still dance in my living room."*

The Ryans follow Chloe, and Matt and Ellis go to the bar for another round. For a moment, in the noise and pleasure of life, Autumn is alone, at a sticky table, covered in glitter because someone decided it was a good idea to celebrate midnight with glitter raining down from the ceiling. There's a good chance she swallowed a lot of it.

Autumn has only known these friends for a few years, not long enough for anything about her to be noticeable. But New Year's never fails to bring a cloud over her head. It's a reminder of the passage of time and it causes all of her unanswered questions to well up again. Like: Will she die? Or is it only aging from which she is exempt? Though she suspects she's not totally frozen, but aging very slowly. People guess late twenties now.

Autumn is afraid, sometimes, of being caught, whisked away to Area 51. It's not unlike the ways she used to be afraid when she and Victoria would steal a kiss in a dark alley, not unlike the way she still fears for these friends, every time they catch a wrong look.

While she is mostly content to just live, it's nights like this that her mind starts groping for answers in the dark. Her childhood was average, wasn't it? There is nothing in her parents' ever-quickening deterioration to suggest their lives are interrupted. They're normal, aren't they?

She's been watching age consume Mom and Dad, year by year. They had to give up the RV two months ago. Once, when she was ten, Autumn tumbled almost a dozen feet out of the tree house into the creek below. She bounced back from a broken arm like she was made of rubber. Meanwhile, Dad trips on the stairs of their RV, falls a foot, and breaks his hip—and their second-life as hippie vagabonds is over forever.

It'll be the same with her friends, even these ones. Again and again she'll walk with friends and lovers to the edge of a wide river—marriage, kids, retirement, even death. One by one, she'll watch them board a ferry for which she has no ticket. And she'll turn back and start again, young as ever.

Who knows what Sasha would think? Autumn stopped calling a long time ago. It's been so long since they've seen each other, Autumn wouldn't know what to do if she was faced with the sight of Sasha's graceful aging, while Autumn is still the unchanging little scamp. The Pippi Longstocking. The impossible. No. Autumn doesn't want to see her. There's no way she would be able to explain. If she thinks of it too long, the sadness might choke her; Autumn doesn't want to be sad.

Ellis returns alone and smiles at her. Because Ellis is Ellis, their clubbing outfit is a loose knit sweater that isn't even worn in a cool way, just in a loved way, and their hair probably hasn't seen a comb in a year. They hand her a whiskey sour, unpolluted with glitter, and slide back into the seat beside her. "Want to not dance with me?" They're always the one to find Autumn in the quiet moments, when the energy of the world is too much. That's their thing: being quiet together.

"I'll dance later." Autumn leans on their shoulder. Even if Autumn loves dancing, tonight she just feels a little too aged for it.

Ellis hums an affirmative. "I can't wait to be old enough that not dancing at a party isn't weird. I want to be old and eat caramels and swear about 'kids these days.'"

"I'm old," Autumn admits, tequila-honest and warm in the company of someone she thinks would actually believe her. "Born 1965. Too old to be here, probably."

Ellis laughs into her hair. "That's the spirit, kid. Oh well. We'll be geezers soon enough."

Autumn picks glitter off their shirt and settles back in against their collar. Across the floor, Chloe and the Ryans are laughing in each other's arms. Matt's chatting with the bartender, who has a very sexy eyebrow piercing. Ellis is warm and solid against her cheek, chasing her melancholy away. Maybe one day she'll tell them for real.

"I always wondered if I should tell you."

ᏇᎯ

June 2023

Dad's last window is in a hospital. The leaves on the tree outside are flushed healthy and green. Nightingales made a home in the high branches, and in summer the hatchlings learn to fly, all but one, who falls to the grass on a sun-washed day.

And Autumn, mistaken by the nurse for a granddaughter, sits at his side. She didn't correct the nurse.

Mom died five years ago. She and her dad are the only two left in the whole world that call each other family. It's just age, coming for him. Nothing more sinister than that. Still, dread creeps up Autumn's throat at night. *Alone. You are one day closer to being alone.*

"I brought you cannolis from the place down the street," Autumn tries. Some days Dad isn't all that lucid. It's a blessing. He doesn't notice that his daughter, who should be fifty-seven, is too young; in his mind, everything is all right.

Today, he is quiet, but he seems to be here. Death is not always the single cruel swing of a scythe; sometimes it takes in pieces, withdrawing senses and memories like small bills from a bank.

And then, out of the antiseptic silence, Dad speaks. "I always wondered if I should tell you."

Autumn leans forward to hold his hand and try to rub warmth back into his fingers. "What was that?"

He's lost weight. His arms are as small as a boy's. His whole body is small. "Used to joke you just popped out of the ground," he murmurs. His eyelids are practically translucent, like the mother-of-pearl insides of a shell. "Autumn baby with Autumn hair and sky in your eyes…"

"I know." It's the story behind her name. Her first barely red crop of baby hair had surprised her parents. Mom picked her up to examine her scalp, then looked out the window at the late-November leaves which gave the wind an auburn shape. Autumn was originally meant to be Marcia, but at the sight of that hair, Mom said there was suddenly only one name she could give her child. Autumn, for the apple-crisp cold, for pecans falling from crimson canopies. Autumn, for the season of her birth in that little pecan town. "You've told me that, Daddy. I love you." Once, Autumn would say she loved him as a goodbye. Now, she says it as she breathes. Just in case.

Dad knows Autumn loves him. He must know. Autumn has said it enough, hasn't she?

"Mom didn't want to tell you. She didn't think you needed to know." Dad opens his eyes and they're filmy. It may not be the good day Autumn thought. Maybe she's— "You were so cold when he brought you to us," he says dreamily. "Wrapped in his leather jacket. You cried so loud."

Autumn feels her smile freezing. She can't help it.

"Just a newborn…but it happened sometimes in that town. We all knew. No one talked about it, but we knew," Dad sighs. "And god, we wanted a baby. We wanted you so much."

Some great, terrible awareness falls into her, rips pieces of her off and plummets through her body, far into the ground. "Dad."

"You were ours anyway." His eyes are back, rolling on Autumn and away again, unable to focus. "We wanted you so, so much."

"Dad. What do you—what are you saying?"

His eyes are closing again, the weight of the world too great on his fragile mind.

"Dad. *Dad!*"

"I always wondered…"

ↀ

2024

How long has the road been closed?

Autumn stomps on the brake, and the rented little Nissan rattles to a stop. A collection of orange cones stands between her and the only route drivable into town. At first, she can't fathom it. Her energy is sapped from days of driving. The interior of the car smells, and so does she; she hasn't stopped longer than a bathroom break since the state line, and she's only been eating Cheetos and KitKat bars. Blearily, she stares through the windshield and waits for the sight in front of her to change.

It doesn't.

The road and bridge into town is nothing but weather-beaten rubble, undrivable. But the damage looks old. Settled into scars. It's been closed long enough that kudzu has laid claim to the cracks. She steps out of the car, considers going forward on foot—but it isn't her car. She can't just abandon a rental.

This can't be. She hasn't been gone…that long…

But hasn't she?

Unwanted, exhausted tears well up and she folds herself back in the driver's seat, honks once—the sound barely echoes. It's swallowed in that unerring still void.

Fine. This won't stop her. There's always another way into town, and Autumn knows it well.

She wheels around, the world's messiest three-point turn, and drives on.

It took her months, agonizing ones, to settle Dad's affairs and lay him to rest by scattering his ashes in the mountains. Months, with terrible, heavy questions in the back of her mind. And months, to get to know her grief and start to become comfortable with it. Because what is her grief but her love taking on a new form? God, it hurts. She was so afraid to lose Dad, and it's every bit as terrible as she feared. But if she is truly an ageless woman, then grief is going to be a part of her life. She would rather have it as a friend.

Still, losing both parents has uprooted her more than any breakup, more than any move. Autumn knows she was lucky in her parents. Many of her friends were not; Chloe raised herself while her mom drowned daily in a bottle; Ryan's father used a belt when he came out; Ellis's family refuses to let go of their deadname and yet cries when Ellis doesn't return home for the holidays. Autumn's parents were a glorious exception to most of the stories Autumn knows. Even when she introduced a woman to them, they never wavered—at least, not where she could see.

So she will go back home, the place she knows where she may find answers and the place that the three of them once shared.

Within thirty minutes, she's pulling into the parking lot outside the ferry stop. It's empty, not a car in sight. It doesn't look abandoned, but no one's selling tickets or waiting on the rusted benches for the ferry to cruise around the bend of the river.

Worse yet, the other side of the river is a haze of green where she should see the town. Helpless, Autumn turns, scouring the area for some sign of life. It never occurred to her that she might arrive and find nothing. Autumn foregoes the dock and scrambles up the ridge of bank, muddy and messy, desperation driving her like a horse whip, thirsty for a glance of something. She stands there, awash in river air, scanning the far bank. But there's nothing to see. Only endless green.

It cannot all be gone. Autumn can't be too late. No town, no matter how old, simply vanishes, does it?

Autumn scans the tree line, the mottled choke of overgrowth.

She holds her memories of the town in the warm hearth of her heart and summons it as best she can. The kitchen where Dad taught her to bake, the records Mom used to play. Her bakery, with ovens she always thought she'd return to once more, the Clearwater pecans, still the best Autumn ever tasted, the tree house, Sasha's eyes in the darkness, her lips—

Dad's strange words. *Just a newborn…but it happened sometimes in that town. We all knew. No one talked about it, but we knew.* The closest thing to an answer Autumn has to unlock the mystery of herself.

It cannot be gone.

"Come on," Autumn says. Her voice is thready and unfamiliar, even to her. "Please. Come on."

The air thrums and then blooms around Autumn. She smells an aroma any kid who grew up around orchards would know: the welcoming scent of a full pecan harvest. Greedy, she breathes it in, the only scant sign offered to her. Warm and earthy, it surrounds her, and between one blink and the next, the bank shifts, fuzzes, and she sees, somewhere in the distance, a light flicker on, marking where downtown should be. Then two. Then three. Autumn can only watch as it reforms before her eyes, the far bank becoming familiar to her again.

Wind pushes at Autumn's back, pulls her forward, heavy with the rustling of trees. It whispers not with words that speak to her mind, but with impressions that speak to the innate understanding of all living creatures. *Ours, our child, one of us, she is back, she returns—*

And Autumn—

Feels the warm hum of the ovens. Sees the glint of her old bakery tables, where she prepped cheesecakes and cupcakes and cookies, once. The tree house, swinging low over shallow water. She is gathered up in the swell of those words, of that welcome and—

She returns to us.

Leaving the world behind, Autumn returns to town.

ACT III

CHAPTER TWENTY

L IL WAKES UP TO CHILLY AIR AGAINST HER SKIN AND the smell of smoke. Muzzy gray light around her. Heavy dust motes scatter. She rolls onto her side, putting out a hand for Jason, but the Persian rug where they fell asleep—eventually, at some point—is cold. Once, she could sleep on the ground and rise for school without a thought; now she feels the press of wood in her bones. And the phantom press of Jason's hands.

"Jason," she calls. Her voice is so rough she sounds ill. But there's no answer. The glow of the morning after flickers. Weakens.

Lil opens her eyes. The fireplace is black with dust, more than she'd seen the night before, and the walls are filthy. It wasn't like this last night; it wasn't so—

No. That isn't dirt.

Lil sits up, her heart suddenly lunging in her chest. The air isn't heavy with dust, and it isn't dirt coating the walls, the floors, the furniture. It's soot. Ash. And it isn't the chandelier casting light over her body, but sky and sun. Above her, the second floors and roof are gone. They've disintegrated around her, as if a giant scooped a handful of the house out above her, leaving broken, burned boards behind.

Honeysuckle House is destroyed. The vase with flowers: cracked, water evaporated, flowers burned beyond a crisp. Curtains, devoured from bottom to top, the rods cracked and blackened against the walls; one is thrown clear through the windows. The couch is burned to the skeletal frame, but the rug is only covered in ash.

And so is she. It coats her body. She looks like a forgotten thing left to languish in an attic.

It can't be.

Lil frantically brushes at her legs, her chest, her stomach, but as her body wakes up, new pains make themselves known. Suddenly the ache of sex and sleeping on a hard floor is the least of her worries. Red burns bloom all over her body, on her arms, her palms. The worst she can't see, but she feels on her shoulder a building scream of pain.

"Jason," Lil calls, but it dissolves into a fit of coughing. The burn in her throat isn't just dehydration. It's smoke. "Jason!" He's not there. Where is Jason? He wouldn't...leave her. Not like this. Not unless he's hurt, or he can't come back to her. Above her, something deep in the house groans.

Standing, Lil covers herself. She won't cry.

In fits and starts, Lil rushes into the hall. But every step is treacherous. She's barefoot. Nails stick up from cracked floorboards, glass from windows litters the ground. It's arduous work to get through the hall. Too much sunlight reaches her; behind her in the entrance hall, something shatters. She catches her own ghostly reflection in a mirror and can't bear to meet her own eyes or see her own body. She doesn't want to know the damage.

Lil must have passed out. Jason must have risen when he noticed the fire. Fought his way through, seeking an escape route for them both. She imagines finding him collapsed under fallen furniture or ceiling, or burned beyond saving. He must have gone for help, or—he's hurt. The landline at Honeysuckle House doesn't work, so maybe he ran...leaving her there? Alone and unconscious? No, it doesn't make sense. Jason wouldn't abandon her to the flames. Unless he had to. Unless he couldn't return.

She won't cry. She won't cry.

When she reaches the breakfast room, it's burned too, the table collapsed under the weight of its own frame. The counter where she cooked is covered in ashy remains. The carnage of a fire. Jason's clothes are crumbled, covered in ash near the counter.

Lil finds her clothes where she left them, tangled in the corpse of the table. The shirt is ruined, but the jacket remains, sooty but miraculously salvageable. Her jeans still button, and that's all she needs. She dresses as quickly as she can. *She won't cry.*

The air is oppressive. Every breath hurts. Mortally wounded, the house moans again. Boards creak, splinter like toothpicks. It could be ready to collapse around her. Jason could be anywhere inside; the house is cavernous. She can only hope he's outside, unconscious but alive. Lil doesn't bother wrestling into her blackened, curling shoes. She picks them up, tucked them under her arm and inches her way across the floor. It's treacherous. There's no sign of him as she makes her way, quick as she can, out of the house, but she feels watched as heavily as she feels the burns on her skin.

"It's the smoke, not the fire that gets you," Jason told her after his first bad burn, out at the old Texaco near the highway turnoff. He was twenty-three, still in training at the firehouse. When the nightmares kept him awake, she lay with her head on his chest, trying to calm his racing heart, his face flushed like he stood again before the inferno. *"So much smoke, I couldn't see. For a second, I swear I lost my way."*

He wouldn't leave her to the smoke unless he was trapped, unless something held him back from her. She won't—she won't—

Clinging to what's left of her heart, her hope, Lil steps outside of the ruin. The sunlight is bright in the Finch orchard. The leaves are a mix of green and orange, the grass nut-brown. But Jason isn't there. Lil wanders across the driveway in a daze, like a sole survivor of some great catastrophe, alone in an aftermath of dust and smoke. Lil's throat burns and she chokes on a sob.

For all the phantom fires she has seen around this town, has she finally stumbled into a real one?

"Jason?" she manages, one more time. But there's no answer. He's gone.

♋

"Sasha. Your birthday—that was twenty-nine years ago."

Sasha sees the whole thing. She watches Autumn's story unfold, sometimes from above, sometimes from *within* the tale—she can smell the steam of a queer club at midnight, taste the cream-rich bisque of her culinary school kitchen. Sometimes she's nodding, maybe, but it is a nod of habit, of a frantic

grasping for the normal fakeries of conversation. It is not a nod
of comprehension.

This can't be real. Autumn lost herself out there somewhere.
Autumn has a drug problem. It's a fable, a coping mechanism, a
lie. It can't be true.

Autumn tells her that she's fifty-nine years old. They're *both*
fifty-nine, out there somewhere. But she looks the same, just sitting there in front of her, as fresh and crisp as an unbitten apple.

"That's how old Mom was," Sasha tries. *"How could you—but
you don't look—"*

"I'm getting used to the idea," Autumn admits. *She's curled her
arms around herself, the first true sign of self-consciousness. "I think
I'm aging. Just slowly. Sort of—" A laugh bursts out of her, strained
and accidental. "God, sort of like a tree. Victoria, she saw right
through me. I just didn't want to accept it for a while. But it's why
I had to come back. I have to know if—I'm the only one. Or are we
all like this?" She presses a hand to her mouth. "You're the first person
I've ever told."*

More words. No sense.

"You didn't come," Sasha repeats, once or twice. "I didn't
know why you weren't there…" Most unbelievably, it was because
Pip had a *girlfriend*. A girlfriend who wasn't Sasha. Sasha, who
had spent her twenties casually recovering from a stolen, forgotten kiss in a rickety tree-ruin. A kiss that at this point is old news
anyway, apparently, and all of this is too much to believe.

*Here, Autumn doesn't say anything at all for a long time. She only
looks at Sasha and sees too much, with soft eyes that ease back Sasha's
skin, nudge apart her ribs, and touch the center of her. "That was
a long time ago for me," she says. "I always wanted to tell you. But*

you know me. I was never such a quick learner. It took me a while to come to terms with myself and catch up." Catch up. Catch up. *And now, Autumn has lived an entire other life, in a world where Sasha is now outdated, a milk carton left in the fridge too long—*

Sasha leaves through the bakery's back door. The sky is still dark. She walks home along the road, glancing around her every so often at the far-off glow of house fires. Even Honeysuckle House seems to flicker in shadows, but she doesn't give it half a glance. It's all just dream stuff. Her mind wheels. She lands, a bird in a storm, on random branches, random moments of Autumn's telling.

"So you think we're what—frozen in time?"

"I think you must be," Autumn admits. "This town is all the same as it was in the nineties. No cell phones, no gay marriage, and Trump's just that guy from Home Alone.*" Her lip quirks up. "No one's heard of 9/11 or COVID-19, which is actually a little nice." She pauses, shakes herself out of the ramble. "No place is this isolated." Autumn twitches for Sasha's hand but doesn't quite take it. "You can't tell me how long you've been here. I think whatever's doing this doesn't want you to know. Doesn't want you to think about it."*

The house is unlocked for her, and she staggers inside, easing herself onto the couch with geriatric care. It's dark like only early morning is, a dark that is also cold and damp from a long steep in the night air. The TV sits on the floor across the room, where she and Mom and Lil had watched the horrible series finale of that doctor-drama show *St. Elsewhere*, where it turned out that the hospital was just a figment of a little boy's imagination, caught in a snow globe. Nobody liked that shitty ending. Now it feels like it was Sasha herself caught in a glass ball of unreality, rattled around in a child's scrawny grip.

All these trips from one riverbank to the other. Countless nights porting shadows. On that side, the world of the living; on this side, this strange, frozen purgatory. Who have her passengers been? Who can come and go, between human time and the underworld?

Has she been ferrying the dead?

Yet, Autumn got in. She came home.

"But why didn't you tell me as soon as you came back?"

Thumbprint cookies. A walk in the woods. Autumn was lost momentarily for words at that.

"Whatever is keeping you and everyone else under pulled me in too for a minute," Autumn recalls. *"The first few…days? Weeks? I was so disoriented. I remembered certain things, like Netflix, like my friends, but I forgot—"* Tears glimmer to life in her eyes. *"I forgot my parents were gone."* Autumn isn't Lil, who fights grief like it's a straitjacket. Autumn just feels it, lets it pour from her eyes. *"I thought they were just on their trip."* It feels wrong to just watch her cry, but if Sasha is going to comfort her, she'll have to move, and Sasha can't move.

Autumn gathers herself. *"The longer I was here, the more I began to remember the things that weren't right. I asked you how long you were going to be here and remembered I hadn't expected you to be here at all. I saw the pecan children and remembered I'd come here for them. I saw one of Dad's sweaters in my closet one day and suddenly I remembered they were gone."* More pearl-shine tears slip down her cheeks. *"After that, it was easy to remember everything. And I just had to figure out how to tell you."*

There's a ferocious burn on the horizon, but Sasha isn't sure if it's the sunrise or just another phantom blaze.

On the porch, there's a hard *bang*, like a body against the door.

The doorknob rattles, then gives. Sasha stands swiftly, heart thundering in her chest.

Lil crashes into the house. She's barefoot and her clothes are so ruined, so covered in dirt that, for a brief flash of horror, Sasha imagines it's their mother returned from her grave. She doesn't even register Sasha, but catches herself on the frame, raises blood-shot eyes and stumbles toward the kitchen.

"Lil?" Sasha trails after her, stunned by the night's second slap. "Wh—"

Lil collapses at the table, shivering, and then reaches for the phone. Through a gap in her shirt, her shoulder is red and blistered.

"Holy shit." Sasha ducks back into the sitting room to grab up their ancient monster of an aloe vera plant, stuffing the first aid kit under her arm on her way back. "We need to go to the ER—"

Except if Autumn was telling her the truth, there's no way to get there. The road is closed. And despite that longing in her gut, Sasha's never stepped off the ferry onto the other bank.

Could they really be *trapped* here?

Sasha forces down a claustrophobic panic. She lays her supplies on the table. Lil has her ear to the phone receiver, listening to an endless ring. "What the hell happened?"

Lil finally looks at her, rather than through her. "Honeysuckle House burned last night."

There is a long, fumbling silence, Sasha's new preferred form of communication, apparently. She gapes at Lil's injuries: the worst is that burn on her shoulder, which definitely needs a dressing. "*Burned* burned?" she clarifies anyway. "I was on the road and…" But when had she even walked by there? Her own night was a blur too tender to probe. "Where's Jason?"

Lil's reddened fingers tighten around the phone, ringing endlessly. It must hurt to touch anything. Even so, Sasha longs to reach for her, wrap her up tight, prove to herself that at least her sister is still real. "I don't know. I can't find him. I think he might be in there somewhere." Lil slams the phone down. "This is useless," she snaps. "I have to go back."

"Sit still," Sasha cracks back, ripping thick fleshy leaves from the aloe vera for a salve. "You need a bandage on your shoulder."

Lil looks ready to protest, but when she meets Sasha's eye, whatever fight brought her here seems to abandon her. "I don't know what happened," she says. "I didn't notice it burning down around us."

That—Sasha just moves on from that. It's immediately clear what was going on; Jason and Lil have a history of drowning in each other. "You need new clothes—we should just cut these off," she says.

"We have to go back out there," Lil says, but she lets Sasha slice off what's left of her jacket to look at her shoulder. She just presses her knuckles to her mouth and turns away like Sasha would care if she cries. Working with farm equipment, plus a reticence toward paying for outside help, ensures that everyone on an orchard has some basic first aid skills. Sasha swiftly plunders the supplies they have, triages the burns, and sets to work. That blistered place on her shoulder outpaces the rest of the angry red marks. The soles of her feet are almost as bad, cut from walking through debris. Another streaky red mark curves around the ridge of Lil's ribs. It's only when the light hits right that its shape becomes clear. A handprint, swollen, raised, burned into her skin. Sasha stares at this for a long time.

Where *was* Jason?

Soon, she's done all she can. "Take these," Sasha says, shaking several aspirin into Lil's singed palm. "You stay here and rest. I'll go look."

"No." Lil cuts over her, catching her wrist. "You're not going out there alone. I'm coming."

"Dammit, Lil, you're *hurt*," Sasha bursts out, eyes suddenly brimming. It's half exhaustion. The sun is up, but this night feels like it will never end. "Your feet look bad."

"You can't stop me," Lil says and doesn't let go. "If he's there, I can't stay here. And I'm not risking you disappearing too. You try to go without me, I'm walking back out there anyway. So wait for me to change and we'll drive."

For a moment they glare at one another, Sasha caught in her grasp. Swallowing hard, she turns her hand over to grip her sister back, very gently. And then Sasha follows Lil to the laundry room to help her get out of the rags she's wearing and ease into whatever clothes they find in the dryer.

They drive, Sasha behind the wheel, creeping down the road like it might come unbraided at any moment. She turns at the Finch driveway, gasping softly at the smoldering ruin of Honeysuckle House. There are no fire trucks, no cops. The disaster has gone, apparently, totally unnoticed by the town, despite the gutter of black smoke above.

Sasha parks closer than is probably safe and jumps down from the truck cab. Immediately, the dirty, chemical air of the burn torches her lungs and she coughs. "Didn't you say he was going to grill?" she rasps. "Maybe the charcoal was still hot and the wind…" It was an old, dry house. There could be ancient wiring in there, old gas lines, parched insulation…

"We didn't even know it was happening. I woke up and he was gone, but he wouldn't just leave me." Lil stares out at the trees, probably still looking for a figure among them. "It's like I was drunk. Or under a spell. I don't know how I didn't…"

Sasha climbs the porch steps. They moan ominously. The once grand entrance hall is visible, since the front of the house has caved in, no more than a slumping portico and gray ash now. The curve of a staircase is as unreal as a charcoal sketch. "Jason," she calls through the sooty gloom of early morning. "*Jason!*" Picking her way through the debris, the hanging cables, the split kindling of the floor, she searches. Together, they overturn charred remains, peek through improbable crannies created in the collapse, wander through the house's soiled decadence. The chandelier crashed and shards of crystal now scatter across the scarred beams below. Lil limps badly. They shout up the remains of the stairs but don't dare test the second floor. He's nowhere to be found.

Lil finally sits down on the front steps, digging her hands into her short hair. White bandages peak from under her cuff. "Sasha," she says. "What do we do?"

There are suddenly so many reasons to ask this question, and Sasha has no answer for any of them. But, for once, Lil is asking. Sasha *has* to answer. "We have to go to town. We can—get some more help. We need the sheriff. A—bigger search party."

"Yes." Lil stands, stronger now that she has a purpose. "Okay. Everyone will be at the festival. We can find help there."

They get back in the truck, and Sasha turns the ignition over, her eyes still on the house. Nothing smokes now; in fact, the air is cold. The house looks like an ancient ruin, long derelict. Abandoned for decades. And then—she almost knocks her hand on the windshield, craning to watch.

"Do you *see* that?" she breathes to Lil.

Lil follows her gaze.

The house flickers, a guttering candle. One moment, it lies in miserable decay, a moldering wreck. Then, like light splitting in a prism, she tips her head and there is the house, whole, complete, just as she's known it all her life. Another erratic blink and it's skeletal again. There's a blurring, like one of her long-exposure photographs in the dark room, when the shutter can't capture a shift. The haze of unreality.

Shattering time.

CHAPTER TWENTY-ONE

T HE FIRST MORNING OF THE PECAN FESTIVAL IS IN full swing. Carnival music jumbles over the crowd from the carousel, and someone's complaining about the spiced cider running low by midmorning. And Autumn sits behind her stand, gnawing on a nutty bunny, watching her baked goods dwindle, and trying to pretend this is normal.

With the truth out, all her unspoken words finally spoken, Autumn thought she would feel braver, freer than she does. Maybe it's the way Sasha looked at her last night, for the first time like Autumn was some kind of alien. Maybe it's returning to the Pecan Festival to man her stand, surrounded by her old neighbors who are unburdened with the knowledge she has.

Autumn poured out thirty years of bound-up heartache. And Sasha listened. Questioned her. Protested. They talked late into the night, and in the morning, Sasha begged off. *I need to think*, she said. *Okay,* Autumn replied. *I'll stop by later,* Sasha promised. *No, yeah, of course. That's fine,* Autumn assured her, but it wasn't. Finding Sasha back in her life was a miracle she'd stopped hoping for out in the world. But it happened; Autumn got Sasha back. And now Sasha likely wanted nothing to do with her.

The longer it takes for Sasha to return, the more frequently the anxious tidal waves hit her. She feels the roil in her stomach and braces herself for the next one.

Across the street, a little ghost crosses between two tables. She starts, sitting up fast. Was that—

"—tumn? Autumn, dear?"

Someone's speaking to her. Autumn pulls herself out of the murk and shades her eyes. Cork stands over her with a genial smile. The sun shines so brightly, his cheeks, temples—those places where bone protrudes—are thrown into sharp relief. Cork, the elderly, wispy janitor at the town hall. Before Autumn left, before the town became this nightmare, he was already getting on in years. It was taking him longer and longer every day to sweep the steps. She left in 1989, last spoke to Sasha in 1995, which means that, like a fly preserved in amber, he should be *dead*—

"Goodness, dear, you've gone pale," Cork says and offers her his hand. "Can I get you some water?"

"No, thank you," Autumn says. Returning his gesture, she cranes her head, searching over his shoulder for the little bare feet, the mane of matted hair. "I'm just tired."

"I just came to buy some pound cake. But can I do anything?" he asks.

"No, I just need..." Behind Cork, the small figure darts through the shadows. Autumn shoots to her feet. "Actually yes. Watch my stand."

"Sure, if that's what you—"

"Thanks, Cork." Autumn is off already, rushing to meet the child who creeps around the side of her bakery.

She finds Wyn pushing at the doorknob at the back door. He glares suspiciously over at her approach, poised to flee—but instantly relaxes when he sees who it is. That trust slightly soothes the hurricane in her gut. "Loud," he complains, kicking in the direction of the square.

"I know." Autumn grins at him and comes forward to unlock the door. "I'm glad to see you. Want to go inside? It's a lot... quieter..."

He's holding something protectively close to his stomach, a tangled web of twigs, angles carefully wrapped in reeds. It's one of those Cajun bird traps, quite a bulky burden for him to have brought here. At its heart, an enormous insect. It has been painstakingly preserved, the delicate wings the color of milky jade. A lunar moth, carefully pinned in place. "I made this," Wyn whispers. "So he don't get you."

The hungry man. A grotesque folktale come to life. Maybe the monsters of children are always more real than adults want to think. Autumn kneels beside him and reaches out. He places it in her hands. "Thank you." His little face is familiar now. Despite herself, she wants to find some similarity in their features. There isn't any, but her heart has felt something in common with him from the beginning. Some sameness under the skin, something in how they were made that rings true together. "What do I need to do with it? Put it up in my bakery?"

Wyn considers this, pushing his small fingers into his cheek thoughtfully. He points toward the front. "Put it—um—put it in that big window." They go inside, and he shows her where, just at

the corner of the front window, close to the front door. "There."
He has found one of her trays of festival goodies along the way
and is cramming a maple bar in his mouth.

Autumn spends too much time setting it just so, turning it so
that the wings catch the light. "You know..." *Courage, Autumn.*
She barely touches one of the legs of the altar. "You could stay
here sometime if you want. It's cold out, and I have room if you
need a warm place."

Before he can quell it, the quickest spark of hope lights in
Wyn's face and nearly cracks her heart. "Neel," he reminds her.

"I want Neel to come," Autumn assures him. "I know he
doesn't want to yet, but if he got to know me a little better, that
could change."

They both ponder for a moment as Wyn chews. Then he
makes a cautious suggestion. "Maybe...maybe we go out there
and we try again."

She takes a chance and sits close enough to him that he can
reach out if he wants. "What you said to me about...the hungry
man...was really scary. If you were here, I could keep you both
safe." In the window, the trap stands strange and lovely. "We
could keep each other safe."

They sit there together, the wings of the moth shivering.
Slowly, she feels a cold hand slip into hers. The small fingers are
slightly sticky from syrup. "Okay."

⁊

Lil's throat aches from the combination of dehydration and
smoke by the time she and Sasha walk into the Pecan Festival.

But she won't admit it any more than she will be deterred. Her body thirsts for sleep, aloe, and a warm, soft place where she can heal. But she can't listen to it. Lil isn't made to be coddled, even by herself. And fear won't let her rest; it's louder than her pain. Her best medicine is action. Answers.

Slightly hunched, Sasha stays close to her side. The strain is clear in her face, the tight, miserable pinch of her mouth that makes her look so much like Mom. She's checking on Lil every fifteen seconds or so. Children run close to their legs, and one of them knocks into Sasha's knee so it overbends, and she huffs out a pained breath.

Under the proud banners of Mom and Marigold Finch, the Pecan Festival has risen to the challenge of Lil's dreams. Her hopes. Strangers, unrecognizable faces, rush around her, buying roasted pecans, flooding the streets, and not a single fire is glowing on the ridge. Kids giggle past. A live band, slightly off-key, echoes just off the square. Lil's head feels attached by an ever-thinning tether.

Just yesterday, she and Sasha walked the same route to the festival. The air tasted like promise, and she'd dared to leave with Jason, dared to drink his wine and eat at his table. But this morning is a crueler, darker mirror of the day before. She and Sasha are the only ones who have changed. They pass the bakery's table, but Autumn isn't there. Cork rocks on his feet, hocking the goodies like he made them himself.

"It's the twins," he quavers out, holding out a pecan cluster on a paper napkin. Neither of them takes it.

"Hey, do you know where Autumn went?" Sasha asks him, and it sounds strange to hear her say her actual name, rather than

"Pip." It comes out so smoothly, like it's been well polished by a repetitive going-over in Sasha's thoughts. Too intimate.

Cork hasn't lowered the offered treat, so it hovers in the air between them, paper napkin trembling. "Well, let's see now," he mutters. "There was a little boy runnin' around by the bakery, and she chased after him."

"Wyn." Sasha glances at Lil, wide-eyed. "How long ago was that, Corkie?"

"Hmm." He frowns up at the sky, as if to check the sun. "Been a good long while."

They look back at the bakery, and Sasha gasps. "See that *thing*?" she murmurs, nodding at the window. There's something crouched in it, brown and spiderlike. "That's one of those bird traps I told you about." It looks almost archaeological, a frail bundle.

Lil sees the silent scream of panic building in her. And there's no choice. "Go," she says. "Take the truck."

Sasha winces. "You sure? I can—"

"I'm sure." Last time, Autumn had come back bleeding. If Autumn doesn't come back whole this time, Sasha won't be whole either. "Go."

Sasha holds Lil's gaze for a long moment, and there's more tenderness there than any touch could convey. "I'll find you, okay? Just find some help, and then you *have* to rest."

"Yes, Mom," Lil teases. *See? It's okay. Everything is okay. We are okay.* And Sasha *runs* like her heart is ahead of her. Lil always figured it was that way, with them.

She goes on. Her feet hurt worse now. Her right sock feels… off. Wet and warm with every step. She misses the usual burnished line of heat in the air that defines Southern autumns. Chill hangs heavy in the wind.

"Goodness, you look peaky, dear," Agnes calls when she passes her volunteer stand, her scarf pinned with a glittering cicada brooch.

Speaking requires pulling herself up from a deep well. "I'm tired," Lil murmurs.

"Poor dear." She has her special-occasion lilac glasses slipping down her nose and a clipboard in hand. One of her eyes bleeds red from a burst vein. "You won't be young forever, Lilian."

Oddness lurches through her. "What did you call me?" Lil asks.

Lilian. Her mother.

"Those twins run you ragged," Agnes chuckles and pats her wrist right over the *bandaged burn*—pain fireworks behind her eyes—and Lil jerks free. Agnes's smile doesn't even twitch. "Get yourself some coffee."

Lil pulls herself away. She continues across the square. But when she reaches the far end of the stalls, the closed library, where the festival turns around—an empty volunteer post where someone is meant to be—and she has nowhere to go but back. Here, at the brink Lil recognizes the awful, secret prayer she's nursed the whole way here: that she'll see Jason in the crowd like nothing happened. Arguing with Cesar, ordering someone to get more marshmallows for the hot chocolate stand, running the carousel, directing the older patrons. Funny how hope might only reveal itself as it's dashed against the rocks.

She crosses into the park, just beyond the bounds of the festival. It's deserted enough here at the far end that she hears the gossip of leaves on the wind and familiar steps on the pavement, approaching her from behind. It must be Jason. His warmth, coming up to crowd her, resting his fingertips on the small of her back.

Instead, Theon walks past her, squinting up at a shuttered storefront. "Not looking so good, Lilith."

The place on her back, the place he touched, simmers.

"Why," she breathes, "is it always you? Why can't you leave me alone?"

Theon's gaze scrapes away at her. He touches on the place over her ribs that aches in the shape of Jason's hand, and she flinches away. "Believe it or not, I didn't think you'd be here," he says. "But I guess I should have known. You don't sit still." He doesn't look great himself. The sense of casual disregard he always carries feels harried this time. His skin strains over his forehead like ill-fitted fabric. Like he wants to crawl out of it.

"But here we both are," he murmurs. Deceptive softness. "I didn't even mean for us to be. Isn't that funny."

Lil stalks away. She just needs to get help for Jason.

"Lil. Can we just talk—"

Then she can leave.

"*Lil.*"

Then she can—

"How many times?" Theon calls after her. She pushes on. The warmth in her sock is less of a warning now, more like a sopping mess, but she won't be stopped and she won't listen to him. "How many times will we keep doing this?"

"Until you leave me alone," she calls back.

This time, something like desperation cracks through his voice. "Dammit—I wish I could."

A fight, her Achilles' heel. Lil might have been drawn right back in if not for Jason's name pounding a tattoo against her chest. "Find some other town to ruin." She speeds up. "No one says it has to be here."

"*You* say it has to be here. *You* do," Theon snarls. His footsteps sound after her. Lil walks a little faster. So does he. She casts her eyes around for an ally. People laugh around them, and all her neighbors are here, everyone, and finally, there's Cesar, flirting with the apple seller. She's so close, she just needs to *get there*.

Fingers ghost at her elbow. She rips away and around to face him. "Don't touch me."

Theon's face is tortured, beseeching, as if she's the plague here. He grabs again. She catches her fingers in his stupid suit jacket, and the scent of burned wood fills her mouth as she shoves him back a few stumbled steps.

Lil channels every ounce of anger and disdain into her voice, her only weapons. "Leave me alone, or next time, Theon, I swear—"

"I can't!" Theon shouts. "You're the one doing this to me."

It stops her cold. Around them a couple breaks apart, circles them, and embraces on their other side. The crowd moves like a river around a stubborn rock.

"What," Lil breathes, "did you just say?"

Lips pursed, Theon pushes his hands up into his hair. There's a red streak on the side of his neck, like he's been scratching an itch. "You're the one doing this to me," he murmurs.

"I'm the one doing this to you?" she hisses.

"You and your—" Theon breaks off. Squints at her, confused.

"*I'm* the one *doing* this to *you*?" Lil rages forward and shoves him again.

Theon stumbles back, something like comprehension dawn-
ing on his face.

"I don't want you here. I don't ever want to see your face again.
I've never encouraged you. I've never even been polite to you. I
want you gone," Lil snarls.

Theon stares at her. "You don't *know*."

Lil can't. She turns, running for where Cesar stands. "Hey,"
she calls. "Hey, Cesar—"

The moment she reaches out to touch his arm—

He is gone.

Lil stumbles to a halt. Behind him, the firehouse, moments
ago blue and beautiful, is a charred ruin. The red door has fallen
in, lost under pine needles and trash. Dark green kudzu vines
twine up the broken columns, the fractured facade, an insidious
blanket over a long-dead corpse. The silence is deafening.

"What…?" she twists.

And it's back—carnival music and children singing and
vendors calling that there are still roasted nuts, more cider on the
way—

Just as suddenly, flicking of a cosmic light switch—

The festival vanishes. The town is gone. Leaves scatter the
pavement. Kudzu creeps along the streetlights. And one by one,
the library, the town hall, the bakery light up with flames. She
cannot breathe under the weight of Theon's eyes.

And then it's all back. Light. Sound. Color. Cinnamon sugar
in the air. Barbecue smoke. Lil staggers back down the steps,
away from the firehouse, away from Cesar. And a hand catches
her collar.

"You don't know what's here and what isn't anymore," Theon

murmurs in her ear. "It's confusing. Even gone things come back here. Fires burn one second. And then they don't."

His breath is too hot on her ear, the stench of blood in her nose. "You're so worried about Jason," he says. "But how do you know he's even gone? For all you know, he's here, and you just don't *see*."

Before her, the festival looks safe. But she's seen the rot. She can't blink, in case it flickers. In case everything she knows—

A sharp nail brushes against the back of her neck. "How long will you hold on, Lil?"

She twists out of his grasp, and for the first time since she's known him, been haunted by him, she *runs*.

CHAPTER TWENTY-TWO

DESPITE ALL THE FOLKS AT THE FESTIVAL IN TOWN, the road is quiet enough that Autumn can march straight down the highway's dashed yellow median without fear.

It'll be harder with Neel than with Wyn, she knows. The day they met, with Neel's shotgun between them, Autumn saw the shadow of the children she used to play with out there in the brush and broken-down cars west of town. They'd talk to her, pepper her with questions, even play tag—but the moment night fell or one of the nearby farmers drove by, they'd scatter into the trees. Eventually, with enough mistreatment, enough abandonment, a child stops looking at adults with hope. Neel has passed that point. But he loves Wyn. Surely, that's a thread Autumn can use to tug him back.

She had tucked Wyn in a blanket on the couch with her own worn stuffed tiger, Bastian. Her last sight of him was of a warm, cared-for child pulling on Bastian's whiskers and watching her. Those not-words of his tree talk, birdsong, and leaf rustle are so familiar it seems all it would take to catch their meaning is strain-ing a little harder. She's so close to understanding him.

With careful prodding, Wyn gave her enough to go on to find the little house. No way is she dragging him back into the kudzu-choked woods—not when it took this long to get him out of there. So she laced her boots and started the long walk down the highway. She'd made only one quick stop downstairs to tape a quickly-scribbled note on the door of the bakery.

Just in case someone comes looking.

A loud corner of her heart still cries that she should wait for Sasha rather than go alone. But Neel can't wait, and there's no telling when Sasha will be ready to see Autumn. But on the slim chance Sasha does want to see her, at least she'll know where Autumn's gone.

After getting caught in that mountain lion trap, Autumn stays out of the woods as long as she can. So she follows the road. She'll climb over the barricade of the construction work at its end. It's what Wyn says he's done before: crawled under the "orange branches." She's mulling over the potential routes when she becomes aware of the sound stalking her from behind.

Honk, honk, honk honk hooooonk, HONK, HOOOOONK…

Autumn starts. The silence is broken, a far-off morse-code blaring that, for a stuttering moment she thinks is the train.

She turns, and around the bend toward her flies a familiar rusty pickup. By the time she's in view, it's close, close enough to flinch—but it swerves to the roadside and rocks off onto the grass. Sasha takes her hand off the horn, relief clear even through the windshield. She jumps out of the cab and hurries over, hands in her pockets.

"Hey," she breathes, a puff of cold air visible between them. "You might've called. Or we need some radios or something. Dammit." She stomps her feet against the chill. She's visibly irritated. "Wasn't sure I'd find you."

"I'm glad you did," Autumn admits. She itches with the urge to throw her arms around Sasha and breathe in the scent of her hair. "I can't just leave Neel—"

Sasha is already nodding forcefully. "We'll go get him." She glances around at the road. "Can we take the truck to—wherever he is?"

"They're camping out somewhere past the construction zone," Autumn says.

"Great." Sasha looks worn, as well as annoyed. "Get in."

They drive.

Autumn has so much she wants to ask her. Has she processed anything Autumn told her; does she see Autumn differently now? Is she angry? Has everything changed? She drums her fingers on the armrest, and the road ends before either of them can think of anything else to say.

Sasha stops the truck, rummaging behind the seat for her camera. Once flooded, the highway here is now a chapped lip, parched and cracked.

Not long ago, Autumn drove up on the other side of this construction block. She stood just beyond it, and felt like the only person left in the world.

"What will we do about the, uhh—shotgun situation?" Sasha mutters, huffing slightly as they clamber over the orange barrier fences and skirt a mammoth earth mover.

"Wyn thinks they ran out of shells a few days ago." Meaning

he and Neel were alone in their house with no protection, no weapon against the hungry man or anything else in these woods.

They don't pass the obstruction to the wrecked bridge just beyond, but hook southward. There's a bit of a jump over a deep mud ravine where even this dirt road has been taken out, where the land has slid out toward the destruction and nearly washed it away. But beyond, on the road toward the tracks, the earth is firm. Once they're past the mudhole, Sasha turns and stares at the construction zone for a few moments. Cast in the harsh shadows of afternoon, the machinery sits there in dark, monumental repose. Sasha pockets her lens cap and takes a look through the aperture of the camera. Autumn hears the slow click of the shutter. Then Sasha slings the camera over her shoulder and follows her.

The dirt road is narrow, bounded by dense evergreens on one side and waving grasses on the other. Sasha is quiet. Eventually, when the road peters out, eaten by vegetation, they leave it and go into the dense brush. Autumn can only hope she's going the right way, that she isn't imagining the gaps in the bushes, the grass tamped down by little feet. They trudge through wheat-colored grasses, prickly bushes and burrs sticking to their jeans. The fields are opening up to the west, so flat she can almost see the curve of the earth. The gnarled and spindly pecan trees crouch low to the ground, like arthritic hands. It feels like this airless plain goes on forever. Every so often, there's a low *crack* as someone's heel comes down on a small bone.

But there, a few hundred yards away, leans a rotting shotgun house, gray and paintless, the small windows broken out, the door swinging. And Autumn comes to a stop. "I think...I think that's it. He said it was a gray house."

To call this corpse a house is almost dishonest, and they both stand there a little too long, breath taken by trying to escape the thickening kudzu snaking across the ground here. To imagine children living in this ruin, huddling together as winter came on—there is nothing to say.

Finally, Autumn picks her way nearer the wreck. "Neel?" she calls. "Are you in there?"

Silence.

"Look at that." Sasha gazes at a now-familiar bundle of twigs that sits on the path to the house. Three little skulls, maybe of field mice, watch them, bound with bits of grass and string to the small sculpture. A breeze stirs and Autumn is struck by a rancid smell coming from the thing, which seems to tremble, wavering before her eyes, flickering...

Because it's on fire.

"What's happening?" she breathes.

"There." Sasha nods to another protective altar on the sagging steps and then—another. Perched on a drooping windowsill. All flaming, their little offerings twitching in the fires they fed, exoskeletons collapsing, cobwebs billowing like toy boat sails. Sitting at the lowest hanging of the roof, a carefully formed pentacle of yellow grasses perches, charred and dancing. Children's best attempts at protection, up in flames.

In her bones, Autumn knows it can't be natural. The hungry man is hunting.

Neel.

Autumn dashes up the porch and pushes open the door, bile rising in her throat. Inside it's cold, somehow even colder than the air outside, a dank icebox odor. There is a hobbled table next to a camping stove; here is a nest of blankets; here are crayons in twenty-four colors and pictures pinned to splintery walls. It's home enough for more than two children—once, maybe not so long ago, there were more.

And all of these things, every stick of furniture, every relic of a home, are scorched. Great licks of soot shoot up the walls. The floorboards curl, nails melted. Even Autumn's first step inside creates an ominous trembling.

There's a loud blast from somewhere much closer than expected, and they both jump hard. The train. They must be very close to the tracks here.

At the sound, a lithe jackrabbit form springs away from them, tearing out the back. Neel is a blur of singed and dirty fabric.

"Neel!" Autumn bolts through the house, out the dangling door.

Behind her, Sasha swears as her foot goes through the rotten boards of the back porch. Autumn hears the clatter and snaps as Sasha pulls her foot free and jumps off the porch, landing with a crunch of bones. "Neel?" Sasha calls, and they run after the sound of crackling leaves. Neel is darting up a steep hill, toward a break in the trees; the train track that runs through the forest. *Stay away from the tracks*, Lou's voice echoes in her head. "Neee—*eel!*" Sasha tries again, her voice ripping raw right at the end. The air is dense and charcoal-scented. He's climbing up and away from them with a speed granted only by terror.

There's a hush of displaced air and Autumn looks back. The shack is burning again, fire raging inside with a heat that billows out to nip at their backs.

It shouldn't be a chase, but what else can they do? They scrabble after Neel, up the tree-lined incline, kicking up great clods of loose earth. Autumn hauls herself up with roots, up an incline no one's meant to climb. It resists her every step.

And coming from around the bend in the tracks, the train is barreling toward them. Ravenous, it eats up the land, sparks bursting under the wheels. Autumn is snared in the glare of headlights for a breathless, sharp second, in the sharp tang of metal in the air. She is seen.

Neel spots it and freezes at the crest of the hill, eyes round and full with animal panic. Where's Sasha; where's anyone to help them? Wyn waits in her home, with a tiger and all the trust he placed in her, and here she is in free fall. The train, her body, the boy are all held in a deadly balance.

"Come back," Autumn calls. "With me, with Wyn!"

He doesn't even seem to hear her, only the train that's surging closer, the sound hammering in their ears.

"I just want to help you," Autumn cries. "I'm like you. I'm one of you—"

And finally, Neel glares at her. "No one helps us! Nobody *ever* helps us!"

Neel climbs onto the tracks and glances at the oncoming train. Then, without another pause, he launches his body off into the dense greenery of the other side. Somewhere, Sasha is shouting a warning.

But now Autumn can hear nothing; everything is engulfed by the blare of the oncoming train. The kudzu is so dense up here that the earth might as well be made of it, miles of ropey vine strangling every tree and telephone wire in an endless green monoculture. Neel is struggling, running like his shoes keep catching in the vine. Autumn can see it snapping the air at his heels like whips. *Chuck Vickers*, she thinks, and her body surges with a new, vast panic.

"Neel!" Before Autumn can think, she's charging his way, straight at the tracks, straight at the train. "Neel, come back!"

She stops on the edge. The timber slats are warped, ready to catch her, trap her, break her ankles. *Don't get on the tracks.* But it's beyond, in wild enough land to be the edge of the world, where Neel, nobody's child, has slowed, dragging his body forward in captive jerks, the kudzu curling up his legs. He's wading through quicksand, and maybe he knows it now, because he turns, catching her eye, and opens his mouth to say something. She can't hear him, or anything, through the wind and squealing metal in her ears. The train bears down, rattling her teeth in her skull.

With a snap she feels but can't hear, another kudzu tether rockets from the ground to grab at his wrist. It pulls at him, hungry to heave him under. "Neel!" she sobs, and even she can't hear it.

She gauges the distance, the gap between her and the train, and leaps—

Her last view of Neel is of his gaping scream, vine looping around his neck in savage twists.

Because something has her too, a thick restraint, like steel, slips around her waist and hurls Autumn back from him, throwing her to the ground, catapulting her down the hill. Autumn screams into the brush, choking on leaves and debris, her body striking rocks and sticks and animal bones as she's tossed down, down.

The fall knocks the breath from her. It's very dark, tethers seizing her. She drags uselessly at the air, fighting what holds her, clawing at the kudzu that wants to bury her, bury all of them—

"It's me, Pip—it's me," Sasha yells at her. She's barely audible over the train crashing by above them. "You idiot. You fucking—idiot." It sounds like she's crying, too. "You threw yourself in front of that train." Autumn writhes, wrestling hair and leaves from her face, lungs still roaring for air. She's lost a shoe somewhere, her bare foot scuffing the cold ground. But as she catches her breath, her pounding, screaming heart seeks out Sasha. She focuses on her face. Sasha looks as wrecked as Autumn feels, battered from the fall and Autumn's blows.

"Sorry," Autumn gasps out. "I'm sorry, sorry."

Sasha is already dragging herself to her feet, listing drunkenly, ripping vines at random. "C'mon," she mouths, offering her hand. It's not easy to stand, but Autumn hauls herself up and they rescale the hill, getting as close to the passing train as they dare. Neel is just beyond.

"I can't see him," Autumn says.

"I know." Winded, Sasha holds her side. "It'll pass. We'll look." The train's sleek body seems to stretch on forever, running boundless on the track. An age goes by, and another. All the endless years of her life have passed in a blink compared to this. The never-ending hours at her dad's bedside. The train just goes gleefully on and on.

And, of course, when the railroad is finally quiet, the field beyond is empty.

Neel is gone.

CHAPTER TWENTY-THREE

S ASHA TELLS THE STORY AGAIN. TO HERSELF, IN HER head. About that road that closed, a long, long time ago. About a town, imprisoned in time. About a birthday party, and a girl who finally stood her up. And a boy, really a very little boy, running for his life down a lonely railroad into an endless swarm of green.

It is night. She is in the story's darkest hole.

Before: the long walk to the truck, the numb drive to Wyn at the bakery. Sasha waited outside, and Autumn was gone a long time as she spoke to him. When they appeared, Wyn had a tiger hanging from his small hand. Then they drove to the Clearwater orchard.

Lil is here, face scrubbed, eyes red. She gives Wyn a cinnamon roll and goes rummaging for clothes in the drawers upstairs.

They sit in the living room at the house. No one cries. It's too much—it is beyond tears. They are dumbstruck.

Several times, Lil says something to Sasha, asks a question about where something is, maybe, and waits an age, and then Sasha answers, a second too late, when Lil has already left the room.

Will the house catch fire around them? They know now that even phantom flames leave wounds.

Where the hell is *Jason*?

The kettle is wailing, but no one rises to take it off. Because Lil is listening to Autumn. Listless and silent, Wyn is tucked into Pip's side. She's saying it all again, the polished-stone version, learning from any stumbling, any confusion, in the midnight confession she gave to Sasha the night before. Now they all know.

Sasha stares into an empty hearth. She confirms nothing.

They'd been so close. She'd seen Autumn bracing herself, ready to risk her life to leap in front of a train.

Somebody has to remember this story.

℘

Later, Lil would always wonder if she should have known that day, that something was wrong. But she's gone over it time and time again and there wasn't a sign. No twist in the wind, no cold front, no vultures circling over the high branches. Instead, the air in the orchard tasted of summer's fresh blush. Sasha called that very day, telling her about her half-pint apartment in the East Village. Lil balanced the phone between her chin and shoulder as she stirred together peach preserves on the stove and tried not to sound wistful, or worse, bitter in her responses. She'd gone to the porch to call Mom in.

Only Mom didn't answer.

Call you back later, Lil sighed and went to ask how Mom wanted her eggs. She looked out over the orchard, but didn't spot the bright-red ribbon Mom sewed on the brim of her gardening hat. The truck was parked near the front gate because Mom liked to drive out at sunset and walk back. They fought about it all the time, how inconvenient it made Lil's morning shipping runs to Su's. The morning was pleasantly breezy. She went back inside to continue her tasks.

It wasn't unusual for them to miss each other while they both went about the business of the orchard, since there was so much to do. But when Mom didn't come up to the house for lunch either—that was odd. So Lil walked their property, calling for her, the seed of uncertainty blossoming into outright fear.

It was afternoon before Lil thought to check the pond.

"Mom. Oh god, Mom, get out of there. Mom. Mom!"

Mom was in the water up to her chest. Her head rested on the bank like a pillow, her face pointed to the shaded canopy overhead. Her hair wasn't even wet. They called it a drowning anyway.

Lil never told Sasha the whole of it. Rushing into the frigid water to drag her out. How heavy her body was. Mourning in the shade of that place. Pulling her as far as the edge of the orchard, as far as the sunlight before giving up. Lil remembered the rules. She didn't let anyone see the pond. She removed the cracked pieces of golden husk Mom still clutched in her hand and stuffed them in her pocket before calling the sheriff. Sheriff Connelly liked Lil and didn't ask many questions about the dirt on her hands and feet, the water dripping from her clothes. It was an irresponsible act of kindness. But what could she tell him? What could she tell Sasha? She didn't know why Mom ate a golden pecan. She didn't know why after so long, Mom had—

And, Lil didn't know why she hadn't *known* the instant Mom was gone. She hadn't felt the orchard become hers. It gave no coronation. Lil lived hours on that blissful, peach-scented day before she realized the life she knew was over.

ᔔ

The night Autumn and Wyn come to stay, Lil spends as much of herself as possible caring for them. She distracts herself by finding clothes for Wyn. By setting him and Autumn up in a guest room—Mom's old room, practically untouched. She busies herself laying out fresh towels in the bathroom. Gorges herself on the noise of their footsteps. But finally, there's nothing to be done, no more diversions for her mind to escape. The dishes sparkle, the spare blankets are in Autumn's arms, even Sasha has gone to bed, all done staring into the ether. The house falls quiet, and Lil can no longer stand it.

She feels bile rise in her throat. She spills herself into the velvet night, runs until she reaches her place of horror and comfort, grief and love, danger and deepest devotion. As always, the pond gleams for her in the blackness, the moon captured in its still bowl. Lil walks in up to her ankles, then her knees, then thighs, and stops.

The chill is bracing. It soothes her mind like a honey balm against a migraine. Today, it doesn't grasp at her and pull, but rests with her. Lets her draw from its strength.

She has woken up a dead woman. She has woken up a ghost. Or maybe she hasn't woken up at all; she is a memory. How many years have passed through her like smoke?

How is it that she never knows when her life ends until it's too late?

"I don't know what to do," she pleads to the water, to Mom—
to anything that might hear. "Please, I don't know…"

Tonight, she is wrecked enough that she might have let the
water swallow her. But tonight, it holds her up as she collects the
shambles of herself.

Lil retreats when her feet feel numb. She draws her legs up
and sits on the bank until she can breathe. She scoops a handful of water and spills it down her back; the burns left by the
Honeysuckle fire ease tenfold.

Dawn bleeds pink over the ground, and it's reasonable that the
others will soon rise. Lil stands and brushes herself off. While she
sat her vigil, a cluster of four golden pecans have hit the ground.
She considers them. And what to do.

When she gets to the house, Sasha is already up, sitting at the
table with the coffeepot beside her. The door to the basement
is ajar, and there's a light chemical odor in the air, like she's been
down in her photography darkroom. Several lenses are scattered
across the table. The sound of the screen door cracks the silence.

Lil clears her throat. "Hi."

"Hey." Sasha waves the coffeepot at her in greeting, pushing
the other chair out for her with her foot. "At least there's still
coffee here in the underworld."

Sasha pours her a cup. Footsteps creak overhead: Autumn or
the boy. Wyn.

Between them, Lil reaches out and puts two golden pecans on
the table. Sasha gazes at them, wordless.

"I've been thinking," Lil says quietly. "About when Mom died."
Sasha's eyes flick to hers.

"She ate one." Lil wraps her hands around her mug for something to hold, something warm and grounding. "Now I'm wondering if maybe she was trying to stop...something like this."

"Something like...a town trapped inside a camera?" Sasha holds up a fish-eye lens and peers into it. "All the bouncing light is captured inside. On film, it looks like one still image." She places the lens on the table again. "You think Mom might have guessed this was possible?"

Lil shrugs. "I always wondered if she knew more than she told me."

They ponder this for a moment. Sasha idly rolls one of the pecans beneath her fingertip, musing.

"We aren't the only ones who know. I think Theon does too." Lil braces herself. "Yesterday, I saw him at the festival. I didn't find Jason." Saying it is sinking a knife into her own stomach, knowing it will hurt. Accepting it. "But Theon really wanted to talk to me. And when I wouldn't..." She describes her strange vision of the town flickering in and out of ruin and wholeness. The ruthless kind of sense Autumn's story made. And Theon's strange place in her own personal nightmare. "Theon saw it. I think maybe he *did* it. I think..." She darts a look at Sasha in case she's off the rails. "Maybe he's doing all of this."

Sasha's pondering the lenses again, frowning. "Maybe."

"But we're safe here." Lil realizes it's true even as she says it. Hasn't she felt it, strong and proud in her body, every time Theon tried to approach a fence and she successfully pushed him back? The orchard has always felt like a sacred duty; that's how Mom saw it. A blessing. A burden. But a covenant that starts at a pond as deep as the world. Theon has tried for—by Autumn's telling—thirty years, and still, he can't step foot inside the Clearwater orchard.

"We're protected. As long as we're on this land, he can't get in. Not without our permission." Yes, she sees it now, the shape of his growing hunger, his frustration the longer she holds on. "It's why he's after me the way he is. He wants me to give in and I won't." Emboldened, she raises her eyes to Sasha. "*We* won't. Maybe he's literally buying time, trying to force us to give him what he wants." She feels the press of arctic water in her marrow, her own wellspring of strength. "Something he can't just take."

CHAPTER TWENTY-FOUR

BEFORE THEY SPEAK IN THE KITCHEN, WHILE LIL spends her morning in the orchard, Sasha retreats to the basement darkroom and holds negative after negative up to the light. At first, she studies each image, spends minutes on it, even uses the enlarger to focus them. But soon, she's only scanning, scanning, scanning. They all show her the same thing.

There's so much film down here. Baskets of it, drawers of it; tiny film canisters stuffed into bags, piled high in the wastebasket. Not a year's worth of film. A career's worth of film. No—not quite that. Not an artist's career. A lifetime of a distracted hobbyist snapping shots in between a hundred other odd jobs.

Twenty-nine years of on-the-side dreaming.

There's no project. There's no end date. These negatives are the scrabbling, desperate handholds of a life unmoored. Maybe that's why she's never developed any of them, not a single one. Just hoarded them under the house and scurried back upstairs into make-believe.

Sasha has her big cry down here in the darkroom, her goggles fogged as she mixes chemical baths: developer, stop, fixer. Mom and Lil gave her this space and gear in high school, as several Christmases and birthdays put together. It's not set up for color film, but Sasha developed lush, slightly overexposed black-and-white prints in here as a teenager.

She has no desire to develop most of this film. The shots are strange enough in ghostly negatives, in their neat little rows of silvery blurs and shadows. Images of muddled decades. Some canisters repeat others; how many times has she gone out to the Keller Orchard? By the looks of it, she's shot out there again and again. Her pictures look like long-exposure images where her subject just couldn't keep still. There's the old abandoned house, with missing rails and sloped, destroyed roof, half-consumed by kudzu—and softer, just beneath, there's the house when it was whole and full, the windows uncracked, the paint complete. From another strip: there's the Keller house on fire, silver licks of flame, white shimmer of char. Overlaid, the vines, pulling it down, quenching the blaze, suffocating it. Two stages of phantasmic decay. She blows this one up, blood turning to ice water. The top floor, just at the corner of the window, peeping out of a single frame, a blurred, impassive face. A child watches her from within the burning.

She and Lil have been sitting inside this decay (or this inferno?) just as placidly, it seems.

Sasha scrubs at her face, then grabs for her camera hanging on the basement's inner doorknob. Rewinding the film, she pops it out to take a look with the loupe.

Same, all the same, a monotony of apocalypse.

She pauses on one image.

Safelights on, lights off. Back in the enlarger. She fiddles with the f-stop.

Big multigrade paper. It's a slapdash job, her test print, but it more or less gets the idea. She's more careful the next time, watching from too close as her image appears in the developer, that comforting, acrid smell in her nose. Ten seconds in the stop, thirty in the fixer. That same old alchemy.

As it dries on her line, Sasha's chest loosens. It's a fixed photograph, free from duplicates or auras. The walk on train tracks, the horizon. And Autumn, in a velvety grayscale, looking back at her, sticking her tongue out.

Autumn.

Her eyes are amused, a little question in them, like, *How many more distracted lifetimes are you gonna waste, huh?*

Sasha flicks off the red light and jogs upstairs.

☙

Autumn's a little relieved when Sasha pulls her away from the house, out of breath and bright-eyed. She doesn't even question where they're going when they leave the orchard and the sense of sanctuary inside the fences. Sasha leads the way with a long stick, poking at the ground as they go for snakes, or traps in the mulchy debris. It doesn't take long for Autumn to figure out where Sasha is leading her. But she doesn't know why.

By any measure, on any fucked-up timeline, it's been a long time since anyone has been out here. The land in this direction is soggy, half swamp as they get closer to the grassy creek, the rainbow cypress knees jutting out from the low water. It's nearly sunset, the tree line crowned with a tangerine glow. Their despondent day is breathing its last gasp, and no one has noticed their absence.

The orchard house is away behind them, Lil and Wyn quietly at work on a five-hundred-piece Donald Duck puzzle Sasha found under the twin beds. Somewhere, too, the Pecan Festival is churning on without them, by the sound of it, a slightly discordant carnival tune jangling out over the woods. Cork is probably still loyally watching Autumn's stand for her.

Sasha stops at the sodden waterline of the creek, giving a hulking half-dead tree a critical once-over. Autumn pushes her hands in her pockets and follows her gaze.

"The rope ladder is busted up," Sasha says, frowning. "I'll have to give you a boost to the higher rungs..." Autumn only stares. She sees the shape of the pieces, how they must fit together, but she can't quite muster her courage to—"You game?" Sasha adds.

Autumn looks at Sasha, caught in her honeyed eyes, and back at the sloping ruin of their tree house overhead. Even sunset's light isn't doing this place many favors. The smell of mildew and cypress drags hard at Autumn's memory. She is eighteen again, her feelings unsullied by time and distance.

"Thank you, tall woman, on behalf of all shorter women," she says and steps up to the tree. "Go on."

Sasha cups her hands and hoists Autumn up to where the hairy ropes are still intact. She grapples her way up from there, on a ladder that trembles and bucks but doesn't give. She hoists herself onto that uneven platform and scoots back to give Sasha room. Autumn half expects to see a discarded brownie tin covered in leaves in the corner, or a crumpled can of TaB. Some ghost of the girls they'd been.

It certainly can't be safe up here. It was barely safe when Autumn first found it in the 1970s or when they were acting a fool up here in the '80s. The platform has soured, darkened with rot on the far end that jags out over the water. The safety railing has a big crack that never used to be there. But the tree itself is strong and accommodating, the branches growing around the tree house, forming a sturdy cradle for what's left of their refuge. Overhead, the canopy is resplendent, despite the many bald spots that have begun to show as leaves fall. The view is the same. Water wending away toward the river and copse of trees. Distant dots of houses on the ridge.

Autumn hears Sasha make the leap for the ladder; then she scrabbles into view. At the last second, there's an awful *snap!* as one side of the rope ladder gives way. Sasha seizes the fraying knot and swings up into the tree house, gasping. "Well, we live here now," she pants, giving Autumn a windswept grin.

"We're too old for this," Autumn jokes. She rests her back against the trunk of the tree, where it presses against her spine. What would it be like if she found some key to twist to send them back to simpler times? When they could laugh and tease and while away whole days as sweet as cake, when they could look at each other, flush, and blame the innocent cold. When she could relax, knowing that just a short walk down neighborly streets, she'd find Mom and Dad, shouting to each other across their little house about what to make for dinner. A part of her has been restless since they passed.

They sit in an idle silence for a while, catching their breath. The old composition is resumed. Now is when the deck of cards appears from a sleeve, or the gas station comic book, a portable radio, or the latest seventh-period gossip. Except Sasha is quiet, thumbs running over, under one another.

Autumn is aware of the warm balm of her eyes on her.

Crickets. A breeze turning chill.

"Autumn," Sasha says at last, after far too long, when the silence should be impenetrable and night is on the welcome mat. "I have to speak. I mean—I need to say something."

"Okay," Autumn says. Her voice sounds sudden and high-pitched. "Sure. Go on—" She's rambling. She stops, catches her breath. Waits.

Sasha seems caught off guard by the invitation, as if that was as much as she'd planned. She huffs out a breath and adjusts from one casual position to another.

"Look," she begins—but there's nothing to look at in the swiftly falling darkness. "I mean, didn't you see? Everyone else saw everything!" She's restless. "And now I'm thirty or almost sixty and having to figure out how to explain this thing that everyone knows and that I thought you didn't want and I had to just...get over." She swallows. "For a long time. You never noticed or—didn't care?"

Sasha swipes at her hair. "But now it's the end of the world, and I'm just sick to death of trying not to look like an idiot in front of you. I tried to preserve this friendship for too long." She sits up to glare at Autumn. Sasha straightening up in the tiny space is enough to bring them very close together. "We may live in hell, but the Pecan Ball is happening on the riverboat and I'd like you to go out with me." She pauses. "Romantically. On a date. A *lesbian* date." She pauses again. "With me."

Autumn's ears fail her. She can't hear anything beyond the stut-
ter of her own lungs. Sasha has spun sentences out of thin air that
change everything, a spoken-word riot of color and possibility.

But there's one thread that snags her, holds her fast. "I—I
cared," she stammers. "Oh god, I always cared. So much. You
don't know how I've thought about you, obsessed about you—
Sasha—" Autumn scrambles into her space. Her fingers want the
edge of her jaw, the soft curve of her neck, to be buried under her
hair. She doesn't know where to grasp so instead, she finds her
hands. "Yes, please. *Please, yes.*"

Last time, a lifetime ago, here in this same space, Sasha kissed
her. But she may have spent her share of courage, and whatever
is left should be saved, because outside of their tree house…their
world still has teeth. So Autumn inches closer, gives in to the
urge, and touches Sasha's face, tilts it toward her. This time, she
kisses Sasha.

It's a tentative touch, and for a moment, Sasha is stiff, tense
from grand declarations and nerves and exhaustion. But Autumn
gives her a chance to catch up, and Sasha warms, easing into
her. There's something familiar in this, but also new. They've
both lived a lot since that first on-purpose accident they crafted
together here during that last summer. How have they concocted
this second chance? Sasha winds around Autumn, tipping her
gently off balance so they're flush on the splintery tree house
platform.

They explore. It feels easy, dreamy, high. And then, with a
sudden roar of heat, *intense.* Breath catches in little stairstep
hitches. Hasty, impatient, Sasha shrugs free of her shirt, and
Autumn presses flush with her, her fingertips running hard down

her back. She catches the clasp of Sasha's bra to toss it up into the branches of the tree. Autumn's sweater is soft and heavy, and Sasha nuzzles the bare skin beneath it, making her gasp. They roll, and someone, one of them, *shrieks*, because they'd almost toppled from the tree but for a well-placed knee. There will be bruises. A lower lip drags over exposed flesh, sending tremors up two spines. Sasha's hand is buried in her own hair as she moans, and Autumn watches devilishly, hungry, urging them farther, faster. She has three decades of desire to spend, of experiences to share—because they waited too long already. Damp leaves prickle under her back, the tickle of pine needles. Sasha touching her. In the wake of that fluttery schoolgirl anxiety, there comes the steady slow burn, and the glow of safety, utter belonging, that Autumn remembers.

And the space is rough and damp, but no cold can touch them as they tangle together, with not even birds to overhear.

CHAPTER TWENTY-FIVE

L IL HASN'T SEEN SASHA LIKE THIS FOR A LONG TIME. Sasha is usually well-veiled, concealed beneath her humor, the casual drape of her facade. Now there's something irrepressible in her, a hope busting through her seams.

Autumn and Sasha returned from their walk together holding hands, declaring that they were going to the party—if Lil didn't mind babysitting, of course. Lil's idea of a good time is certainly not the festival's party on the riverboat, surrounded by people who don't know the frightening truth. But she empathizes a little with why they're happy to have found a spot of joy in their wasteland. Why they want to spend their frozen time with each other.

Yeah, of course, she says. *Take all night if you want. Just be safe.*

No one in town called today to ask where the Clearwater girls have been. No one's called at all.

Jason hasn't called.

The past days have left her burned, and she can't think of a single thing to do to fix it. Going to Honeysuckle House accomplished nothing. Going to town to look for help was even worse. Lil's fear, her anger, her grief, they're overwhelming her. But at least Sasha and Autumn can have one night to be happy. In order to make that happen, Lil would sacrifice much more than one evening to babysitting. Besides, Wyn is a pretty interesting child.

She catches Sasha in her room getting ready and leans in the doorway. Down the hall, Autumn and Wyn are in their room, Autumn's laugh bursting out here and there.

"That's a good color on you," she offers.

Sasha has delved into some of her clothes from New York, from those moldering boxes in her closet, that don't quite fit in in town. She's wearing a tailored suit in emerald velvet. The long jacket is slung over her arm as she stands in her shirtsleeves and stares out over the dark yard. She turns to give Lil a rueful smile. "I know this is kind of a strange time for this," she admits, drawing closer. Lil can follow the bow of her dark brown lip liner. There's a bolo tie at her throat, clasped with one of Mom's broaches—an amber tiger's eye. "But, you know, there's never really a good time, or much space for—for us." She sounds a little apologetic nonetheless. "You sure you'll be okay?"

"I'll be fine." Lil crosses the room, fiddling with the tie even though it's perfect. "This is a good thing." In another life, she and Jason would have been the queen and king of the Pecan Ball. She would have worn that slippery lavender dress and a spritz of her best perfume. Surrounded by lights and happy, tipsy people, she would have danced with him. They'd have been the last to leave, the Clearwaters and their dates. But that won't happen. Jason isn't here. She can't even voice the horrible idea that's begun to creep into her head, heavy the way only truth is, that maybe—no. She can't. "Seems like nothing here has been real. For a while. You deserve something real," she says instead.

Sasha steps in, wrapping her arms around her. They're two halves, together, a complete whole. "This is real," she promises, against Lil's ear. "Us. And the orchard. We'll figure this out. I swear."

Lil nods against her shoulder. There's the creak of footfalls in the hallway behind her.

They pull apart to see Autumn. With the help of a couple of safety pins at the bodice, Lil's old dress from junior homecoming fits her well: off-the-shoulders mauve satin with ruffled sleeves. It's distinctly out of time, but she's charming with her sneakers, a wide grin, and her eyes falling full and awed on Sasha.

"Hi," she says, without looking away from her. "Here to pick up my date."

Sasha skids across to her in sock feet, grinning all over. She leans in the doorway to say something to her, very quietly, but Lil hears it anyway: "You're kind of perfect, you know that?" Autumn tilts into Sasha's space like she's a gravitational center.

"Go on then," Lil says. "I've got Wyn. And everyone will be lining up for the boat by now."

"Thanks, seriously," Autumn says, sobering a little and glancing at Lil. "We'll try not to be out too late."

Sasha shrugs noncommittally. Her smile is a little roguish. "Well, time is fake, so…"

They go downstairs, where Wyn is stirring the Rice Krispie blob he and Lil have been putting together. He looks up at them for a moment, but he's busy with his project, which is best. He seems to do pretty well with tasks, little steps to focus on, to keep his mind calm.

Sasha takes the truck keys from the peg and steps outside, waving to Lil from the porch.

She watches the truck trundle down the dark rows of trees until they reach the fence and the turn off to the road. Lil flips the porch light on to illuminate their way back and returns to the house.

⁖

The night deepens, but Lil and Wyn are both too alert to sleep. He's kept night-owl hours his whole life, knowing the dangers that come out in the dark, so she hasn't the heart to send him to bed. Instead, they retreat to the kitchen, where they'll be able to see the moment the front door opens—maybe Autumn's return will allow him to drop his guard and rest. Lil teaches him to play Go Fish with their battered old deck, some novelty thing with oversized cards and colorful cartoon fish. Some are stained with indefinite substances, but Wyn stares at them with deep concentration.

"You have—um—do you have—seven," he asks.

Lil hands over her sevens. "You're getting good at this, kid."

He offers a small smile, just a slip of his gap teeth.

Her mind will drift to Sasha and Autumn if she doesn't distract herself. It takes her whole stubborn will to ignore the dark premonition that anyone who steps foot outside the Clearwater orchard will be gone like they never existed.

"Sixes," Lil calls. With that same tiny smile, he shakes his head. Lucky the kid knows how to count. Neel taught him, he'd explained and then gone very quiet.

Wyn knows the secret darkness she has been blind to. Lil

wishes she could ask about it. Something like: *Do you think people can just disappear here?*

Waking up alone in an ashy relic of a house has altered something in her. Some anxious piece of herself is unbound now, whispering warnings in her head. But any insight he could give her isn't worth how it would further terrorize him to relive it.

"Do you want more hot chocolate?" she offers instead. "I've got—"

Beyond her, beyond the house, beyond the trees, she feels the heavy tread of footsteps. She's always felt it on some level. When she'd wake in the night disturbed, or look out the window just before a car flashed past. When she'd feel eyes on her neck and turn to see *him* haunting her gate. Someone is approaching. That sensation heavy in her ribs is the oily press of an unwelcome presence at the boundaries of her land.

Lil stands and lays her cards as calmly as she can on the table. "Wyn, I'm going to step outside for a couple of minutes," she says. He stares up at her with narrowed eyes. He is not a tender child and is not fooled. "Stay here," she adds, a plea in it. "I'll be right back."

Lil steps into her boots and casts a look over her shoulder to make sure he's staying put. He's perched on the edge of the couch, watching her. "I'll be right back," she promises again and grabs the old fireplace poker she left by the door. Just in case.

Out in the night, the trees rage, a gust of leaves slapping against her as she strides down the road toward the gate. And standing outside the barrier, he waits, shrouded in shadow.

Lil refuses to be goaded into shouting. She keeps her pace, steady and unrelenting, and keeps her silence too.

Theon shows up in pieces: the white of his wrinkled shirt, the glint of eyes in the darkness, the sharp cut of his jaw. He isn't smiling this time. One hand stays in his pocket. On anyone else, it would look relaxed, but she sees the heart of him. He is never relaxed. He is a coyote sleeping with one eye open in tall grass, ready to break a deer's heel in his jaws.

She stops within arm's reach of the gate. Lets him look, taking in her expression, her weapon.

"You can't come in," Lil says with no small sense of satisfaction; the wind flares against her back. "You aren't welcome here."

His mouth twitches. "I just want to talk."

All of her instincts rear. She wants to rebuff him, bowl him over with her refusals if she can. But she won't. She knows better now. In a way, he must love the fight as much as she does. As Jason does. What else could be keeping him here? "So talk," Lil says.

Theon's expression softens. Maybe he's confused.

"Well?" Lil prompts. She forces herself to stay calm. In her mind, she is as cool and still as the pond in its peace.

"Every time I try, you leave." He watches her every breath.

"You've got permission. Talk. This is your only chance."

Theon is too still today, she realizes again, too still and too proud. He isn't standing in his usual lazy slouch. "You don't like me. But this isn't what you think. There's a lot I can explain to you."

When she doesn't respond, Theon leans forward, something like hope in his eyes. "I'm not what you think I am. When I came here, I knew this place, your place, was special. I thought...it doesn't matter what I thought would happen. But I changed." His face transforms, and flicker of passion and righteous—

Lil blinks.

For a single moment, she thought she saw—but no. Theon is

back to normal. He is himself again, the familiar face she's come to dread. But the whispered warning in the back of her mind is beginning to rise.

"I changed, Lil. Because of you." He grips the fence with both hands, eyes wide and pleading. "So many years, so many cycles of this, this same old story with you," Theon continues.

A flash: his dark hair changes. It burns blond.

"I've been everywhere. I could tell you everything—" His mouth is suddenly plush and loved. Then it is Theon's again. "I've never felt like this before."

Lil sees, even if she can't comprehend. But she can't deny it.

She's incapacitated with horror that is quickly congealing into grief. She can't even hear his words. They don't matter. Because Theon is changing. He is flickering like a burning-out light bulb. With each awful flicker, each impassioned word—there, hateful eyes turn to eyes that smolder in her dreams—he doesn't notice it. He doesn't know what he's showing her, clear and damning as a death knell.

"I can't explain it," Theon breathes. "It isn't even just the land anymore." And for a startled moment, his face changes, all at once in dreadful harmony. Lil holds her breath and forces herself to look, breathe in the sight that makes her want to rip out her own ribs. Counts. One. Two. Three.

"God, Lilith," Jason whispers, clutching the fence with one hand, reaching for her with the other. "I don't know how to make you understand the way I feel about you." The poker slips from her hands.

And from behind Lil, Wyn screams. Nothing but that could have jerked her away. He's followed her, his toothy mask bravely balanced on his head, but he's pale now, shaking all over. Lil whirls to him.

"Hey," she breathes. "Hey, it's okay." She catches him in her arms.

"It's"—his breath is hummingbird fast—"him. It's. Him. The hungry man."

Their boogeyman. The thing that stalks children in the night. Lil whips back to the specter at her gate, putting Wyn behind her. He holds tight onto her hand. The intruder is Theon again, the moment over, and he glares at the boy in her arms.

"Don't listen to that mutt," he snaps, petulant. "Send him away."

"Tell me one thing," she demands. The face looks wrong on him now. Elongated, ill fitting. Like there's something under the skin he wears. "Was Jason ever here? Or was he always *you*?"

Theon blanches, utterly caught out. "I—" He can't deny it. "Look," he says, almost desperate. "The two of you kept cycling through the same old story. The same empty year. The same harvest. The same people leaving. You don't even know you're the only ones left here. Everyone else is gone, Lil, there's no one left but us. Let me in."

Shock electrifies her. Everyone? It can't be…

But how many times had she stopped in town to find no one there? How many times has she felt like she and Sasha were all that existed?

"Can you even remember this town's name? The state you're in? What's the name of the river? You don't even know, do you? It's all eroding. You're ghosts living in a ghost town, living the same year over and over again for thirty years," Theon says.

Lil picks Wyn up and holds him as fragments of Theon's whole insidious speech find her. They burrow under her skin like poisoned needles, a stain she may never be free of.

"And Jason? Coming for the funeral? Staying in town for you? Bringing up the Pecan Festival? That isn't what happened. Is it?"

Suddenly, blood pulses in her ears. She sees Jason, standing on the tired porch of Honeysuckle House. *"I'm sorry, Lil. The Pecan Festival is a great idea. You have so many great ideas."*

Of course. The banners in his attic. *She'd* shown *him*, the first time. It was her idea, her appeal to Jason. To get him to stay. And he'd said—he'd said—

"But I can't stay. This isn't my home anymore."

"Jason hasn't been here for thirty years. He's been a ghost," Theon snaps. "Until…this time, he became me."

Jason hugging her one last time. Her steely anger. *"Don't come back this time, if you don't intend to stay,"* she'd said, only she hadn't meant it, and by his sad smile, even Jason knew it. His car, vanishing down the horizon. She's been trying to bring him back and find a way to make him want to stay ever since.

It was the last nail in the coffin. The morning after their thirtieth birthday, she'd seen it, hadn't she? The sign on the Finch orchard, red letters on the white and blue Realtor's sign. SOLD.

One of the last great houses, gone. To *Theon*.

"I'll never leave," she'd promised the trees, the water, the earth, the house that night. *"Even if everyone else leaves, I'll stay."*

"We've been caught in this cycle so long, I thought I'd change it up. Try getting you to let me in as him, rather than me," Theon murmurs. "This time, when I met his echo at the funeral, I had the idea. To become him. I slipped into his skin, bit by bit. I showed you the fires from the hill. And it was different. You and I felt something. It was us. Let me *in*—"

She wants to vomit. It wasn't Jason with her that night at Honeysuckle House. It had been a lie, Theon wearing his skin and she'd—believed. Heart, body, and soul, she'd believed. He made her trust him. "You sicken me," she breathes.

Theon hunches like a kicked dog. But he isn't. He *isn't*. He is a monster. She sees it now, the strangeness of him, the feeling of him, like he is rage and hunger barely contained in a paper shell.

"I loved Jason," she spits, with all the hatred burning her up inside. "I will never love you."

Raw hurt shines in his eyes. Almost like tears. He looks lost with it.

Lil takes a breath and locks her knees, because if she doesn't, she might crumple. "No matter how many times you come back or how you trick us, what form you take, Sasha and I will drive you out. Every time." She tucks Wyn's face into her shoulder and stares their monster down. "I don't want you, you—you *thing*."

Theon's struck dumb one moment. And the next, fury morphs over his face. Without a sound, he disappears.

In the silence, Lil could weep. She can't. There's someone who needs her more, shuddering against her collar. Wyn is too young for this.

She shifts him in her arms enough to check on him and wipe a few tears from his eyes. "It's okay," she says, over and over again. "It's okay. It's okay…"

But it isn't. She's never seen Theon angry like that. He's always played human before, but never made such a vulnerable play. Now she's coldly aware that all bets are off.

And she doesn't even know what he is.

Sasha has the truck. But the Smiths next door have a tractor. And they never lock their barn.

"We need to go get Autumn and Sasha," she says, putting Wyn down. "Can you be brave with me? A little longer?"

After a moment, he lowers the mask over his face. It glowers up at her. She takes his hand and they start running.

CHAPTER TWENTY-SIX

WHEN THE WORLD IS YOUNG, HE CRAWLS OUT OF the hot mud on his belly. He has been spit from the slavering, volcanic maw of the earth, and the starshine above him aches. And he is hungry, so hungry his insides eat themselves.

He limps his way in darkness to the gleam-flicker of fire—warmth that burns against whisker and fang. It is not fire which draws him, but the other warmth. The warm red river-pulse inside the figures who have built the flame. Whining, he comes on his belly for help. But they kick, bellow loud from their chests and he flees—quick to hide, or they club at his tender places. He is young too, like the world. Easy to hurt.

But he cannot stay away. He licks his own blood, chews his own limb and tail and bone, and it does not sate him; he is so hungry *he is so hungry he is so hungry*—

So he learns. When they sleep, he sneaks back. He wears a new form, a facsimile of what the fire-builders are. It is all shadow, too long of back, too sharp of fang, legs that do not bend as they should. But it is strong. *He* is strong. Hunger snarls in his belly as he steals one away, gathers one of them up in his new arms and tosses it over unwieldy shoulders—and he runs on false legs.

In the darkness, he and his first prey discover that the throb of fresh heart in his throat soothes him. As does the scream. As does the fear. Because as he learns under his first moon, the hunger of his body is small compared to the empty need of his being, the hunger of himself. He eats and eats and is empty, so empty, like the mouth of the earth he crawled from.

ℭℐ

He lingers, follows the people as they squirm across the dirt of the young world. He steals from their beds and their tables, eats in the darkness, revels in his growing strength. Until one day they rise as one and attack. They corner him in the dark cave where he has made his first home and strike his tender places. It is a shock, pain and blood and fear—his attackers leave him for dead and flee. He lingers. But then he heals. And eventually, he follows, weak as he is, pitiful creature he has been reduced to. He has nowhere else to go, no company in this world but the people. He will have to be more careful. He fears their clubs and kicks.

And so he learns new forms. He can be a rustle of wind in trees, he can be deer with antlers built high, he can be ravenous gleam-flicker-*flame*. But the nuances of their own shape still elude him; he struggles to speak their throat-sounds. So he does not fit in. If he comes near as one of them, he is caught out and chased.

They know he haunts them. They give him a name. Though they spit it like a curse, it is nice to be known. They try to ward him off with blood on their doors. He does not realize it is meant to deter when he first laps it up with hungry tongue. Initially, he takes it for an invitation.

When they move on, frightened by the babies torn from their beds, by the graves dug up, by the abandoned camps consumed by fire, he follows. He is growing strong again. And he has come to like the taste of their scraps.

∾

As eons pass, he becomes new forms. The human form, once such a mystery, with practice, becomes a convenience. He is man, he is woman, he is running water eating shoreline, he is howling wolf pack, he is screaming train, eating and eating of the land. He is a thousand hungers. He is consumption itself. He remains fond of his first ones: the begging coyote, the shadow with antlers, the ever-starving flame.

He gives himself a name, to talk to them. He makes it up himself. Theon. If he asks nicely, humans give him his meals now. He finds the lonely and lost places, comes to them at their death, and eats what's left. Theon loves what humans do to the earth. He loves the way their hunger leaves the earth scorched and ravaged until it cannot sustain them and they have to leave. And it is all his.

Until one day, he comes to this town. And at its heart, a pond. A tree. Theon has never smelled anything like it. He doesn't know what it is. But he knows it's old. It's eternal and bottomless like him. Finally, a meal that matches his hunger. And he is ravenous for it. He knows that the pond and its tree are meant for him. It's the first time he's ever been close to something that will fill him. He wants, so much, to be sated.

But he has barely approached the woman who guards it, barely asked to buy—there are more elegant ways to eat now than scrounging at a firepit—before she chases him away. Here is a place he cannot gnaw to the bone because of two sisters sustaining it. There is the old magic, the pond and tree that grow strong at the heart. He cannot get it. It has been long since he has been denied like this, but it will only make the eating sweeter.

Fine. A long game. He has the language now to play games as men do. And while he waits for the pond, the land feeds him. It gives orchards, fallow lands. And children. Tenderest of all, this land is peopled with plenty of abandoned, forgotten children. They remind him of his first taste of blood. They grow of the trees, so humans don't care for them either. There are so few creatures like him anymore who grow in strange ways. The kinship he feels with them is more proof that this place was made for him. They are fun to hunt. He wastes happy years tracking them down, one by one, easy pickings as he waits for his feast. He is content to stay. He is so hungry.

He is train, he is fire, he is eminent domain. He is suffocating miles of kudzu growing over trees and grass, greedy for sunlight. And so he *eats everything the town has to offer.*

Until one day, he is locked out of the orchard entirely and cannot step foot on the land.

It must be the fault of the sisters. Theon stands at the edges of the fence, screams, salivates, and burns—but he has been pushed out. It is unthinkable.

For ages, he runs the edges of the barrier on coyote feet, he claws at the firm husk that keeps him out when he wants *in*. Full of rage, he burns houses and buildings, and blankets himself over them as living green. He eats at the town because they won't let him in the orchard. For years and years, they hold fast.

Until he feels a new pull. Eager, ravenous, he follows it. It's a pull from inside the husk. A longing from the very woman who has denied him, time and time again. For she, herself, craves. He feels it under her skin, awash in her pulse, in the shine of her eyes. She is tired of grief and loneliness. Theon is not welcome. But Jason is longed for.

But he missteps.

He only means to taste Jason's form. Jason is a creature who burns too. Theon pulls him over himself like a mantle, little by little. He learns his ways. Jason is welcome in the orchard, he sees. He wants that.

But when he wears this skin, Theon forgets *himself*. He is ancient, and she is just a woman—but no one has *wanted* him in any form before.

And he answers her desire.

He answers again, yes and yes, and yes.

He carries Jason's memories, has picked over them like carrion, has sucked in his love and lust until Theon knows Lil as Jason did. And he forgets that he is not Jason. At their first touch, Honeysuckle House burns around them. It's the first fire he didn't intend to set since the form of flames was new to him. Around them it burns with abandon and he is helpless. He too is burning inside.

Waking before her, there is nothing he can do but run. Theon only wanted to drink from the unending well of the pond. And yet, Jason didn't look to the pond, the land, the scraps for his satiation; he found it in Lil.

Could Theon?

Is this love?

But Lil will not let him in again, nor will she accept him now that she knows the game. She will not let him have the pond, the tree, herself. Humans always bellow and club his tender places. He was a fool to expect different of her.

Yet he knows her tender places now too. He knows what will make her relent. The other sister is on open water, out of their sanctuary. And Lil won't hold so firm a line alone. Eventually, even she will be lonely.

He is so hungry.

But not for much longer.

CHAPTER TWENTY-SEVEN

ASHA NEVER GOT AROUND TO PREPARING THE STEAM-boat for the Pecan Ball, but it sits on the river like a paper lantern. A warm golden glow emanates from the deck lights, framing the guests with soft auras. She parks in the grassy field that acts as an overflow lot. They can hear a jazz band tuning up on deck as they wait to board.

Autumn is close beside her, and there's another thrill low in her stomach that she's actually managed to *speak* finally. Standing there in line, she wishes fervently that they could just be alone, actually, with none of their neighbors around to fog the clear window of this joy. She glances over at Autumn.

By and large, she's unchanged: her swept-up hair is a little messy, she has that same impish grin, the same unladylike mannerisms. She's still Sasha's Pip, who wakes her up by pouncing on her bed and tickling her, and borrows Sasha's hands for thumbprint cookies. Only now, Sasha knows what Autumn feels like, skin to bare skin. What she looks like with nothing between them but moonlight. She knows what it's like to kiss her, slow, lazy, and sated while water hushes by underneath their tree house.

"Guess I'm not on duty tonight," Sasha notices, nodding at Tim, one of the jolly shipmates who runs the ferry when she isn't there, behind the wheel. He looks excited, and she doesn't blame him; they don't get this boat out of its covered storage space often. It gleams with an improbable luster tonight.

She people watches. It's fun to see the town, usually behind counters or sweeping up shops, bedecked in their (somewhat humble) finery. There's Su and her string bean of a husband, talking to the high school vice principal, little glasses of cordial in their hands. Freddie, their town librarian, adjusts his bow tie in the reflection of a brass pole. It looks like Pop has brought his daughter for a date, and she wears a corsage of burnt-orange mums.

There are some faces missing, of course. Somehow, death and loss can still reach them here in the snow globe. Russ. Jason. These are jarring absences, but no one else seems at all aware of anything off. She casts an eye for Lou, but Autumn slips her arm into Sasha's elbow, and she is distracted.

"Ooh, puff pastries," she says. "You tackle the caterer, I grab the whole tray?"

Sasha laughs. "I think—" But the steamboat's whistle interrupts her. Beneath them, the boat rumbles. They're some of the last aboard. The steamboat is getting underway. They chug out onto the dark water, the same misty currents Sasha has traversed so many times before. Quietly, she urges the shorelines to hold them snugly, and allow nothing, no bad winds, no thunder, to puncture the evening for her.

First, they do a tour of all the hors d'oeuvres floating around the deck, and each receives a full critical review. Almost always, Autumn has made a more delicious version of each delicacy, or has ideas about how she might. Sasha snickers, jabbing several smoked oyster canapes into Pip's mouth.

They drift over to the bar for glasses of spiced cider. Sasha leans against the rails, gazing out at the rush of the river. The band is in full ecstasies on the upper deck. Back toward the town, and up on the ridge, twinkle bright, flickering stars. More phantom fires. "No one knows," Sasha murmurs. "No one knows but us."

"Yeah." Autumn leans the other way, facing the people making a go of dancing under the string lights. Autumn tilts enough that her hand finds Sasha's shoulder. "Is it bad that I'm happy?" she hedges. The turn of her neck makes it hard to meet her eyes, hard to see anything but the shine of her hair, and the butterfly clip keeping strands out of her face. "I'm kind of used to being—left behind," she grits out. "I'm okay. Mostly. I've had a really good life. Mostly. But it's hard to see people change. So finding you of all people again…even as messed up as all this is…" She swallows. "I'm just glad you're here."

They're brave words, a confession that seizes Sasha by the heart. She dips her head, lips brushing Autumn's, pulling her in to crowd Sasha into the banister. Pip smells of fall. "I guess I know what I've been waiting all this time for," she says against Pip's mouth.

Autumn's breath catches lightly, and Sasha's hand tightens against her hip in response.

"I'm actually kind of starstruck by you in a suit. So if I say something dumb, you better forgive me," Autumn murmurs, tracing the lapel of her blazer.

Sasha snickers. "Say some more dumb things, please."

The song ends upstairs, to a crackle of applause. "Dance with me?" Pip asks.

"I—yeah." It feels like she's lit from within by a warm lamp. Sasha twines their fingers together, and they trail up the stairs into the middle of the ball. They have barely an instant to take in the scene, the crowd of bodies, the color, the static press of the party, before the band fires up again and Sasha pulls her in. The trumpet player launches into an acrobatic solo, and Sasha does her best impression of a lindy hop. From somewhere close, cider flies into the air in a fragrant, boozy spray. They cling to each other, cracking up, as what feels like every person they've known their entire lives dances like it's their last night on earth.

Once they're out on the floor, Sasha doesn't want to stop. Not because she loves dancing—actually, she's spent most of her life in an introverted hunch, just off-screen, her camera as good as a mask for protecting her from unwanted eyes—but because the rhythm draws a heady flush into Autumn's face, and Sasha wants to watch her forever. They mostly act like fools, laughing and bowled over with the flavor of it, sides aching, everything raw and sharp and so fucking beautiful.

And then the band slows, centering the sax, and couples find each other. They're hot and panting, still giddy. Suddenly, Sasha feels slightly shy. It isn't effortless, to do this here, where they know everyone and even that, maybe *especially* that, doesn't make it safe. Sasha opens her arms anyway, and Autumn melts into them, and they sway.

There can be happiness here, she thinks. People can watch if they want. Let them see this. Let them see them like this, happy.

The dance is slow, and no one leads. They find every way to be close to each other.

It's when her eyes are closed, her cheek pressed against the top of Autumn's head, that Sasha feels it. Maybe it's air currents, an icy wind moving through the labyrinth of bodies, like the erratic drafts in the winding hallways of an old house. Or, no, it's not air—the feeling is more visual, a rapid blink of shadows over her eyelids, like sun shooting between the limbs of trees on a long car trip. Except it's not quite that either.

Sasha opens her eyes. The song's time signature skips into a frenzied three-four, and she sees it—and finally, she understands.

"Pip," she says quietly. "They aren't—look at them."

Autumn stirs. It takes her a minute to see it too.

The dancers, their neighbors, drift in and out of focus under the boat lights. They look like a tape, a fuzzy TV-to-video recording unwinding into someone's VCR. And noticing it—Sasha gasps. Noticing has made it worse. Now they flicker, one instant a crowd dense and laughing, the next, the boat is empty. It's deserted, adrift in blackest midnight, far from shore. They're alone.

They're all alone here.

"What—" Autumn begins. There's a shattering of glass.

The tape breaks. The lights are cut, the people gone. Somewhere far below them, a low *boom* quakes the deck.

And that's when the fire starts.

༆

The boom from the bowels of the boat vibrates through Sasha's body.

She clutches Autumn. Cork, who'd been two-stepping in the corner, is gone. Gladys, who brought pictures of her son's new baby, is gone. The jazz band is gone, leaving empty microphone stands, covered in a veil of cobwebs. There's no one else; it feels like there's no one left anywhere in the world.

"What was that?" Autumn asks. The shore is so far away. The water has lost its romance. Now it's a serpent undulating beneath them as the riverboat lurches hard to one side and begins to turn its nose in the direction of the far bank. Some great mechanism beneath them coughs, sputters. Falls silent.

In the new quiet comes the sound of approaching footsteps.

How—Sasha squints, trying to assure herself that her eyes aren't, once again, deceiving her. But every part of this place tries to deceive her now. She can't trust any of this to be real anymore. They're in a double-exposed photograph, image and afterimage in a blur. They can't deal in realities now; all they can do is face whatever comes, be it fact or folklore.

Jason saunters toward them on bare feet, even as the riverboat gives another ominous shudder. In his hand is a tray of three champagne flutes. "Sorry I'm late," he says.

How is he here?

"Where have you been?" Sasha asks. A low-grade panic is rising in her body. "Lil's been looking for you."

Jason offers them the champagne. "Just saw her, actually. She"—his breath hitches—"isn't coming tonight. Just us."

"We shouldn't be here either." Sasha speaks slowly, deliberately, like he won't understand. The disconnect between them feels vast. "Something's wrong with the boat. We need to—"

"A toast," he cuts over her. "To the good people of this

town. To their waste." He takes one of the glasses and salutes Sasha.

Sasha listens to the crack and groan of the boat. "We have to check on the boiler," she insists. "We're not safe—" She starts over toward the stairway that leads to the lower decks.

Jason steps in front of her with a wide, empty smile and pushes the tray of champagne against her stomach. "It's rude to leave when someone's talking."

Cold rushes through Sasha's body. There's something off in his voice, in the quivering lines of his frame. He is loose and bony, dislocated, his clothes hanging off him like he's nothing but rags. His golden hair is singed and straw-like. The town's perfect son is reduced, a scarecrow dummy dragging itself across the deck.

"What's wrong with him?" Autumn asks behind them. "What's wrong with you, Jason?"

His head snaps back, his gaze fixing on her. The lost expression on his face sharpens. "I got all the rest of you," he confides, grinning at her. "You saw. You know."

Autumn shudders in sickened alarm. "What are you talking about?"

Jason taps his champagne glass against another on the tray. Below them, the boat rumbles; the golden liquid shivers in its slender flutes. "Right, my toast. To you, Sasha," he bites out, a bitter edge to his voice. "To the forgotten sister. Should have been left to the spirits, but they'll claim you now."

Her mind feels sluggish as she grasps desperately at what Jason is saying. It echoes, reminds her of an earlier conversation out on this river, one that could've happened yesterday or decades ago… one to keep, one to give away.

"That's not Jason," she murmurs, taking a step back. "It's—"
but how?

Fury morphs over that familiar face, twisting it into new
shapes. "I am," the thing wearing Jason snarls. Theon under a
mask snarls. "I'm as much him as anyone ever was."

"What the hell," Autumn gasps.

Theon moves too fast, the glasses from the tray shattering
against the deck. He has Autumn by the throat, bending her
back as he chokes her into the railing. "I need—i need i need
ineedineedineed…"

Autumn claws at his hand, her face a rictus of shock.

"You're older than the others from the unwanted trees." His
wild eyes roll over her. "How will you taste?" Autumn's shock
morphs into rage.

"You're—the hungry man," she rasps. "Neel—"

"Last one left," he growls.

Sasha lunges, but the boat lurches under them, and she falls to
the deck, chin knocking on the hardwood.

Autumn is already fighting. She throws her knees up into his
ribs, wrestling with her whole body against his grip, and Theon
breaks out in hoarse, painful laughter. She wrenches, slamming both
her feet into one of his. Theon's laugh chokes off into a hiss. Again
and again, even as her eyes bloom with scarlet, she brings the weight
of her body down on him. He's nothing like Jason standing there,
his mask slipping away as he stares at her, snaps his teeth at her face.

Sasha searches clumsily, cutting her hands as she grapples for
a weapon among the shattered glass.

"They all struggled too," Theon snarls. Autumn's nails rip at
the flesh of his hand. And Sasha—her fingers find a substantial

shard of glass. She straightens just as the miserable, destroyed mass of Theon's foot seems to give and Autumn, with the last of her rage, tears herself out of his grip. She gasps for breath through painful coughs, and he takes a ponderous step back, seemingly fascinated by his own mangled foot, the remnants of her rage.

Sasha feels the glass slicing into her palm as she draws her arm back and drives it at this monster—

The shard slides over the emaciated cheekbone, curving with the eye socket, and Sasha runs it into him with her whole body, feeling the give and release of the eye all the way up her arm. Theon howls with agony as she pushes the glass straight through his eye, gouging as deep as she can. Blood and viscous matter flood from the wound, and Theon's animal pain fills the night, bouncing off the ridge and resounding over the river. Sasha can't form words, but she screams back at him, a territorial snarl from some long-silent misery in her chest, with every pain she's ever quietly borne. It's that feral sound that seems to send him stumbling out of his shock. He barrels backward, bloodied hand still clasped over his destroyed eye. Knocking first against the boat rail, he throws himself over it, down into the water below.

The boat shudders. Red light gleams on the water.

"Pip? Christ, I'm so sorry. You got him. He's gone." Sasha kneels beside Autumn, taking in the ugly red marks at her throat, the desperate whistle in her attempts to fill her lungs with air. Her gory weapon hits the deck just as the riverboat lists hard to the left and they nearly topple. "We have to move," she says, getting her arms around Autumn to haul her to her feet. "I think it's the boiler."

"I'm—okay," Autumn mouths, steadying herself. Sasha can't afford to double-check if she's telling the truth; in moments it'll be too late. They rush down into the darkness, into the ominous orange glow.

Oily smoke belches up into Sasha's eyes. She coughs. Reaching the stairs that retreat into the deep workings of the steamboat, Sasha takes a step toward the inferno.

"Don't," Autumn croaks, reeling her back. "We need to—steer? Or get on the lifeboats. Or something that isn't *going into fire.*"

There's a fire extinguisher a little ways down the stairwell, and Sasha pushes forward to it. She has blood on her suit, and fear can't touch her anymore. "Maybe I can fight it," she huffs, dragging the extinguisher off the wall. "If it's small, I can save the—"

The boiler, left unattended, bleeds out in putrid black gusts. There's much more smoke than actual flames. But it's sweltering down here, the walls radiating heat rabid enough to burn if they were to bump into them. Coughing, Sasha unleashes the extinguisher in the direction of the boiler, which is almost eclipsed in the smog. The extinguisher shushes loudly and the boiler hisses in response, a feral cat unwilling to be calmed. Sasha winces, advancing, her face lit by sparks and flecks of soot.

There's a momentary flush of hope, as if, maybe—

The steamboat gives a long, low groan, and the hull nearest the boiler buckles in toward them. Water busts in at a seam, and the world lurches hard, listing right this time. Gravity shifts, and they're nearly thrown into the fire. Autumn grabs onto the banister, wrenching Sasha upright with enough force that Sasha's feels her shoulder creak in its socket. "Run," she screams hoarsely at Sasha, water crashing in from every side. They plunge upward—what was once *up*—a miserable lunge toward a deck that is screeching down to the water. Autumn staggers up, hoists herself over the rail out over black writhing water.

Together, they leap, and together, they hit the icy churn of the river.

But, of course, once Sasha is caught in the flow, she is alone. Sucked deep in fast currents, everyone is alone.

This riverboat, this bend in the river, has always been her place, almost like the pond, it turns out, has always been Lil's. But water is a fickle friend. Sasha struggles when she should relax, fighting for the surface—she opens her eyes, and there he is, a dark stain like an oil spill seeping through the water around her. Caught only in the dwindling reflections of the fire above, she can make out that single eye. He rushes at her, a dash that feels like rage and panic, and Sasha is cast farther below. Her head collides with some mangled debris from the destruction above, and Sasha drifts into unknowing.

⌀

Autumn flails beneath the surface, buffeted by the current like a toy. The dark shape of the sinking wreck. It's too dark to find the way up. The languishing steamboat tugs at her, ripping at her ankles as she kicks back from it. Sasha's gone, their hands pulled apart by the furious current.

Autumn holds her breath, dreading the sucking grip of the riverbed. Through the water, some massive broken-off piece hits with a grounding shudder, bubbles escaping, rising past her nose—bubbles. Up. There's up. Autumn kicks off her sneakers and fights her way from the density of the water into the density of night.

Her head breaks the surface into harsh air and a riot of shouting. The land tilts at an angle—a wave rushes over her head. River currents, swift and dangerous. She kicks blindly toward the first bit of land she sees, and hopes it's the right way.

"—tumn! *Autumn!*"

There's the shore, the dock, looming ahead of her, but she can't go yet, not until she finds—

"Sasha!" Autumn screams, ripped from her sore throat. "Sasha!"

She can't find her in the darkness. A fear colder than the river grips her even as she stumbles onto the shore, mud sucking at her feet. The prow of the boat is sticking out above the surface, but it's sinking so fast. "*Sasha!*"

Warm hands find her shoulders and drag her back out of the water but she fights. She can't leave, she has to find Sasha.

Familiar dark eyes invade her vision. Lil, frantic and fierce, searches her gaze before whipping around and running up the bank, racing to get ahead of the current. She braces herself before charging into the water and stroking powerfully into the river of ink, toward the white-frothed mouth of the river where the boat is making its final descent. Smoke drowns the moon.

Autumn casts around the water for some help—

Someone stands on the bank. She can't see much, just a slight, masculine frame and a jagged shadow like antlers above his—

"Autumn!" Lil calls from downstream and Autumn whirls back. Lil's barely above water, battling the current to reach a sandbar. Because she's struggling with a limp weight around her shoulder. A body in a soaked emerald suit.

No.

Autumn stumbles down the bank, reaches the Clearwater twins where it's shoulders-deep and pulls half of Sasha's weight against her.

"She's okay, she'll be okay," Lil's babbling. "She's okay."

They lay her on the bank with a wet slap.

"She isn't moving," Autumn stammers.

"I know." Lil's voice is calm. She's all focus even while Autumn wants to crumple into a ball at Sasha's side. So she shores herself up.

Autumn tilts Sasha's head back while Lil brushes aside her blazer and starts compressions. Her mouth is a thin line. Water drips from her fringe. One. Two. Three. One. Two. Three.

Sasha's impossibly pale, and Autumn brushes her hands across her forehead, clears water from her eyes where it mats her lashes shut. A small figure appears at her elbow, a familiar mask over his face.

The silence feels very long, and a sob builds in Autumn's throat. And then—

Sasha splutters weakly, water from her lungs dousing her face. Immediately, she heaves herself over onto her stomach and coughs, coughs, coughs again.

Lil hunches over her, hands falling on her shoulders, clumsy, broken sobs erupting from her chest.

Autumn wants to kiss her everywhere, bleed warmth back into Sasha's skin, feel the assurance of her breath. She leans forward and rubs her back. Soothes her, calls to her gently.

Sasha's shoulders shake hard, and the hoarse coughs turns to a desperate gagging.

"She's choking," Autumn says uselessly.

Eyes wild, Lil slaps Sasha on the back.

With a full-body spasm, Sasha expels something into the mud. Blood, Autumn registers dimly. At first, it looks like *tonsils*—or teeth?

And then Lil rolls Sasha away, onto her back, where she lies still.

There in the mud, the mass of blood and phlegm seems to glitter. Something golden, like a ring or a coin. Lil is gaping at it, her face as white as her twin's. Entranced, Autumn picks it up, rolls it between her fingers.

It's a pecan. A golden pecan.

CHAPTER TWENTY-EIGHT

THIRTY YEARS OLD.

Thirty years ago.

Thirty (twenty-nine and some) years ago, the twins turn thirty. It's a small party (about twelve) in a large venue (the orchard). The affair is subdued. Sasha sulks continuously, drinking rainy punch until she's very day-drunk and then, because she's thirty now, very hungover. She's been home for a few weeks. It's a headache. Everything is a day-drunk headache.

Autumn isn't coming. She called to say so, days ago, but Sasha still stares at the gate, mood growing worse by the minute. Finally, she ditches that party, the grocery store chocolate cake, and her sister, who is trying really hard. She is frayed, too, heartbroken, too. Because Jason left for good, after he made all the arrangements that become necessary after a death. Jason left, and Russ is buried, and Honeysuckle House is quietly for sale. Sasha abandons their birthday and goes walking.

That's when she wanders too deep into the orchard, when it takes her places she hasn't been invited before. Maybe it's the land that decides. Maybe it is the last plea.

Sasha finds the pond, and Lil finds her, and for the first time, they fight a fight they'll have again and again and again.

They've been here before. Here are the highlights:

Sasha, soberer by the minute: *I should be surprised. I should be completely thrown by the fact that you would have hidden whatever this place is from me our entire lives. And Mom too. But of course I'm not. Of course you did this. And then you still resented me leaving! Who wouldn't leave?*

Lil, her eyes full of fear and righteousness: *Of all the parts of the orchard, Sasha, I swear…this is the one part I'm supposed to protect you from. There's only one, okay? Two of us, sure, but there's only one person who takes this task. I can't—I can't—I can't share it with you and be sure you're safe. But I was wrong. No one is safe. Not even me.*

Sasha learns the secret she was disinherited from by their mother. She hears, for the first time of many times, the riddle of the tree's offering, and the pond's hunger, and the Clearwater responsibility.

Lil: *Mom said that they're an offering. The tree is an arm the pond reaches out to us. They're a—gift.*

Sasha: *Or a trick?*

Lil: *She always said the gift was too great for anyone to bear.*

It's a conversation they'll repeat many, many times to each other, forgetting and remembering in endless cycles. Again and again, they try to save the town, telling the same story together like players to an empty auditorium.

But not the first time. The first time, they break everything.

There is no festival. It is a few days after their birthday, and Sasha still has the pecan she took. She holds it until it is warm, then forgets it in a pocket, and finds it again. Things get rapidly worse. No one has seen Lou, who is either locked in his shop or taking long walks in the fallow orchards alone. Dale's wife, Kitty, loses her leg to a trap she stumbled upon in the woods. Some bureaucrat from the city has looked over their bridge, the one bridge on the one road in or out, and found it unsafe.

Sasha goes out to the Keller Orchard, the house eaten through with vine where tiny animal bones crack underfoot. Later, she's in the kitchen, making an omelet. That's when Lil bursts in, eyes wild and enraged, storms past her to brace herself against the sink.

"He sold," she snaps out. "To *Theon*."

One of Sasha's eggs slips from the counter and cracks on the floor. Theon. That newcomer who seems to be everywhere these days, chatting up the people who are selling, buying dying farms, doing nothing with them but letting them rot. Sasha has been surveying for Dale and seen the evidence for herself.

"Jason sold to him," Lil repeats as if she still can't believe it. "That's the last one. The last of the major orchards besides us." She hunches her shoulders. "We're all that's left."

Sasha puts her spatula down. She leaves her *tortilla de huevos* to burn. She can see it all now. Their whole lives, the generations before, reduced to rubble. This land was once undesirable for farming besides pecan trees, but the corporations will find a way. Tear out the trees and level the ridge and fill this place with some cheap, soil-stripping crop. A monoculture. Fields of corn like marching soldiers. The kudzu will swallow the town whole.

What do you care? a part of her whispers. *This place doesn't want you. You are an exile. Let it all go, and never look back.*

Her body says no.

"What do we do?" Sasha murmurs, watching her sister's face closely.

Lil raises her head, and she's coldly determined. "I won't sell. I'll die first."

The house will dry to kindling and burn, or it'll fall into the ground. And maybe Sasha can escape, rip out her roots and go—but Lil never will. She'll haunt these rooms, tend scab on these trees, live food stamp to food stamp. She'll grow stooped and bitter and *lonely*, but she'll remain.

"It's our home." Lil's eyes return to the trees. The anchor that will drag her down. "Even if I wanted to sell, I think it'd kill me anyway."

How long will you hold on when your world is gone? Sasha wonders, but doesn't have to ask.

Forever, Lil will say. *Forever*.

It's seeing that future in the desolation on Lil's face that has Sasha reaching in her pocket for her last trick.

"What are you—" Alarmed, Lil swipes at it.

"Stop." Sasha holds it out of her reach, feeling the cool weight in her palm.

"That could kill you!" Lil eyes it again, poised like Sasha's holding a knife. "We don't know what they do. Mom didn't know and she…"

"I don't think it will." Sasha hasn't been privy to this secret for very long, but she's lived with enough of her own, trying to bear truths alone, long enough to put two and two together. "You just told me you'll die here anyway. And I just realized that I'm not leaving you here alone again. Ever."

The air crackles with summer lightning, the day sitting heavy around them. It's now or never.

"I think I understand the gift," Sasha says. She holds out the gilded treasure she stole from the pond.

It's too great for anyone to bear. Any one. One. Lil watches her, face tight with horror that melts into grim resignation. And just a hint of peace.

Mom did it alone.

We can do it together.

They break the husk between their palms and fish the golden pecan from inside the depths. It falls apart in two pieces in Sasha's hands.

In their kitchen, all they can hope for is more time. For protection as strong as the husk of a nut.

Lil takes her sublime fragment with hesitation. Her eyes tentative with wonder. *Are you sure? Are you* sure?

"It's you," Sasha says. "And me."

Together, they eat.

CHAPTER TWENTY-NINE

THE PECAN GLINTS IN AUTUMN'S HAND, AND LIL remembers everything. Sasha declaring that they would make their stand. Her own sour fear, Mom's whisper in her ear, *Maybe one day you'll eat one…maybe one day I will…*

And the taste of it, the best pecan she ever tried, crisp yet tender. A hint of honeyed delight. She hadn't felt the sacred boundaries closing around them, but Lil knows them now. She's felt them all along, in some small way. Every time Theon tried to step foot on Clearwater land, she'd felt it. How many times had Lil paced the fences, repairing and strengthening the heart of their territory? And how many times had Sasha unconsciously done the same, cruising in the riverboat along the outer boundaries of their little world? Driving into town to keep the lights on at the grocery, the library, the bakery?

All this time, they'd kept the candle burning in their home, enclosed inside. Preserved, sanctified, guarded.

One person could not maintain it alone. But two?

They've been cut off for so long, they forgot everything, even how they did it.

Sasha's breathing is ragged and rattling. Autumn draws her head onto her lap, brushing back her hair, murmuring to her, the golden pecan still cupped in her hand. Wyn hovers at her elbow.

"What does this mean?" Autumn asks without looking at Lil. Holding their bomb, Autumn is painstakingly real. A solid person jolted into the misty two-dimensional watercolor that Lil and Sasha painted.

"It means…Theon didn't do this to us. Sasha and I did it," Lil answers. "It's only been going on this long because of us."

Autumn catches her gaze, then looks down at Sasha's half of their bargain. "It's not just a pecan."

"No." Running through her body, an electric current blares a warning. Sasha's not awake to eat her pecan again. There is a crack in their foundation. Theon has never crossed the boundaries of the orchard, but that doesn't mean he can't now, not with Sasha brought to her knees, all of their facades falling away. He might be powerful enough to force it tonight. And angry enough, finally, to do it.

Lil pats Sasha down—thank goodness. The truck's keys are caught in a fold of her sodden pocket. She wrestles them free. "I need you to stay here."

"We need to get her back to the orchard," Autumn cuts in. "It's safe there, right? No one can—"

"It's not safe," Lil interjects. Sasha's eyelids are pale blue under the moonlight. Lil stops. Presses a hand to the side of her sister's neck. Reassures herself once again of her pulse, the living rush of blood under her skin before standing. "Stay here. Stay together."

"What? Why?" Autumn's eyes are narrow. She's cold too, bare shoulders still covered in drops of water.

"This is my fault." Lil turns from her. "But I'm going to fix it." The cool night air tastes like dry leaves and smoke. The hook attached to *him* is buried in her stomach, wanting to pull her back to him. She ignores her heart, lying unconscious on the ground. Her truck is parked down near the docks.

"Hey," Autumn calls, her voice turning sharp. "Wait!"

Lil walks away.

ᏋᎧ

Autumn watches Lil vanish into the darkness and turns back to Sasha.

Nearby, Wyn shivers, and she takes his hand. It's small but rough from survival, and strong, too. Stronger than a five-year-old hand should have to be.

"I don't know what to do." She's drenched. She could follow Lil in the ancient tractor she and Wyn seem to have driven here. Only she won't leave Sasha. Clearly, Lil knew this when she left. Autumn keeps holding the gory hunk of pecan. It seems like maybe Sasha needs it. The night is cold, lonely, but quiet now. She can do nothing but sit. Nothing but wait.

The town is totally dark, not a light on anywhere near them, and the sky is bright and complex above. Total silence buries them. On the ground, Sasha is restless, but doesn't wake. Autumn glances back at the tractor, considers how to get them onto it and back to her apartment. But before she can move, she hears something very close.

An old car drives slowly over the grass toward them, headlights blinding her. The driver cuts the engine and jumps out.

Autumn squints at the silhouette, disbelieving. The last ghost in a town out of time approaches. He's very close before she catches sight of his face. "Lou?" she breathes.

"Hi, honey," he says, his face grim as he takes in their little huddle. "I heard the shell crack. We better get inside."

"W-what?" she stammers. "Lou, you…" He *knows*. Autumn holds back a sob and lets him help her lift Sasha and carry her to the car, laying her out in the back seat. Wyn clambers in and sits by her legs, and Autumn collapses into the passenger seat.

Lou smiles, relief clearing the clouds from his face. "You found him after all. What about the other boy?"

At the mention of Neel, Wyn goes utterly still. Autumn lays her hand on the seat between them, an offer. Rather than taking it in his, he lays down, pushes his head into her palm.

Lou glances between them, with quiet, tired understanding. "Nice to meet you, kiddo," he offers instead.

Lou twists the dial to blast the heat as he makes the short drive to his junk shop. The town is empty now. Whatever power Lil and Sasha held, practically willing it to stay fresh and loved, is gone. The place is unmistakably a relic left to turn fallow. The buildings are faded with chipping paint and broken glass in empty windowpanes. A car with flat tires is absolutely buried in leaves and detritus. Lou slowly circles the square. The road is buckled and cracked, no one to keep up the care, and a stray dead power line sags to the ground, relieved of its burdens. Her bakery is different too. The awning is torn completely free, leaving black spokes behind, and the furniture she swore she left out just days ago, bright and shining red, is broken and gone to rust.

"How long have you known?" Autumn asks finally, to break the interminable silence.

"Oh, it took me a little while," he admits, as they pull up outside his shop. It's the only building that seems unchanged, its sign as fresh as it ever was, its toys and trinkets and dreams all in place. "We cycled four or five times before I caught on to it." They heave Sasha through the narrow shop, her trailing legs toppling treasures as they push through to the back room, where the trains whir in their orbits. Wyn helps, keeping one of Sasha's arms aloft. Lou busies himself, putting one of the many teakettles on to boil and gathering scratchy army blankets and a heap of old clothes from a half-blockaded closet.

They settle Sasha on a faded yellow love seat with a cigarette burn in the arm and what looks like cat scratches mucking up the leg.

It's only later, after Wyn is transfixed by viciously taking apart one of the model train cars, and Autumn has changed into a sweater and Razorback sweatpants, that she is strong enough to broach the subject again.

"You didn't say anything," she murmurs to Lou. She holds Sasha against her stomach, the blankets wrapped around them both. "All that time? How could you bear it?"

"I've been saying something for years! And doing my best with it." His eyes are fierce on hers. "I stayed for those kids out in the trees, because nobody else would lift a finger for them." He scatters crumbly biscuits on a place. "I would never had realized this town was a trap in the first place if I wasn't like them. Like you."

He turns to gaze at her, a little shyly, and nods at Wyn. "I remember when I found you out there, swaddled in the tree boughs. Just like that old lullaby…" He clears his throat and turns away again as the kettle begins to whine. "I came from those orchards myself. Long time ago. And I gave you to your mama and daddy, made sure you and lots of others had good families like I had." Of course. It's the only reason he wouldn't be pushed out or faded like everyone else; the same reason Autumn was pulled inside the husk. The trees know their children. They were born hardy, built to survive. Lou doesn't look it, but he must be *very* old, she calculates, more than a hundred years. Two hundred?

"Someone should have told me," she says. "I spent so long thinking I was wrong and not knowing why."

"You're right." He passes her a mug, his expression softening. "It just wasn't how we did things. People just never know what to say, do they?" Wyn shies away from the cookie Lou offers him, so Lou just lays it nearby. "The Clearwaters' protections are powerful. But they've got short memories. That's the trouble with most folks. You and I, our memories are long."

"What about the rest of us?" Autumn asks. "Where are they?"

"There never have been many. Used to be even fewer. It's always been easiest to leave, slip out into the world and become a stranger. Maybe they'll come back. They're out there somewhere. Like you were."

"But you want to stay when everyone is gone?" She wraps her hands around the mug, nearly cries at the warmth of the steam. "Why?" Sasha shifts restlessly against her.

Lou rubs at his face and folds into the chair across from her. He looks older, very tired. "Those kids are the closest thing you and I have to blood," he says simply. "That's what matters most to me. But for a long while, it was for Russ too."

Autumn stares at him, uncomprehending. "But Russ is dead."

"He's alive," Lou interjects. "At the beginning of each cycle. For a little while longer." He shakes his head, staring into his tea. His eyes are the color of warm bark. "I love him. And each time he goes, and we have the funeral, again and again, I swear it's the last time. That I'll quit it. Because it hurts so much. But...knowing I can see him again, for just that little while...I never have."

Autumn holds Sasha a little closer. Looking at her face, the tangle of her hair, a sharp, helpless need bowls her over. Can she blame him? "Is it over now?" Tears threaten at the edges of her vision.

Lou is thoughtful, watching Wyn gnaw savagely at the edge of his train car. "I'm not sure," he murmurs. "Their husk only cracked. But—I think that was the last time. I don't think that Russ will be back again." His voice is rough with tears. "Thank goodness."

Autumn feels Sasha jerk. She looks around, her heart pounding so hard Autumn feels it in her own body. "I—" Sasha's voice sizzles out immediately, like an awful case of laryngitis. "What happened?" Her eyes roam around the dim space, panicked. "Where's my sister?"

⚭

The orchard is quiet except for the crickets when Lil arrives and parks in the middle of the dark road. It isn't like there's anyone else here to inconvenience. Her neighbors have been shadows for a long time. She hops the gate and flips on the old searchlight propped over it, letting the glow bathe the old blessed trees, their mailbox, and their big wrought iron sign: CLEARWATER ORCHARD. She unlocks it from the inside and pushes the gate open a crack.

Amid gnats and mosquitoes vying for the attention of the light bulb, Lil waits. He'll be here. There's nowhere else to go.

In the back of her mind, she swirls like fog over the pond and the golden pecan tree that drops blessings and curses. She feels its calm chill in her body. Lil is its guardian. This is a duty only she can do.

Theon approaches from the tracks with a limping gait. He smells like smoke but not like Marlboro or Lucky Strikes. No, this smells like burning oil, like the blackened hull of a faithful riverboat, like ash on water. He is more ragged and less human than he's ever looked, his semblance of humanity cast aside to reveal a cold hint of other. Blood slicks from a hole where his eye used to be, soaking all the way down his shoulder. He stops at the open gate, face in a pained snarl, and grazes his knuckles along the curve of the C in CLEARWATER. She feels each bump of bone along her cheek and refuses to offer him the satisfaction of a shudder.

"You win," she says and pushes the gate open wide. "Come on in."

CHAPTER THIRTY

THEON AND LIL HOLD THEIR BREATH AS HE INCHES UP to the boundary line. His remaining, distrustful eye darts, searching for a trap. But the bait is too sweet. He lifts one foot and steps into the orchard. He moves in a lopsided limp, but his laugh is soft and amazed. He can't believe it either.

Theon touches a tree, then another with a child's stunned glee, smearing blood on the bark. But he composes himself just enough to meet her on the edge of the light spilling on the grass, the line where they both stand.

"Hello, Lilith Clearwater," he breathes. Blood drips down the side of his face, catches in the corner of his mouth. The thick scent of it coats the back of her tongue.

"What happened to you?" she can't help but ask.

He winces, teeth flashing white in the moon. "Your sister bit back. But it won't last."

There had been blood on Sasha's cuffs. Pride riots inside her.

"I'll be fine by morning." He doesn't wear the mutilation with the horror a human would feel, losing an eye; he isn't fussed about the blood, or even bothering to stem its flow—he isn't driven by the same instincts that would have clamped onto an actual person. But he is in pain, distracted and disheveled by it. He's weakened. The realization is a glimmer of light. "Are you worried?" He reaches out, hand deceptively tender, to touch her face.

Lil steps back, out of reach, but only just. "Wait. Not yet."

Frustration flares in his eyes. He drops his hand back to his side.

"I want to know a few things," she continues. Behind her, the house and the trees hold very still. "What brought you here?"

He looks surprised and then a little flattered to be asked. He stuffs his hands in his pockets, considering his answer. His shadow stretches longer than hers, flickers here and there. For an instant, she sees not the head of a man, but the maw of a coyote grinning at her from the ground. "This town was wasting away before I got here. That's my kind of thing. But there's power here. I felt the pond. It called me. And that? Captivated me, like a light on a hill." His breath comes quicker. Hungrier. "It led me to you."

"The Pecan Festival? You were just messing with me?"

"We were playing," Theon replies lightly. A cat who feels no guilt over taunting a mouse. It's impossible to know what most people are to him, other than prey.

She narrows her eyes. "Sasha?"

Theon hesitates a beat. "I thought she'd give up way more easily than you. Guess I was wrong there." He presses a hand gingerly over the wound. "But I did something, didn't I?" He opens his mouth, a snake scenting the atmosphere. "I can feel it. You're weaker. The boundary is all cracked open now. Are you mad?"

Is she *mad*? She wants to tear open his veins with her teeth. Lil nods against the knife in her throat. Theon has been playing human for a long time, but he still doesn't comprehend love. He'd never have struck at Sasha if he knew.

"I thought maybe she'd die, but she didn't, did she?" He reads her face, finds the answer. "Nah, she didn't."

Theon has been striking blows wherever he can, hoping to get right here: Sasha, injured and out of commission; Lil, alone, boundaries susceptible, no recourse left.

This time, when Theon stretches out his hand, she doesn't flinch. Lil stays as still as a deer on the other side of a rifle as warm fingers, tacky with blood, touch her cheek. He spreads his palm along the line of her neck and jaw. It's different from Jason's broad, sure touch, dispelling the memory like dust. Lil endures. Theon's mouth goes soft with triumph.

"I win," he breathes. The orchard shudders. The trees will brown over winter and turn barren and hard. Maybe, one day, they'll even drop infants at their roots. And Theon, unrelenting, will consume it all, drop by drop, leaf by leaf, person by person, until there's nothing left of them. Nothing left of her, because where else can she go?

"You'll stay," he says as if reading her mind. Perhaps he is. "I don't want you to go. I can be Jason if you want. Or I can be—I can be whatever you want me to be. You'll see."

Again, she says nothing, just breathes, in and out, as if his thumb, grazing her cheekbone, doesn't feel like the curve of a claw.

"I want to show you something." She glances in the direction of the orchard's cold, dark, and still center.

Theon follows her gaze. "Show me."

As they walk through the orchard, he lingers over her, a dog nipping at her heels. They don't speak as the trees grow wild as fables, the ordered rows that have been Lil's whole life dissolving into brush and undergrowth, vines and thorns.

Theon's breath is short and panting. Pain, she thinks. "Wait." He clenches her shoulder for support.

Lil stops. Bearing up under his touch. Theon suppresses a snarl, swallows it back down. "Slower," he says grudgingly.

Glancing down, one of his feet is also…not right. She hadn't noticed in the dark, but blood mottles it too. The limb, when he steps, flops, like there isn't solid bone in it anymore.

She makes no move to help him, but lets him lean on her.

Deeper they go into the trees, into a blanket of shadow. She steps over roots and stones and he follows her exact path. More than once, he slips, catching himself with nails that dig unnaturally far into her shoulder.

But she ignores the claw that's slowly shredding into her. Lil throws her thoughts, her soul, into the suffocating stillness, the water that's calling to her. What she hoped, once, Jason could love and that Sasha might never have to see.

They come out of the thickets and into the clearing.

Theon shudders when he first lays his eye on it. Lil has always been in awe of its beauty too, of the sky's reflection captured underwater. But Theon, slumping to the ground at its edge, breaks that spell. She pictures Mom in her desperation, kneeling at its base, cracking a shell open between her palms, prying it loose. Sasha, in her faith, doing the same. The water trembles, lapping higher, eating always at its own edges. Everything can be lost here, at the edge of the water.

Theon spits a mouthful of blood on the hallowed ground.

"It's so…much," Theon says, tender with awe. He crawls to

the edge, where he stops, trembles. Salivates. He tips back his head and gazes in wonder at the tree, the moonlight turning golden treasures to silver stars above them.

Lil keeps her eyes on the pond, its surface silken and dark. With every breath, her body grows colder and colder.

Theon reaches for the water and jolts back. Staring at his feast, no idea where to start. He stands and backs up a step, then lurches forward to the edge again, a heady whine building in his throat.

Lil moves to stand at his side. Sunless water flows through her veins.

Theon's longing fingers twitch. She slips her hand around his wrist. It draws his attention back to her. "Your skin is so cold." Theon flips his palm around and holds hers too, like he's learning from her. Like he thinks she means to teach him. "Thank you, Lilith. Really. Before you, I've never loved—"

Lil steps into the water.

She pulls.

"What are you…?" Theon's voice trails off.

Knee-deep, Lil faces him, clamped onto his wrist, and the look on her face stuns him in place. He scents the trap. His nostrils flare, feet skittering at the edge of the pond. And another hand shoots out from the water and seizes his bad ankle. It is the pond's. But it is also hers. The mirror of the hold she has on him, her grip's reflection. Theon stops, snarls, jerks against it. But it doesn't let go. Lil walks backward, deeper in, fingers tightening on his wrist. He twists his hand and claws at her skin, rending into the tender inside of her arm, but she doesn't feel the pain. Trying to strike a wave is useless; it bends and flows on, untainted. She tugs—the pond tugs—and by ankle and arm, Lil yanks him into the water. Into herself.

"What are you doing?" Theon asks, twisting against her grip. He grabs a handful of her hair in his fist. Lil stares at him from two places. From her body. And from inside the pond. It's numbing and stinging all at once. She tugs. Waist-deep. Another hand surges up, snatches him by the back of his head and plunges him under.

Lil holds him and holds him and holds him down. The surface ripples and boils as Theon thrashes. His shape shifts and unfolds enough to snap his arm free. He bursts up screaming and lunges for her.

Claws sink into her shoulders and he snarls in her face. "Let me go!" Animal shock burns in his remaining eye. "You said I won. I won. *I won*—" Lil grabs him by the hair again. This is the duty and burden Mom passed on. With every pecan Lil tossed to the pond, the covenant between them deepened. Lil has cared for it faithfully for decades, and it answers her call now, pouring itself eagerly into her, embracing her into itself until they're one body.

She pushes him under; the water pulls him down. And Theon sinks again.

He thought to consume them. He thinks his hunger is endless—he does not know what eternity tastes like. But he will.

Once again, Theon fights his way to the surface and this time he shoves away from Lil, toward solid ground. He snags onto a root. "I don't like this," he threatens. "Stop it, I don't like it. I'll kill her, for real this time, if you don't—"

Lil and her reflection grab his ankle again and dig twinned fingers into his broken foot until he yowls and breaks his grip to swipe at her. She doesn't feel human skin but skinny bone and fur under her hand. The creature is appearing under the human mask, the one that turned her home into a brutal hunting ground, that ate at their hearts, their *children* without mercy. No more. She pulls him deeper.

Bloodied, one-eyed, Theon meets her gaze and fear floods his expression when he beholds the death in hers. Then pain. His scream becomes a heartbroken howl.

"But why?" Theon sobs out. He is desperate to breathe; she is forgetting what breathing is. "I don't understand. You let me in. I thought—" He shudders and—Jason's panicked face peers out at her, his lips bloodless, water spilling from between them. One of his warm brown eyes is an empty, gory canyon. "Lil, why? I *love* you."

Lil stops her steady tugs. She lunges at him, grasps that hideous, familiar face and *drags*.

They both go under.

Here, there is no more screaming. They fight in the moonless infinity as the cold grows deeper and purer, claws scoring her belly, her fingers digging into the soft places where he already bleeds. Air escapes his mouth in bubbles. Rise toward a faraway surface.

And down they go.

This thing that is Theon has never felt anything like drowning before, and probably could never have drowned if he hadn't put on such a human face for so long. He'd made himself just human enough to die at the mercy of Lil's love.

He twists and thrashes. One moment, she's holding cheek and an ear—the next, her fingers grip antlers—then a wolf's jaws snap too close to her neck. But water can subdue any struggling, panicked thing. Even as untenable as a riptide is, it has a tight hold.

Minutes. Hours. Maybe even eons pass. Until he stops fighting. Claws ease from her skin. Teeth fall out of their death snarl. Limp hands slip from Lil's. He aches with hunger no more. Heavily and soundly, he sinks.

Lil floats. Water around, above and below and in her. She might linger in the forever of the pond, stay here where there's no up, no down, no sound, only great, unknowable eternity. Will someone tend to her then? Offering her whatever golden pecans grow from the roots fed by her waters? Will Sasha?

Water rushes in her ears and she closes her eyes.

It's very still in the deep.

"Lil!" A familiar voice is close. A palm taps anxiously at her face, nearly a slap. "Lilith! Wake up!"

And Lil coughs herself awake. Her throat is a slice of pain as water dribbles weakly down her cheeks. She gasps in a noisy, desperate gulp of air.

Where is she? She was—in the water. Now—

"You're alive," Sasha sobs, heaving her into her arms. "You're okay."

Lil comes back to herself slowly, in ebbs and flows. More pain: her arms flare with deep scratches, her lungs burn for oxygen, her muscles tremble with exhaustion. All she is, actually, is pain, because she has a body again, and the fight is catching up with her.

Lil recognizes the roots of the tree, her fist tightly squeezed around mud, and her sister, right there beside her, here in the place they now share. Faint stars peer through the branches overhead, enough leaves have dropped to allow moonshine to fall down on the pond. She lies on her back, her head pillowed on the torn, river-soaked material of Sasha's knees. The rest of her is cradled by the pond. It let her go.

"I'm here, okay?" Sasha mouths, a rasped oath. "I'm here."

The night is quiet. There's no blare from the train, no growl of a hunter beyond the fences. And there's not a ripple in the sated water.

EPILOGUE

I T'S THE LAST GOLDEN-SYRUP DAYS OF THE HARVEST. SASHA sleeps in, and when she wakes, the breeze carries the first stir of December. She looks out her window at the orchard. Autumn is with Wyn, walking among the trunks. He's been telling her all the wild things he knows and teaching her the language of the trees. It's her mother tongue too. They can whisper together now in treesong, share secrets.

Sasha smiles, spying as they wander inside the fences, picking ripe husks off the ground. She pulls her camera from the dresser, holding the two of them in her viewfinder. As she watches, Wyn bashes a pecan against a tree to get at the meat inside, while Autumn cracks hers under her sneaker. Wyn is wide-eyed at the abundance of the harvest; the trees near his and Neel's home were barren. Slim pickings for hungry children. To him, the grasses and tangles of roots offer nothing short of a kingly feast. They invent their own games and chase each other around the reliable, sturdy rows. Another day, she and Sasha raked piles of leaves and introduced him to leaping into that mess of color. There are no hungry men to fear anymore.

Sasha snaps a picture.

She and Autumn leave the bed unmade on principle, and it's always a rowdy tangle. Being with Pip feels as green and full of promise as spring leaves, even as frost gathers on their window pane.

Sasha pulls a chunky sweater over her head, careful not to tangle it in the chain of her necklace. Autumn made it for her, threading her half of the golden pecan like a pendant. *It's too important not to keep it safe*, she'd said and looked at her bashfully through her lashes. *Besides, I didn't think we'd ever be ones for rings.* Sasha never takes it off. It's always right there, over her heart.

Downstairs, it smells like mulling cider, the windows thrown open. Sasha flips through their vinyl, and puts a Nat King Cole album on. Lil is in the kitchen, opening the oven to pull out the sticky buns inside, wafting spicy caramel scents through the first floor. Autumn comes in with Wyn, and she bends to help him untie his shoes.

They are finding a new rhythm. It's been a month since the steamboat sank. At dawn, the morning after Sasha found Lil at the pond's edge, the grass was frosty and rigid underfoot at the Clearwater orchard. After twenty-nine years of endless cycles of fall, winter is setting over the land.

Some things are the same: Sasha still gets voicemails from ghosts, asking her to take over the same shift after shift in town. She goes when she feels like it. The town is still empty but relatively well-preserved, their own doll's house. Together, Lou and Autumn are custodians of the fallow orchards, watching for newborns among the boughs. In and out of his shop, he's still fixing things, and he comes over for dinner most nights. Sometimes there's a window to fix in an old building. Lil repainted the firehouse door a glossy red. They do their part to keep alive what they can.

Some things are changed forever. No more fires blaze on the ridge. Nothing flickers in and out like it might dissolve. Their snow globe is cracked; it's holding, but it's changed. Sasha can't see all the ways that will matter yet.

Autumn helps Wyn out of his jacket and hangs it with hers by the door, next to Sasha's.

"Hey." Lil appears at her elbow and pokes her side. "Breakfast's out of the oven, but it's got to cool. Are we doing this?"

It's been their habit the past few days to take a small drive in the morning, somewhere different every day. Part of it is Sasha's restlessness, her claustrophobia, and another part is Lil's need to find and understand the crack they all can sense in the hull. So far, they've driven the length of the river inside their boundaries, thinking that since Sasha coughed the golden pecan up along the banks, the crack would have formed there. But, finding nothing, they've continued along the far edges to the north, where the neighborhoods bleed into kudzu-heavy trees, and down the southern edge where the abandoned train tracks have started to fuzz over with green vine. Without Theon screaming along the railroad, the tracks will soon disappear beneath the tangle.

Lil starts the truck, and they roll down the driveway to the dusty highway. They pause there, uncertain.

"Try left," Sasha suggests lightly. They glance at one another, just from the corner of their eyes. Why not?

They bump down the road, avoiding the same old potholes. Sasha peers into every shadow, on every property. She's planning to continue the surveying project, just on the off chance they'll find any more small faces peeping through the leaves.

Sasha stares at the road. Some things are gone that can never be reclaimed. Sasha's beautiful, grieving New York is ancient history, and the world out there is full of new problems she knows nothing about. And it's possible that they're now trapped here forever anyway, unaging, locked in a cell of their own making. Sasha sacrificed her escape for a home where she never fit. And yet—she can't regret it. There, on the steamboat, dancing with Pip, she'd forged her own joy, rebelliously, in spite of pain, and history, and imminent destruction. They carved this town out for themselves, and made it safe, and made it theirs. If the circuit on that love is closed, and there's no way out, well then, Sasha can just about live with that. She has everything she needs right here, in this pocket they made in the universe.

But what about her twin? Can Lil bear it? Since the crack, she and Lou have both shed their favorite phantoms, their most seductive haunts. Russ and Jason are gone now, and they won't be back.

"Do you regret it?" Sasha finds herself asking. "Any of it?"

Lil rolls down her window, letting the wind feather up her hair. Most of the burns Theon left on her skin have faded, but she didn't come away unscarred. There will always be patches of pinched red on her shoulder and the curve of her rib. Many, many nights, late into morning, they've talked about the nightmare of Theon and Jason, Theon as Jason. Sasha's held her as she's raged and cried, trying to unspool the real from the lies. It's a job that will never be done.

Lil takes a shuddering breath. "Is it bad if I say yes?" She lets it out slow and easy. "I don't regret that we saved this place. It's too much a part of me. But now…the world is gone forever. I spent my whole life here, and I told myself it was enough. Mom made the choice for the both of us and it's…" She ignores traffic signals and stop signs, cruising the middle of the road. "I used to dream about college. Then I dreamed about having a life with Jason, and I never did any of it. I want that," she admits in a rush. Her fingers flinch on the wheel. For a moment, she's filled with the passion of her teenage self again, when she was so hungry for freedom, before she learned to quiet herself. "I want the years of my life back that I never got to live, because I was all alone here. I want to go back to school. I want stupid twenties in a big city, making bad decisions. I want to fall in love again. I always wondered if I could be more than this purpose, and now I'll never get to find out."

Sasha feels the pain of this confession in her own chest, rubbing her sternum since she can't wrap her arms around her twin as she drives. Lately, Sasha has been a fountain of emotions, tears prepared for any occasion. Something in her has cracked open too, and it feels right. But Lil—with all the secrets their mother forced upon her, all the sacrifices she made for Sasha's liberty, for the orchard…even in this preserved place, where they seem to stay young and safe forever, is this town her locked closet? Her readied grave? "Lil…you deserve all those things," Sasha murmurs. "You deserve everything you want."

Lil glances at her with a tightness to her eyes. "I'm making my peace with it."

"To hell with that." Sasha begins to plot. The crack hasn't destabilized their protections, but it may have bent the rules.

She's never been able to get off the boat on the far shore, but…"I still have one riverboat. We can crash it into the dock on the other side and maybe—"

Some far-off siren begins to toll in her mind, and Sasha frowns.

Lil senses it too. The truck drifts to a stop. They've come to the turnoff to the south, and before them is the bridge that's been closed as long as Sasha can remember. The earth movers, bulldozers, and mounds of steel supports are gone. Before them, a flat expanse of open land and a long thin highway. They've found the crack.

Lil's breath catches in her throat. It's the only sound—other than the rush of distant cars, over on the interstate. It's only a few miles now. That city where the fresh starts await is just over the horizon.

"Well, your twenties are basically over," Sasha remarks, giving her a slow smile. "But there's still your thirties."

"I…hear your thirties are supposed to be better anyway," Lil manages.

"Definitely." Sasha doesn't wait. She kicks open the passenger door and hops down from the truck. She'll walk home from here.

Lil looks down at her, indecision warring with confusion. She's still gripping the wheel, the truck rumbling like it's ready to run. "What are you doing?"

"Go." Sasha blows her a kiss. "I'll take care of this place." She swallows the emotion building in her throat. "We'll be here when you get back."

Lil's eyes dart between her and the crack, and hope flushes over her face.

The road is open.

READING GROUP GUIDE

1. Like many small towns, Lil and Sasha's hometown has steadily declined over their lifetimes. Their memories of their home, and the reality of its current state, are drastically different, yet both versions of the place are real to them. Do you have places, or even people, from your life who have undergone such transformations over time? How do the characters cope with this in different ways?

2. Lil is stubbornly loyal to her land and the covenant her mother passed on to her. How does this responsibility impact her life? Is her relationship to the orchard a gift or a burden?

3. After Sasha returns home from New York, she keeps very busy doing odd jobs around town. She runs the ferry, does survey work, picks up tasks at local businesses, and works on her photography—but she never helps with the orchard. Why do you think she stays so occupied? How do the twins approach work in different ways?

4. Though Theon initially appears as a rich man trying to buy
    land, he is slowly revealed to be a shape-changing monster,
    driven by his hunger to consume everything in his path.
    At what point in the book did you begin to suspect Theon
    was more than he initially appeared? What do you think he
    represents?

5. Jason is the old flame Lil never let go of, in part because her
    life has been brought to a standstill. Though he is real to
    her, the only Jason who appears in the book is his memory.
    Where do you think the real Jason is in the present? How is
    his haunting weaponized against Lil?

6. Autumn's friend Matt refers to the "Homecoming Effect,"
    the pressures a person might feel to conform, blend in, or
    become an earlier version of themselves when they visit
    home. Have you ever felt this pressure? How does the
    Homecoming Effect impact Autumn and Sasha in the story?

7. The pecan children, like Wyn and Neel, are marginalized
    outsiders in the town, overlooked by the residents and easy
    victims to dark forces. How did the people of the town
    manage to ignore them for so long? Who in your commu-
    nity is most like the pecan children?

8. The Autumnal Interlude is an abrupt break from the world
    that Sasha and Lil know. It's also a coming-of-age story
    for Autumn, who searches for her identity as both a queer
    woman and, eventually, a child of the pecan trees. What

stood out to you about the many lives she leads? What do you think this interlude says about the journey we're all on to discover who we are?

9. Sasha and Autumn both often reflect on their last night hanging out in their tree house as teenagers. What happened that night, and how did it have a lasting impact on their relationship? What secrets have they kept from each other, and why?

10. Is there local folklore that you remember learning about when you grew up or that was passed down in your family? How do you think we're shaped by our homes and the stories we grew up hearing?

11. Lou, the oldest child of the pecan trees, has an interesting relationship to time. As a Black man in the South, he's lived through deeply painful history. Yet he owns a shop for old things and willingly goes through the time loop again and again to be with Russ. How would you cope with living forever? What do you think is next for Lou?

12. From Theon's fate to Lil and Sasha's final choices, every character ends in a different place from where they began. Did the characters' endings feel earned? What do you imagine happens to Lil, Sasha, Autumn, and Wyn after the epilogue? What feeling lingered with you at the end of the book?

ACKNOWLEDGMENTS

There are so many people we would like to thank for joining us in our pocket universe these last years. To our agent, Amy Stapp (the third Quinn!), thank you for always fighting for us. And to our editor, Mary Altman, your love for this book has given us more courage than you can imagine.

Thank you to Sourcebooks Landmark: our marketing team, headed by Cristina Arreola; our designer, Erin Fitzsimmons, for producing another perfect cover; and our copy editors, Jessica Thelander and Meaghan Summers. And to our sensitivity readers, thank you so much for your insightful notes and your time.

To the booksellers, librarians, archivists, event organizers, and, most importantly, the readers who have come along with us from Lake Prosper to this old pecan town, you have our most sincere gratitude. Finally, our truest thanks to each other. From one Quinn to another: there's no one else I'd rather be trapped in a time loop with.

Alex: All my love to my parents, big sister, and the rest of my extended family. Thanks and love as well to my found family: my closest friends (you know who you are) and my mentors, who have guided me here. And finally, the loved ones I've lost. You live in my heart.

Robyn: I am so blessed with the folks in my life who have continued to support me unconditionally. My most heartfelt love to my parents, my best friends, my aunts and uncles, and my professional mentors and colleagues. You inspire my work in every way.

ABOUT THE AUTHORS

 Quinn Connor is one pen in two hands: Robyn Barrow and Alex Cronin.

Both writers from a young age, Robyn and Alex met at Rhodes College in Memphis and together developed their unique cowriting voice. Whether Robyn is doing art historical fieldwork or Alex is reading on a subway in Lower Manhattan, they write all the time. It's their preferred form of conversation.